Corrupted Seduction

A Strangers to Lovers Captive Dark Mafia Romance

Kiana Hettinger

This book is an original production of Hardmoon Press.

HARDMOON PRESS

By Kiana Hettinger

Corrupted Seduction is the seventh book in the Mafia Kings: Corrupted Series.

Mafia Kings: Corrupted Series

#0 Cruel Inception

#1 Corrupted Heir

#2 Corrupted Temptation

#3 Corrupted Protector

#4 Corrupted Obsession

#5 Corrupted Vows

#6 Corrupted Sinner

#7 Corrupted Seduction

#8 Corrupted Deception

Standalones

Stolen Bond

Brutal Oath

Forbidden Romeo

Your Exclusive Access

Thanks a million for being here. Your support means so much to me.

The best way to keep in touch with me is by signing up for my newsletter – sendfox.com/authorkianah (I promise I won't spam you!) and by joining my readers' group, Kiana's Kittens – facebook.com/groups/KianasKittens

You'll receive bonus chapters, inside scoop, discounts, first access to cover reveals and rough drafts, exclusive material, and so much more!

See you on the inside,
Kiana Hettinger

Author's Note

I knew it was high time for a Luciano hero in the Corrupted series; a man like Amadeo has the world in the palm of his hands, the world is his oyster. If he wanted to truly find something special, he had to dive.

After all, not all treasure is silver and gold. Amadeo sought for his *perla*.

K

Table of Contents

Prologue

Heidi

I couldn't breathe.

I couldn't scream.

A hand pressed hard over my mouth, muffling any sound that tried to escape.

Panic flooded my small body, my heart pounding against my chest. like a wild drum. Desperate, I reached up, trying to free myself from the suffocating grip.

But then, through the haze of fear, I heard a hushed voice, a whisper that sounded familiar.

"Hush, luv, don't make a sound," my mother whispered urgently.

Relief washed over me, mingling with confusion. Why was Mama covering my mouth? Why was she awake? Hadn't I just gone to bed?

As my eyes adjusted to the dimness of the room, I caught a glimpse of her face, her eyes wide with terror.

"Hush, darling," she whispered again as she took her hand away from my mouth and brushed her trembling fingers across my forehead. "Everything will be okay, I promise." She tried to smile, but her lips trembled.

I strained my ears, and that's when I heard them—the sounds that made my heart skip a beat. Men's voices, loud and angry, seeped through the cracks of my bedroom door. They shouted and argued, their words a jumble of chaos.

A heavy feeling coiled in the pit of my stomach, and a cold shiver crawled up my spine. Who were they? What did they want? The questions lingered, unanswered and terrifying.

Tears welled up in my eyes. I clung to my mother, burying my face in the warmth of her embrace. She held me close, her trembling arms a protective barrier from the chaos outside my room.

But amidst the chaos, I heard it. My father's voice.

Why was Daddy shouting too? Was he in trouble?

"It's going to be okay, luv," my mother whispered, her voice quivering. "Just stay quiet, and everything will be all right."

But the noises grew louder as we huddled together in the dark. My heart raced and I trembled. Even my mother's warm arms couldn't drown out the dread that consumed me.

And then, as if in a terrible dream, the bedroom door exploded open, a thunderous crash as it slammed against the wall. Two men barged into the room—one tall, one short, both of them dominating the space. Angry eyes locked onto us, freezing my blood in its tracks.

"Get out here, now," the tall one bellowed, his voice dripping with authority. He sounded like us. He was from home! And yet, the sheer force of his words sent tremors through the room, rattling the very foundation of my being and leaving me paralyzed with fear.

My mother's grip tightened around me, and I pressed myself harder against her chest, like I could burrow into her and hide.

"Please. Please, she didn't do anything," she pleaded, her voice quivering but resolute.

The tall man's lips curled into a malicious sneer as he stepped closer, his eyes burning with twisted satisfaction. "No, but *you* did, you slag," he spat, his voice oozing with contempt.

The room filled with a palpable tension as the two men advanced toward us. I clung desperately to my mother's side and squeezed my eyes shut.

Wake up. Wake up. Wake up, I pleaded silently.

But my mother's scream made my eyes fly wide open as the men grabbed us both by the hair and dragged us out of my bed and across the room.

"No!" I cried as my mother screamed and flailed.

She looked savage, wild, as she kicked and punched and yanked madly against the tall man's grip.

My feet caught on the hem of my nightgown as they dragged us out into the hallway, and I stumbled, crashing into the wainscoted wall.

The man didn't stop; he kept dragging me along the short hall to the sitting room where he threw me down onto the gray carpet.

My mother followed, landing right next to me with a terrible thud.

She scrambled up onto her knees and wrapped herself around me. Her dark hair hung down over my face as she covered me with her body until I felt like a turtle tucked inside her shell.

My eyes darted around, searching for my father. And there he was, already on the floor, his knees pressing into the carpet. Tears streaked down his square face, leaving glistening trails in the dim light. I wanted to run to him, but another man held my attention.

He stood tall, maybe even taller than the tall man, his eyes filled with a dark intensity that sent shivers down my spine. There was a stark white scar on his tanned cheek, round in the middle, then branching out like spider legs. I swear I could see them moving.

In his hand, he held a weapon—a gun, shiny and black. My breath caught in my throat, and my body trembled uncontrollably. The world around me seemed to blur, distorted by the sheer terror that gripped me.

"Please, Dorian," my father's voice cracked. "Please, just let them go."

"You think you can beg your way out of this, you wanker?" the man with the spider scar sneered.

My mother held me even tighter, her body trembling against mine. I clung to her, my small fingers gripping her clothes as if they were the only anchor in this storm.

My father's face was etched with anguish, his light gray eyes filled with a mixture of sorrow and fierce determination. "They haven't anything to do with this. Let them go."

The man with the spider scar smirked, a cruel twist of his lips. "You should have thought about that before, shouldn't you?"

I couldn't understand the cruelty in his words, but I felt it deep in my bones.

Through tear-filled eyes, I glanced at my father. His eyes locked with mine for a brief moment, a silent, secret message passing between us. "*Your mum and I love you, Heidi,*" he said without saying.

"*I'm so scared, Daddy,*" I told him.

When he flinched like I'd struck him, my heart hurt, and I wished I could take it back.

"Bring the slag here," the man with the spider scar barked at the tall man who'd dragged my mother from my room.

"No!" I screamed as her cocooning warmth was wrenched away. She reached back to me as the tall man shoved her down on the floor next to my father.

I was alone. Separated by mere feet that felt like miles.

Crying, I scrambled after Mama on my knees, but my nightgown caught beneath me and the man with the spider scar stepped into my path, his eyes gleaming down at me with a twisted satisfaction.

"Stay quiet, little one," he sneered, making the spider legs move more.

I shrank back. I cowered closer to the floor.

The short man from my room crouched down next to me. "You're going to want to watch this, poppet," he said right before he grabbed my hair again and yanked my head up.

I tried to fight. I tried to be savage, punching and kicking like my mother had.

But the man just laughed and gripped my hair harder, making pain shoot through my scalp like lightning bolts. Then something cold pressed against my temple. Without seeing it, I knew what it was. This man had a gun, too.

My heart pounded, threatening to burst from my chest. I stopped fighting; I wasn't brave and fierce like my mother.

"Let her go!" my father barked, but the man with the spider scar hit him over the head with his gun's barrel.

And then the spider-man was coming toward me.

"Please!" my mother cried. "Please, don't do this, Dorian." She reached out her hand toward me. It was right there, but I couldn't take it, I couldn't reach her.

"Not in front of her, for God's sake," my father begged.

Then all three of the men were beside me, one on either side of me and one behind me.

I'd fallen into a pond once. It had been early winter and the water so cold it stole my breath and seeped into the core of me in a flash. That's what this felt like, surrounded by cold, shivering to the bone, gasping for breath.

There was a sharp, sudden explosion.

Deafening. So painful, I screamed as hot vibrations gusted past my ear.

Then another explosion.

I screamed, but it made no sound. Only ringing, high and sharp. The whole world was ringing.

I covered my ears as my parents flopped to the floor. They stared at me, eyes lifeless, as blood spewed from their foreheads.

And all the while the world kept ringing.

My head kept spinning.

And then the world went black.

Chapter One

Heidi

The pungent odor of antiseptic permeated the emergency room, but beneath the sterile scent, the coppery tang of blood clung to the air. It was always there, a visceral reminder of old stab wounds and broken bones, and an ever-present omen of the lacerations and severed limbs still to come.

But right now, in this moment, it was calm. Too calm.

Not empty—not nearly so. Every treatment room was occupied, patients waiting for splints or stitches—or, in the case of the young gentleman behind curtain number seven, a tetanus shot for the rusty nail he'd landed on arse first.

I cringed as I dropped the man's chart down at the nurse's station, and my own backside twinged in sympathy. But as the blonde spiky-haired nurse who'd helped me treat him sidled up next to me, I fought the urge to rub away the vicarious pain.

"It'll be some time before that kid gets drunk and takes another stroll through a junkyard," she joked.

I didn't know her name, only that she was quick to joke and just as quick to buckle under pressure.

"It's quiet tonight," she mused, looking around, then she flinched. "I mean, it's calm tonight," she said, enunciating each syllable carefully.

Really. It's not like I'm going to break if somebody says the wrong thing. I made an effort not to roll my eyes at her and gave her a tight smile instead.

Calm for now, perhaps, but the storm was coming. I could *feel* it.

"Enjoy it while it lasts," I said, but I'd barely gotten the words out when the emergency room doors flew open and a giant of a man burst in, drenched in sweat, his clothes stained with blood. He staggered under the weight of another man, who lay motionless in his arms, bleeding profusely.

A cold weight settled in the pit of my stomach.

It hadn't always done that. When I'd started my residency here, I'd had little instinct for who might live and who might die. But now, I could see it. There was a laxity in the man that spoke of more than injury; it spoke of surrender, the body's capitulation to the greedy hand of Death.

"Clear a trauma room, stat," I called out, because whether Death had come for this man or not, it was my job to stand in His way.

And I could be one hell of a roadblock.

The calm was over; the storm had come.

The staff on the ward moved like the storm's lightning. In thirty seconds, the man was on a stretcher and in a trauma room, with the big man who'd brought him here close on his heels.

The big guy was muttering a steady stream of obscenities the whole way, but I could barely catch them with the way his face was twisted in rage. Looked like all the usual words, plus something that might have been "Luke" or "lush" or "Lucianos".

I couldn't be sure, though; I only had half an eye to pay attention to his lips. Someone needed to get him out of here, but I didn't have time.

"Primary survey first," I called out. *Airway, breathing, circulation.*

I grabbed a pair of gloves and yanked them on, the cold latex snapping against my wrists as the nurses in the room sprang into action.

"I want the airway secured," I said to the spiky-haired blonde nurse who'd followed me in. "Intubate, please."

She paused, her expression uncertain. It was no more than the span of a breath, but it was one breath more than I could afford.

"You," I said, nodding in her direction. "Out."

Her expression fell and the whole room paused for a fraction of a second. I could hear the silent jeers. *"Control-freak." "Tyrant."* And of course, *"Bitch."* Those weren't the worst of the things they'd called me—they forgot sometimes that I could read lips.

But I didn't have time to explain to them that nurses who buckled under pressure killed people. And it wouldn't have mattered if I did. I was the ER bitch, and nothing was going to change that. And I was fine with that.

"I've got it," Raven said, moving into position with a laryngoscope and endotracheal tube in hand.

I didn't know many of the nurses by name, but this one was good under pressure. I liked that; I respected that.

"Thank you, Raven," I said curtly as the blonde slunk out of the room, her shoulders slumped. There would be fresh pejorative terms for me circulating through the ward by morning, no doubt.

With expert hands, Raven inserted the endotracheal tube while another nurse—a tall, gangly man with a shockingly white-blond mop of hair named... Tom, maybe?—cut away the patient's clothing, revealing a bleeding canvas of gunshot wounds.

This man hadn't just been shot; someone had tried to turn him into a human sieve. Six bullet wounds. I envisioned their paths as best I could. Damage to the liver, the right kidney, duodenum, possibly the pancreas. But the bullet wound to the chest? I could see its path right through the thoracic aorta.

Damn.

Death was here, circling above me.

"Tube secured," Raven announced within seconds, and the patient's chest rose and fell in rhythm.

"Let's get access," I said, ignoring my racing heart and Death's cold presence. "Large-bore IVs, blood products on standby."

Raven and Tom scrambled to find veins amid the patient's blood-soaked skin, skillfully threading catheters into place. Bags of fluid hung from IV poles.

"He's tachycardic and his BP's dropping," Raven called out loud enough I could hear her.

He was on the verge of cardiac arrest. He needed an OR, but he'd never make it there.

The big man who'd brought him in surged across the room, still covered in blood. He stopped right next to me, puffing himself up, glaring down at me.

"What the hell, *troia*? Do something," he seethed loud enough I could hear most of the words.

I fought the urge to slink back from him and stood up straighter. "I am doing something; I'm trying to save his life," I said in a tone I'd practiced plenty, that blend of professional confidence and empathy that had made a good number of patients' worried relatives and friends back down.

This man just stood up straighter, puffing himself up impossibly more. He was the breadth of two of me and stood at least six inches taller.

"You're wasting time," I said, refusing to be cowed even if my knees felt an overwhelming desire to turn to Jell-O. "Time he doesn't—"

He pulled a gun from the waist of his trousers, so fast it was a blur until it was pointed right at me, so close, I could feel the icy chill of the barrel.

"Hey!" Raven snapped while Tom tried to disappear into the wall behind him. "Put that—"

"Save him," he seethed at me while his eyes flashed with menace. "Save him, or I paint this room red with *your* blood, Heidi. *Capisce?*"

My heart raced, but it didn't show on my face. On the outside, I was the "Ice Queen"—I'd seen that name on more than one set of lips here.

He'd called me by name, though. He knew me, but how?

"Who are you?" I asked him, searching for anything familiar in his oblong, pockmarked face, looking for a way to connect with him, to defuse him.

Because, deep in my stomach, the cold weight was still there, and Death was circling ever closer.

"Never mind who I am," he said, his finger hovering over the trigger. "Do your fucking—"

Raven took a step forward from the other side of the gurney, drawing his attention.

"If you want her to save his life," she said, her features as unruffled as my own, "you're going to have to let her work."

I couldn't help but wonder if it was a façade, if below her composed exterior, her heart was racing like mine.

The man swung the gun in her direction.

"Enough," I snapped. "Stay out of my way if you want your friend to live."

But this was the ER, and the ER had a sick sense of humor. So, of course, that was precisely when the ECG strip on the cardiac monitor decided to flatline.

Raven spun around to the monitor, no doubt drawn by the continuous, high-pitched drone I couldn't hear.

For one brief moment, I couldn't stop the terror from racing down my spine.

"Save him, or I paint this room red with your blood, Heidi," he'd said.

My heart pounded like a drum. My hands grew cold. I waited to feel the blow, the fiery burn of a bullet through my chest.

Then I tucked it all away.

Save the patient—that's what he wanted and that's what I wanted. Even though he didn't realize it, we were on the same side.

"Defibrillator," I said as I forced the world to narrow.

As I commanded the room to fade away.

As I made the man with the gun disappear.

No one existed for me but those who could play a role in thwarting Death, in serving as roadblocks with me.

"Push one milligram epinephrine," I told Tom as I clasped my hands together, one on top of the other, and started compressions, counting them out in my head while Raven readied the electrode pads.

Even with the world narrowed, I could still feel the coldness of the gun's barrel, inches from my temple. I swear it was ticking, like a time bomb, waiting to detonate the moment Death smashed through this roadblock.

When I finished the first round of compressions, I leaned back, grabbed the defibrillator paddles Raven had readied for me and put them to my patient's chest.

"Clear!" I called.

The patient's body jerked a little.

But no change.

"Save him, or you die, Heidi," the man with the gun barked, like maybe I'd forgotten.

Raven's gaze flickered toward the door. She must have pressed the hidden panic button; she was watching for the police.

I resumed compressions, round after round while the gun sent icy chills across my temple and down my spine.

Still no heartbeat. No police.

Sweat trickled down the back of my neck and beaded on my brow.

But just as my back started to ache like someone had hit me with a baseball bat, I saw a figure move outside the door out the corner of my eye.

"How do you know me?" I asked, hoping to keep the gunman from noticing.

I think he scoffed, making the gun bounce in his hand. "I know all about you, Heidi Dawson. Where you live…"

The trauma room door opened.

"Where you eat…"

A lone figure slipped in. An older man dressed in slacks and a cardigan.

"Who you're fucking…"

The lone figure crept forward.

"I know everything—"

The newcomer's arm snaked around the gunman's neck, his surprisingly large bicep bulging against the gunman's throat.

Caught so off-guard, the gunman's eyes flared wide as he dropped his gun. He flailed, but it didn't last long. Within seconds, his eyes rolled back, and he flopped, unconscious, in the newcomer's arms.

I kept up compressions, but something wasn't right here. One lone officer? And where was his uniform?

"Who are you?" I asked as he lowered the gunman onto the floor, face-first, and secured his wrists in restraints behind his back.

"Off-duty police officer, Doctor," he said. "I happened to be in the building."

I nodded as I held out my hands to Raven and she placed the defibrillator paddles in them.

The threat had been neutralized, but I still had a job to do.

"Thank you," I said to the officer, then turned my attention back to my patient for another round of compressions and then another.

The officer slung the gunman over his shoulder and carried him out of the room.

"Push another milligram of epinephrine, Tom," I instructed.

He looked at me, hesitated, then nodded. But I knew that look. "*Why bother?*" it asked.

"*Because I have to,*" I answered to no one in particular and kept going.

But each time I paused to assess, the result was the same.

No heartbeat.

I glanced up at the clock. Twenty-five minutes had passed since we'd started CPR.

I'd lost.

Death had won.

Fuck.

I stopped compressions but left my hands against the patient's chest. I always did that, like maybe all the high-tech equipment was wrong and I'd feel his heart beating all on its own.

But the equipment wasn't wrong.

Bloody hell.

It felt like a blow, a solid punch to my solar plexus, making it just a little harder to breathe.

"Time of death, eleven-oh-five PM," I called out, then stepped back, my cool exterior carefully intact.

"Tom, could you please contact the mortuary affairs team?" I asked as I yanked off my blood-soaked gloves and tossed them in the rubbish bin, fighting the urge to kick the can across the room.

Tom nodded and left the room, but Raven lingered.

I wished she hadn't. The adrenaline that had been pumping through me all this time writhed in my veins, searching for a way out.

"Are you okay?" Raven asked. It was easy to see the worried quirk of her mouth through the Clearmasks we used in the ER.

I blew out a breath and nodded. I don't know how long I'd been standing here, staring down at the rubbish bin.

"Yes, I'm fine," I replied. *Just really in need of a good punching bag at the moment.*

She smiled—light and easy, like what had happened here with the mad gunman hadn't affected her. It seemed she really was as unflappable as she looked. Or maybe she was in shock?

The Ice Queen wouldn't give a damn, my brain taunted me.

So, I stood there with the question frozen on the tip of my tongue.

"*Sí,* I'm fine," she said as she tossed away her own gloves. Her lips curved up in a knowing grin. "Just in case you were wondering. It wouldn't be a day at the office if there weren't crazy jerks with guns popping up left, right, and center."

"You stayed calm; you did good." I offered up a modicum of the praise she deserved.

She smiled like there was a secret there somewhere. "It's no problem," she said with a shrug. "I've been in a tense situation a time or two before."

Chapter Two

Heidi

I wondered, sometimes, what my parents would think of the choices I'd made in my life thus far. I swear I'd felt them smiling down on me the day I'd graduated from medical school. It was warm, like a ray of sun even on a cloudy day. At other times, I'd felt their disapproval like a cold, faint brush of wind against my shoulders.

As I stared up at the Palatial Towers, one of the ritziest buildings in New York City, I could feel that cool gust.

"Good evening, Doctor Dawson," the doorman, Emmett, signed right before he opened the door for me. He was in his sixties, but he had a thick mane of silver-gray hair that stuck out in every direction from beneath his uniform cap.

"Good evening, Emmett," I signed back.

He was generally an excessively chatty man, but he'd learned recently that his two-month-old granddaughter was deaf. The very same day, he'd enrolled in a sign-language course and started reading every book under the sun about supporting a child with a hearing disability. He knew of my own hearing impediment, so of course, I'd become an opportunity for him to practice his budding skill.

He propped the door open with one foot to free up his hands. "Mr. Bianchi isn't home yet," he signed with increasing dexterity.

"That's all right," I signed back. "I'll wait for him."

He nodded. "Have a good night then, Doctor Dawson."

"You too, Emmett."

I took the elevator up to the thirty-fifth floor and let myself in to the lavish three-bedroom apartment with floor-to-ceiling windows. It felt like only yesterday that I'd met Elio Bianchi of Bianchi Industries, but somehow, I'd started to spend most nights here in this souped-up luxury suite.

"It's closer to the hospital," Elio had reasoned.

Closer, perhaps, but I missed my renovated nineteenth century flat on the other side of the city. There was barely enough room to move around in it, but it was mine. My own private space.

I dropped my key card back into my purse, set it down on the Fendi Casa entryway table by the door, and headed across the stark white sitting room for the Poggenpohl kitchen on the other side.

But as I reached the doorway to the L-shaped kitchen, I could smell it—the metallic tang of blood, assaulting my nostrils

I rounded the corner into the room and froze.

There was a man in the dining room beyond the kitchen, his back toward me, but it wasn't Elio.

Elio had a swimmer's build, sleek but not overly muscled. The man standing in the dining room could have been an MMA fighter, with his broad shoulders and thickly muscled arms, expertly displayed in a charcoal gray suit.

In front of the intruder, partially obscured by his broad frame, a man was tied to one of the dining chairs. His back was toward me as well, but he had a familiar narrow frame and dark hair. Blood pooled below him on the white marble floor beneath him; red smears and spatters marked the marble floor and Boca do Lobo dining table.

My breath tried to come in great, panicked gasps, but I silenced them. The man hadn't seen me. I could still leave, turn around and run for help.

But leave Elio? There was no deep-seated emotional attachment between us, but still, something kept my feet rooted in place.

My eyes fixed on the pool of blood, slowly spreading across the cold marble. But how much blood?

My mind switched into a clinical analysis, detached from the urgency of the situation. I began calculating, attempting to gauge the extent of the blood loss, assessing the size of the pool, its density, and the rate at which it expanded. Amidst the danger, my brain couldn't help but engage in its instinctive habit of seeking answers, seeking order.

Half a liter, my mind determined. Approximately half a liter of Elio's blood was no longer in his body. Not immediately fatal, but he had no time to spare.

Just leave, the Ice Queen cajoled. I'd spent seventeen years looking out for number one. Now wasn't the time to change philosophical principles.

And yet, I crept forward not back, eyeing the knife block on the sleek, black granite counter. My hands were shaking. God only knew if I'd be able to hold the knife, never mind stab the man with it.

I think they were talking, loudly, but not loud enough that I could make out any words. Only sounds, some of them angry, some of them desperate.

I kept my eyes on the broad fighter's back as I reached for the nearest knife and gripped the handle in one trembling hand.

Calm down, I barked silently. *It's just like a scalpel. Simple. Easy. An extension of my arm.*

I took a step forward, then another. I could only assume my feet moved silently because he didn't turn around.

One more step, and I was right behind him, my view of Elio still obscured. But even more vivid than the fighter, or his sandalwood and bergamot scent, or the contrast of his charcoal gray suit against his sandy blond hair, was the shiny black gun in his hand, his finger poised on the trigger.

He was going to kill Elio. He was going to kill him right in front of me.

I felt the cold, just like in the water, surrounding me, making me shiver to the bone and gasp for breath.

My hand shook as I raised my arm, gripping the knife with every ounce of strength I possessed.

"No!" Elio cried. "Please—"

The gun went off, a muffled explosion in comparison to the ones I'd heard before, but it brought to mind the ringing. The blood. The holes in my parents' heads and their lifeless eyes. The spider. I could see it, crawling all over the man in front of me, burrowing into him, *becoming* him.

Kill it, I screamed silently.

Instinctually, without forethought, I brought the knife down. Hard. Fast. It punctured his suit, then his skin and went deeper. Subcutaneous tissue.

And then the blade hit bone.

The sudden stop jarred my arm all the way up to my shoulder.

He yanked himself away and spun around.

There was no spider on his face. Nothing about him that I'd expected at all. No pockmarked skin or tall forehead. No beady eyes or snub nose.

This face was chiseled jaw, sharp cheekbones, unmarred skin, and full lips.

This man was… beautiful, and utterly masculine.

He took a step back, the gun raised in his hand.

I still had the knife, but it was like brandishing a plastic fork against a majestic lion.

A majestic lion who hadn't killed Elio; the man in the chair wasn't him. I could see the man with the swimmer's build now—his long, narrow face, his hooked nose, his lifeless brown eyes. This was Owen Thompson, Elio's VP.

I'd risked my life for a complete stranger, a man who'd made my skin crawl the few times I'd laid eyes on him.

You bloody fool.

"*Buenasera, signorina,*" the man with the gun said, his full lips quirking in the faintest hint of a smile as he spoke. "It looks like you've won a front-row seat to my little show."

Don't cower. Don't show fear.

"Not exactly the show I was hoping for," I said dryly, drawing on the Ice Queen like never before. I needed to be cool and calm—unflappable. Raven—the nurse from the hospital—sprung to mind. I don't think the gunman had even made her blink.

Don't blink.

He laughed. The sound was loud enough for me to hear, but short and cold. "Maybe not, but the man deserved—"

"And you're what? Saint Francis of Assisi?" I spat, feeling the Ice Queen's coldness in my veins, making me blissfully numb. Numb to Owen Thompson sitting in the dining chair, his head flopped forward and blood seeping from a jagged hole in the back of his head.

The blond man's brow furrowed, then he barked another short, cold laugh. "The patron saint of peacemakers?" He shook his head. "I am not that, *signorina.*"

It hit me like a tidal wave.

His lips had formed the word "*signorina*" more than once—an Italian word, not that I knew many of them.

He was Italian. He wore an expensive suit, tied people up and murdered them in their homes. And he didn't seem the least bit perturbed that I'd stabbed him in the back in the middle of his "show". It was possible he was a nutter, but I had a terrible feeling this man could have walked right out of *The Godfather.* Organized crime. Organized and destructive and bred from the vilest evil.

The ice wall started to crack inside me. I could feel the fissures forming as my heart raced faster and my cold hands shook.

"Just leave," I said. I could feel the trembling in my own voice, knowing the demand was pointless.

He chuckled, shaking his head slowly. "Oh, sweetheart, if only it were that simple. But I have a reputation to uphold, and witnesses tend to be rather inconvenient. So, you see, we have a problem."

I glared back at him. I knew exactly what kind of problem he was referring to—the "walking, talking, could identify him in court" kind of problem.

And from where I was standing—in Elio's dining room with a cold-blooded killer—there seemed to be only one solution to his "problem".

My hands shook harder, and my heart pounded against my ribs while my mind screamed at the only option left. I felt like one of my patients, struggling to hold on when the body had all but given up.

Please, don't kill me, was on the tip of my tongue. But I wasn't going to beg. I'd begged once before. My mother had begged. My father had begged. And they'd laughed at us.

I wouldn't give this tosser the satisfaction now.

If the only thing I could do was go down swinging, then that was exactly what I was going to do.

I drew my arm back. All it would take was one quick move, and I could slash his throat. Even if he managed to fire a shot, I'd take him down with me.

But his eyes slanted to the left.

Too late for me to spin around. Too late to confront whatever new horror approached from behind.

A hand gripped my wrist. Another one wrapped around me, trapping me against a solid wall at my back.

I yanked and jerked. I stomped and kicked.

But the hand gripped my wrist harder, so hard it forced my hand to let go of the knife.

My only weapon was gone. It dropped to the floor. I imagined its clatter against the hard, unyielding marble.

I kept it up, though, flailing and fighting, savage and wild like my mother.

They were talking, their voices raised enough I could make out the indistinct sound. To me? To each other? I couldn't tell.

The arm around my ribs gripped tighter, making it harder to breathe, crushing my strength, my fight.

The man with the gun came closer. He took hold of my chin and forced my head up to look at him.

"Calm down," he said, so close I could follow his lips loud and clear even with my vision blurred by tears. "I don't intend to shoot you."

I stopped struggling, looking back and forth between his lips and his eyes. They were hazel, maybe, or brown, so pale they almost looked amber.

"Why not?" I forced the words out past dry lips, oblivious to my volume control.

The men who'd killed my parents had left me alive, but I think that was because it amused them to let me live after snuffing out my whole world. This man had no reason to let me walk away.

He dropped his hand, and the man holding me from behind loosened his grip, though he didn't let go entirely.

"What's your name?" the amber-eyed man asked, ignoring my question.

"Why?" There was an angle here; there had to be.

The corners of his full lips twitched up in a smile, but it didn't reach his eyes. "Because when someone walks in on me and sees something they shouldn't see, I like to have a name to go with the face."

"Heidi," I said, trying not to spit it at him like a curse.

He nodded cordially. "It's a pleasure to meet you, Heidi. I wish we were meeting under better circumstances. My name is Amadeo Luciano."

Chapter Three

Amadeo

Vito Agossi looked at me from where he held the dark-haired—and vivacious and mouthy—beauty. His bald head caught the light from above, turning him into a beacon towering over her.

"What do you want to do here, boss?" his eyes asked silently.

Good question. Fuck if I had an answer.

As far as complications went, this one was the hottest I'd ever come across by far. It was a complication, nonetheless. And the few choice solutions that came to mind weren't going to happen unless I'd somehow stepped into the land of every man's fantasy in the past thirty seconds.

"Take care of the body," I told Vito. "I'll take care of the girl."

Not that I had the slightest clue what I was going to do with her.

Vito nodded and let go of the woman.

She took two skittering steps sideways, then looked at me, her chin tilted up now, feigning a confidence that didn't quite reach her eyes.

"What do you mean you're 'going to take care of the girl'?" she snapped.

What she lacked in confidence, she more than made up for in defiance. Too much defiance. Too much determination to resist what had to happen here.

I stood up taller despite the jolt of pain that shot down my back. I towered over her, hiding everything on my face but the cold, hard killer I needed her to see.

"You shouldn't have been here, Heidi. You understand the predicament that poses for me, *sí*?" I said, my voice devoid of emotion.

"I won't tell any—" She cut herself off with a flinch. I bet she could hear the insincerity in her words as well as I could.

A sardonic smile tugged at the corners of my lips. "You expect me to believe you'd walk out of here and never mention our little meeting to another living soul?" I asked, then shook my head in answer to my own question. "You're a liability now, a potential threat to me. And I don't take kindly to threats."

Despite her steely façade, a tear slipped from her eye, trickling down her pale cheek.

Her skin wasn't much darker than the apartment's white marble floor. She looked like a porcelain doll, with an oval face and big blue eyes that were dark for the most part. Up close, though, I could see a scattering of tiny, pale blue flecks in them. She wore no makeup, and yet, when she blinked and another tear escaped, her long, dark lashes fanned out across her cheeks.

The tear trickled down to the corner of her vivid pink lips, which were shaped like a cupid's bow, the upper lip a little too plush, just enough to make her the envy of every collagen-filled pair out there. One look at them, and I was fairly certain that nothing would ever look better wrapped around my cock.

As Vito untied the dead asshole from the chair and heaved him up over his shoulder, her tear-filled gaze flitted back to the corpse, then back to me, over and over again.

Was she wondering what I'd do next? Was she realizing I held her life in my hands, that she was entirely at my mercy?

It was sick as shit that I got off on that kind of power, but there it was in the shock of heat that shot through my body and the image that filled my mind of the woman naked in my home… and entirely at my mercy.

"Come, *signorina,*" I said, nodding toward the apartment's door. Not that I expected her to come willingly. But willing or not, I had no intention of standing around in this apartment indefinitely.

She ignored me, her blue-eyed gaze intent on the corpse now, even as Vito strode through the kitchen with a parting nod and disappeared through the kitchen doorway.

Her whole body was trembling. She had her hands at her sides, but she was eyeing the knife on the floor. I'm not sure if she realized it, but she was shaking so hard, she'd just cut herself with the damn thing. If I couldn't leave marks on her body, then I sure as hell wasn't going to stand here while she did.

"Enough," I snapped, more harshly than I'd intended.

She jerked her gaze away from the knife and looked up at me, taking a step back at the same time.

"'Come'? You think you can call me like a dog? You're mad if you think I'm going to walk out of here with you," she said while her eyes snapped defiantly. She held her hands out in front of her like she had any hope of fending me off.

I almost laughed.

"Mad? You think I'm insane?" I raised an eyebrow. "No, *signorina.* I prefer to think of myself as creatively misunderstood."

She opened her mouth, then snapped it shut without saying a word.

"Here's the deal," I continued, my voice dripping with sinister charm. "You have two options. Option A: You come along with me, and we embark on a thrilling adventure filled with danger, intrigue, and a questionable moral compass. Option B: I send you on a different trip," I paused—for dramatic effect. "To the land of eternal silence."

"Go to hell, you monster," she spat back with insolence etched into every line of her porcelain face. She clenched her hands into fists, so tight that her knuckles turned stark white.

"Monster?" I chuckled again. There was no humor in the sound. "You've seen nothing 'monstrous' yet, Heidi, but I assure you, I'm capable of things you couldn't even begin to imagine."

To this woman, I was the embodiment of evil, a heartless killer forcing her into a fate worse than death. And yet, she didn't cower. She didn't shrink away.

A surge of reluctant respect coursed through me. I admired her spirit, even if it was proving inconvenient at the moment.

But while she was brave, no one was unbreakable.

I took a step toward her, closing the distance between us. She smelled like vanilla and soft musk and something... clean that called up a potent desire to make her dirty.

I could see the urge to run in her eyes, but she stayed put, glaring up at me.

"I could kill you," I spoke, slow and clear, emphasizing her vulnerable position. "I could do anything I wanted to you, and there isn't anything you could do to stop me. Do you understand that?"

She needed to understand that I was in charge here. She needed to believe that her obedience equaled safety, and that disobedience would have consequences.

Her whole body shook. She hesitated, her fierce gaze faltering for a moment. The weight of her predicament finally settled on her shoulders, and the fire in her eyes flickered. She nodded her head.

"Then, tell me, why haven't I hurt you?"

Her gaze skittered away and then back again. A furrow formed between her brows. "You want something from me."

"Smart girl," I said with a nod of approval.

"What is it you want?" she asked.

"For now, all I want is for you to come with me."

"Where are you going to take me?" she asked like she wanted to weigh her options.

Pretty much anywhere was better than six feet under, wasn't it?

I took a step back, giving her some breathing room.

"Somewhere safe," I said. And then, once I'd deposited her 'somewhere safe', maybe I could see about getting someone to do something about the goddamned knife wound in my back. That son of a bitch hurt.

She scoffed. "I'm just supposed to trust you?"

"This isn't about trust; it's about survival. If you want to survive, you'll do as you're told."

She scowled. I don't think she liked that answer. But since most men in my position would have put a bullet in her head and been done with it, I was clearly being more than reasonable here.

"You won't get away with this. Someone will—"

I smirked, my amusement not quite hidden beneath my menacing façade. "Oh, *signorina,* I'm always getting away with things. It's what I do best. But as you can see," I said, motioning between us to emphasize the distance I'd given her, "I'm not hurting you. I have no interest in hurting you. But you *will* come with me, one way or another. Don't make this more difficult than it needs to be."

Her eyes flickered to the doorway, and I could feel it—I could practically see the wheels turning in her head, telling me exactly what she was going to do. I don't think she appreciated just how reasonable I was being.

Nevertheless, I was prepared for it when she turned on her heels and darted back through the kitchen. What I hadn't expected was that the woman would be so damn fast.

She'd made it through the kitchen and halfway across the living room before I caught up to her. I wrapped an arm around her waist and yanked her back to me, ignoring the warm, soft feel of her lithe body against me.

But this was pointless. The stubborn woman wasn't going to see reason. How many times had I argued with Greta, only for her to go and do whatever the fuck she wanted anyway?

Before Heidi could start flailing again, I reached into my jacket pocket and withdrew the syringe that had been intended for Elio Bianchi.

But since the man wasn't here, I yanked off the cap with my teeth and jabbed the needle into Heidi's neck.

She squealed in shock and tried to jerk away from me, but it was too late. The injection did its work fast, making her knees buckle and taking her away into sweet oblivion within seconds.

She collapsed into my arms, and I lifted her up, carrying her out of the apartment and down the service elevator to the car waiting for me in the lot below.

When I imagined having this woman at my mercy, *this* wasn't what I'd had in mind.

Chapter Four

Amadeo

Four hours. A four-hour drive to the middle of fucking nowhere. My back was aching, the leather seat of the slate gray Bentley Bentayga was covered in blood, and my stubborn little witness was starting to come around in the back seat.

She'd been silent, near-motionless throughout the long drive, but now, as I pulled into the long gravel driveway that led up to the Luciano's… cabin, three hours outside of New York City, she began to make quiet noises, not quite a breath, not quite a moan, that were making their way into my ears and heading straight to my cock.

As I shifted the Bentayga into park at the top of the drive, I pulled out my phone and dialed my father's number. Enzo Luciano, the don of the Luciano family.

Had I deliberately waited to let Vito share the news about the turn of events this evening? Hell, yes.

"I'm at the cabin, *Papà*," I explained to him the moment he answered his phone.

He made a rumbling sound in his throat. My father was fond neither of phones nor surprises.

"*Sì*, Vito filled me in on this evening's events," he said in a voice that sounded very much like an impending earthquake. "I assume you didn't eliminate the woman. What is it you plan to do with her, Deo?"

Good question. I had no better answer now than I had four hours ago. At least, not in the long run. For now, she had a purpose to serve.

"She's involved with Bianchi—she let herself into his apartment. And since the asshole in the apartment didn't know where to find him, she might. I'll see what she can tell me."

"And you think she'll be amenable to handing over that information?" he asked, his tone full of doubt.

Amenable? No. Scared into offering it up to save her own hide? Absolutely.

I didn't much care for scaring the shit out of innocent women—as opposed to scaring the shit out of sinful women, which I kind of liked—but this was more than business; it was personal. Even Greta would understand.

"I'll get the information," I said. There wasn't a doubt in my mind.

"*Bene*. You find him, Deo."

"I will, *Papà*. And when I do, he's going to die a slow and painful death."

My father made another noise in his throat, but this one was filled with approval.

I hung up the phone, slipped it back into my jacket, and peeled myself off of the seat. Blood had soaked right through my shirt and jacket, making the latter try to stick to the leather.

When I got out of the SUV and opened the rear passenger door, it struck me for the first time how small and fragile the woman looked, her dark lashes fanned out across her porcelain skin, her plump lips just barely parted as another quiet sound slipped out.

The warring urges to protect something so delicate-looking and to tie her up and use her in every deplorable way made my head spin. Or maybe that was a combination of blood loss and hunger. Maybe it was both.

I lifted her up off the seat and into my arms. Even with my back aching like a son of a bitch, her weight was nothing.

I carried her inside the cabin where the hardwood floors gleamed and the floor-to-ceiling windows in the living room offered a wide view of the property. No blind spots.

The cabin was cleaned and restocked regularly, but no one had stayed here in quite some time. Years, maybe, since we'd made use of the cabin's isolated location and the soundproof basement beneath it.

With more care than I thought I had in me, I laid Heidi down on the leather sofa across from the hearth, supporting her head. I stood back and watched as her eyelids fluttered, then finally opened, signaling her return to consciousness.

As she gradually regained her senses, her gaze darted around the unfamiliar surroundings. Confusion etched itself across her face as I could see her trying to piece together the events that had led her here.

Finally, her eyes locked with mine, flaring with heat before her brain fit the last puzzle piece into place.

The heat vanished. A mixture of fear and defiance swirled in her eyes instead. Storm clouds rising in those blue-flecked eyes.

She jerked herself upright, but the moment she did, she winced and grabbed her head like she was trying to hold it together.

"What did you do?" she groaned.

I shrugged, once again donning the "creatively misunderstood" man she'd met back at Bianchi's apartment. "I solved a problem," I explained simply.

She glared at me, hands still clamped to the sides of her head. "Is that how you solve all your problems with women? Drug them?"

It was meant to be sarcastic, but I could hear the genuine, fear-filled question in her tone. I imagine part of her was wondering if I brought other women here, maybe hacked them to pieces out on the back deck. I could work with that.

"I prefer handcuffs, but when the situation calls for it..." I said, allowing the thought to dangle out there in the air. I needed her scared.

And I also needed to do something about the damned stab wound in my back.

I grabbed the elaborate medical kit we kept in the coffee table in front of the sofa and tossed it down next to her.

"You're going to fix this," I said simply.

A mix of surprise and defiance flashed across her face. I watched as she mustered her snarkiest expression. "And what makes you think I'd help you with a bloody thing, you prat?" she retorted, her voice dripping with sarcasm.

I couldn't help but smirk at her audacity. She was a firecracker, that was for sure. I gestured to the seeping wound on my back, evidence of her failed attempt to defend herself.

"Well, you see, when you so kindly stabbed me in the back—not actually a nice thing to do, by the way—you managed to give me quite the souvenir," I replied, taking off my jacket and showing her the bleeding proof of her handiwork. "I'd *appreciate it* if you stitched it up."

Her eyes flared with satisfaction. "Stitch your own wounds," she suggested matter-of-factly.

I chuckled, appreciating her stubbornness. "I would if I could reach," I replied, a mischievous glint in my eyes. "But I'm afraid I'm not much of a contortionist. I saw a show once," I said, waggling my brows. "The woman really had no use for a man with all the places she could reach."

Heidi scoffed. "Then I suppose you'll just have to keep bleeding. Don't worry; I'm sure it'll fester quickly."

She looked very satisfied with that idea.

Me, on the other hand, I was tired, hungry, and sick of feeling my back throb in time to my heartbeat. Altogether, they were making me a bit cranky. "Since you're the one who stabbed me, *you'll* clean up your mess," I snapped.

"Then *you* probably shouldn't have kidnapped me. It's not a good way to make friends."

She said it so prim and proper, I could envision her in Buckingham Palace, giving the royal family a lecture about proper friend-making etiquette.

I turned away, scrubbing my hands through my hair, then winced when the movement hurt the damned stab wound.

Prim and proper or not, I'd had enough.

"If you prefer, I can handcuff you to the bed," I said, nodding toward the hallway beyond the living room, "so I can drive all the way back to the city to get stitched up." I shrugged. "It's a long drive, a long time with no food, no water... no bathroom. But it's up to you." I turned back to face her, waiting for an answer.

"Well?" I said, cocking an eyebrow when she didn't respond.

"Well, what?"

"Make your choice, *signorina*."

Uncertainty flashed in her eyes and her brow furrowed, like she really had no idea what I was talking about.

Christ, it had been a long fucking night. "Do you want to stitch it up or..." I turned toward the window.

"Fine," she said, cutting me off. She looked more flustered than I'd seen her thus far.

But at least that had been easier than I'd expected. I'd been half-prepared to wrestle her onto the bed to cuff her there, and that sounded like one hell of a bad idea. Actually, it sounded like one hell of a good idea... which was precisely why it was a bad idea.

"*Bene*," I said, thrusting everything else out of my head for the time being.

I unbuttoned my shirt and tugged it off. The dried blood clung to my skin and the shirt, and I had to yank harder to peel it away. Fucking wonderful.

I could feel her eyes on me the whole time, roving over me appreciatively. She could hate me with her mind all she wanted; her body had other plans. Those star-flecked eyes of hers were definitely heating up—I'd decided that's what they looked like; rings of twilight sky filled with pale stars.

I tossed my shirt on the coffee table and sat down on the sofa cushion next to her, my back facing her.

"Don't bother trying to run, Heidi; there's nothing around here for a hundred miles. You'd run into animals or collapse from exhaustion long before you made it back to civilization," I warned her. It was a genuine warning. Coyotes and wolves and even bears weren't unheard of in the area.

She didn't answer; she was already opening the medical kit and sifting through the contents inside.

I turned to look at her. "Can you stitch?" It came as an afterthought.

Most of the people in my world had good reason to know their way around a medical kit. But this woman wasn't from my world, and suddenly, I had visions of her stabbing me in the back with a suture needle just for the hell of it.

She shrugged. "I suppose we'll find out, won't we?"

She tugged on a pair of gloves, grabbed a package of gauze and the bottle of alcohol, then shoved me back around none too gently. Which turned out to be nothing in comparison to the fiery hell that followed when she doused the gauze with the alcohol and rubbed it across the open wound. I swear she kept it up far long than was necessary.

I clenched my jaw and stayed silent. I had a feeling she'd take great delight in hearing me groan. *The little sadist.*

When she'd finished with the fire in a bottle, she placed it back in the kit. There was a syringe of anesthetic in there, but she ignored it, readying the suture needle without it. She'd just touched the tip of the needle to my flesh when her fingers hesitated.

She put down the needle and reached for the anesthetic.

"Don't worry about it," I told her. "Enjoy a little payback, *signorina*." It was the least I could offer her.

But once again, she ignored me, picking it up like I hadn't said a word.

I turned to put a hand over top of hers, and she dropped the syringe, yanking her hand away, eyes wide, arms drawn in close to her body when I looked back at her.

Scared is what I'd wanted, right? *Mission accomplished, asshole.*

"Just get it over with," I commanded. "Don't worry about the anesthetic."

Her brow furrowed as her gaze went back and forth between me and the syringe. She nodded after a moment, then picked up the suture needle, her hands steady—which surprised me.

I turned back around and let her get to work.

She dug the needle into my flesh and threaded the first stitch through. Then again and again. I kept silent the whole time, but goddamn it, had the woman really needed to stab me in the first place? I mean, what good had it done her?

Sweat had broken out across my brow, but fortunately for me, she was finished faster than I'd expected. Maybe she stabbed a lot of people and stitched them back up afterward.

"*Grazie,*" I said as she finished applying a bandage and sat back.

I stood up and shrugged back into my bloodstained shirt, leaving it open for the time being.

Heidi remained seated on the sofa, staring at the med kit now. The scalpels and scissors, the tweezers, the unused syringe. All potential weapons.

I couldn't blame her. I would have been looking for a weapon had the roles been reversed.

But I slammed the kit closed and stepped closer.

Now, for the next order of business.

Chapter Five

Heidi

"Food," he said. At least, that's what it looked like he said. What on earth was he talking about? Was he really thinking about food at a time like this?

His lips kept moving as he turned away and motioned beyond the grand stone wall with the hearth in the center of the interior floor space. Presumably, there was a kitchen on the other side. He started walking in its direction, but I couldn't hear him, couldn't read his lips to follow what he was saying.

I considered following him to find out, but there was no way in hell I wanted to get any closer to him.

I glanced toward the front door, calculating the distance—fourteen steps, maybe. And then what? I'd refrained from asking him where he'd taken me, as disorienting as it was to have no bearings. But I hadn't wanted to put any thoughts in his head about me escaping.

He stopped at the open archway next to the hearth wall and turned back to me.

"Well?" he said, one eyebrow cocked, arms crossed over his chest.

I decided to glare at him in silence, since I had no idea how to respond.

He dropped his arms to his sides. "This doesn't have to be difficult, Heidi," he said. *It could be easy,* his eyes said in tandem.

Could I use that? I wondered. He was attracted to me. Men could get very stupid when hormones were involved. But I'd have to be sly about it. Anything obvious, and he'd figure out what I was doing fast.

"Come here," he said. There was no expression on his face. What did he want? What was he going to do?

I stood up slowly but stayed where I was. At least until his lips started to move and he turned around again.

Bloody hell.

I stomped across the sitting room and followed him around the stone wall into a long galley kitchen fitted with every appliance under the sun.

He paused halfway down the galley, just before I'd caught up to him, and he swung around.

"Aren't you a little old for the silent treatment?" he asked with an expression that hovered somewhere between amusement and aggravation.

I contemplated telling him about my hearing—or the lack thereof—but decided against it.

"What is it you want?" I asked, striking a haughty pose with my arms crossed over my chest and my chin tilted up.

"Can you do anything with this?" he asked, nodding toward the cupboards. He opened them up, revealing a multitude of canned foods and dry goods.

I pretended to survey the contents of the cupboards for a moment, then shrugged. "I could hit you over the head with one of those cans. That's something, right?"

He laughed. The tiniest, faint lines appeared at the corners of his amber eyes when he did, and it somehow made him even more attractive.

"You're feisty," he said—which was not an attractive thing to say at all.

"That's an admirable trait in a chihuahua," I spat back. "I assure you, I'm no ankle-biter."

44

He cocked an eyebrow. There were no lines at the corners of his eyes now, but their amber depths filled with heat. "Then where do you bite, *signorina?*"

"Come closer and I'll show you."

On the surface, I'm sure it sounded like some twisted flirtation, but I meant every word. I would have been more than happy to sink my teeth into the tosser. Preferably his neck, where I could tear right through his jugular in the process. Or his carotid. Honestly, I wasn't picky.

He smiled lazily. "Tempting," he said. I imagined his voice like smooth whiskey, the amber liquid—like the color of his eyes—gliding over ice. "Though, if I did come closer, you wouldn't be the one sinking your teeth into flesh." His eyes were intent—no longer *warm,* they felt scorching.

I looked away, denying that he was having any effect on me and focusing on the odd conversation at hand.

"You've brought me here to cook for you?" I asked in a haughty tone that matched my stance.

"No." He didn't elaborate.

I was about to tell him to make his own bloody food, but my stomach chose that precise moment to clench uncomfortably around the nothing inside it. The last I'd eaten had been half a sandwich in the hospital cafeteria, hours before my shift had ended. How long ago had that been? I wondered. I wasn't really sure how much time had passed, and that was disorienting me just as much as my unknown surroundings.

I huffed, dropped my arms, and looked through the cupboards in earnest this time, grabbing cans of vegetables here, a package of cavatappi noodles there. A handful of spice jars and a bottle of olive oil.

Making food wouldn't only serve to satisfy my hunger; it would allow me to familiarize myself with the kitchen. The knives. Scissors. The glassware that could be broken and used as a weapon.

"Pots?" I asked.

He eyed me for a moment, like perhaps he was deciding if I was planning to hit him over the head with them.

Apparently, he determined the threat was minimal because he leaned down in front of the cupboard next to the deluxe Bertazzoni gas range and withdrew two pots and a frying pan. Stainless steel. Too bad; cast iron could have done some worthwhile damage.

He set them on the counter, and I got to work—if it could be called work—boiling water for the noodles and filling the frying pan with olive oil and the canned carrots and green beans, mushrooms and peas.

As I worked, I opened drawers and cupboards under the guise of searching for can openers, spatulas, and dishware.

Finally, I added a few spices from the cupboard that contained a heavy looking pepper grinder, and *voilà*—the kind of meal that had kept me fed through my teenage years. No one had exactly been jumping through hoops to feed me, so I'd figured it out myself.

By the time I'd transferred the food to plates, my captor was looking at the concoction skeptically, like it couldn't possibly be edible, but he made no comment.

It felt like some strange domestic scene right out of the Twilight Zone when he took the plates and transferred them to the oak dining table at the end of the galley. He pulled out a chair and stood behind it, presumably waiting for me to take a seat.

I glared, because this was not some romantic dinner between lovers. This was survival.

"Suit yourself," he said after a moment, then took the seat next to it, leaving the chair pulled out for me.

I left the chair where it was, grabbed my plate, and took it to the other side of the table. It didn't escape my notice that if my plan had been to escape by seduction, I wasn't off to a very good start.

All right, new plan, I thought to myself as I dug into the pasta dish. I'd sneak a knife into my pocket from the drawer next to the sink under the pretense of putting away the dirty dishes. Then, I'd wait for him to fall asleep—because even psychotic killers needed to sleep—and then I'd slash his throat.

It would be quick. Effective. And final.

Murder?

My stomach turned. But it wasn't murder; it was self-preservation, no different than what this man would have done had the roles been reversed.

"I'm trying to do this the nice way, Heidi," he said, pausing halfway through his plate.

"You killed a man. Then you drugged me and kidnapped me. This is your idea of nice?"

He nodded slowly, eyes meeting mine intently. "This *is* the nice way," he said, sending a cold shiver down my spine.

The food I'd eaten sat like a heavy lump in the pit of my stomach. But food equaled strength. It equaled the energy I'd need to survive whatever happened between now and the moment I dragged a knife straight through his jugular. So, I forced down bite after bite until my plate was clean.

"That was surprisingly good," he said, the moment I set down my fork. "*Grazie*, Heidi."

"Don't thank me. I would have doused your food with poison if I'd had any handy."

He laughed, full and hearty, making those tiny lines crease at the corners of his eyes. "I don't doubt it," he said, shaking his head. But he sobered quickly and met my eyes once again.

"The police are a problem," he said, "but not an insurmountable one. You're here because what I need from you more than your silence, is information."

Information? I had plenty of that. "The human heart pumps an average of sixty-seven million gallons of blood in a lifetime," I said.

His brow furrowed in perplexity.

"You wanted information, right? Now you have some."

He barked a laugh, shaking his head slowly. "You really are something. You don't scare easily, do you?"

No, I didn't scare easily. So, it spoke volumes that I was terrified to the bone right now. But fear gave the wielder power, and I wasn't about to hand that over to him.

"I need to know about Bianchi," he said.

"Elio?"

As I spoke the name aloud, a ghost of what I'd felt when I saw him tied and bleeding in his apartment shivered through me. Except, it hadn't been Elio.

But did my captor know that? Did he believe he'd killed the CEO of Bianchi Industries? If he did, then I couldn't let on otherwise.

"What is it you want to know?"

"What are you to Bianchi?"

The question brought me up short. I hadn't been expecting it, nor did I have a word to explain it; we'd never put a word to it. Lover? That sounded too intimate. Boyfriend? Too immature, plus it implied a sort of liking that I just didn't have.

My captor's chest deflated. He had a name—he'd said it—but I hadn't been able to fully make it out.

He reached into his trousers' pocket and pulled out a phone. He pressed a few buttons, then held it out to me, screen up.

There was a picture on the screen. A picture of Elio with a blonde woman on his arm.

He swiped the screen and another appeared, this one of Elio and the blonde at a restaurant.

"…is his girlfriend," I caught the last few words of what he was saying. "So, what are *you*?"

I looked back at the screen, waiting to feel… what? Rejection? The sting of betrayal?

I felt neither, no more than the emotion that came from losing a decent vibrator.

"I'm a convenience to him," I said simply. *And he to me.*

"And yet you had a key to his apartment?" he asked as his gaze turned increasingly suspicious.

If this man had been hoping I had the codes to Elio's bank account or the keys to his safe deposit box, then he was sorely mistaken.

"We shagged," I said bluntly. There was no point in beating around the bush.

His eyes widened just a little, but he covered it quickly, shaking his head slowly. "You look too prim and proper to have a fuck buddy, Heidi."

"And you look too civilized to drug and kidnap women. Clearly, looks can be deceiving."

He didn't laugh this time. Something akin to guilt flickered in his eyes, but surely, it was my eyes playing tricks on me. Despite the drug-induced nap, I was more tired than I'd been in a long time. It felt like there were weights attached to my eyelids, and the tabletop looked as appealing as my own bed at the moment.

"You're not going to make this easy, are you?" he asked.

I shrugged, feigning nonchalance. It lost its effect somewhat when a yawn forced its way out and made my eyes tear up terribly.

He eyed me for another long, contemplative moment, then nodded as if coming to some decision.

He stood up and motioned for me to follow. "Come," he instructed.

I glared at him, unmoving. "As I said, I'm not a dog."

He smiled tightly. "Come with me, *per favore.*"

I eyed him warily. I couldn't follow him yet. I needed a knife from the drawer next to the sink.

"I can pick you up and carry you, if you prefer," he said, his eyes glinting with a mixture of malice and desire.

Maybe now was the time to play on his attraction. But how? Any move I made would be obvious. So, as I stood up, I just looked back at him, meeting his eyes, letting the physical attraction that was there shine through in mine. There was no sense in denying it. I'd watched the play of the muscles across his back when I'd tended his wound; I'd felt them beneath my fingers. The man was an incredible specimen with a model's face and a fighter's body.

His body tautened, and his amber eyes darkened. I could imagine what was taking place inside his body, his heart pumping a little faster and his lungs drawing deeper breaths, innately fueling itself. His pupils dilating. Blood filling the spongy tissue of his cock.

It was all medical, clinical, and yet, I found those things fascinating, the workings of the human body, the thousands of shifts and changes happening inside it at any given moment. All the tiny things that had to go just right to become something more, something alive.

I looked away first, overwhelmed by my own body's response. Rationally, it was nothing more than the physiological response to stimuli. It didn't bother me that looking at my captor made me wet; it wasn't disturbing that my breasts felt heavier or that my nipples had tightened almost painfully. It was innate. Human nature.

What did bother me was the potent urge to act on those physiological responses. Which I had no intention of doing.

The corners of his lips quirked in the tiniest of victory smiles. He'd won. Without knowing it, we'd engaged in a game of "chicken", and I'd come out the loser.

He nodded in the direction of the hallway, back the way we'd come through the galley kitchen.

I opened my mouth to ask where we were going, but he'd already turned away. I wouldn't be able to see his lips even if he answered me.

I waited, lingering. If he turned the corner, I'd make a grab for the knife.

But he paused at the entryway and turned around, eyeing me expectantly.

Arrogant sod.

I followed him, and it was utterly pathetic, the tiny breath of relief my lungs took as I walked past the drawer with the knives.

He led me down a broad hallway to a large bedroom. Its walls were painted a pale gray except for the wall with the window and queen-size bed, which was covered in the same kind of stone as the hearth wall.

Outside the door, he paused, motioning for me to enter.

So, *this* was what he'd intended all along.

My insides turned cold and my gaze swept around the room, searching for anything that could be used as a weapon.

There wasn't much. A pair of candlesticks in pewter holders on the dresser in the corner. Drawn by them, I entered the room, but even if I reached them, they seemed like poor weapons.

I bet you wouldn't have any qualms about dragging a knife across his throat now, the Ice Queen taunted.

"I'm not going to have sex with you," I said, forcing my words to come out slower than the racing beat of my heart.

He followed me, stopping where I stopped next to the dresser, and he leaned in closer, but so slowly, I almost felt like a frog in cold water, oblivious to the rising heat.

"I wasn't asking, *signorina,*" he said, though, by the dark desire in his eyes, I could imagine the huskiness in his tone.

Then he moved, lightning fast.

Something cold wrapped around my wrist, trapping it.

He yanked me toward the bed by the cold cuff around my wrist and fastened the other to the wrought iron headboard, so fast I had no time to respond, to escape. Not enough time to do more than shriek in protest.

"No!" I shouted, trying to scramble away as far as the short chain between the cuffs would allow.

"*Buena notte*, Heidi," he said.

Then he turned around and left the room, flicking the light off as he went and closing the door behind him.

Bloody hell.

My knees gave out, and I collapsed onto the edge of the bed.

My heart raced; my body shook. It felt like he'd pulled a rug out from under me, leaving me reeling for balance.

He'd been one step ahead of me, already anticipating my escape.

Tomorrow, I'd look for an icepick I could take to the cuffs. Had to get out of those before I could go slitting anybody's throat, didn't I?

Chapter Six

Amadeo

I scrubbed my hands through my hair as I stared at the closed bedroom door. *El víbora's* face flashed behind my eyes—the sick fuck who'd dealt in women until we'd taken him down. And Javier Domínguez, the man who'd kidnapped people for ransom.

And here I was, standing on the same goddamned side of their twisted fence.

I had no qualms about being a criminal; the people I killed deserved it, and I had no illusions about where the Lucianos' money came from. Guns. Drugs. Skin—consenting skin that was well-paid.

And the truth was that I'd do a hell of a lot worse to get my hands on Bianchi—evident by the stubborn, defiant beauty cuffed to the bed.

Kidnapper, that's what I'd become. I could practically feel a familiar pair of hazel eyes glaring at me. Greta Agossi was going to give me hell.

I sighed and turned away, but I hadn't made it two steps back down the hallway when my phone rang. I pulled it out and checked the number. It looked vaguely familiar, but tired and frazzled—and more than a little in need of a mind-clearing fuck—it took me a moment to place it.

"*Pronto*," I said as I answered the phone and put it to my ear.

"I have a feeling I got to see your handiwork up close and personal last night," a feminine voice spoke. A familiar, feminine voice.

"Raven?"

"Take a look," she said, and my phone *dinged* a second later.

I checked the photo she'd sent, which turned out to be a quickly taken snapshot of a corpse on an operating table. The blood in my veins coursed a little faster and my free hand curled into a fist. I had a feeling that corpse belonged to one of the men who'd gotten away from us earlier.

"Interesting pastime you have there, *amica*. Taking photos of dead men?"

She scoffed, but there was laughter in the sound. "Maybe the next time you or your men shoot somebody, you could do those of us who work in the ER a favor and make sure they're actually dead. The jerk who came in with him pulled a gun on me and the doctor who was trying to save his life—which is kind of a crappy thing to do, in my opinion."

"My apologies," I said, trying not to laugh. Raven could hold her own, though she always reminded me of a spirited squirrel. Or maybe a cockatoo—intelligent, energetic, and prone to nip if you got too cocky. And after the night I'd had, some asshole waving a gun in some arrogant doctor's face hardly made it onto the "shit I'm going to worry about" list.

"You could at least try to sound sincere, you know?" she said.

"Someone dealt with the asshole with the gun?" I asked, though I was certain of the answer.

"*Si.* Aurelio came in, posing as an off-duty police officer, and scooped him up."

"*Bene.*" Maybe he'd had better luck getting information than I had tonight.

I was getting ready to hang up the phone, but I paused. "The doctor the asshole pulled the gun on—he's all right?" I asked.

"*She's* all right," Raven said breezily. "She's tough. No worries."

I hung up the phone a moment later, just in time to see Vito come in through the cabin's front door.

"*Buenasera*," I greeted him. Or was it morning yet? The sky had begun to lighten to a mottled gray.

Vito turned dramatically and looked out the door before he closed it, then turned back to me while the corners of his lips twitched.

"*Sì*, it's been a long night," I said.

"Did you manage to get anything out of her, boss?" he asked, scrubbing his hand over his mouth, covering his smile.

"A lot of attitude and sarcasm. And a decent meal—does that count?"

And there were those few moments when she'd stopped bothering to hide her attraction. Moments that would have made the night worth it had I not had to cuff her to a bed and walk away. My cock had been all in favor of cuffing her to a bed; the walking away part, not so much.

"Sounds worthwhile to me," he lied. "She is one hell of a looker, isn't she?"

"That's one way of putting it." "A wet dream come to life" was another, possibly more apt, description.

Vito looked past me, down the hall, like he was hoping to catch a glimpse, but he shrugged after a moment. "Aurelio found one of the assholes from yesterday at the hospital, but it doesn't sound like there was anything useful to get out of him. He's on his way here with a team of three others——Mario, Bruno, and Carmine. I'll have them stationed around the cabin outside as soon as they get here. Why don't you go get some sleep, boss? You look like you could use it."

"*Sì*." That was one of the things I needed. "*Grazie*."

I left the living room and headed back down the same hall. My cock jerked as I walked past her closed door. I swear the scent of her still lingered in the hallway. It was vanilla and soft musk and that clean, fresh scent that had my mind conjuring all the ways to make her dirty.

The room beyond the one where I'd deposited her was the master suite. I went inside and closed the door behind me. The room was a palatial version of a "man cave", decorated in deep hunter greens and navy blues, with a fully stocked bar in the far-left corner and a big screen television on the wall opposite the king-size, four-poster bed.

I ignored the bar and headed across the dark oakwood floor for the en suite, an en suite where the white marble floor and walk-in shower were far too reminiscent of Heidi's porcelain skin.

I could see her here as I turned on the water, ditched my clothes, and stepped into the jet streams. Pale hands pressing hard against the pale wall as I pounded her cunt from behind.

The cold water sluiced over me, but it wasn't doing a damn thing to cool the images that flooded my head.

I shifted the faucet dial to hot, then braced one hand against the shower wall as I dropped my free hand to my already-hard cock. It jerked against my fingers as I wrapped them around my shaft and let the images take over.

She has the perfect size tits, just big enough to press together and shove my cock between them. I fuck them from over top of her, watching the tip of my cock reach for her chin with every long, slick stroke.

The image was so vivid, I could almost feel her tits around my cock as I pumped it slowly. But thoughts of her chin sent my mind upward, to those ridiculously plush lips.

I have her on her knees the first time she sucks my cock. I wrap my hand around all that thick, dark hair and use it to control her speed, her depth. I have a vibrator in her cunt so I can feel the vibrations of her moans around my cock. And then, when I'm ready, I use my grip on her hair to hold her still while I fuck her mouth.

My hips jolted as my fingers caught the sensitive ridge of the head of my cock. Christ, that felt good.

When I'm finished with her mouth, I have her on the bed on her stomach. I cuff her wrists to the headboard and shove her knees up under her, giving me a perfect view of her sopping wet pussy and the vibrator I still have inside it.

I work it in and out of her, watching her writhe, hearing her quiet gasps turn to breathy moans. I work her right to the brink, then yank the vibrator out of her. When she whines, I slap her heart-shaped ass and watch my handprint raise across her flesh. It stands out in sharp contrast against her pale skin, and I fight the urge to do it again and again, to cover her in the proof of exactly who she belongs to.

My hand moved faster on my cock, gripping it tighter. The tingling started at the base of my spine; it grew and spread out, reaching for my balls.

When she settles, I move in closer behind her, staring at her glistening wet pussy and the tight bud of her anus.

I line up my cock with her slit and thrust in. Hard. Fast. No warmup.

She cries out, gripping the bars of the headboard tight, but even as I fill and stretch her, she presses back against me, wanting more, craving that sinful mix of pain and pleasure that's better than the best high the world has to offer.

I tightened my fist and worked my cock faster. The tingling had reached its pinnacle as my balls drew up, and white-hot pleasure shot through my body as my cock spurted ribbons of come across the shower floor.

I stayed there, my hand braced against the wall and the hot water jets pummeling my shoulders and back, while my heartbeat returned to normal. Then I shut off the water and stepped out of the shower, lingering just long enough to dry off and throw on my pants before heading back out to the bedroom. I flopped down in the center of the king-size bed and closed my eyes, not surprised to find the dark-haired beauty there behind my eyelids.

Christ only knew how the girl was involved with Bianchi, but there was one thing I knew for certain: Heidi and her killer body had just rocketed to the top of my list of favorite fantasies.

Chapter Seven

Amadeo

The door handle clicked.

The door began to open.

"Boss," Vito said even as I shot out of bed, grabbed my Sig Sauer P229 from the night table, and flipped off the safety.

"It's me," he said as my eyes adjusted to the darkness. Thanks to the blackout curtains, there was no light inside the room, only the spill of it from the hallway.

I flipped the safety back on but kept the gun in my hand. Vito hadn't barged in for no reason.

"We've got company, boss," he said as he flipped the light switch by the door.

"Fuck, that was fast."

I grabbed my shirt and threw it on as we made our way to the surveillance room. The door wasn't locked; Vito had been keeping an eye on the property since I'd gone to bed what felt like a few minutes ago. On the right wall, a bank of monitors flickered with images of the surrounding woods. My heart raced as I saw a dozen figures stealthily advancing through the dense foliage, still a hundred and fifty yards away.

"We're outnumbered two to one," he explained. His eyes flicked from screen to screen—calculation, not fear.

I shrugged. "Better odds than we usually have. Seems pretty good to me," I said as I fitted an earpiece into my ear. "Let them get cozy and think they're taking us by surprise."

Vito smiled while an eager light shone in his eyes. We all got off on this shit; killing assholes and protecting what was ours.

Confidence pulsed through my veins, mingling with the adrenaline that surged at the prospect of imminent danger. I scanned the monitors intently, analyzing the enemy's movements and their coordinated approach, moving in a skirmish line formation through the trees and bushes. They were moving slowly, heads swiveling, watching for threats. Their line was sloppy, though, and their movements felt jerky. They were anything but a well-oiled machine.

There was no doubt that they knew we were here, though, and the burning question whirled in my mind: how did they find us? I'd had no tail on my way here, and I was certain Vito and my men hadn't had one either—we were never sloppy like that.

Then, like a bolt of lightning, realization struck me.

Driven by suspicion, I stormed out of the surveillance room. "Carmine, get in here," I spoke into my earpiece, which connected me to our men outside.

I threw open the door to the room where the girl was sleeping peacefully. Christ, she looked like a goddamned angel with her dark hair fanned out around her head.

"Get up," I snapped, striding across the room.

No response.

"Get up," I said again, shaking her shoulder.

Her eyes fluttered open, then went wide as saucers as she scurried across the bed as far as her restraints would allow.

"We've got a problem," I said.

Confusion clashed with the fear across her face.

"There are people outside, Heidi. Do you know anything about that?"

Her brow furrowed, but nothing else about her countenance changed. No relief. Just bewilderment.

There wasn't time for this. The assholes outside would be on us any minute now.

I unfastened her cuff, pulled her off the bed, and dragged her out of the room, back down the hallway to the surveillance room where Vito and Carmine were waiting for us inside.

She yanked against my hold on her the whole way there, but the moment we stepped into the surveillance room, she froze.

Her eyes widened again as her gaze flickered first to Vito, then to Carmine, who was nearly as big as Vito, in his mid-twenties, with a thick, dark head of hair and a beard to match.

"They're not here to hurt you; we've got bigger problems," I told her.

But still, she tried to jerk her arm backward until her eyes swiveled to the monitors and a quiet gasp escaped her lips.

"Friends of yours?" I asked.

Her wide eyes met mine, innocent and puzzled.

A wave of doubt surged through me, but time was a luxury I couldn't afford.

"You'll stay here," I told her, "and watch what happens to people who try to fuck with me. You don't leave this room. Do you understand me?"

She nodded, almost imperceptibly.

I turned to Carmine. "Stay in here and watch the monitors. Tell us what's coming at us and when we're clear."

"*Sì, Signor*," Carmine said in his raspy, deep voice, hiding his disappointment. No one liked missing out on the action.

I turned to leave, then paused. While it seemed fairly certain she was working with whoever was coming at us, there was no guarantee. She could be in as much danger as the rest of us.

"You keep her here, Carmine," I said, nodding at Heidi. "If they breach our line, you know where to take her."

I glanced at the monitors—seventy yards and closing—then once more at Heidi. Victim or enemy? Time would tell.

Outside, as I left the cabin, the air was thick with tension and eager anticipation as my men took up strategic positions around the cabin, prepared for the inevitable clash.

With each passing moment, the tension grew, and the silence became suffocating.

"They're within firing range, *Signor,*" Carmine's voice crackled on my earpiece.

But the silence stretched on. The kind of quiet that only came on the precipice of pandemonium.

And then the silence shattered as the first shots rang out, cutting through the forest like thunder and sending birds scattering into the sky.

Bullets whizzed past us, biting into the cabin's wooden walls. Splinters filled the air like confetti.

I returned fire, my shots aimed with lethal precision. Each pull of the trigger propelled me further into the heart of the firefight, where survival hung in the balance.

It was a symphony of chaos, punctuated by shouts and the roar of gunfire. The acrid smell of gunpowder mingled with the earthy scent of the surrounding forest. Adrenaline surged through my veins, sharpening my senses and narrowing my focus, blocking out the chaos around me.

There was a faint shadow of movement in the cluster of trees ten yards in front of me. I aimed, waiting.

The shadow emerged—a man dressed in black, armed with a semi-automatic, aimed right at me.

I fired first.

The man fell.

Beyond him, another figure dropped to the ground amidst the underbrush. It was possible that he'd been hit by a bullet, yet I remained patient, watching for the telltale glint off the barrel of his gun.

And there it was, seconds later, even closer. I didn't need the reflection, I could *feel* the heat of it tracking me as I adjusted my aim and pulled the trigger.

A bullet zipped right past my ear, so close I could feel the heated rush of air right before it slammed into the cabin behind me.

The gunfire ceased, and a hush settled over the forest. Fallen adversaries lay scattered amidst the underbrush, their once-intimidating presence reduced to lifeless forms.

"All clear, *Signor*," Carmine's raspy voice came across my earpiece.

I stood up. "Search the area," I called out. "If you find one alive, I want him."

I strode toward the trees and brush directly in front of me. One of the two men I'd shot there was still alive, his breath labored, determination etched across his face as blood pumped from a bullet hole to the right side of his chest. I kicked his gun away and crouched down next to him.

He couldn't have been more than nineteen years old, and his eyes were wide as he gasped for breath like he hadn't seen this coming.

A kid. A kid completely unprepared for battle.

"This is what happens when you fuck with the Lucianos," I told him, fighting the guilt that had no business welling up inside me. He'd made his choice.

"You can lie here until you bleed out, or I can end this quickly for you," I said, holding up my gun in explanation. "The choice is yours."

The goddamned kid groaned and his body convulsed.

"What… do you want?" he panted when he'd recovered himself.

"Information, *amico*. Why are you here?"

He coughed, spewing out a copious amount of blood.

Shit. The guy had seconds left, maybe a minute, before he drowned in his own blood.

"Answer me," I snapped as I held his head upright, trying futilely to keep the blood from blocking his windpipe.

"The... girl," he choked out, then coughed some more, painting the green grass and fallen leaves red.

So, this had been about Heidi.

"She's working with him?" I asked.

He opened his mouth, but all that came out was blood.

He coughed once more, and then it was too late.

His eyes rolled back in his head. His chest stopped moving, and his hands went slack against the ground.

"Dumb fucking kid," I cursed at him as I gently laid his head down on the ground.

This had been no hardened criminal, no well-paid mercenary. A goddamned fucking kid, still wet behind the ears.

I closed his eyes and stood up, but the moment I did, a volley of gunfire exploded.

All I could do was watch as Aurelio's body jolted with each bullet's impact. I could feel them, one at a time, ripping through something inside me.

He fell to the ground, ten yards from the cabin's front door.

I looked around, searching for the source. And there he was, hiding amid a dense cluster of oaks.

The asshole should have run when he'd had the chance.

I fired at the same time as Vito, filling the lone straggler with bullets.

His body jerked and jolted with each impact, then collapsed, dead ten times over by the time he hit the ground.

"Fuck, I'm sorry, *Signor*," Carmine's voice crackled in my ear. "I'm sorry; I didn't see him, I swear."

Every man on the property was already moving, heading straight for Aurelio. Vito and I grabbed hold of his arms and dragged him inside, laying him out on the living room rug.

My heart was pounding as I stared down at the blood that soaked through his cardigan.

"I don't know what happened, *Signor*," Carmine said as he came out of the surveillance room with Heidi in tow, his hand wrapped tight around her arm, pulling her with him. "I swear I didn't see him. I—"

"Quiet," I seethed as Vito dropped down and yanked open Aurelio's cardigan.

I glanced over Heidi, surprised by the small bubble of relief that came from seeing her uninjured. But the relief didn't last long.

"*The… girl,*" the kid had choked out. This had been about her. I'd killed that kid because of her. Aurelio had been shot because of her.

"Bianchi's just a man you fuck?" I seethed at her. I shook my head. "No goddamned way."

Bianchi had sent men straight for her. A lot of men. Whatever reason he wanted her, he wanted her bad.

"It doesn't look good, boss," Vito said as he ripped open Aurelio's shirt beneath the cardigan.

There were two bullet wounds to his abdomen, bleeding profusely. This far out, he'd never make it to a hospital in time.

My heart clenched, and the guilt I'd been pressing back surged like a tidal wave.

Because Aurelio was going to die.

Chapter Eight

Heidi

He wasn't my problem.

The blood leaking from his body and soaking into the Persian rug meant nothing to me.

I recognized the man; it seemed he was no "off-duty police officer". He'd lied. He was a criminal. He deserved every ounce of his agony.

That's what I told myself. That's what I kept telling myself over and over again.

I turned away from the harsh lines of agony written across his face. I tuned out the vague sounds of chaos emanating from the men all around me.

You took an oath, the Ice Queen chastised me in her cool, imperturbable tone.

"I will apply, for the benefit of the sick, all measures that are required… I'd promised. *"If it is given me to save a life…"* I was a doctor. I raised roadblocks in Death's way at every opportunity. No matter what I thought of the people He came for.

"Bloody hell," I cursed under my breath as I yanked my arm out of the stranger's grip and grabbed the medical kit from the coffee table.

"Get out of my way!" I demanded as I pushed my way closer and dropped down next to the man bleeding on the floor.

I could feel the astonished gazes of the men upon me, their confusion palpable.

Ignoring their incredulous stares, I grabbed a pair of gloves from the kit, but a hand wrapped around my arm from behind. A large hand with long fingers that were just a little callused. My captor's hand.

"It's okay," the man on the floor wheezed. His voice was all but gone, but I could see his lips move clearly. "Let the doctor work."

The grip on my arm loosened, but his hand remained there, wrapped around my bicep. I turned to look up at him.

"The doctor?" he said, his brow furrowed with confusion. If I didn't have a man bleeding out on the floor, I'd have to laugh.

"That's right, you sod. You thought I just magically knew how to stitch you up? That everyone just walks around with that kind of innate knowledge?"

I yanked my arm out of his grip and tugged on the gloves. This time, he didn't stop me.

Time seemed to slow down as I leaned over the wounded man, took hold of his hip, and turned him partially onto his side, looking for exit wounds.

There were none. Both bullets were lodged inside him.

"Bloody hell," I muttered under my breath as I laid him back carefully.

I grabbed packets of gauze and compressed both wounds, thinking.

"How far are we from a hospital?" I asked, turning to look up at my captor.

He pressed his lips together, silent. Of course, he wouldn't offer up that information easily.

I huffed before I automatically schooled my face to professional composure. "If you want him to survive, I need to know how far," I said, meeting his eyes with all the cool, clinical detachment I could muster. "The choice is yours."

"Two and a half hours," he said, his gaze never leaving mine like he was watching to see what my brain would do with that knowledge.

If either bullet had hit anything vital, my patient didn't have that kind of time. I'd have to retrieve the bullets.

"Do you have more than one medical kit?" I asked my captor.

He nodded.

"Get it." I spoke with the same calm and confidence I would have used to direct anyone in the hospital. And as much as they hated me there, my clinical assurance conveyed to everyone in the room that I had complete control and the ability to manage any situation that arose. It was no different tonight.

My captor nodded at the big, bald man who was still on his knees across from me, hovering over my patient. He got up and strode out of the room without a word, presumably to retrieve more medical supplies.

I grabbed the bottle of antiseptic from the kit and carefully cleansed the area around the wounds.

"What's your name?" I asked my patient as I readied the anesthetic syringe. I didn't often make small talk, but these were extenuating circumstances. I was going to have to operate with this man wide awake.

"Aurelio Carbone," he said. His face was so pale, the deep lines of pain stood out in sharp contrast.

"I'm going to help you, Aurelio," I said, "but I have no way to put you under right now. The anesthetic–" I held up the syringe. "–will numb the area. You'll feel no pain, but you will still feel tugging and pressure," I explained. "It will feel very odd."

Aurelio nodded while I checked his pulse.

"I'll need you to do your best to stay very still. Can you do that?"

He tried to nod, but it made him flinch. "I'll do my best, *signorina*."

I nodded, then turned away, running through a mental checklist of items I'd need.

"I need a torch or a cell phone light," I said to the man from the room with the monitors. "Hold it on an angle from above, but not directly over the wound." It was the best I could do to keep the area clear of contamination.

Then I looked around at the remaining faces, searching for the calmest one. Not surprisingly, it was my captor's face that looked the most composed. Those amber eyes were worried, but his expression was calm, a calm that communicated itself to the men who were watching him.

"I need you to keep the surgical site clear," I told him. "Stay on the other side of him, put on gloves, and be ready with gauze when I say."

I looked back down, not waiting for his response. He was either going to help me or he wasn't.

Fortunately, he moved around my patient, dropped down to his knees next to him, and retrieved a pair of gloves from the medical kit.

At the same time, the big, bald man reappeared from the hallway, and he placed a duplicate of the first medical kit down next to me.

All right, that was it.

With the light above me and my captor-turned-assistant clearing the field for me, I administered the anesthetic and examined the path of each bullet, tracing it through the layers of tissue and muscle. The impact had caused considerable internal bleeding, but I didn't think any vital organs had been damaged.

Using a scalpel and forceps—the only ones available in the medical kit—I made precise incisions to access the bullet fragments embedded in the abdomen. The metallic glint of the foreign objects contrasted starkly with the vivid crimson of the blood-soaked tissue. Gently maneuvering the forceps, I extracted each bullet fragment, being cautious not to cause any further damage.

The world around me had disappeared and time blurred, my focus consumed by the intricate dance between life and death. My back ached from the awkward, bent position, but even that pain was something distant, like it throbbed from behind a semi-translucent curtain.

As I worked, I sutured the damaged blood vessels and tissues, meticulously repairing the internal structures that had been torn apart.

All the while, my amber-eyed captor's hands were there, sopping up blood, clearing my site each time before I could ask him. It seemed as if he possessed an instinctive understanding of when I required assistance, surpassing the capabilities of most nurses I had encountered. Some detached portion of my mind couldn't help but wonder how he accomplished such a feat.

Once the bullets had been removed, I ensured there was no active bleeding, meticulously tying off any remaining vessels. I applied sterile dressings and bandages to protect the wounds, then sat back on my heels.

The world around me came back into focus. As it did, I rather wished it hadn't.

The men surrounding me had their gazes fixed upon my patient, their expressions reflecting a blend of concern and sadness, as if they genuinely cared about the wounded man. I wasn't sure what to think of that. Individuals like my captor, hardened criminals, were devoid of empathy, resembling monstrous beings more than humans. It was a clear-cut, undeniable truth that I had experienced firsthand.

I looked away and focused on checking my patient's vitals, envisioning the flow of his blood through arteries, then arterioles, then capillaries, then its long return to his heart through venules and veins.

"How are you feeling?" I asked him stiffly.

"Like I've been shot, *signorina,*" he said with a weak smile.

"That could be because you *have* been shot," I said, but stopped the rant that was bubbling its way up my throat. "Your wounds are serious, but now, not fatally so," I finished instead.

I looked up at my captor as he stood up across from me and tossed his gloves onto the bloodstained rug.

"He'll need—" I began, but he turned away from me.

"Get a car ready for Aurelio, Bruno," he told one of his men, a tall, wiry man with a blond buzzcut and a scar that cut across his face from his right temple to the left side of his jaw.

When my captor turned to look at me again, his eyes were snapping and the muscles in his jaw twitched.

"Take off your shoes," he said. The look on his face said his voice probably sounded like pure ice.

I should have been cowering; the logical part of my brain knew it.

"No," I snapped back. Not that I had any particular fondness for my shoes, but I bloody well wasn't handing them over to this churlish sod. "I just saved your man's life—"

"*Sí,* you did," he interjected. "But you're also the one who put his life in jeopardy. Now, give me your shoes. I won't ask again."

I glanced around, but if I'd been hoping for any assistance from the men here, I was a sorely mistaken fool.

I stood up and yanked off my shoes, wishing I was the kind of woman who wore stilettos on a day-to-day basis. They would have made much better weapons than my sensible, comfortable pumps with modest wedge heels.

"Coldhearted tosser with a bloody shoe fetish," I muttered as I chucked them at my captor.

He caught them in mid-air with lightning speed, snatching away any satisfaction I would have gleaned from the impact.

"Take her to her room," he said to the big, bald man.

I almost fought. Almost. But an image of the window by the bed sprung to mind. If the big, bald man didn't cuff me to the bloody bed, then escape was right there, ripe for the taking.

I glared at my captor and took a step back—if I didn't put up at least a nominal struggle, he'd know something was amiss.

"I'm not in the mood to argue with you, Heidi. Go," he demanded.

There was no humor dancing in the recesses of his eyes. It had been there, I realized, from the very first moment I saw him in Elio's apartment. I hadn't realized it because it had been ever-present. It was gone now, though. In its place was an imminent warning, one even the Ice Queen had the good sense not to ignore.

She did not, however, have sense enough to keep her mouth shut. "If he doesn't get a dose of broad-spectrum antibiotics soon, you might as well rip out those sutures; the end result will be the same."

The big, bald man moved to grab my arm, but I'd had more than enough of being man-handled. I stepped quickly away from him and walked—barefooted—to "my" room.

His footsteps followed me, but I didn't turn around until I'd crossed the room's threshold.

"I think I can manage from here," I said, chin up, eyes defiant.

He smiled like he was looking down at a feisty toddler. "I can see that, *signorina,*" he said as he nodded.

He turned to leave, paused, and turned back. "If you were hoping to make a quick escape," he said, gesturing toward the window, "you should probably know the window doesn't open. And it's bulletproof glass."

Bloody hell.

Chapter Nine

Amadeo

"How did you know she was a doctor?" I asked Aurelio as Carmine and I helped him up off the floor and onto the sofa. Mario was currently monitoring the perimeter from the surveillance room and Bruno was readying one of the vehicles for Aurelio's transport. I'd deal with Carmine and his fuck-up later.

Aurelio groaned as we eased him down, and his hands shook, but the moment he was settled, his hands relaxed and the harsh lines of pain on his face eased.

"Raven Luca sent Vito a message from the hospital last night when someone came in muttering about the Lucianos," he explained. "I was already headed in that direction. It sounded like it might have been just what we were looking for. When I went in, she was there," he said, nodding down the hall, presumably in Heidi's direction. "Dr. Dawson, her nametag said."

I sat down on the coffee table in front of him and dropped the tracker I'd found in the heel of Heidi's shoe on the floor. I slammed my foot down on it, crushing it into tiny, useless bits of metal.

"An ER doctor," I said, lacing my fingers at the back of my neck. "That means she's smart. So, what the hell is a smart woman doing jumping into bed with a man like Bianchi?" I mused aloud—and I didn't mean "why was she fucking him". Whatever the two of them were up to went far beyond sex.

Aurelio shook his head. "I think the more pertinent question, *Signor,* is what does Bianchi want from the ER doctor?"

He was right. Bianchi had been keeping tabs on her, had sent his men here to get her. *She* was vital to him. But how?

"He deals in pharmaceuticals," I said, dropping my hands. "She could be stealing drugs from the hospital for him." But I shook my head right away, dismissing the thought. "That's not a good enough reason to send men to retrieve her."

"She's locked down for now," Vito said as he came back into the room. He sat down in the recliner next to the hearth and dropped his elbows onto his knees. "But we should move. Fast."

"*Sì.*" I glanced at my watch. "You move in five."

And I planned to be gone as soon as Aurelio was out of here, but I wouldn't be taking Heidi out the front door—just in case.

He nodded, but tension continued to tauten his shoulders. Vito wasn't much for sitting around with nothing to do. None of us were.

"What's your take on the woman?" I asked him.

Vito grinned. "She's spunky. And good with a needle—I like a woman who doesn't faint at the sight of blood. Hot as hell, too, but she's got a giant 'fuck off' sign across her forehead."

Aurelio laughed, then winced, sucking in a breath. "Prides herself on her skill," he said when he'd recovered. "Justifiably," he added, glancing down at his abdomen.

Vito nodded. "And I agree with what you were saying, boss; I get the feeling she's too high and mighty to be pilfering from the hospital to line Bianchi's pockets."

All true, but none of it got me any closer to an answer.

"As soon as you're on the road, I need intel, Vito. Everything you can find out about Dr. Heidi Dawson. Start with hospital records and work backward from there."

He gave another sharp nod, then stood up, glancing back down the hallway. "High and mighty" she might be, but I had a feeling Vito still wanted to hit that.

Not happening, the greedy fucker in my head snarled. If anyone was getting a piece of "that", it was going to be me.

For now, though…

"Did the asshole from the hospital have anything to tell you?" I asked Aurelio. The man was particularly good at making reluctant men talk.

He shook his head. "I would have contacted you if he was of any use. He and his brother—the man the doctor and Raven were working on—had been hired by one of Bianchi's men—probably his vice president, Owen Thompson, by the description he gave. It was a simple grab job, they were told. They didn't even know who the target was."

"You're certain?" I asked, though it corresponded with the information I got from Thompson before I'd killed him.

Aurelio nodded. "It only took two toenails and a finger, and then he was singing like a canary. Couldn't shut him up."

The cabin door swung open and Bruno walked in.

"We're ready, *Signor,*" he said.

Thank Christ. "*Bene.*"

I called for Mario, and stood back, letting my men help Aurelio up off the sofa and across the living room.

"Carmine," I called when they'd just about reached the open doorway.

"*Si, Signor?*"

"You'll protect Aurelio with your life," I said. Fair, in my opinion, since it was his fuck-up that had gotten Aurelio shot. "If anything happens to him, you might as well use your gun on yourself because it will be a hell of a lot kinder than what I'll do to you. *Capisce?*"

"*Si, Signor,*" he said, nodding while his eyes flickered away with chagrin.

I turned away, dismissing them, and grabbed the broken tracker off the floor.

Now, to move the doctor to a new location.

But I paused halfway to her room. There was one source I could tap for information about Dr. Dawson with minimal trouble.

I pulled out my phone and dialed the number that had called me earlier.

When Raven answered the phone, she sounded breathless; I decided not to inquire why.

"The doctor you work with—Dr. Dawson—what can you tell me about her?" I asked.

Raven scoffed. "The Ice Queen?"

Maybe. I supposed I could see it.

"Dark hair, blue eyes, killer body?" I asked, just to be sure.

"*Si.* Why?" she responded, her tone suddenly tinged with suspicion.

"She was in the apartment of a real scumbag. Aurelio says she's the doctor from the ER last night. I'm just trying to learn what I can." The rest of the details could wait.

"All right, what can I tell you? Well..." Raven paused and the line fell silent. After a moment, she chuckled. "Not much, actually."

"That isn't as helpful as you might think."

"Sorry, *cugino.* She's not exactly the chatty sort."

"You called her the 'Ice Queen'; why?"

The line went silent again.

"Raven?"

"It's what most of the staff at the hospital call her. She's... she takes her job very seriously, that's all. I like that about her; others, not so much."

I sighed. "That's it, huh? You don't know anything else about her?"

"I'm afraid not. Oh! She's deaf."

"What?" My own hearing must have been playing tricks on me.

"Well, she's not completely deaf. She can hear louder sounds in her left ear. I somehow doubt that has anything to do with the 'real scumbag' you were talking about, though."

Heidi was deaf?

"How?" The question slipped out unbidden.

"I don't know," Raven replied as if the thought had never crossed her mind.

"*Grazie, cugina,*" I said, then hung up the phone a moment later.

I thought about all the time Heidi had spent watching me. I'd just chalked it up to the way any captive would watch her captor like a hawk. But she hadn't just been keeping an eye on me; she'd been watching my lips. The few times I'd presumed she was giving me the silent treatment were actually moments when I'd been faced away from her, and she hadn't been able to hear me.

Great detective work, asshole, my mind taunted.

I shook my head as I slid my phone into my pocket and continued on to Heidi's room. Because whatever else she was, she was the woman who'd drawn Bianchi's men here, the woman who'd gotten Aurelio shot. The woman Bianchi was using somehow.

"Let's go," I said the moment I opened the door. But she was standing at the window with her back to me, looking out at the forest that stretched for miles behind the cabin.

For one brief moment, fantasies of the woman flashed through my mind like a porn reel. Her hands cuffed behind her back, her tits thrust out toward me; her lips wrapped around my cock; her legs spread wide open, giving me access to every inch of her slick cunt.

My cock jerked.

Christ.

I crossed the room, but before I could tap her on the shoulder, she spun around. Either she could hear better than she let on at the hospital or

76

she was very intuitive. Picking up vibrations in the floor, maybe? Noticing shadows out of the corner of her eye?

I opened my palm and held out the scraps of the tracker I was holding, curious to see how she'd respond.

Her dark brows drew together as her gaze flickered back and forth between my hand and my face. But now I could see how she'd managed to keep me fooled. Her gaze didn't quite linger on my lips; it swept up them to my eyes and back down again. It looked watchful and wary, and nothing more.

I waited for her gaze to reach my lips on its next pass.

"*This* was in the heel of your shoe," I said, letting the scraps fall to the floor. "You were being tracked," I explained—as if she didn't already know. "You knew Bianchi would be coming for you. I'm guessing that's why you've had no problem giving me a hard time."

"I—"

"I suggest you be more careful from here on out, Heidi; you've got nobody coming to your rescue now."

She glared at me, but before she could get out any more irascible remarks, I decided it was time to get this show on the road.

"It's time to go," I said, motioning for her to follow me.

"So soon? I was just starting to settle in," she said, glaring defiantly. "Or is it that you have more men with holes in them you'd like me to patch up? I hope not," she said, shaking her head with mock sympathy, "because I'm afraid I have a quota. Only one vile criminal per day."

Christ. The woman had no sense at all.

"Move," I instructed her in my not-so-nice voice. Maybe she couldn't hear it, but I was pretty sure my expression spoke volumes.

It spoke loud enough, at least, that it got her hot ass moving, out of the room, through the kitchen, and past the dining table. When I punched in the code to unlock the door at the end of the room and swung it open, though, her feet stuttered to a stop.

"You've got to be kidding me," she said, stumbling back.

I shrugged. "Nothing bad ever happens in basements," I said off-handedly.

She just glared at me some more, clearly not in the mood for humor.

"You're the one who decided to lead your bed buddy right to us, so now we need new accommodations."

"And you think Elio won't be smart enough to check the basement?"

That was debatable given his recent undertaking. "I don't credit Bianchi with much in the way of brainpower, but I do figure he's mastered how to turn a door handle," I quipped. "But you'd have to tell me, Heidi; is he skilled with his hands?"

The moment the words were out, I regretted them. Thoughts of Bianchi's hands all over her awoke something feral inside me that made me want to come all over her.

"That's none of your business," she said, all prim and proper.

Christ, how much goddamn fun would it be to break through that tight-laced exterior to see what lived beneath it?

"Then I suppose we're done talking," I said, ignoring *that* thought. "Get moving," I said, nudging her forward.

So, of course, she turned and darted away, flying back through the galley kitchen.

I caught up to her in four long strides, just as she was reaching for the drawer next to the sink.

I wrapped my arms around her from behind, which pressed her body back against me so that every one of her curves molded to my harder frame. *Christ.*

"You can keep running, Heidi," I said, speaking loud and clear in her left ear. "I don't mind chasing you one bit," I said, fighting the urge to grind my hardening cock against the small of her back. Not completely successfully.

She gasped and her body went as still as a store mannequin.

"Take your hands off me," she said in that haughty, prim and proper tone that, apparently, drove me fucking crazy. Seriously, she was killing me here.

I let her go, since yelling in her ear seemed like a shitty way to have this conversation.

She spun and lunged a step back at the same time.

"Do you want to walk down those stairs, or would you prefer I carry you? The choice is yours, *perla*," I said. A pearl, that's what she was. Rare and refined, and so pale she almost seemed translucent.

"Don't touch me, you tosser," she hissed, then spun and stormed back across the galley to the open doorway that led downstairs.

At the bottom of the stairs, she paused, taking in the big concrete room and the two doors that led off of it. Behind one of those doors, more than a few enemies had met a very gruesome end. But there were cuffs suspended from the ceiling in there. Cuffs that would be perfect for Heidi's wrists, keeping her arms stretched high above her head while I stripped her. Tasted her and touched her. Fucked all that 'prim and proper' right out of her.

Get a grip, asshole. She's not here because she's into your kink.

Signorina 'Prim and Proper' probably didn't even know the meaning of the word 'kink'. She and Bianchi probably had endless hours of prim and proper vanilla sex.

Ignoring the room and the possibilities inside it, I led her across the open, concrete-floored expanse to the only other door and punched in the code. Behind it was a long, concrete tunnel, studded with the occasional recessed light that lit up when the door opened.

"Bloody hell," she whispered under her breath when she saw it. It seemed to be her favorite phrase.

"It's not that far of a walk," I said when she turned to look up at me, the defiance in her eyes wavering amid the disbelief and fear that swam in their blue depths.

"That's easy for you to say," she snapped. "No one took your bloody shoes."

I couldn't say I'd personally walked along the rough concrete barefoot, but maybe a pair of aching feet would take some of the fight out of her.

"You know, big, bad, scary guy here," I said, pointing to myself. "Do you think it might be in your best interest to curb that combative tongue?"

"Because otherwise, you might, what? Stick a needle in my neck? Kidnap me? Cuff me to a bed? Steal my shoes?"

"Do you really think those are the worst things I could do to you?"

She shivered as fear flickered in her eyes. "No, I don't. But a man like you does what he pleases, does he not? I hardly see how my 'combative tongue' will sway the outcome one way or another."

"Clearly, you haven't spent much time in the company of many big, bad, scary men," I mused as *El víbora* and his men jumped to mind, and what they would have done to her if she'd talked back to them the way she'd been spewing snide comments at me. I may have teetered precariously on the line between kink and twisted fuck; they'd blown that line into oblivion.

I was waiting for a snarky retort, so it surprised me when she didn't have one. I took advantage of the momentary silence, and led her down the mile-long tunnel to another set of stairs at the opposite end.

Up the stairs led us into a well-concealed one-car garage where a gunmetal gray Mercedes-Maybach was waiting there for us.

"Get in, *per favore*," I said when I opened the car's front passenger door and she stood unmoving in front of it. "Unless you prefer I put you in the trunk?"

I was rewarded with another glare, but she relented, sliding into the bucket seat and slamming the door closed behind her. And then she proceeded to glare out the window in silence.

It was music to my ears.

***

"Where are we?" Heidi asked, speaking up for the first time as I slowed the car, approaching the gated driveway that led home.

"We've had a similar conversation before, have we not?" I said as I turned into the drive and the tall iron gate opened up.

She huffed. "I can read road signs; our general location is hardly a mystery."

Ah, how I missed this.

I didn't respond as I shifted the car into park at the top of the driveway. Maybe I should have. I certainly should have seen it coming when she threw open the passenger door and bolted.

Fuck.

She was making a beeline straight back down the driveway, her bare feet slapping against the pavement. Even barefoot, she was fucking fast.

"Heidi, stop!" I yelled, chasing after her, but she couldn't hear me. *Fuck. Fuck. Fuck.*

She only made it another ten yards before Carlo, one of our men, stepped out into her path, gun in hand. Even without the gun, he would have intimidated the hell out of most people with his linebacker build and thick, dark beard.

She stuttered to a stop, too arrogant to put her hands up, too stubborn to surrender.

I couldn't see her face, only the slight jerky movements of her head as she glanced left and right, cataloguing her options.

She couldn't hear me approaching, and it gave me some sort of sick satisfaction when I wrapped my arms around her from behind and she jolted, a quiet squeak escaping her lips.

Without taking her eyes off Carlo, she tried to yank herself out of my grip. Her skin felt colder than it should have, and through my grasp on her, I could feel her body trembling.

"I've got her, Carlo. *Grazie.*"

"*Si, Signor Luciano,*" he said as he holstered his weapon, staring at Heidi a heartbeat too long before returning to his post.

"Get your hands off me," she seethed as Carlo walked away.

I almost laughed. If only she knew what I was thinking with her writhing body pressed up against me… my hands probably wouldn't have been the biggest worry on her list.

Chapter Ten

Heidi

He loosened his grip, and I didn't waste a second. I yanked and broke free.

I thought about running. I wanted to run. But there was no point.

"No matter how many times you try to run, I'll catch you," he said. There should have been a creepy look in his eyes, but there wasn't. It was all very matter-of-fact. "Even that stubborn brain of yours has to be piecing that together by now."

"Go to hell," I hissed, taking another pointless step back.

He was ready though, muscles coiled, eyes watching. If I bolted again, I wouldn't make it two steps.

"One day I'll make a trip there, maybe, but not today, *perla*. Today, I have a job to do."

"Kidnapping women hardly qualifies as a job."

He pinched the bridge of his nose like he was staving off a headache, shaking his head at the same time. "You really need to rein in your claws before we go in there," he muttered, nodding toward the enormous gray stone mansion.

Claws? "I'm not a dog. Or a cat."

He laughed like that was somehow funny. "I was thinking more of a prim and proper Tasmanian devil.'

Well, actually, I rather liked that—not that I'd admit it aloud.

His smile fell away, and he was back to pinching the bridge of his nose. "Sit down," he said, nodding to a bench in the gardens off the main driveway amid a cluster of Japanese lilac trees.

I shook my head. I wasn't trembling, I realized. The man with the gun had walked away, and I'd... what? Relaxed? That wasn't the word for it. I was still on guard, but it felt like I was waiting for an attack from the side or from behind, not from the man who stood directly in front of me. Which was ridiculous, of course.

"Sit. Down," he said again. This time his lips moved in exaggerated enunciation, which made it feel like there were worms writhing beneath my skin. The exaggeration was common to people learning that I read lips. It made me feel like an infant with people speaking to me in slow, exaggerated tones. I didn't think that was this man's intent, but it had the same aggravating effect, nonetheless.

But rather than reveal the effect he was having, I huffed— exaggeratedly—and stomped across the grass to the bench, sitting down neatly at the edge of it.

He sat down right next to me, his thigh pressed up against me. I expected it to feel warm; what I wasn't expecting was the way my thigh tingled all along where he made contact. I tried to draw myself further away, but I'd foolishly positioned myself right at the edge. Any further, and I would have fallen right off.

I moved to stand instead, but stopped. It would probably give him satisfaction to see me flustered.

"That asshole you've been fucking was tracking you," he said. There was a certain twist to his lips as he said the word "fucking" like it repulsed him in some way. "Bianchi wanted to know where you were every minute of every day. So, that leaves me with two options: Either you're in league with him, and I can't let you out of my sight. Or, he's stalking you, and you should be damn grateful you're here with me because it might be the only goddamned place you're safe."

Safe? Nothing since I'd found this man in Elio's dining room with a gun in his hand had felt safe. I opened my mouth to tell him he had a very skewed understanding of safety, but I paused.

He was a criminal, no doubt. But that didn't mean every word out of his mouth was a lie. In fact, the best liars often relied heavily on the truth, did they not?—peppering in fibs only where necessary. It was possible, then, that there was some truth to what he was saying about Elio.

"How can I know you even retrieved that thing you claimed was a tracker from my shoe?" I asked. "You could be lying."

His chest deflated even as it shook with a half-hearted laugh. "Do I look like a five-year-old who has nothing better to do than play games?"

I looked him over, but the perusal only served to make me painfully aware of the tingling in my thighs, the way it branched out, spreading until it set off sparks low in my abdomen.

But putting aside the innate response to his physical appeal, it did seem that "playing games"—as he put it—was beneath this man who carried around him a potent air of power and authority. So, why lie? He'd proven he could take what he wanted. The lie made no sense. Not that I had any intention of admitting it.

"You most certainly do not look like a child," I said. "You look like a murderer. You look like a man who kidnaps women and keeps company with men who have no qualms with that."

He nodded with no hesitation. "You're right; my men are loyal to me. And they know if I'm keeping you here against your will, there's a damn good reason for it."

"A good reason?" I shook my head emphatically. "There is never a good reason to abduct and terrify a human being."

"You hardly look terrified, *perla*." There was a light in his eyes as he spoke that I couldn't quite put a name to at first, but then it came to me. Respect. Begrudging, perhaps, but respect nonetheless.

All right. He'd never be able to convince me he wasn't evil, but he seemed bloody certain Elio was evil as well.

"You were in Elio's flat. You… tortured and murdered a man in his employ. Why?" The words felt ridiculous on my tongue. There was no excuse that could justify what he'd done.

"Those men—Elio Bianchi and Owen Thompson—fucked with my family, my flesh and blood, Heidi. So, whether you're helping Bianchi or not, maybe you can understand why this man is a problem for me, why this would go a whole lot smoother if you stopped fighting me and helped me?"

My jaw dropped. Help him?

"You thought if you spouted the word 'family', I'd be helpless to fight the empathy that welled up inside me and I'd rally to your cause, however vague that cause might be?" I cocked an eyebrow at him, fighting down those very same empathetic feelings I was bashing. Or maybe it was sympathy? Because how could a woman who had no family truly empathize with a man who did? I shook my head. "Even if what you're telling me—very vaguely, I might add—is the truth, how is any of it my problem?"

"You're a doctor, right?" He raised his eyebrows at me. "Don't people do that shit because they're all about helping people?" He flashed me a sexy grin. Combined with the flare of heat in his eyes, it told me he was used to getting what he wanted using one power or another.

Perhaps it was time to get one thing straight.

"I've seen the way your men jump to your every command, and I have eyes," I said, forcing my gaze to graze over him coldly. "I have no doubt women clamber all over each other to do your bidding. So, I'm sure you're quite unaccustomed to a man who doesn't obey you or a woman whose sole purpose for existing isn't to please you. But your life and your problems are precisely that—yours. I learned a long time ago that sad stories don't make people just jump to your aid." Not even for a child. "Perhaps it's time you learned that lesson as well."

"How did you learn it?" he asked. There was no calculation in his eyes; it was a genuine question.

That threw me off; I hadn't been expecting it.

"That's none of your concern," I told him, sitting up straighter, arranging my features in the same way I did for a med student who walked into the ER, thinking they were God's gift to emergency medicine.

"You really are the Ice Queen, aren't you?" he said, shaking his head.

My breath froze in my lungs. He couldn't know that term unless he'd been stalking me, unless he'd been listening in the hospital's halls.

He was looking at me, watching me. It felt like he was stripping me down, peeling off layer upon layer with his piercing gaze.

"Where did you hear that?" I asked.

"Raven Luca."

A weight dropped like lead in my stomach.

"What did you do to her?" I snapped, my voice half-strangled in my throat.

He cocked an eyebrow at me. "How is that your problem?" he mocked. "Aren't you all about looking out for number one?"

I looked away, silently cursing myself. He'd caught me. He'd walked me right into a trap, and I'd been none the wiser.

"If you hurt her because of me—"

"You'll what? Refuse to help me?" he asked with a wry grin.

"If you hurt her because of me then you really are the monster I pegged you to be."

He scoffed. "That's interesting."

Was it? I didn't see how.

"You seem very concerned about Raven, but I was under the impression you had the utmost disregard for criminals?"

I nodded, but he was shaking his head, laughing. It felt like he was laughing at me.

"If that's true, then your concern for Raven is seriously misplaced."

What?

"Raven Luca is about as steeped in the 'criminal' world as a person can get."

"You're mad." The competent, unflappable nurse hardly struck me as a coldhearted criminal.

"Am I?" He shrugged dismissively. "I still prefer to think of myself as creatively misunderstood. As for Raven, what you might not know is that she's the youngest child of the Luca family, cousin to the Lucianos. And fiancée to the don of the Costa family. All very powerful 'criminals'."

He could have been lying, but again, games seemed beneath this man. "Well, then I suppose that explains why she had no qualms in telling you all about me."

"It seems there wasn't much to tell," he said. There was a speculative light in his eyes I didn't like.

"I keep my professional and personal lives separate—not that it's any of your concern either," I said, forcing the words out past a lump that had suddenly formed at the back of my throat.

It didn't help that he kept watching me. His eyes were doing that piercing thing, trying to strip off layers.

I turned away. Because any sight had to be better than watching him try to strip me down like that.

"I take it this is my new prison?" I said, ignoring the lump in my throat, as my gaze settled on the enormous gray mansion surrounded by elaborate gardens all around, then I turned back to face him.

"*Sì*." He nodded, looking over at the house with a contented smile on his face. He was comfortable here; he belonged here. "You're going to love it, *perla*. It's filled with all of us *criminals* you love so much."

A shiver shot down my spine as images of tall men and a short one flashed behind my eyes. A spider scar; I could feel it creeping down my spine.

I didn't realize until my teeth started to clack together that I was trembling from head to toe.

He put a hand on my knee, and my breath caught in my throat. I didn't yank my leg away or brush off his hand. I just stared at his long fingers—I don't know for how long—disgustingly comforted by their warmth.

"Tell me what you know about Bianchi," he said when I finally looked up at him. I swear that beneath the scrutiny in his gaze, his eyes were just the tiniest bit beseeching. It seemed out of place. This hardened criminal didn't beseech; he took. A burglar with a loaded gun didn't say please. A murderer didn't implore his victim to lie down.

"Nothing," I replied, but I had a feeling it came out like a breath, like a whisper of the wind. Because the feel of his hand on my thigh unnerved me. Because that look in his eyes had shaken me.

But mostly, because it was a lie.

Chapter Eleven

Amadeo

There was a crack in her armor. A thread-like fissure amid the impenetrable shield that seemed to surround her. It was there in the way she left my hand resting on her knee. In the way her lies slipped out like wisps of smoke, not blazing flames.

The crack was a way in. Usually, those cracks formed from beatings and blood. From knives and razor blades. Nails. Guns. Fire. Those were the tools with which I'd always extracted answers, pulled them out through those cracks that inevitably formed in every enemy I'd tortured.

But here sat my enemy, unscathed, cracking beneath simple touches and calculated guesses. What a mindfuck.

"Come," I said as I stood up. I needed time to regroup.

She opened her mouth, a snide comment fresh on her tongue, no doubt.

"Come with me, *per favore*," I said before it could slip out. I wondered if she could hear the no-bullshit tone in my voice by the "don't fuck with me" look in my eyes.

She stood up, lips pressed together, gaze swiveling back and forth between me and the house.

I reached out to take her arm, but she sidestepped me.

"I'm capable of walking on my own," she said in that prim and proper tone that was turning into some fucked up aphrodisiac and making me hard. Christ, this woman was all kinds of difficult.

"It seems when I don't have a leash on you, you're quick to scurry away," I replied, definitely not thinking about how fucking incredible she'd look in collar and leash. My cock jerked against the uncomfortable confines of my pants.

She glared at me, but she was right. Not touching her was definitely the wiser move at the moment.

I motioned for her to go ahead, and she turned, walking tall even in bare feet. She marched all the way up the drive, right up the front steps to the door, but then she paused, body tense, back to trembling. And didn't that make me feel like a first-class ass?

She's working with Bianchi; don't you dare feel sorry for her, dumbass.

That was all the motivation I needed to brush past her and walk inside. She lingered slightly behind me, to my left, but to her credit, she followed, shoulders back, even if they were trembling.

My father was already standing at the other end of the big marble-floored foyer, in front of a tall, rock waterfall wall. He had his hands behind his back, an unreadable expression on his face.

The moment Heidi caught sight of him, her feet stopped moving.

"*Buongiorno, Papà,*" I greeted him, not missing the way Heidi moved a little closer to me. *Interesting.* I'd gone from monster to protector, had I? Though I had a feeling it was more of a case of "the evil you know".

And then the pair of hazel eyes that had been glaring at me from the back of my mind ever since I'd "run into" Heidi appeared at the top of the tall, spiral staircase.

"*Buongiorno,* Deo,*" Greta Agossi called down the stairs, fluttering her fingers at me as her gaze swiveled to Heidi.

Shit.

Heidi's gaze kept flickering between my father and Greta, and every few seconds, it ended up on me. It made her look skittish, but thanks to Raven's intel, I knew better. What she was really doing was watching lips, trying to keep up with whatever was being said. And Christ, it looked exhausting.

"*Buongiorno,* Greta," I said, though I would rather have just pretended she wasn't here at the moment. "I'm going to get Heidi settled; then we'll catch up, *si?*"

If Greta was going to chew me out, it was probably better Heidi wasn't around to witness that. It might shake her confidence in my scary-ass monster persona.

"Looking forward to it, *amico,*" Greta replied with a "*you so better have a good explanation for this*" look in her eyes as she descended the stairs. She might have gotten her start working for the Lucianos, but she'd earned every bit of the respect we gave her, and she knew it.

As I motioned Heidi toward the staircase, my father raised an eyebrow at me. He said nothing, but the gesture spoke volumes. *We have a nice, cozy 'interrogation' room in the basement for your... guest,* it said.

I shrugged and continued toward the stairs. Clearly, I'd be making an appointment to get my head examined tomorrow. But the thought of Heidi in my bed, her hair spread out around her like a dark halo? Yeah, I was a totally sick fuck.

She didn't say a word on the climb up the stairs or down the hallway. When I opened the door to my suite, her shoulders stiffened, and I waited for her to try to bolt.

No bolting.

She walked into the room, then spun around to face me. "Why am I here?" she asked with as much haughtiness as she could muster. It wasn't much.

"You'd rather be down there with them?" I asked, curious how she'd respond.

"I'd rather be at home with a book and a glass of red wine," she said without missing a beat.

I laughed. The girl was a chore, but Christ, she was entertaining.

"Books," I said, nodding to the nightstand beside my four-poster, king-size bed where a stack of sci-fi books and a few business journals had been sitting for the past few months. "The wine will have to wait, but I'll see what I can do."

Her brow furrowed. "I don't think you've read many kidnapping guides, have you?"

"Is there one you'd recommend?"

That seemed to catch her off guard, but not for long. "No, but I believe the '*United States Criminal Code*' might be a worthwhile read for you."

"Nah." I shook my head. "I've heard a few spoilers; completely ruined it for me."

She pressed her lips together. If I didn't know better, I would have sworn she was fighting a smile. She shook her head after a moment and all traces of humor fell away.

"I don't understand," she said. Fear had climbed back into her voice, even if she was doing her damnedest not to show it. "If I'm such a threat, shouldn't you be pulling out fingernails or breaking my kneecaps?"

"I've taken and confined many people against their will, *perla*." *And every one of them has met a very unpleasant end.* I decided to leave that part out. "If I'm telling you to rest and read a book, don't look a gift horse in the mouth."

She crossed her arms over her chest, though the way her fingers curled around her ribs made it look less haughty and more like a self-comforting gesture.

She dropped her hands all of a sudden like she realized she'd been caught in the act.

"No handcuffs this time?" she asked, trying to cover up her error.

A bolt of heat shocked through my body. "Do you want me to handcuff you?" The words slipped out before I could stop them. Or maybe I didn't want to stop them. Maybe the 'Ice Queen' needed to learn what happened when she played with fire.

She lifted her chin and turned away without a retort, so unless I wanted to shout, it seemed the conversation was over.

I left the room and locked the door with the app on my phone—the Lucianos were very fond of high-tech shit, particularly high-tech security shit. In the brief moments I'd been gone, Vito had returned; I could hear him conversing with my father as I descended the stairs.

Vito nodded to me as I reached the foyer. "The doc says your doctor did one hell of a job," he filled me in. "Aurelio's going to be fine."

A small knot of tension in my gut eased. Aurelio had been with the Lucianos since I was a child; he was like family.

"*Your* doctor?" Greta said. "Presumably the woman upstairs?"

I nodded.

"She saved Aurelio's life, and you're keeping her locked up like a prisoner? Remind me never to save your life, *amico*," she jibed, though there was no venom in it. As much as Greta might not have liked the situation, she knew me well enough to give me the benefit of the doubt before she went all "crazy superwoman" on me.

But first things first.

"How's Freya?" I asked, my gaze swinging back and forth between my father and Greta.

My father sighed and nodded to Greta, letting her fill me in since, presumably, she was just upstairs with her.

Greta's lips curved upward in a half-smile. "Shaken, but not stirred. She's stronger than you guys give her credit for," she said, daring to swing a mildly accusatory glare at my father. Greta was probably the only person on the planet who could get away with that.

But talking about Freya flooded my head with fresh memories. Memories that would stay in my head for the rest of my goddamned life.

"We're close, boss," Bruno says. "We just left L'Ultima Cena, two blocks away. Aurelio's with me."

"I'm coming. Hold them off, Bruno." But even as I say it, something twists up painfully in my chest. It's too far. I'll never make it.

And then the sounds come all together. The crack of a gunshot. The shatter of glass. My sister's scream.

I grip the phone so tight, it's a wonder it doesn't crack as I fly out of the parking lot, listening, helpless, as a volley of gunfire continues.

The volley subsides, but I hear no voices. Not Bruno's. Not Aurelio's... not Freya's. Endless minutes. Endless traffic.

When I finally arrive on scene, the car in front of our white Lexus LS is squealing away. There are two men in a dark blue Nissan and a puddle of blood on the ground next to where it had been parked. Another three men dead near the car behind ours. Not my men.

The dire urge to go after the Nissan pumps through my veins, but I race to the Lexus instead, my heart pounding, trying to prepare myself for what I'm about to see, trying to prepare myself for Freya's bullet-riddled, lifeless body.

But she's not there. The car's empty. No sign of her but for a smear of blood on the rear passenger seat.

"We've got her, Signor," Aurelio's voice comes from way down low on the other side of the Lexus.

My chest unclenches as I hop over the hood of the car. Freya's on the ground. I crouch down next to her. There's blood on her arm, a few inches below her shoulder. Enough blood to bloom through the sleeve of her cream-colored shirt, but not enough to be alarming.

Just infuriating.

As I stand back up, I survey the dead men on the ground. Their clothes, their faces. The first two are strangers; I've never seen them before. But the third one, I know that face. I've seen it before.

And the man who'd sent him has just made a very big mistake.

"Get her home, Bruno," I say as I help Freya to her feet. "Aurelio, I want you tracking the ones who got away."

As for me? I'm heading straight for the source.

By the time I'd gotten to Bianchi's apartment, the cowardly fuck was long gone. He should have taken his scumbag VP with him, though. That fucker squealed like a fucking pig when I cut him.

"All right," Greta said, making herself comfortable in one of the wingback chairs in my father's office. We'd moved there at some point in the past thirty seconds. Can't say I had much recollection of it. "I get why we're after Bianchi. What I don't get is why Bianchi was after you, *Signor*— or after Freya, in this case."

My father shifted in his seat behind his mahogany desk. He didn't generally discuss Luciano matters with anyone but the closest men in his top circle, but Greta had become an exception. I think it might have been the aura about her that said she could handle shit, and more than that, it said that she wasn't going to go away, so you might as well let her in.

My father cleared his throat and steepled his fingers on the desk in front of him. "Elio Bianchi wants two properties owned by the Lucianos. When he couldn't bribe me out of them, he tried to threaten me with legal ramifications." He scoffed at the ridiculous notion. "When that didn't work…" He trailed off, brow furrowed, murderous rage flashing in his eyes.

"Two properties?" Greta's frown was almost a mirror of my father's as she sat up straighter. "This seems a little extreme for a bit of real estate, doesn't it? The guy had to know what he'd be going up against when he went after Luciano property… and then his *daughter*," she said with barely a telltale hitch in her tone.

Freya was my father's only legitimate daughter, but I had a feeling Greta knew that he truly had two. I'd seen it right away, when she'd come into our lives after growing up in LA. Others had, apparently, been slower to see the resemblance.

"I can help with that, *Signor*," Vito said, addressing my father as he placed a file folder down in front of him. "After the attack on *Signorina* Luciano yesterday, we finished tearing apart Bianchi's finances and his company. Essentially, he's broke. He and his vice president, Owen Thompson, have been cooking the books, but there's no money and a lot of debt. It looks like he may have needed those properties to close a development deal that would have gone some way in paying off what he owes."

My father looked over the files, nodding to himself every once in a while.

"This," Vito said, holding out another folder like he wasn't quite sure where to put it, "is that information you asked me to get," he said to me. "It's all we could find on the girl. We'll do more digging…"

I grabbed the folder and opened it up. There was plenty here. Work records, college records. High school. Social services and foster care documents. Police reports and news clippings. All the way back for seventeen years. And then nothing.

No birth certificate, no passport. No medical records. No school records. Absolutely nothing.

I perused the police reports and news clippings as an uncomfortable sensation settled in my stomach. According to these, her parents had been murdered when she was nine years old, right in front of her. She'd lost her hearing that same night—both eardrums blown out when the assholes had fired their guns right beside her ears.

When she'd recovered, they'd tossed her into foster care. She'd had no family that she knew of, and not a single identifying document in the family's home to point social services in the right direction. It was like she and her parents had appeared out of thin air.

I put the folder down, and Greta picked it up.

"She's not from here," I said, like that somehow filled in the giant black void of missing information prior to the night of her parents' murders. "And she really hates criminals," I mused aloud to myself aloud. "I suppose I can't blame her." Not that we were well-liked in general, but a childhood experience like that could justify a lot of hate.

After some time, Greta dropped the folder back down on the desk, shaking her head.

"All right, so, smoking hot British girl drops out of the sky just in time for a really shitty childhood. She busts her ass through school despite being tossed from foster home to foster home, completes her residency in emergency medicine… and then gets herself involved with a tanking corporate CEO who's dumb enough to go up against the Lucianos?" Greta kept shaking her head. "In what universe does this make sense?"

Vito laughed while my father looked over at her, eyebrow cocked at her colorful summary, but there was a flicker of humor in his eyes. Which was not something that flickered in my father's eyes often.

"Are you suggesting she's innocent, *cara mia?*" he asked.

Greta pursed her lips, tapping her lime green fingernails on the desk. "That would be too simple, wouldn't it?"

I nodded in agreement. "Bianchi's been tracking her, and he had men coming after her the minute I absconded with her."

""Absconded'?" Greta said, cocking an eyebrow while her lips twitched. "That's the word we're going with?"

"I thought you'd like it better than the alternative." Abducted, kidnapped; those weren't some of Greta's favorite words. "But my point is," I continued, "he's seriously invested in her. She says she knows nothing…"

"But you're not buying it?" Greta speculated.

I shook my head. "I don't know if she's outright working with him or if she just knows something, but she's definitely lying."

"She's a woman, right?" Greta asked. "Has a heartbeat and a pair of eyes?"

"*Sì.*"

"And you haven't thought about maybe putting all of *that* to good use?" she said, with a flick of her fingers that indicated my whole body.

I scoffed.

"Are you telling me she's immune?" Greta dropped her jaw in mock astonishment, but recovered quickly. "I can try talking to her," she offered with a shrug.

Usually, I'd say Greta was a force to be reckoned with, and she was. But in this case? "I think I might have met your match, *amica*."

She looked at me expectantly, waiting for me to elaborate.

How exactly could I describe her? "Heidi's…"

"Uncooperative?" Vito filled in for me.

That was one way to put it.

Greta waved a hand dismissively. "Well, she did see you shoot a guy in her boyfriend's apartment, followed up by drugging and kidnapping her… Hm, I can't imagine why she's not feeling very 'cooperative'."

"Ah, *Signor?*" Giovanni said, poking his gray-haired head in the office doorway. He was the butler of the estate, but the title seemed too small for the myriad responsibilities he undertook on a daily basis.

All three of us turned to look at him.

His lips were pressed tightly together like he was holding back laughter, but his eyes were narrowed with what might have been concern. "My apologies, *Signor,*" he said, nodding first to my father, then to me. "But the *signorina* is… on the roof."

Chapter Twelve

Heidi

I stared into my captor's bedroom from the slanted, shingled roof where I stood. This had certainly seemed like a better idea from *inside* the room. Out here, the ground was laughing at me, throwing up a checklist of all the bones I could break: tibia, fibula, tibial plateau, femur, hip.

The window I'd climbed out of was a dormer, set back from the edge of the roof by four or five feet. It gave me a surface to climb out onto—albeit a slanted, rough surface—so I could ease my way to the edge of the roof where I would then be able to hang-drop to the ground. Ten feet down, I'd gauged when I first peered out. Now, I wasn't so sure. Twelve seemed like a more accurate guess.

"Doable," I said aloud. Less than seven feet once I was hanging from the roof's edge.

I eased myself down onto my knees and crawled to the edge, muttering obscenities about beautiful criminals the whole way. It was certainly preferable to focusing on what I was about to do or how, even if I managed to make the drop unscathed, I still had to get away from this place without running into any more men with guns.

A long shot? Absolutely.

I reached the edge of the roof and looked around, scanning the tastefully landscaped grounds and gardens for men with guns.

What the bloody hell are you doing, *Heidi-girl?* It's what my father called me, and I swear I could hear his voice, whispering inside my head. There was no cold, faint brush of disapproval blowing against my shoulders, though. He couldn't be completely opposed to my plan.

I'm getting out of here, Daddy, I told him as I maneuvered onto my stomach and stretched out my legs. I hadn't spoken to him like this in a long time, not since I was in high school. It was comforting to think of him here beside me, to think that he was more than a warm ray of sun or a cool gust of wind.

You'll be all right, luv, my mother crooned.

It seemed my mind was calling in all the big guns for encouragement today.

I took a deep breath and flexed my arm muscles, testing them. Thanks to morning runs and the occasional weekend afternoon at the gym, I was in reasonable shape, but I didn't have the muscle of a bodybuilder. I'd only have to support my weight for a moment, though.

My hands shook—which was not at all useful to my task—as I lowered one leg over the roof's edge. I looked down one last time—which was not at all useful either—then endeavored not to look down again as I grabbed hold of the gutter. It was metal, not plastic, which meant it had a much better chance of holding my weight long enough for me to swing my other leg over and drop down.

I squeezed the gutter as hard as I could and swung my leg over.

The metal bent and bit into my fingers as I swung free, and my shoulders screamed in protest.

I took a deep breath, tried to relax my body for the impact, and let go.

I dropped.

I dropped so fast it took a moment to register that I didn't hit the ground.

Arms wrapped around me, gripping hard, crushing my ribs.

Then my feet lowered to the ground, slowly, gently, and the vise around my ribs loosened.

"Where the bloody hell did you come from?" I screeched as he let me go and took a step back. My captor, of course. Who else?

"You're welcome," he said as the corners of his eyes creased and his lips quivered with silent laughter.

"You expect me to thank you? There's no way you just happened to be passing by, so if you knew I was going to go out the window, why didn't you just stop me?"

"And miss the show?" The laughter broke free.

I'd never felt the compulsion to hit another human being before. I'd never considered myself a violent person. But plenty of violent urges were crawling up my spine.

"What exactly was your plan?—to drop, break your ankles, and army crawl your way to freedom?"

"I had no intention of breaking my ankles." The chances of that happening were twenty percent at best, placing the odds firmly in my favor.

He shook his head, still laughing at me. "I'm not sure gravity would have been terribly concerned about your intentions. It's pretty stubborn that way—you two would get along great."

"I'm not stubborn; I'm tenacious. If you think I'm just going to——"

"Let's go, *perla*," he said, gesturing in a grand sweep toward the front door. "Your great escape will have to wait; I'm tired."

"You expect me to just follow you back inside?"

He looked up at the window, then back to me. "Unless you'd rather climb back up?"

"Insufferable sod," I muttered under my breath as I made my way back to the front door. Fortunately, there was no one in the foyer as we stepped inside this time. Less than fortunately, he led me right back upstairs to the suite of rooms that I had no doubt belonged to him.

He unlocked the door with an app on his phone and walked right in.

I watched him as he took in the condition in which I'd left his rooms, and I felt a moment of triumphant satisfaction, quickly snatched away when he didn't bat an eyelash.

He strolled across the Aubusson rug to the mini bar in the far-left corner of the sitting area. The bed and walk-in closet were on the opposite side of the room where I'd wreaked the most havoc. I'd emptied bedside tables, dresser drawers, and one conspicuous black duffel bag that I rather wished I hadn't opened. A bag I'd been quite hopeful would be filled with weapons or even old gym socks I could use to make my captor keel over. A bag that had, instead, been filled with every kind of erotic fetish implement known to man; cuffs and whips, blindfolds and clamps, vibrators and plugs.

"Here," he said once he'd poured two glasses of Scotch and held one out to me.

In less than twenty-four hours, I'd been held at gunpoint in my own ER, witnessed a murder, been kidnapped, and each of my escape attempts had been thwarted—and those were only the highlights. If ever there was an appropriate time to get sloshed, that time had come.

But I hesitated. Alcohol depressed the central nervous system, leading to an overall decrease in brain function. Slower reflexes. Impaired judgment. Decreased coordination.

"No, thank you."

He tipped back half his glass, then set it down on the bar. "You're afraid you might forget how much you hate me and jump into bed with me, am I right?" He waggled his eyebrows in a way that was at the same time both comical and enticing. Neither of which I noticed, of course.

"I assure you, there's no risk of that."

"It's one drink, *perla*. You saved a man's life today; you've earned it."

"I save lives everyday. And generally, those lives are worthy of being saved. I'm not sure I can say the same thing about *this* day."

He stopped talking. It felt like I'd overstepped some boundary, but I wasn't going to apologize for it. Kidnappers and murderers were bad men. This was rudimentary knowledge, in my opinion.

He picked up his glass and finished off his drink. I stayed by the door. It was only during this lull in the conversation that I realized my body wasn't shaking, my hands weren't cold and clammy. My heart beat at a—relatively—even tempo.

I wasn't afraid of him. At least, not in the same all-encompassing, primal manner in which I had been. I looked him over, searching for a change, for a difference, flitting back to his lips every few seconds to watch for movement.

"It must be exhausting," he said on one of my passes over his face.

"What must be exhausting?"

"Constant vigilance," he explained.

Was he trying to empathize with my role as kidnap-victim? If so, I don't think he could fully appreciate it from his position as kidnapper—slightly different perspectives.

"The lip-reading, I mean. I know you're deaf, Heidi, or at least mostly so."

It felt like he'd cut me off at the ankles again.

"How did you know?" I forced the words out, oblivious to my volume.

He shook his head self-deprecatingly. "I didn't. I don't miss much, but I missed that."

"Then how?" I was quite certain I hadn't brought it up.

He stared at me for a moment like he was ruminating over what to say. "Raven," he replied eventually.

It was like a slap in the face. Not that I had a right to expect any kind of loyalty from the staff at the hospital, I supposed.

"I asked her what she could tell me about you. I don't think she thought it was any kind of secret."

"It's not," I said too quickly. It wasn't a secret. But knowledge of my impediment revealed a weakness to my enemy. I felt uncovered, exposed. "It's not a secret; it's common knowledge," I assured him, downplaying the raw feeling inside.

"Why do you want to kill Elio?" I asked, jumping subjects. That I'd rather discuss murder rather than my partial deafness shocked me to some degree.

"Why don't you seem terribly distraught over it?" he returned with a question of his own.

"Because I'm not emotionally invested in Elio," I lied. Sort of. I think I was more numbed by the events that had taken place than I was indifferent.

He shook his head as he poured himself another drink. Perhaps he'd drink himself unconscious. A woman could hope, could she not?

"Somehow, *perla*, I doubt that's the reason."

"Because you know me so well?" I replied, raising an eyebrow at him.

"Because I'm a damn good judge of character."

I scoffed. "Perhaps you're not as perceptive as you think…" I paused; I could feel my brow furrowing. "What's your name?" I asked. "You said it, but I couldn't… I didn't catch it."

"Amadeo Luciano," he said with a flourished bow.

I liked that he spoke normally, rather than carefully enunciating it like I was a child.

"My friends call me Deo."

"Amadeo." I formed the word without making a sound, testing it on my lips.

"You approve?" he asked. His lips were back to twitching with amusement again.

I looked up, meeting his gaze. He really did have the most stunning eyes I'd ever seen, amber and deep-set and piercing. I could imagine them—

I choked off the thought before it could fully form. Physiological responses to sexual stimuli were one thing; fantasies were entirely another.

"I wouldn't have thought criminals had many 'friends'," I said, too flustered by my own partially-formed thoughts to invent something better. "But you didn't answer my question, Amadeo. Why do you want to kill Elio?"

"I don't," he replied like it was common sense.

"I don't believe you," I said, shaking my head. No part of this felt like he was looking to sit down and have a friendly conversation with Elio.

He pushed away from the bar, striding slowly back toward me. "This isn't what I wanted. Believe it or not, torturing men, kidnapping women, gunfights, and watching my men get shot aren't how I want to spend my days." He paused, his eyes contemplative once again.

"Bianchi threatened my family, *perla*; he tried to kill my sister, Freya— or maybe what he was after was worse; I don't know. In my world, that shit can't slide. It just can't. It's my job to do whatever's necessary to put him in the ground."

His words made the room feel just a little bit colder. "You live in a very violent world."

He stopped in front of me, close enough, he'd be able to reach me if he just stretched out his arm.

"You live in the same world, Heidi. You know firsthand the bad shit that happens in it—I know you do. I just don't have the luxury of pretending it doesn't exist. And even if I did have that luxury… I wouldn't want it."

"You think I'm pretending?" I said, crossing my arms over my chest defensively.

"I think you suffered shit no child should ever suffer. I think you spent years never feeling safe, always waiting for whoever killed your parents to come back—to come for you.

"If I were you, I would have spent every night wide awake, listening for sounds of them coming for me. For you, you were trapped in silence; you didn't even have the comfort of knowing you'd hear them when they came for you. That kind of terror stays with a person. And I think you were scared shitless that I was just like them, but I also think some part of you is learning that I'm not."

I took a step back as the coldness in the room seeped inward. I'd never told anyone at the hospital about my childhood—including Raven. This wasn't information he'd learned from a casual conversation with her.

"You… investigated me." "Violated" felt like a more appropriate word.

"I had no choice. I know there is some connection between you and Bianchi. That means you and everything about you are my business."

This nightmare got worse with every passing second. I'd always been a private person, but this man had ripped me out of my world and kept tearing through more and more layers, exposing pieces of me I'd never offered to anyone. It needed to stop. "If I tell you what I know, will you let me go?"

"He sent his men after you, Heidi. It might not be safe for you."

"But being here, with you… that is safe?"

Heat flared in his eyes as he shook his head slowly, never breaking eye contact. "Probably not," he admitted.

The unsettling sense of my own exposure mingled with the blatant desire in his eyes and trembled down my spine in half-tingling, half-prickling ripples of heat. I couldn't bring myself to look away.

"Tell me what you know, *perla*," he said, and though his words had no volume, I could feel the huskiness in his voice by the dark, heated look in his eyes. His gaze had the allure of a snake's, mesmerizing its prey. I could feel the draw, pulling the information he sought from my brain to my lips.

"I don't know that any of it will be useful," I confessed. "I know you think I'm involved in some clandestine plot, but I'm not. I'm still not convinced Elio is either."

"There was a tracking device in your shoe, Heidi. Do you think someone else put it there? Do you know of someone who would want to be tracking your every move?"

I shook my head.

"Just tell me what you know."

I sighed; I imagined it was a tired sound. Maybe the bits of information I had were somehow my key out of here.

"Owen Thompson—the man you *killed*," I said, "he used to come at odd hours of the night. When he did, Elio wouldn't return to bed for an hour, sometimes longer. I spied on them a few times," I said with a shrug. They'd been in Elio's sitting room, not behind a closed office door.

"I didn't really expect to see them speaking about anything clandestine, but after the first time…" I shook my head, trying to find an explanation for what had drawn me back.

"It wasn't anything particular they'd said—that time I only managed to glean a handful of words—but the way they sat, their heads close together, it struck me as odd, that's all."

Amadeo was nodding. "So, you spied on them some more," he said. There was no accusation in his eyes.

"I did," I confessed, though I didn't see how most of it was relevant. "They talked about debts and money… searches… something about birds and a man or a place named 'Belemonte'."

His eyes flared, and his jaw quivered just once, like he'd bit down hard.

"You know the name?" I asked. I suppose I could have looked it up on the internet, but it had never struck me as terribly important.

"I've heard it before," he confirmed what I'd already gathered from his reaction.

"It was just little snippets like that, except for the last time, perhaps two weeks ago."

"What did you overhear, er, oversee?" he corrected himself.

"Owen said, 'We need the Luciano property; the money's got to be there'. Then Elio nodded, but he looked angry. Very angry. I assumed he was talking about a real estate deal, but now that I… know you, I don't know what it means. And I don't see at all what any of that has to do with me. So, you see, it makes no sense that Elio would be tracking me. Whoever those men were at that 'cabin', it's far more likely they were there because of you, Amadeo, not me."

"Do you know anything about the Luciano property he was talking about?" he persisted.

I shook my head. "I have no idea what property you or your… family own." Why would I?

He looked at me, eyes assessing. In such a short time, I'd come to notice he did that often. He nodded to himself after a moment like he'd come to a decision.

"The Regalton Arms and The Beresford. Those are the two properties he came to my father about."

I gasped; it just slipped out. If I'd had more experience dealing with dangerous criminals, I might have done a better job covering it up, but, thankfully, I had little experience.

"You know them?" he asked, though there was no question in his expression.

There seemed little point in denying it. "They're old flats… apartment buildings. My father used to—" I had to swallow past the lump that formed in my throat. "My father did maintenance work there. When my mum had to work, he'd take me with him. He'd let me play in the hallways so long as I stayed on the same floor he was working on."

"Did you ever tell Bianchi this?" he asked. His lips moved more quickly.

I nodded, feeling a new coldness try to creep in.

"He said, 'the money's got to be there'," Amadeo repeated the words. His eyes were thoughtful like he was mulling them over.

"I never said anything to Elio about any money." I scoffed; the thought was absurd. "My family wasn't… well-to-do. My father never had more money with him than the loose change in his trouser pocket."

"*Grazie, perla,*" he said, but his eyes were still caught up in thought. He strode right past me toward the door but paused there and turned around.

"Stay put, Heidi. Don't make me cuff you to the bed. You see that shit?" he asked, nodding toward the contents of the conspicuous black duffel bag I'd dumped out in my search. "That's the shit I get off on. So, be a good girl, and don't make using it any more tempting than it already is."

He strode out of the room then, presumably locking the door behind him, while I stood in a strange man's bedroom—a bedroom I wasn't permitted to leave—and pretended the heat tingling through my veins had nothing at all to do with my captor.

Chapter Thirteen

Amadeo

"According to Heidi, her father did maintenance work on The Regalton Arms and The Beresford," I said, sitting across from my father at his desk with my hands laced behind my neck, massaging muscles that were way too tight.

"That seems like more than a coincidence," he mused. He had his fingers steepled on his stomach and an untouched glass of Scotch on the desk in front of him.

Greta nodded her head from where she sat next to me.

"And for some reason, Bianchi thinks there's money there," I finished summing up what Heidi had revealed. "Thanks to Vito, we know that neither of her parents have any history. And someone with no history usually has a lot to hide."

"So, you're thinking they were involved in something?" Greta asked. "Maybe hid the money in one of these buildings when someone started sniffing around?"

I nodded. "It makes sense. And I might know how Bianchi got his hands on that information."

My father cocked an eyebrow, waiting for me to continue.

"Harry Belemonte." The man had dealt in plenty of shit, but the one commodity he'd prided himself on most: information.

"That asshole's dead," Greta jumped in, shaking her head.

"He's dead now," I conceded, "but he wasn't not that long ago. And according to Heidi, Bianchi's been talking about 'birds'. I'm thinking she meant the Free Birds—Belemonte's gang of thugs."

"Son of a bitch," Greta muttered under her breath. "The guy's dead and he's still managing to make waves?"

"*Sí*, it seems to be too much to ask dead men to stay dead. I couldn't figure out how Bianchi could be up to his nuts in debt and still manage to pay men to work for him, to attack Freya, to come for Heidi, but now…"

"You believe he has the Free Birds working for him?" my father asked.

I nodded. I was almost sure of it. "The Free Birds were a piss-poor collection of thugs—no real skills, not enough street smarts to make it on their own after Belemonte died. It explains the kid I killed at the cabin too," I said, feeling a ghost of guilt whisper through my veins. "Belemonte would have had no qualms about taking on kids. I'm guessing Bianchi has no qualms about it either. It's all about the lowest bidder, and what's left of the Free Birds have got to be desperate, so they're at the top of that list."

"All right, that's it," Greta said, shaking her head. "The next time we put an asshole in the ground, all his piss-poor henchmen go there with him."

"Agreed," my father said. He wasn't joking.

"But if Bianchi has the Free Birds treasure-hunting like goddamned pirates, why the continued interest in Heidi?" I wondered aloud. "Why send men after her?"

"Maybe she knows more than she's letting on?" Greta speculated.

I mulled over the possibility, but it wasn't sitting right. Heidi wouldn't have revealed as much as she had if she was after that money too. It seemed she'd handed over information to Bianchi unwittingly.

"I want that money," I said, sitting up straighter.

Greta laughed. "Because you're so hard-up for cash?"

"Because if Bianchi discovers I have the money, there's no reason for him to go after Heidi."

Her eyebrows reached for her hairline. "I always knew you were a big softy at heart, but really, Deo? Going to all this trouble for a woman you didn't know existed two days ago?" She shook her head exaggeratedly. "You must think she's got one magical pussy, *amico.*"

"As magical as a unicorn," I joked. Or was it a joke? Christ, there was definitely something about the woman that was doing a number on my head.

But for the time being… "I'd like to send some of our men to sweep the buildings and see what they can find," I said to my father, dropping my hands, giving up the hope that the muscles there would ever relax. At least not so long as a particular dark-haired, defiant doctor and her—possibly magical—cunt were gracing my bedroom.

"You don't want to go with them?" my father asked, his eyebrows raised in surprise.

I shook my head. "I'd like to go cage one of the Free Birds and see if I can make him sing."

Greta laughed. "Now, that sounds more like the Deo I know and love."

"Do you want to come along for the show, *amica*?"

She waved her hand in the air dismissively. "Nah, I'll stick around here and see what trouble I can get into."

I sighed, wishing she was kidding. But I knew she wasn't.

***

"How do you want to play this, boss?" Vito asked from the front passenger seat of my Ferrari 488.

We were parked outside The Coliseum, a bar that had once belonged to Belemonte but had closed after he vanished off the face of the earth— at least so far as the cops knew.

113

But closed bars didn't usually have people moving around inside them.

"Tell Bruno and Carmine to head around back," I told Vito.

They were parked in the Mercedes behind us, maybe just as eager to make some birds sing as I was. After all, these men were in league with the men who'd shot Aurelio.

Vito typed a message into his phone, and the Mercedes pulled out around us a moment later, circling the bar and disappearing around to the employee entrance in the back.

"We'll give them a minute to get in place, then we'll go in the front door," I told Vito as I withdrew my Sig Sauer from its holster and checked the clip. "If they try to run, Bruno and Carmine will have the only other way out of the building covered."

Vito nodded and flipped the safety off his guns. "How many of them are we keeping alive, boss?" he asked.

"It looks like there's five or six men in there," I said, squinting to watch through the gauzy curtains that covered the windows like we'd been doing for the past several minutes. "We only need one. But if any of them are kids, shoot to wound, not kill." I didn't need any more dead kids on my conscience.

Vito nodded. "Maybe a bullet hole or two will make the young ones think about a new career path," he joked like maybe we were doing them a favor.

"I'm all about empowering youth."

A minute had passed. I got out of the car, keeping my gun tucked inside my jacket for the time being. There was no sense in drawing an unwanted audience to this show.

Vito followed suit, and we crossed the street, keeping watch on the bar's window. There were no signs of movement there at the moment, no indication we'd been spotted.

Outside the door, we paused, listening. The murmur of several raised voices seeped through the Coliseum's door. They were arguing, but the sound was too muffled to make out the context of the dispute.

"Wait," I said, holding up a hand. "The sounds in there will cover the lock; pick it," I told him. It would give us the best shot at taking them by surprise.

He nodded, holstered his gun, and pulled out a lock kit, and I stepped behind him, blocking the view of any passerby as he deftly worked the lock free.

Perfetta.

I held up my fingers for a five count while Vito traded out the lock kit for his gun.

Then four fingers.

Three. Two. One.

Vito grabbed the door handle and yanked it open.

A rush of adrenaline coursed through my veins as we burst into the dimly lit bar, my heart pounding in my chest. I felt charged, lit up inside; I'd long ago accepted that I lived for this shit.

The smell of stale alcohol and cigarettes assaulted my senses as my eyes quickly adjusted, taking in the startled faces of the five men and one teenager who stood around the bar. Which one was the ringleader?

That one, I decided in the blink of an eye as I homed in on the one the others were looking to for direction. He wasn't overly tall, but he was stocky, and he had his chin tipped up higher than the rest.

And now he was a dead man.

I aimed and fired, taking him down with a single gunshot to the head.

"What the hell?" a dark-haired scruffy looking man shouted as the remaining five scrambled for their weapons.

"I wouldn't do that, *amici,*" I said, adjusting my aim on a new target as Vito followed suit.

They froze. We'd caught these dumb assholes completely unsuspecting.

"This bar's closed, *stronzo,*" the scruffy man sneered. He hadn't spared a glance at his fallen comrade. "Get the hell—"

"That's not very polite," I said, shaking my head disapprovingly. There might have been five of them and two of us here at the moment, but the odds were stacked against this disorganized cluster of thugs.

"You walk into our bar with a gun," a gray-haired man with a pockmarked face said, puffing up his chest, "killing our fucking men, and you say we're impolite?"

"I'd say stalking a woman was impolite. Shooting at my sister was... most definitely discourteous," I said to the room in general, then turned my attention to the scruffy man. "I'd also say that if you move that hand one more inch, I'll blow it right off."

His fingers were creeping slowly into his worn and faded jacket, but they paused.

"Now, put your hands down," I told him, keeping my gun aimed at him as Bruno and Carmine crept forward from the long hall that led to the office and storeroom behind them.

The asshole glared back as he obeyed while the men around him shifted nervously.

"Come here," I said to Scruffy.

His gaze swiveled from me to his comrades, lingering on the tall, gangly teenager a heartbeat too long. Then he crossed the room toward me, slowly, his hands clenched into fists and his lips pressed together beneath his wiry beard. He stopped five feet from me.

"Who have you been working for?" I asked, already knowing the answer.

"*Vaffanculo.* We ain't working for nobody. In case you haven't heard, Belemonte's dead."

"I have heard that, *sì.* But you're lying to me, aren't you?" I asked, adjusting my gun's aim from his heart to his shoulder.

"No, I ain't," he spat.

I fired.

His body jerked back as he screamed and blood bloomed through his jacket.

"*Papà!*" the kid hollered as he took a step forward before the others grabbed him and pulled him back

"You asshole," Scruffy seethed. "You goddamned son of a—"

"My mother was a lovely woman; do not insult her. Now, sit down," I instructed him, pointing to the floor at his feet.

He glared at me, panting hard as he pressed his hand to his wound and blood leaked out between his fingers. Eventually, he lowered himself down onto the dirty floor.

I turned my attention to the men still standing. "It seems your friend here might have a hard time answering questions at the moment. You," I said, nodding to the gray-haired man. "Do you have a different answer for me?"

He glared at me, but this one wasn't as stupid as his bleeding friend. "His name's Bianchi," he said, confirming my suspicions.

"How long have you been working for him?" I asked.

"A couple months," he spat.

"Doing what?" Of course, we already knew about the treasure-hunting, but I wondered if there were any more pieces to the puzzle.

The gray-haired man didn't answer. He glared at me with narrowed eyes while the pockmarks along his chin rippled with the twitching of his jaw.

"Silence is the same as a lie, *amico*. And as you can see," I said, nodding to scruffy, "I don't like lies. They tend to make me cranky."

Vito scoffed. "Almost as cranky as when he gets hungry," he added, ever so helpfully.

He wasn't wrong, though. "So, perhaps you have something to say?" I persisted.

"He's had us trailing after some doctor, following her like a dog after a bitch in heat. Had us searching a bunch of places too."

"What places?"

He pressed his thin lips together, and his eyes narrowed even further, like he could shoot me down with laser beams. The man wasn't a quick learner.

I adjusted my aim and shot him in the foot, making him scream just like Scruffy as he hit the floor hard.

Vito chuckled. "He warned you he gets cranky, *coglione.*"

"How about you?" I said, shifting my attention to the next in line, a dark-haired man in his mid-twenties who I probably would have said was attractive if I swung that way. "Do you want to tell me what places your new owner had you searching?"

"There were a bunch," he said reluctantly, likely not in a hurry to join the men bleeding on the floor. "A bunch of apartment buildings, an old convenience store. One house—one that looked like it hadn't been lived in for years."

Heidi's childhood home, maybe. My gut told me all of these properties were somehow linked to Heidi or her parents.

"And where is Bianchi now?" I asked.

The guy cringed. He opened his mouth, then closed it. "I don't know. I swear I don't." He cringed some more while his eyes fixed on the barrel of my gun and his feet took a small step back. "He only contacts his men when he needs something."

He really didn't know; I could see it in his eyes.

Vito shifted beside me. "Do you want them dead yet, boss?" he asked.

That was usually how this kind of "meeting" ended, but it wasn't sitting right. Not one of these assholes had the eyes of a killer. They were the kind of men who had done Belemonte's grunt work and were now doing the same menial shit for Bianchi.

I shook my head almost imperceptibly, but Vito got the message, easing his finger up on the trigger.

"From what I knew of Belemonte," I said, "most of the men he had working for him were coerced and fucking desperate." I looked from one man to the next. "Every one of you looks desperate. But Bianchi's a dead end; the man's living on borrowed time. So, I suggest you give him a message for me and then get your asses as far away from here as you can. If I see any one of you again, you're dead men. *Capisce?*"

Most of the men stared back at me, silent, but the dark-haired one who'd been cringing nodded his head.

"What message should we give him?" he asked.

"Simple. Tell him I'm coming for him. And you," I said, turning my attention to the teenager who was shaking like a leaf. "Stop spending time with your dumbass father who's only going to get you killed, and get your ass in school."

There, I'd even done a good deed for the day, motivating youth and all that shit. I was practically a saint.

Saint Amadeo of New York. It did have a certain ring to it, didn't it?

Chapter Fourteen

Heidi

If the window wasn't an option, maybe I could go out the roof. I was beginning to think it might be easy, given how close I was to climbing the walls.

No phones. No weapons—not unless a giant dildo counted as a weapon. Maybe I could beat him over the head with it, if I could get him to stand still long enough.

The bedroom door opened, and I seriously considered making a grab for the giant dildo, but it wasn't Amadeo who walked into the room. It was a woman. The woman with blonde hair, hazel eyes, and lime green fingernails.

"Whoa," she said, looking first at me, then around the room.

"You're gorgeous, *amica*, and either Deo's a real slob, or way to go, gorgeous stranger," she said, winking at me.

She had a warm and likeable energy radiating from her, but still, I wasn't letting my guard down. I wasn't even sure what that looked like after having my guard up most of my life.

"Who are you?" I asked, watching her warily from the sitting area.

"I'm Greta," she said as she came toward me and plopped down on the sofa like she'd been here countless times.

Oh. Amadeo's lover? Girlfriend?

My eyes flickered to the overturned duffel bag, and my cheeks suffused with warmth as my mind conjured images of Amadeo's big hands using the rope from the bag to tie the woman up. I wasn't at all prepared for the hot jolt of desire that shocked through me, nor the prickling discomfort of jealousy that followed it.

I thrust the thoughts and feelings aside and focused on the woman's lips. He was my bloody captor, not my lover.

"I work for the Lucianos," she said.

I ignored the ripple of relief I had no business feeling.

"I'm also Raven Luca's best friend," she continued.

This woman seemed too… easygoing in comparison to the serious intensity I saw when I'd seen Raven work at the hospital.

"Why are you here?" I asked, standing awkwardly on the Aubusson carpet in my bare feet and yesterday's clothes while this woman reclined on the sofa, looking like she'd just walked off the runway.

"Well," she said, crossing one long leg over the other, "I'd like to say I've come to put your mind at ease, but since that's not an easy thing to do after a person's been kidnapped, I imagine I'm just here to keep you company."

"If you work for the Lucianos, I think your ability to put my mind at ease may be limited," I said, but even so, I took two steps forward and sat down in the wide armchair opposite her, perched on the edge of the seat.

"I get what you think of Deo—probably the same thing you're thinking about me—but things aren't always as black and white as they seem," she said with a shrug.

"Let me guess, Amadeo might murder and kidnap people, but he doesn't go around kicking kittens, so he's really a good man deep down?" I could feel the tiny spark of hope in my voice as I said it and wondered where on earth that had come from.

"Good?" Greta laughed like the notion was absurd. "No," she said, shaking her head emphatically. "Definitely not in the traditional sense of the word. But he is the kind of man who spent weeks rubbing elbows with the scum of the earth just to put the fuckers in the ground. Those are the kind of men he hurts; those are the kind of men he kills. The same kind of men I kill. And the same kind of men Raven would kill."

She looked at me for a moment like she was waiting for a response.

"They're the kind of men you don't want breathing air, Heidi," she said when I remained silent. "So, you should be damn grateful there are men like Deo out there who don't mind getting their hands dirty."

"Regardless of what else he may or may not be, he's still the man who's keeping me here against my will."

Greta shook her head as she uncrossed her legs and stood up. "He's keeping you here for your own protection, *amica*. But you're right," she said. Then she turned away and walked across the room to the door.

If she kept talking, I couldn't hear her.

She turned back to face me at the door.

"It should be your decision," she said, and then she opened the door and stood aside.

It could have been a trap, a game. If I walked out of the room, there could be someone standing there in the hallway, ready to pounce. But what was the point? This woman didn't strike me as the type to play games any more than Amadeo did.

"A word of advice, though," she said as I stood up and dug my bare toes into the carpet.

"Don't go back home," she said. "Don't go anywhere there aren't plenty of people around. If Bianchi comes to you, don't let him get you anywhere on your own. And if you don't have a gun already, I suggest you get one." She pressed her lips together like she had more to say but was holding back.

She shook her head after a moment, apparently dismissing whatever it was. "I'm going to go downstairs now. I suggest you take a few minutes to think about it, and then, whatever you decide…" She shrugged. "Well, at least it was your choice, *si?*"

And just like that, she turned and walked out of the room. I was really free. I could leave.

"Thank you," I called after her.

She didn't stop, but she nodded her head as she started down the tall spiral staircase.

I stood in the open doorway, watching as she reached the landing and disappeared somewhere further inside the house.

My feet weren't moving. Why weren't they moving? I should have been flying down the stairs and out the front door. I should have been running as hard and fast for freedom as humanly possible.

Good? Definitely not in the traditional sense of the word."

"*He's keeping you here for your own protection.*"

"*You should be damn grateful there are men like Deo out there who don't mind getting their hands dirty.*"

Bloody hell, maybe she had been playing games with me, getting inside my head.

A door across the hallway opened and another blonde woman stepped out through it, one who bore a vague resemblance to Greta. She was wearing silk pajama pants and a camisole, and her upper arm was wrapped in a bandage, the reddish-pink tinge of blood just beginning to seep to the surface.

She came to an abrupt stop when she saw me.

"*Buongiorno,*" she said with a faint line forming between her perfectly arched eyebrows.

I nodded, not quite sure what to say to this woman.

"I'm Freya," she said, her bafflement seemingly long forgotten as she crossed the hall with a kind smile on her face. "I assume you're Deo's…" she trailed off, looking at me like she was waiting for me to fill in the blank.

And how would I do that? Kidnap victim? Could I even call myself that if I wasn't making a beeline for the exit?

"I'm Heidi," I said instead.

She flashed me a small, knowing smile that had me looking away uncomfortably.

My gaze settled on her bandage-covered arm. "You should see about having that bandage changed," I said, nodding at it.

"*Sì*. I've been waiting for *Papà's* doctor, but he seems to be taking his time."

"Do you—" I slammed my mouth shut, but Freya just looked at me, waiting for me to continue.

Well, I'd already mended one criminal today; why not help another?

"If you have the supplies, I can change the dressing for you," I offered.

Her brows drew together.

"I'm a doctor," I explained in case she thought I had some strange wound fetish.

"A beautiful woman with brains too?" she said, smiling. "My brother would be wise to hold onto you."

Yes, it seemed he was of a similar mind, though the image that sprung to mind wasn't of syringes filled with sedative. The handcuffs and rope I'd found in his room flashed behind my eyes. His big hands and long fingers. His amber eyes changing from smug certainty to heat and need–

Bloody hell.

"The doc left all the supplies in my room," Freya said right before she turned away and headed back through the doorway from which she'd come.

I followed her into the room and felt at once like I'd stepped into some strange realm where all periods of history merged together. Old-fashioned clocks, antique furniture, curio cabinets filled with knickknacks that most certainly had not come from this era.

Freya sat down at the edge of the ornately carved Victorian bed and motioned to the collection of modern medical paraphernalia laid out on an antique bedside table.

I perched next to her, pulled on a pair of gloves from the box on the table, and unwound her dressing. But as the gauze fell away and I loosened the bandage, revealing the wound beneath, I gasped.

The wound ran through the anterior aspect, through the deltoid muscle. I adjusted her arm carefully and discovered a corresponding wound. An exit wound.

"This is a gunshot wound," I said, staring at the evidence but finding it difficult to believe. "You were shot?"

She shrugged, then grimaced at the movement. "It's not all that bad, really. It's kind of nice not to be the only one around here without any war wounds."

"That's my problem too; not enough bullet holes," I joked. I actually joked. About a gunshot wound.

Freya laughed, but then sobered quickly. "So, how did you meet my brother?" she asked as I split my attention between applying a new bandage and watching her lips.

"He kidnapped me," I said, wondering if that would catch her off-guard as easily as her bullet wound had caught me.

Her eyes widened, and her lips parted.

"I was locked in Amadeo's room until a few minutes ago when a woman named Greta gave me the option of leaving."

I secured the bandage and began wrapping it in fresh gauze.

Freya's eyes returned to normal. "Well, if Greta says it's all right, then no worries."

That was it? "I was under the impression most... families like yours were patriarchal."

She smiled. "My father is definitely the boss of the Luciano family. Greta's kind of the boss of... well, everyone."

That wasn't as difficult to believe as it should have been. The woman's presence had certainly commanded attention.

I finished with the gauze wrapping and pulled off the gloves, depositing them in the small rubbish bin next to the bed.

"*Grazie*, Heidi," she said, the appreciation on her face so genuine it was difficult to reconcile it with the face of a criminal.

"I think I should be going," I said as I stood and took a few backwards steps toward the door.

Freya shrugged. "Of course. But, Heidi?" She swung her legs up onto her bed, probably trying to appear as non-confrontational as possible. "If Deo brought you here, there was a good reason for it. I wouldn't take that lightly if I were you."

"So I've been told."

I turned then and left the room before she could say anything further, shutting the door behind me.

The moment I stepped out into the hallway, though, the front door opened. Amadeo walked in with the big, bald man beside him.

I should have run, maybe back into Freya's room, but I just stood there, staring down the stairs at him. He wore a scowl on his face, deep in conversation with the man next to him, but like he sensed me there, he looked up, finding me unerringly, and the scowl vanished. He stopped talking.

His eyes met mine, and without breaking eye contact, he left the big, bald man and started up the stairs toward me.

Every fiber of my being wanted to run, but what I saw in my mind was not a terrified, frantic escape attempt. I saw him running after me. Catching me. Slamming me back against his hard body. I imagined his muscular arms wrapped around me, pinning my arms to my sides. The hard length of his erection digging into the small of my back. He'd be rough when he took me, maybe right here in the hallway.

I blinked. My heart was beating faster and my whole body felt warm, my clothes suddenly tight and constricting and my clit pulsing with blatant need. Where the bloody hell had that come from?

He'd reached the top of the stairs by the time I'd gotten my wits about me—or at least some semblance of them.

I took a step back as he got closer, then another, but his legs were longer, his strides wider. He was standing right in front of me in just four big steps, and I'd backed myself up right through his doorway and into his room.

"Tell me the truth," I said, grappling for composure as he stopped so close, I could feel his warm breath against my forehead.

"What truth?" he asked.

"Any of it. All of it." Something to explain why the hell I hadn't bolted when I'd had the chance.

"All right," he said with a nod. "'On the first day, God created light...'"

I huffed. "You killed a man. And you kidnapped me. But you say you want to keep me safe, and it seems everyone I conveniently run into sings your praises. And I..." I hesitated.

"You what?"

"I'm not a good judge of character, Amadeo. I'm a good judge of diseases, of trauma. I can recognize when a person is all but banging on Death's door, but you..." I shook my head. "I don't have a lot of experience reading people."

The left corner of his lips pulled up in a smile that would have been a boyish grin if it weren't for the very adult heat warming his amber eyes.

"I'm a killer. I hunt down assholes who take advantage of other people, and I take great delight in snuffing out their lives. I sell bad things to bad people. And I hurt people when I have to... and when I want to." Desire flashed in his eyes, so vivid and so potent it left me feeling breathless and in no doubt about the context in which he enjoyed inflicting pain.

My throat had gone dry. I had to swallow before I could go on. "What is it you want from me, Amadeo?"

I hadn't meant for the question to come out breathy and needy, but I had a feeling it had. The truth was, regardless of how we'd come to be standing here, I'd never been so blatantly attracted to a man. I could go days without thinking about the occasional fifteen minutes of quasi-enthusiastic sex with Elio, but this man, he was big and dangerous and powerful. It awoke something inside me that had forever been asleep. A part of me I wasn't at all sure I liked.

"What I want from you right now, *perla,* is your help."

My help? The words felt like a bucket of ice water.

"You want my help?"

He nodded, his heated gaze still fixed on mine.

Of course, he did. And wasn't I just fool enough to give it?

Chapter Fifteen

Heidi

"What is it you need my help with?" I asked as I took a small step back from him and tried to regain my wits. Because this wasn't desire radiating from him; this was seduction. He was trying to use my attraction to him to bend me to his will.

"I need you to take a look around those two properties I told you about, Heidi."

I drew myself up taller, remembering our roles here. Not lovers. Not friends. Captor and captive.

"That seems like a rather odd request," I said.

"You said you spent time there as a child. I need you to see if anything jumps out at you—a faux wall, a hiding spot in the floor."

"Why on earth would you want me to–" I clamped my lips shut as the answer dawned on me. "You really think there's money there—the money Elio was talking about. And you want it."

I did my best not to feel slighted by the realization that money was all this man was after.

He shook his head and looked at me like I'd sprouted a second head. "I don't give a flying fuck about the money, *perla*. I've got more than enough to last me several lifetimes."

I eyed him doubtfully. From what I understood about rich men, one thing they all had in common was the desire to become richer.

"Then why?"

Instead of answering me, he stared at me. Perhaps he was grappling for a noble reason that might sway me.

"You're a smart woman, Heidi," he said after a long moment. "Why do you think I want that money?"

Apparently, I was to concoct my own noble reason for his endeavor. Rather lazy of him, in my opinion.

I opened my mouth to spout the obvious explanation, but then paused as another possibility jumped to mind.

"If you don't care about the money, then what you care about is making sure Elio doesn't get his hands on it."

He nodded ever so slightly.

"But he'll know you have the money," I continued, "and that means he'll have to come after you to get it." Not that I expected to find a pot of gold hidden under the floorboards of an old building.

"*Sì.*"

I took another step back as an uncomfortable sensation writhed in my veins.

"You're trying to goad Elio into a confrontation… so you can kill him."

I was tempted to imagine two bulls butting heads, but this man was a lion, strong and powerful, and Elio was a gazelle. The gazelle didn't confront the lion; it ran.

But Amadeo was shaking his head. "I'm trying to draw him away from one target and onto another. But yes, I will kill him."

"What if you're wrong about him? If you have the money, then can you not just leave him be?"

"That isn't how this works, *perla.*"

"But you say you're trying to draw him from one target to another—to you, presumably. What if he doesn't come after you?"

"Then I'll find him."

I shook my head. "I can't let you do that."

He looked down at me with an amused smile on his face, like he was looking at an ornery toddler and not a full-grown woman. "I'm asking for your help nicely. Don't make me ask for it the not-nice way."

Despite his smile, a cold sensation skipped down my spine. I should have run when I'd had the chance. But like before, I wouldn't cower now.

"I can't be party to Elio's death any more than I could have let your man bleed out on the floor. That's not who I am, Amadeo."

He looked back at me, those piercing eyes peeling off layer after layer. What I wouldn't have given to do the same to him, to see exactly what lay beneath.

He looked away after a moment, then nodded.

Was he conceding? Had I won? It seemed unbelievable.

"Help me," he said, "and I won't make a move on Bianchi unless he makes a move first."

Not a complete win, then. "And if I refuse?"

He shook his head slowly. "I wouldn't do that if I were you."

I shivered, clenching my hands tightly to hide it. "Fine," I conceded. "I haven't anything better to do anyway, it seems," I said, trying to retain some sense of autonomy.

Somehow, I think I fell about a mile short.

***

"They look terrible," I said, looking up at the six-story, red-brick buildings that stood nearly side-by-side. Half the windows were boarded up and the molding around them looked like it was crumbling, nothing like the vague recollection I had of them. "Your family bought these properties?"

Amadeo nodded.

"I didn't think the mob dabbled a great deal in the rental market." Never mind the dilapidated and 'just about ready to fall down' rental market.

It seemed the drive into the city had taken the edge off. My surroundings were more familiar now, and away from that house, it didn't quite feel like there were men with guns lurking around every corner, even if I could see them plain as day in the cars parked behind us.

"The buildings haven't been tended to in years," Amadeo said. "They were on the verge of being condemned when my sister, Freya, stumbled upon them."

I wasn't sure how that explained his interest in them.

"Freya has a doctorate in archaeology, and she's working on another in anthropology." He shrugged, but an affectionate smile flickered across his face. "She's a huge fan of old shit. She couldn't stand the thought of them being torn down, so she asked my father to buy them so she could restore them and rent them out to families who could use a break on the rent."

"Your family bought these buildings... to help people?" I asked, though, surely, I'd gotten it wrong.

Amadeo laughed. "Seriously messes with your whole bad-guy theory, doesn't it, *perla?*"

"I think you're the one messing with me, Amadeo."

He blinked, just a little too long. I wondered why.

"Let's go," he said, motioning toward the building on the left.

We entered through the wide double door entryway off the main street, but the moment we stepped inside, I stopped moving.

It wasn't the two men in suits standing in the foyer that gave me pause. It was the ghost.

Memories of my childhood had been sketchy at best, but when I stepped inside the narrow, wood-paneled foyer, I could see my father with his toolbelt around his waist and a screwdriver in his hand, fiddling with the interior entry door that had perhaps come loose on its hinges—I never knew particularly what my father was doing. No eight-year-old cared about loose hinges or faulty wiring or leaky pipes.

"What is it, *perla?*" Amadeo asked. He'd stopped beside me and had his eyes narrowed in on where I'd been looking.

"It's nothing." Nothing that meant anything to him. But I had no photos of my mum or dad. Seeing my father here, now, was the most vivid he'd been in a decade and a half. Vivid, and private.

Before Amadeo could inquire further, I started walking again, through the interior entry door and down the narrow hallway lined with doors to each individual dwelling. I ran my hand along the old, faded wallpaper as I walked, my fingers catching on a peeled-up edge here and there. But I could call to mind no loose panel in the wainscoting, no section of floor my father had lifted up. The whole floor had squeaked—I remembered that, so vividly I could hear it now, imagining it with every step I took.

We walked all the way around the building, but no memory jumped out at me, not until we came to the maintenance door that led to the basement. My dad and I had spent a great deal of time down there, if my memory served me correctly.

I tried to turn the handle, but it wouldn't budge. It was locked.

"Here," Amadeo said, retrieving a ring of keys from his trouser pocket and inserting one into the lock.

My father had had a keyring just like it—no keychain, just a ring of a dozen keys or more.

When Amadeo pushed open the door, the aromas of dust, rust, and oil washed over me and broke open something inside, something raw and tender. I turned away, hiding the moisture that welled up in my eyes.

I'd played down there. I'd spent countless hours in that basement, listening to my father whistle while he banged on pipes. I could hear the strange cacophony in my ears like he was down there even now.

Amadeo put his hand on my shoulder, turning me back toward him.

"Are you sure those stairs are safe?" I asked before he could speak.

It was a valid question. The stairs that led down were as old as the rest of the building. The wood treads were clearly rotted out in some places, and there was no railing.

"I'll go first," he said, moving a step in front of me while keeping his face turned toward me. "If I don't fall on my ass, you should be safe." He waggled his brows then stepped down on the first stair.

I imagined it creaking beneath him, maybe groaning, ready to crack, but he kept going. Once he'd reached the fourth stair down, I followed him as memories of this place tickled my brain more and more with each piece of the cracked concrete floor that came into view. And the pipes that ran all across the ceiling. The big boilers in the corner of the main room.

"Bloody hell, this goddamned thing is older than Moses," my father had cursed as he banged away at the big boilers. Then he'd see me standing there and mutter something about swear jars. *"Don't tell your mum, Heidi-girl, or I'll be broke by morning."* He'd smile and I'd smile back because all my father's cursing felt like our little secret. "Bloody hell", that had been his favorite. Mine too.

My breath was trapped in my chest. I'd never returned to any of the places I'd been with my parents. I'd never imagined how potently the memories would rush back.

"Heidi?" Amadeo said, tilting my chin up toward him.

Something warm trickled down my cheek, and my breath came out all at once. I was crying. There were goddamned bloody tears streaking down my face like rivulets.

"I'm fine," I said, yanking my chin out of his grip.

"We can leave," he said, his eyes sympathetic. "We don't have to do this, *perla.*"

But we did. Not because of the money, but because I did remember something, or more accurately, *somewhere.* A place my father might have left something of himself behind. A photo? One of the quickly scrawled love notes my mum would leave for him and he'd shove down deep in his pocket?

"This way," I said, crossing the room to the boilers and then around behind them.

My father hadn't liked me playing freely down here while he was working. Too many hazards, he'd said. So, he'd shown me his secret place and made me promise never to tell anyone about it.

Something squeezed painfully in my chest as I looked for the telltale bolts in the wall. I supposed I was breaking my promise to him now.

And there they were, not quite the four corners of a perfect rectangle, but close to it. I reached for the first one and turned it slowly. The long bolts used to spin right out for me, but they were stiffer now, rusted with disuse.

"Those two," I said, pointing to the two bolts that made up the top and bottom left of the rectangle.

When we had all four bolts removed, Amadeo looked at me, waiting for what came next.

"Just pull," I said, putting my hands against the section of the wall that looked very much like concrete, but was not. My father had never said what it was made of—perhaps he didn't know—but whatever it was moved easily, like the whole section of wall couldn't have weighed more than thirty pounds.

Amadeo followed suit, and we pulled the section of wall out toward the boilers, revealing the small, hidden room behind it.

Aside from thick cobwebs, there wasn't much here. An old shelf with ancient canned goods stacked neatly on it, two stools and a storage bench in front of them where my father had stashed all my crayons and coloring books. There was also a big, old toolbox in there that must have been left by the last maintenance man, my father had said.

I knelt down in front of the bench and slipped my trembling fingers beneath the lid. If the contents had remained untouched, then there would still be the coloring books inside that my father and I had colored in together. But what else?

If he'd had any inkling that his life was in danger, would he have left something here for me? A letter written in his own hand? A picture of the two of us together? Some way to remember him beyond the sketchy pieces drawn from a child's imperfect memory?

With my heart in my throat, I lifted the lid.

And there they were, the stack of generic books filled with outlines of clowns and cats and lollipops. The crayons were there too, and the doll in the pink frilly dress that I'd carried with me everywhere for a time. But there were no notes, no pictures. Nothing else but for the old, dusty toolbox.

The sound that escaped my lips wasn't pretty. I could hear it muffled like most of the sounds I made. A choked croak that sounded more like a frog than a breaking heart.

I was about to slam the lid shut when the sight of the toolbox stopped me. It was just as dirty and dust-covered as it had been the last time I saw it, nothing that would ever have tempted an eight-year-old me.

There was no lock on the box, just a latch. I reached in and flipped it open and slowly lifted the lid, now dreading what I'd find inside. I wanted there to be rusty tools in the box. Lots of pencils—my father was always losing pencils.

I rolled my eyes at him as he patted his hands down his chest, over the pockets of his shirt, then slipped his hands into his trouser pockets, searching and coming up empty.

"I'll get one, daddy," I said as he sighed, shaking his head at himself for the umpteenth time.

"What would I do without you, Heidi-girl?"

"You'd have to get your own pencils," I joked, then skipped down the hallway to the small office on the main floor.

There was never anyone in the office but sometimes there'd be a pencil or two. I was allowed to take them from the desk top, but the desk drawers were off-limits. This time, there were at least half a dozen, freshly sharpened, on the desk, and like I'd found a pot of gold, I scooped them up and skipped back with my shoulders chuffed up.

I'd taken it on as my personal responsibility to keep him well-stocked after that. I even convinced my mum to buy the pretty blue pencils with yellow flowers on them from the shop, just to ensure I had my own steady supply for him.

But there were no tools inside the toolbox now. And no pencils.

There were gold bars. Diamonds. Stacks of fifty-pound banknotes. Altogether, I had no idea what the contents were worth.

And I didn't care.

I sat back on my heels, staring at the toolbox but not really seeing it.

Could you see a feeling? I think it's possible. Because all I could see were the colors and shadows of heartbreak, greed, and betrayal. My father had hidden these here. He'd taken them and hidden them, knowing all the while that someone would come for them, for *him.*

He'd cost me a life with him and my mum. He'd cost me my hearing. He'd used this treasure to buy the empty seats at my graduation, and the foster families who'd tossed me on from one to the next—a partially deaf foster child with trauma issues was no prize.

Amadeo crouched down next to me, tilting my chin up to look at him once again. But there were no tears in my eyes this time. My eyes were dry, empty, like the rest of me. Hollowed out. Gutted.

"It wasn't what you were hoping for, was it, *perla?*" There was no mockery in his expression. His pale eyes were still sympathetic.

"It's just a little overwhelming, that's all."

He didn't fight me when I turned away from him and looked down at the box.

"I imagine it's heavy," I said, staring at the diamonds that seemed to be winking back at me sardonically. "You should probably get some of your men to help lift it."

Then I stood up, and I left the small room, the room that had been a special secret between me and my father. But it wasn't a secret any longer, and it certainly wasn't special.

Amadeo followed me out and grabbed hold of my wrist before I reached the stairs.

"As soon as it's safe, all that is yours, Heidi," he said, like he thought I was mourning the loss of a fortune I hadn't even known existed.

"I don't want it," I said, then I pulled my wrist free and left the sullied secret behind.

Chapter Sixteen

Heidi

I'd learned to put things into boxes. 'Compartmentalizing', they called it. The loss of a patient at work; that went into one box. The jeers and snickers from my co-workers; that went into another box. The terror since I'd walked into Elio's apartment; it had another box too. The lid kept trying to pop open, but for the most part, I'd managed to keep it shut tight.

But now, no matter how hard I tried to cram and shove, it felt like there wasn't a box big enough for what I'd found today.

"It doesn't mean he wasn't the man you knew, Heidi," Amadeo said as he poured two glasses of Scotch from the mini-bar in his room.

I was grateful this time when he'd ushered me right up the stairs to his room. I didn't want to see the big, bald man. Or the older man who looked a great deal like Amadeo. Or even the vibrant blonde who'd tried to offer me an escape.

Amadeo handed me one of the glasses, and I swallowed back the Scotch in one gulp.

"He was a thief who cared more about money than he cared about being here with me," I said through the burn, still grappling with the box. "That's who my father was."

He watched me while he sipped on his own drink. "Do you really think it's that black and white?"

I shrugged, hoping the movement looked more natural than it felt. "What else am I to think?"

"That if he hadn't loved you, you wouldn't be missing him so much now."

"Perhaps. But love is more than a feeling; it's a priority system. Those things you cherish most, you protect at all cost."

He nodded, conceding. "But he's not here, Heidi; you can't ask him why he did what he did. All you can do is trust he was more than the contents of that box."

That box. It seemed life was just a series of boxes, some of which fit neatly into storage, others which were really bombs, threatening to blow the entire storage facility to bits.

I wondered which kind Amadeo was. A bomb, for certain, I would have said twenty-four hours ago. Now, I wasn't so sure.

"I think we should have sex," I said quite matter-of-factly as I set down my glass. It was a rational move, even if there were a few irrational aspects to it.

He scoffed even as a fire ignited in his amber eyes. "That's quite a leap from the 'fuck off' sign you've had pasted on your forehead."

"I didn't say I wanted to be intimate," I said, for there was a vast difference between sex and intimacy. "There's no sense in denying the physical attraction here. And sex is a great escape, is it not? It floods the body with endorphins; it consumes the brain's concentration." I hesitated, reluctant to bare my motivations, even if they were quite obvious. "And I would very much like my mind to be consumed at the moment."

He scrubbed a hand over his mouth like he was hiding a smile, then he shook his head. "I don't 'make love', Heidi. I don't do vanilla sex. I fuck. Hard and dirty. I somehow doubt that shit has ever crossed your prim and proper mind."

"And what if it has?" I asked even as a nervous shiver chased up and down my spine. It was never anything I'd asked for from previous partners, but the thoughts, the images were there. They'd always been there.

One moment, he was standing still, and the next, he was right in front of me. He had his hands wrapped around my upper arms, and when his lips covered mine, there was certainly nothing romantic about his kiss. It was brutal, the way his mouth sought mine and his tongue pierced between the seams of my lips, demanding entry.

The cold shiver along my spine was still there, but the blood in my veins turned to lava, so hot and fast flowing that it chased away the chill.

But he was gone as quickly as he'd come, wrenching his lips away, shaking his head like he was trying to cast off whatever had come over him.

"Don't tease me with that shit, *perla*," he said, the movement of his lips quick and rough. "You play with fire, you get burned."

Burned. I think I was already burning, from the inside out.

I leaned up on my toes, fighting against his hold on my arms to reach his lips. I was just about there when he leaned back, his eyes boring into mine with the intensity of laser beams.

"Last chance to walk away, Heidi. I suggest you take it."

I didn't move, not forward nor back. I thought about the way my lips already felt bruised and how his fingers were gripping me so tight, there were sure to be marks. And this was only the beginning. The knowledge sent chills and thrills up and down my spine in a riotous contradiction. *I want this. No, I don't,* they whispered beneath my skin.

"Too late," he said at the same time his grip on me transformed. No longer holding me at bay, he pulled me to him, crushing my breasts against the hard planes of his chest as he captured my mouth once again—for that's what it was; captured. Claimed. Owned.

I felt branded by the bruising pressure of his lips as thoughts of the rope I'd found in his duffel bag flooded my brain like a drug, lighting up every receptor. The cuffs. The toys. The look in his eyes that said this man could be ruthless and demanding. Not erratic, though. There was nothing chaotic about his presence. He knew exactly what he was doing.

I'd no sooner moved my hands to his broad, muscled shoulders when he broke the kiss and stepped back.

"Strip," he said, loud enough I could hear the muffled sound of his voice.

His command made me pause. There was a challenge in it, a dare. He thought I hadn't what it took to go through with this.

I met his gaze, meeting his challenge, as I grabbed hold of the hem of my shirt and pulled it off over my head. Then my jeans. My bra fastened in the back, which was a good thing, keeping him from seeing the slight tremble of my hands as I worked it free and let the straps slide down my arms. All that was left was my thong, and I'd removed enough Band-Aids in my adult life to know that quick really was the best way of it.

I hooked my fingers into the narrow bands of fabric at my hips and dragged the thong down and right off my feet while his heated gaze grazed over every bare inch of me. Suddenly, I felt at a serious disadvantage here. Not only was I smaller than him, but the sharp contrast of his fully clothed body to my very naked one left me feeling exposed, vulnerable.

He took a step forward, and I took a step back, bumping the backs of my thighs against the back of the sofa. The urge to run was potent; the hope he'd catch me if I did, even more so.

Instead of running, though, I stood there as he slid his foot between mine and shoved, forcing my legs open. I had to grab onto the sofa back for balance.

He pressed a finger to the hollow of my throat and drew it down, straight down the center of me to my clit, but he didn't stop there, he kept going, sliding his fingers along my slit, then plunging a finger inside me.

I don't know how he did it, but on that very first stroke, the pad of his finger grazed over my G-spot, making my hips jolt at the unexpected surge of pleasure.

His very clothed body was close, so close I could feel the heat of him seeping into my bare skin as he worked his finger in and out, hitting that ultra-sensitive patch of flesh inside me with every stroke. All the while, he watched me. Not my body, *me*. His gaze never left mine, and somehow that amped up the power differential far more than even the height and breadth of him did.

He kept up the perfect rhythm inside me as his free hand unzipped his fly.

His trousers dropped.

"Is this what you want, *perla?*" he asked as he pulled his cock free from his black boxer briefs and stroked it with one hard, twisted pull.

Bloody hell. His cock was massive, long and thick. But that wasn't all that had my mouth watering and my pussy clenching around his finger. His cock was pierced. I could almost feel the barbell that ran through the plump head hitting my G-spot over and over again.

"Yes," I breathed because the thrills were winning at the moment, and the chills could just sod off.

"Then beg for it," he said as he let go of his cock. He grabbed hold of my hip, holding me still as he fucked me faster with his finger.

Beg? I'd never begged for anything. But as the pleasure mounted and the lava pooled, low and heavy in my lower abdomen, the pleas climbed up my throat, higher and higher.

"Please, Amadeo."

He grinned darkly. "Please what?"

"Please, fuck me."

With his jaw clenched, he pulled his finger out of me and held it up in front of me, the digit glistening with my wetness.

"You're certainly wet enough, aren't you?" he said. He ran his tongue along his finger, sampling the taste of me.

Then he put that finger to my lips. "Suck," he commanded.

I parted my lips, taking the tip between them. I'd never tasted myself before, but the warm salty-sweet taste was more pleasant than I would have expected.

He pushed his finger in further, all the way to the last knuckle, then out again.

"Good girl," he said. I just managed to see the words on his lips before he spun me around. As he did, I caught sight of the little foil packet in his hand—thank God.

I'd barely gotten my hands down on the sofa's back when I felt the swollen head of his cock against my slit, rubbing up and down.

And then he was inside me. Not gently.

Hard.

Deep.

All at once.

The stretch, the burn, it made me cry out. And yet, it had my body sparking hotter than ever before. No more chills. Just heat.

As he withdrew and thrust back in without pause, every bit of me zoned in on that sexy-as-hell piece of metal. It stroked against my G-spot like it had been made just for me. The sensation was so intense, it shocked right through my whole body, and the cry that slipped from my lips had nothing to do with pain.

"That's it, *perla,*" Amadeo said, right against my left ear. "Scream."

He kicked his hips and thrust harder as his free hand slid around my body to squeeze my breast. And then he caught my nipple between his fingers.

The pull. The twist. Bloody hell, it hurt. And it didn't hurt at all. It was like his cock was twisting up every sensation inside me, turning them on their head until pain looked like pleasure.

By the time he released my nipple, I was whimpering at the loss, but not a breath later, his fingers zeroed in on my clit, pinching, rubbing.

"God, that feels good," I moaned. But it didn't just feel good. It felt wild and fast and out of control. I was climbing so high, so much faster than ever before.

Orgasms during sex had never been a guarantee for me. More often than not, I'd find my own release at the end of a lackluster shag. But now, I could feel it, the intense pressure building between my thighs. So close.

He pulled out.

I'd gone from stretched to the maximum to empty so fast, it made my breath catch in my throat.

It did nothing to help me breathe when he spun me around and threw me over his shoulder.

I squealed; it was a strangled sound to my own faulty ears.

His hand came down on my backside, a stinging slap that made me squeal and moan at the same time. I couldn't even say what that sounded like.

He carried me across the room to his bed in several long strides and dropped me down on the edge of it.

He was in front of me, his cock in his hand, stroking it slowly.

"Spread your lips for me," he said, eyeing my pussy.

I hesitated, feeling the full weight of the power differential here. He still had half of his bloody clothes on!

"I know you saw what I said, *perla*. Do it."

And I did, feeling part erotic temptress, part inexperienced virgin. It was true to some extent, insomuch as I'd never had sex quite like *this* before.

His gaze followed my hands down my body, watching as I slid my fingers along my slit and spread myself for him, his eyes boring into the most private part of me. It helped mitigate how vulnerable I felt to see what it did to him, to see the way the muscles were ticking in his jaw and his cock was jerking in his fist.

"*Perfetta*," he said as he dragged the fingers of his free hand from my clit to my anus.

It worried me when he lingered there, but he dropped his fingers after a moment and stepped closer as he finally shucked his shirt.

My lips parted on a silent gasp. This man didn't just have an incredible cock; every part of him had been sculpted to perfection. Wide, muscled shoulders, defined pecs, a perfect six-pack.

"Don't move your fingers," he instructed as he lined up the plump head of his cock with my slit and thrust in. I could feel his latex-covered hardness against my fingers as he did. To feel him in my pussy and against my fingers at the same time poured fresh fuel on the fire already burning inside me.

He grabbed my hands and pulled them out from between us, instantly letting him drive in deeper, so deep I could feel the head of his cock bang against my cervix.

With my hands in his, I expected him to slam them above my head— which worked for me—or pin them on either side of me—which worked for me too. But he did neither.

He brought the fingers of one of my hands to my mouth.

"Lick," he instructed as he rammed into my pussy hard, then withdrew slowly.

I obeyed, tasting myself once again and wondering what we'd taste like mixed together.

When he placed my other hand in front of my mouth, I expected him to demand the same thing, but he rubbed my wet fingers over my lips instead, circling them again and again.

Seemingly satisfied, he dropped my wrists above my head, pinning them there with one of his much bigger hands. Then he delved for my lips, kissing me for one bruising moment before sucking my lower lip into his mouth so hard, the sensitive skin prickled.

"You taste like heaven, *perla,*" he said when he pulled away, just enough I could see his lips to read them. "Tell me you like the taste of your cunt."

At the same time, he adjusted his position so that every time he bottomed out, his pelvis ground against my clit. I saw stars. Or perhaps there were fireworks going off somewhere nearby. Between his piercing working its magic on my G-spot and his pelvis doing wonderful things to my clit, I had no filter, no room in my head for 'prim and proper', as he called it.

"I do," I said.

"You do, what?" he persisted as he drove in hard, forcing my hips so deep into the mattress, they might never come out again.

"I do like the taste of my cunt," I moaned.

He didn't come back to my lips, but veered sideways, along my jaw and down my neck. No lover before had ever bitten me, but this one did. He sunk his teeth into the column of my neck, making it sting before his cock flipped the feeling on its head and bolts of lightning shot through my body, twisting up the coil that was already wound up tight inside me.

Then lower. He nipped his way from my throat to the upper swell of my breast. When his mouth latched onto one taut nipple, I knew what was coming next.

Except, I didn't.

Instead of biting, he suckled me into his mouth, so hard, so deep. I was so focused on the sensation, I didn't notice his free hand moving until his fingers caught my other nipple between them and squeezed. Hard.

I cried out, but instead of leaning away from the sensation, I leaned into it, arching my back as I wrapped my legs around his hips, holding him closer.

His mouth released my nipple, and he looked up at me. "You like it when I hurt you?" he asked.

I nodded while he tugged on my nipple and rolled it between his fingers.

"*Bene,*" he said, then nipped at the underside of my breast. "Because I like the sounds you make."

He moved over and caught the flesh of my other breast between his teeth, biting down harder, not enough to break skin, but enough that it had me writhing and arching against him.

"I like the way your body moves for me, *perla.*"

"It doesn't feel like pain," I confessed.

"No?" He leaned up further while the pace of his fucking changed, faster but shallower. "Then what does it feel like?"

A word for it? I wasn't sure I had one except for a word he'd used earlier. "Heaven," I said as I dug my heels into the small of his back, urging him deeper.

The heat in his hooded eyes grew hotter. A wildfire, but I had no more than a second to think about it before he slid out of my pussy until only the plump head of him was inside me. And then he slammed back in. Deep. So bloody deep.

My heart pounded as my breath came in heavy gasps. It felt like every fiber of my body was sparking.

He fucked me harder.

Deeper.

The coil wound up tighter.

"Come for me, *perla,*" he commanded. "I want to feel you coming all over my cock."

Perhaps it was only perfect timing, but the moment the words were out, the coil inside me sprung free and white-hot pleasure rocketed through my veins, coursing from my pussy all the way to my fingertips and toes.

I screamed; the sound of my own voice was loud even to me.

He was close. I could feel his cock swelling inside me as he thrust in once, then twice.

"Christ. Fuck. Oh fuck*,*" he shouted as he went still, spurting his come deep inside my body.

I dropped my head back as my inner walls continued to spasm around him. I felt sated in a way sex had never managed to make me feel before. Rather than just a physical workout, it was like he'd worked me, mind, body, and spirit.

And now, it was over. I waited for him to pull out, to flop back on the bed and start snoring, like Elio tended to do. But when he finally withdrew from my body, he ditched the condom in a rubbish bin by the bed and started to dress, once again making me potently aware of the power differential here.

His boxer briefs first, covering up that incredible cock with its magical metal. Then his trousers. I hadn't time to admire his legs before, but they were equally as sculpted as the rest of his body, with long, sinewy muscles down his thighs, lightly dusted in dark blond hair.

He bent down to retrieve his shirt, still without looking at me. I had a feeling this was the silent version of 'wham, bam, thank you, ma'am', and that was fine with me. Sex without intimacy; that's what I'd been after. Great sex, as it turned out.

But when I sat up to retrieve my clothes, he shook his head like he'd been aware of me here watching him the whole time.

"You should probably get some rest, *perla,*" he said as he threw on his shirt, then leaned down to plant a hard, fast kiss on my lips. "You're going to need it for the next round."

So… apparently, this was "wham, bam, let's go another round, ma'am"?

Chapter Seventeen

Amadeo

What the fuck are you doing?

The question repeated itself over and over in my head as I closed the door to my rooms and headed downstairs.

That was not supposed to happen, and yet I couldn't help but smile. I certainly couldn't bring myself to regret it. I'd fucked her so hard, I might have actually fucked all that prim and proper right out of her. Which, I supposed, was too bad. It had turned out to be one hell of a turn-on.

At the bottom of the stairs, I heard voices coming from down the hallway and followed the sound to my father's office. The door was open; he was sitting behind the desk with two blond heads and one bald one facing him. Vito and Greta, I'd expected, but the other blond head…

"*Buongiorno*, Cielo," I said, making my younger brother turn around in his chair. He and I were fairly evenly matched in height and breadth, but Cielo kept his hair shorter, and he was the only one of the Luciano siblings to inherit our mother's ice-blue eyes. When he was pissed off, those eyes could send a chill straight to the bone.

"*Buongiorno*, Deo," he replied as he stood up and crossed the room. He hugged me one-armed and hard, slapped my shoulder, then stepped back, surveying my wrinkled clothes astutely. "You look like shit, *fratellone,*" he said with a grin.

"*Grazie*. I don't know what I'd do without your shrewd observations."

In Cielo's defense, it's what he did; he watched and he scrutinized and he paid attention to every minute detail. On the surface, he was the man who oversaw the family businesses; beneath the surface, he was something else entirely.

At the moment, though, it was Greta's perceptive gaze that was unnerving me, not Cielo's.

"Don't you have a big-ass biker to keep you entertained these days?" I asked her.

Greta—a woman I would have bet money on staying single until hell froze over—had recently hooked up with a biker. The president of an outlaw motorcycle club, no less.

"Don't be jealous, *amico*. No one provides the kind of entertainment in my life that you do." She was grinning like the Cheshire cat.

"So," Cielo interrupted, "it sounds like your treasure-hunting was a success." He settled back into his seat, his movements deliberate as always.

"Is that why you're here?" I asked him, taking my seat opposite my father. "Treasure" was an odd thing to make Cielo come running; normally he removed problems rather than seeking out new ones.

"I've asked Cielo to stay close to home," my father explained. "Matteo will remain at the college, but I've arranged for increased security there."

My father was taking this threat seriously if he was putting Matteo—my youngest brother—on lockdown. Not surprising, I supposed. He'd managed to keep my sister protected from our world her whole life. Until now. And whether he wanted to admit it or not, it had him rattled.

Vito cleared his throat, drawing everyone's attention. "I was just telling your father about the toolbox we took from the Regalton Arms. Our assessor estimates there's roughly fifty million in cash, gold, and diamonds."

"*Sì*, that seems about right," I said. I'd only gotten a brief glimpse before Heidi had flown out of the room like she wanted nothing to do with that shit—not a typical woman's reaction to staring down at millions of dollars of gold and diamonds.

"That's one hell of a find," Cielo said, chuckling. "It explains why this Bianchi asshole was coming at us full force."

"*Sì*," my father agreed, though it came out very much like a growl. "Now that we're in possession of what he was searching for, I want him found and eliminated."

I laced my fingers at the back of my neck and pretended the muscles there weren't knotting up.

"We can't do that," I said, already cursing the bargain I'd made. Greta was going to have a heyday with this one.

My father cocked his eyebrow at me. "It seems like an odd time for a stroke of conscience, son."

Well... just... fuck.

"I promised Heidi we wouldn't go after Bianchi if she helped me find what he was looking for." I spit out the truth; there was no sense in tiptoeing around it.

There was also no missing the way Greta's eyes widened or the knowing grin that followed. She opened her mouth, but I got there first.

"Whatever you're about to say, *amica*, don't. Heidi was dragged into this shit with Bianchi unwittingly. The least I could do was get the bull's-eye off her back."

Thoughts of Heidi's back flooded my mind with fresh and far more interesting images, her lying naked, her cheeks flushed, and her hands on her cunt. Christ, that was going down in the history books as one of the best sights ever.

But before Greta could use the silence as an opportunity to persist, I shoved the image away.

"We can't go after Bianchi directly, but if we get word out that we've got what he's looking for, it's only a matter of time before he gets desperate and makes a mistake or even tries to come directly at us. And then he's fair game. I never promised not to kill him; I only promised not to go after him."

"But you never promised I wouldn't go after him," Cielo said, sitting up straight in his chair like he was ready to move. "If we can get a location, I can be in and out without anyone knowing. I'll make it look like a heart attack, if you'd like, and no one will be the wiser."

"But I'd know, *fratello.*"

Breaking my word wasn't something I did lightly. I'd stand by it even if it meant stirring up shit here.

My father was silent, tapping the pads of his steepled fingers together. The pulse in his temple was throbbing, but he didn't look nearly as pissed as I'd expected.

"You've become a better man than I expected, Deo," he mused, still tapping his fingers.

I'm not sure if it was meant to be a compliment. What exactly had he "expected"? Then again, I wasn't about to ask.

Eventually, he stopped tapping and sat up straighter, placing his hands on the desk in front of him.

"It's not a promise you should have made without first discussing it with me, but I won't cheapen your word by finding a technicality to get around it. We'll—"

Giovanni stuck his gray head in the open doorway.

"My apologies, *Signor,*" he said to my father, then nodded politely to me, then Cielo.

Well, didn't this feel like déjà vu? Visions of Heidi hang-dropping her ass from the roof sprung to mind. Attempt number two? Really? She was probably right that a fall from that height wouldn't exactly be fatal, but did the woman have to be so persistent?

"There's a man at the gate, *Signor,*" Giovanni said, directing his attention to me. "He says he wishes to speak with you."

Was it too much to hope Bianchi had walked himself right up to my home? That would be an aggressive move, if ever there was one. More than enough justification to put that asshole in the ground.

"*Mi scusi*," I said to my father as I stood up, then followed Giovanni out of the office and down two doors to the surveillance room.

The footage from the camera at the front gate had been moved to the large center screen that was surrounded by half a dozen other smaller ones. And in the middle of the screen was one of the men from Belemonte's bar, the good-looking one who'd been more agreeable than the others.

Maybe he had a death wish.

"Let him in, Giovanni," I said, then headed for the front door. I nodded to Vito on my way past the office, and he followed me out onto the stone front porch.

The guy with the death wish pulled up to the top of the drive a moment later. He was driving a BMW 230i Coupe, so he wasn't hard up for cash, but neither was he rolling in it.

He stepped out of the car and held up his hands, away from his body, meeting my eyes dead-on.

"Do I need to have Vito check you for weapons?" I asked as Vito and I descended the stairs.

"No, *Signor*," he said, shaking his head. "But he's welcome to." He held up his arms a little higher.

I nodded to Vito, who proceeded to pat the guy down. He shook his head when he was finished and took a step back, putting himself on the opposite side of the guy so that we'd pretty much boxed him in.

"You do remember what I told you would happen if I saw you again?" I asked.

He swallowed. Nodded.

"And yet, you come to my *home?*"

He lowered his arms to half-mast. Rather brave of him, in my opinion.

"I've come here because I want to work for you, *Signor*."

I laughed. Maybe the guy was dumb as fuck, but he certainly had balls. "I don't recall putting out a want ad."

He lowered his arms the rest of the way, watching me warily. With Vito positioned on the other side, he couldn't keep his eyes on us both.

"I know that, *Signor.*"

"I can refer you to our HR department," I said, nodding to Vito, "but he's not nearly as amicable as I am. I don't think you'd enjoy the 'interview' process."

Vito smiled, all teeth. All ice.

The guy's gaze flickered to him, then back. It was a testament to his mettle that he didn't piss his pants.

"I know this isn't the way things are usually done, *Signor,* but I'm here to do whatever it takes."

Persistent son of a bitch. "What's your name?"

"Antonio Verdi. I grew up in Del Rio, Texas, right off the Mexican border, with my mother, my sister, and my grandmother," he went on without pause. "When I was twelve, my mother and sister were taken—my sister was fourteen years old."

An uncomfortable sensation writhed in my gut. I had a feeling I knew where this conversation was headed. "I can't say I've spent much time in Del Rio, *amico.*"

The guy nodded distractedly. "The man who took them, he sold my sister. My mother was too old for that, which meant he took her for the hell of it."

"What does that have to do with me?" I asked. It wasn't that I was actually as heartless as I sounded, but the scenario he was describing was a hopeless one.

"You killed him, *Signor.*"

I did? "You might have to narrow it down for me. The list of men I've killed is a long one."

"*El víbora*," he said, bringing back memories of the time I'd spent at the asshole's compound, stewing in a sea of twisted fuckers and dead-eyed girls.

"*Sí,* I did help kill that one. I can't take all the credit, I'm afraid." Greta had been there too. And Gabe Costa, younger brother to the don of the Costa family, had orchestrated it. In the end, just about every part of our alliance had taken part in bringing down that compound and the twisted fuckers inside it.

Antonio nodded like he was already aware of that. If he'd also known about my involvement, he probably was.

"I don't know what you're hoping for here. I'm not going to be able to find your mother or your sister." It was the gentler way of saying the people he was looking for weren't breathing air anymore.

"I know they're dead, *Signor,*" he said. There wasn't an ounce of emotion on his face. Either the man felt nothing or he was pretty damn good at hiding what was going on behind the mask.

I exchanged a brief glance with Vito to get his take on the guy.

Vito inclined his head minutely. He was willing to hear Antonio out but not ready to buy what the guy was selling just yet.

"Then what is it you want?" I asked him.

"What I want is a chance to stop even one man like him from tearing apart families like *El víbora* tore apart mine. And I know that the legal way of trying to fix this shit doesn't work. Your way does. I have no qualms with killing assholes, stealing from rich bastards. Anything you need done, I'll do it. I'll do whatever it takes to earn my keep and prove my loyalty."

"How long did you work for Belemonte?—how long were you *loyal* to him?"

He shook his head. "I didn't."

"And yet you ended up working for Elio Bianchi with Belemonte's Free Birds? Explain, *per favore.*"

"Brando, the kid you told to get his ass in school—his mother was cousin to my own mother, and the only family I have. When he told me what his father had him doing, I tagged along to keep the kid safe."

It was plausible. I did remember this man positioning himself in front of the kid in Belemonte's bar.

"But you do understand, from my position, it's just as likely Bianchi has sent you here, hoping to infiltrate my family. There's really no way for you to prove otherwise."

"*Sì*, there is. I know where Elio Bianchi is, and I'll tell you whether you decide to take me on or not. You take him down, and then you'll know I've got no ulterior motives here, none that I haven't laid out for you plain as day."

Well, that was useful. Or at least, it would have been if I hadn't made a promise to Heidi.

"I'll make no promises, but go ahead," I said, nodding for him to continue. I wasn't about to turn down the information.

"Bianchi's been seeing this woman the past few weeks—a real rich bitch."

The blonde from the photos I'd shown Heidi.

"She's got a cabin at Cayuga Lake. That's where he's hiding."

"How do you know that?" I asked, though I'd already made my decision. My gut was telling me this man wasn't full of shit.

"Bianchi called my cousin shortly after you left that shitty bar," he explained. "He didn't give a fuck that the men he'd contracted had been shot or killed." His features twisted with disgust. "He wanted Brando to meet him—at the cabin. I wouldn't let the kid go alone."

"What did he want with your cousin?" I asked.

"He gave him a note to deliver and said he was to leave it underneath the bench at GreenVale Park at midnight tomorrow night and walk away."

So, Bianchi was trying to reach out to a contact.

"Where's your cousin now?" I asked.

Antonio eyed me, his gaze suddenly wary. It didn't bother me. That he was protective when it came to his family was a point in his favor in my books.

He sighed after a moment, then nodded. "I've got him locked down somewhere safe. I have the note though," he said, slowly reaching into his pocket and pulling it out.

"*Both targets are out of my hands. Advise on how to proceed,*" the note read.

"Both targets?" I asked.

Antonio shrugged. "Brando didn't know what it meant either."

The toolbox from the Regalton Arms had to be one of the targets, but the other? Heidi sprung to mind, but that didn't make much sense. She'd inadvertently handed over the location of her father's stash to Bianchi. There was no reason for her to still be a target. So, another stash Bianchi had been after? That was possible.

"But the blonde," Antonio went on, "I know he's got her at the cabin. Her shoes and purse were there, but I saw no sign of her."

"You think he killed her?"

Antonio shrugged again. This time, the move seemed more reluctant. "I think he has it in him. Brando says he had his VP off two men for insubordination. And the woman you took from Bianchi's apartment—Heidi Dawson–"

I nodded warily. I could feel my hands curling into fists. It felt like the guy had just ventured into dangerous territory.

"I have a feeling she's not dead, am I right?" he asked, the tone of his voice almost hopeful.

I nodded again, watching him, looking for the slightest provocation to put a bullet in his head. If he was here trying to get to Heidi, he'd have a hard time doing that with half his brains on the car behind him.

"The thing is," he continued, "when Bianchi sent those men after her, he didn't send them there to retrieve her from you; he sent them there to kill her. When they asked him how he wanted it done, he told them to 'get creative'."

I hadn't considered it. I'd been operating on the assumption that Bianchi was trying to retrieve Heidi, not kill her. But he'd been trying to silence her, the only sure way to keep her from spilling information about the money Bianchi was after.

"You're sure?"

He nodded. "I was there with Brando when he gave the order."

That was it. Promises be damned. Bianchi had just hammered the last nail into his coffin.

I nodded to Vito, then turned my attention back to Antonio.

"You'll remain here," I told him. "I'm afraid your accommodations won't be pleasant. If your information is correct, then when Bianchi is dead, you'll have what you want. But if you betray me—now or at any time in the future—you'll be praying for death long before I grant you that escape."

Antonio nodded. "Fine, but if this stay ends with your man here removing my toenails, I'm going to complain all over Yelp."

I smiled. If I didn't have to kill the man, he might just fit right in here.

"Take him downstairs, *per favore,*" I told Vito. "Then tell my father there's no need to wait any longer."

"You got it, boss," he said, then motioned for our new guest to accompany him inside.

I stood outside a moment longer, then returned to the house and headed upstairs to my rooms. I closed the door behind me, then turned to see Heidi fast asleep on my bed.

Her hair was fanned out around her like a dark halo, her dark lashes stood out in sharp contrast against her cheeks, and her lips were slightly parted. I thought about all the other women I'd fucked, the blurred faces of countless blondes, brunettes, and redheads. I couldn't remember any of their faces, couldn't recall ever standing idle, just watching them sleep. It made me wonder how long it would be before Heidi became a blur just like the rest of them. It was too bad, really.

I shook off the odd sense of loss and headed for my closet to change, but by the time I came back out, she was awake.

Right away, her brow furrowed. "What's wrong?" she said as she sat up, pulling the sheets up with her like I hadn't seen every naked inch of her less than an hour ago. It was cute. And it seemed that prim and proper shit was still intact.

"I'm going to kill Bianchi," I said plainly. I might have been breaking my word, but I wasn't going to lie about it.

"No." She shook her head as she got out of the bed with the bedsheet firmly wrapped around her. "You gave me your word, Amadeo."

Christ, I'd had the same goddamned name for a long time—my whole life, actually—but never before had it sounded like *that* coming from anyone else's mouth. Not the point of this conversation, though.

"He's holding a woman hostage. If he hasn't already killed her, he's going to," I said as I shoved a spare gun into the holster around my ankle. "And more importantly, when those men attacked the cabin, they weren't there to retrieve you; they were there to kill you—on Bianchi's orders. That changes things." Broken vows were a hell of a lot easier to carry around than blood. No fucking way was I going to have Heidi's blood on my hands.

She was standing at the foot of my bed, her teeth digging into her plump bottom lip, conflicting emotions flooding across her face.

"You expect me to tell you it's okay?" she asked. The furrow between her brows deepened. "That would be like signing Elio's death warrant. How can I do that?"

Her breathing was coming faster. She was a doctor; she saved lives. And she took that vow so seriously that she'd saved Aurelio's life when she'd thought he was just another dangerous criminal. She wore that fastidious manner of hers the same way she did a doctor's coat, as armor and status symbol all at once. If she stained it with blood on her hands, she'd lose far more than a little dignity.

This weight didn't belong on her shoulders.

I sighed. There was a surefire way to remove that weight, but man, did it fucking suck.

I wiped every bit of feeling from my face, leaving behind the cold mask of indifference.

"If you haven't noticed, *perla,* I'm not asking; I'm telling," I said dismissively. "You think you have any control over me?" I shook my head and forced a scornful laugh. "I do what I want, when I want. To whomever I want."

Her teeth released her bottom lip, her arms wrapping more tightly around herself even as she tilted her chin up higher.

"But you knew that about me already. That's why you despised me from the first moment you saw me, remember? Me standing there, holding a gun to Thompson's head? I drugged you, kidnapped you. And yet, you honestly think you can stand here and tell me what to do?" I shook my head. "Let me guess, you think you have some magical power over me because I fucked you?"

Her hands had curled like she had claws. She opened her mouth, but I wasn't about to let her turn this around.

"I'll give you one thing, though: you were a better fuck than I was expecting. All that prim and proper exterior you wear? Who would have guessed there was such a dirty little slut beneath it?"

I turned to leave, then stopped. I grabbed her arms and pulled her close without looking at her face. No way in hell did I want to see the hurt and anger written there.

She was rigid against me as I delved for her lips, tasting them one last time. Before she could acquiesce or fight, I let her go, looking down at her with a scornful, knowing smile.

And then I left, locking the door behind me.

If ever there was a woman who would hate me to my core, it was this one. But there was also no way she'd be blaming herself for what was about to happen.

Chapter Eighteen

Amadeo

The sun had disappeared below the horizon, painting the sky a dark blue, flecked with thousands of stars. I swear the goddamned sky was mocking me.

"It's good to see you again, Brute," I said, holding out my hand to the giant president of the Old Dogs MC. According to Greta, he had a vacation home on Cayuga Lake, about half a mile from where we were now standing.

"You too, my friend." He shook my hand, then stepped back and shook hands with Vito, Bruno, and Carmine.

"We thought you wouldn't mind an extra set of hands," he said, nodding to Leo Luca, who was standing next to Greta. Leo—Raven's brother and my cousin—was dating Brute's honorary daughter, so it didn't surprise me to see the two of them together.

"You're always welcome, of course," I said, slap-clapping my cousin on the back.

"Brute says you've got an issue with the man inside," Leo said, nodding in the direction of the blonde woman's two-story cabin about two hundred yards in front of us, "but you won't let him torch the place." His lips quirked in a smile.

"*Sì*, that about sums it up," I said, not forgetting for a moment Brute's crazy obsession. The man seriously liked to burn shit down. "Elio Bianchi might have an innocent woman in there with him, and even if he didn't, I want to see the fucker before he dies."

"You can see a man just fine when he's on fire," Brute muttered good-naturedly.

Greta swatted at him while Vito rolled his eyes next to me.

"Dynamite and Tate are working their way to the back of the cabin," Brute said, settling down to business. "As soon as they're in position, they'll let me know."

"I appreciate it, *amico,*" I replied.

Brute had brought along two of his best men, and although the Lucianos hardly needed the help, I wasn't about to turn it down. It was a strange alliance we'd formed between mafia families and bikers—and even one bad-ass South American cartel—but it worked for us.

I held up a pair of binoculars with night vision for one last look at the target.

There were three men with guns outside the cabin, clear as day. If Bianchi was smart, he'd have at least a few others concealed in the immediate area—those were the ones we'd have to watch out for.

"If Dynamite and Tate can take the cabin from behind," I said, "then the rest of us can fan out and approach from all angles. Any resistance we encounter on the way, we need to take out silently. Knives only."

Heads bobbed around the semi-circle we'd formed. Vito, Bruno, and Carmine already had combat knives in their hands.

Greta withdrew one of hers from a sheath on her back while Brute looked at her with a furrow between his brows.

"I can see that look, Brute," she said without looking over at him.

"You didn't see shit, darling," he said with a resigned smile.

I really hoped he hadn't hooked up with Greta thinking she'd settle down.

Brute pulled out his phone and read a text on the screen, then nodded. "Dynamite and Tate are in position, about fifty yards behind the house. They haven't run into any resistance."

Perfetta. "All right." I checked my watch. "We breach the cabin in five. *Andiamo,*" I said, and like we'd done this too many times before, the seven of us spread out through the dark woods, each one navigating through the trees to take the cabin from a different angle, then moving inward.

The forest was cloaked in an eerie stillness as I moved through the dense underbrush. Each step was measured and deliberate, my senses on high alert. I gripped the cold handle of my knife, the blood in my veins pulsing with adrenaline.

I scanned the darkness for any signs of movement, but even the leaves on the trees above me were still.

Moving from one tree to the next became a well-rehearsed dance. I pressed my back against the rough bark, my body melding into the shadows. I waited, listening, watching for any indication that one of Bianchi's men was hiding close by.

There—a faint flicker of movement ahead, in a tall cluster of maples.

I crouched low, my breathing steady, and observed him from afar.

He seemed alert, his eyes scanning the surroundings, but he couldn't possibly see me lurking in the darkness. I slowly circled around him, my footsteps silent as I moved through the undergrowth. Each step was carefully placed, avoiding any dry leaves or twigs that could betray my presence.

With a keen eye, I mapped out the perfect angle of attack. As I closed in, my heart pounded as I gripped the knife tighter.

I was mere feet away from him now. I took another step, hiding behind the maple at his back. So close. Could he feel it? I wondered. A prickling sensation at the back of his neck?

He turned slightly, and in that instant, I struck.

I lunged forward and wrapped an arm around his mouth to muffle any sound. With my other hand, I brought the knife down, dragging it across his throat in one deep slice that ripped right through his vocal cords.

The only noise he made was a wet gurgling sound as his body struggled, jerking wildly against my hold. Hot blood spurted against my arm, saturating the fabric. Then his body went limp in my grasp, and I lowered him to the ground just as silently as I'd killed him.

I wiped the blade clean and moved on, disappearing into the shadows once more. I could see the tree line and the cabin beyond it, lit by one interior light. I was almost there.

Silently emerging from the shadows, Leo materialized on my right just as I stepped out from the concealing trees. Our movements were synchronized, both of us crouched low as we made our way along a path of ornamental bushes, concealing our approach to the cabin's front door.

Within seconds, we reached the sunken door, hidden from sight by the cabin's façade. I checked my watch. One and a half minutes remained for the rest of the team to get into position.

I sheathed my knife and withdrew my gun; once we were inside the house, there'd be no more need for stealth.

Only one more minute on the clock.

Then the sound of footsteps echoed on the cabin's front steps, breaking the silence.

"Shit," I muttered under my breath, exchanging a quick glance with Leo. We needed a distraction.

Leo's eyes gleamed with mischief. Apparently, we were on the same page.

I nodded, silently swapping my gun for the blade once more. Without a word, Leo stepped forward into the man's path.

"Lookout duty, huh?" Leo quipped, his voice dripping with sarcasm. "Must be thrilling, counting trees and chatting with squirrels."

Before the man could respond, I followed Leo out and my knife found its mark, slicing deep into the man's throat with deadly accuracy, hitting bone before I withdrew it.

As the blood sprayed like a macabre fountain, Leo swiftly caught the man before he could crash to the floor, muffling any potential noise. Together, we eased him down, leaving him lying in a pool of crimson.

"*Grazie*," I whispered to Leo as we made our way back to the door, leaving the man where he lay.

Fifteen seconds.

Ten seconds.

Five.

I took a step back, aimed my gun at the lock. When the countdown struck zero, I fired.

As the gunshot ruptured the silence, glass shattered all around the cabin as the rest of our team breached windows.

Leo shoved the door open, and we slipped inside.

There was a man in the living room, right in front of us. Not Bianchi. I aimed and fired at the same time as Leo, taking the man down with two shots to the chest.

I saw Greta and Vito charge up the stairs as I turned toward the first door off the living area.

It was a bedroom. The light was off, but a sliver of moonlight slipped through the curtains, vaguely illuminating the queen-size bed beneath the window, a bed that wasn't empty.

Leo felt around the wall beside me and flipped on the light, lighting up the burgundy and hunter green room.

And the blonde woman on the bed.

She was naked, staring up at the ceiling with lifeless eyes. Deep purple strangulation marks circled her neck. Her lips and fingers were a bluish-purple, but the tips of her fingers were covered in blood. She'd scratched her assailant, drawn blood, fought with everything she had in her.

She'd fought Bianchi and lost.

"Son of a bitch," Leo muttered under his breath as he grabbed a burgundy sheet that had fallen to the floor and draped it over the woman's body.

If I'd had any doubt about what kind of monster Bianchi was, those doubts were gone. If he'd gotten his hands on Heidi, was this what he would have done to her? Was this what 'get creative' had meant?

Suddenly, the face of the woman on the bed was pale, her eyes a star-flecked twilight blue, her hair spilling out around her like a dark halo.

Something ignited inside me, something raw and visceral.

"I want Bianchi alive," I seethed. The mic in my earpiece would transmit my instruction to the whole team. The son of a bitch was mine.

Leo swept the closet and the en suite bath, and we headed back out of the room. No more gunshots were sounding. Only the sound of muffled footsteps as the team cleared the house, room by room.

"I've got him," Vito called out. His voice came from the upper floor.

I took the stairs two at a time, down the short hallway to another bedroom. The door was open, the room was empty, but the closet door was open too, and I could see Vito standing inside it, his gun pointed toward the far corner.

"Get him out here," I said as the room filled up behind me. Leo, Bruno, and Carmine. Greta.

"The rest are securing the perimeter," Greta said as Vito leaned down and dragged Bianchi up with one arm.

I nodded, but I kept my gaze on Bianchi as Vito pressed the gun's barrel to his head and yanked him out of the closet.

The man was my height, but he wasn't as heavily muscled. His clothing was rumpled and his short, dark hair stood out in every direction. There were tears on his cheeks. Fucking tears. He was blubbering as Vito dragged him toward me.

Bruno and Carmine took a step forward, guns in hand, but I shook them off as Bianchi looked around the room with wide, tear-filled eyes.

"P-please," he blubbered. "I didn't have a choice. I've got nothing. I had to do something."

I smiled like the devil himself. "You did what you felt you had to do, Bianchi. Now, I'm going to do what I have to do. You understand, *sì?*"

"No. Please, no," he whimpered like a coward.

"Is that what the woman I found downstairs said? Did she beg you? Did she plead with you to spare her life?"

He shook his head frantically. "I had no choice. She was going to—"

"I don't care," I said, cutting him off.

"Please," he kept whimpering like he had a hope in hell of swaying me.

I shook my head. "You're not sorry; you're only sorry you were caught. But I'm very glad you don't regret it." It made what I was about to do much easier.

I turned to Bruno and Carmine. "Help Vito secure him to the bed, *per favore*. Strip him first."

They nodded and got to work, stripping him while Vito twisted his arms up behind his back.

They used his own shirt to tie up one wrist, then the belts they found in the closet to finish the job. Thin belts; clearly, these had belonged to the woman downstairs. It was fitting that they should be used now.

Bruno and Carmine worked perfunctorily. But Vito, his movements were sharp and brutal; he was pissed. Somehow, this was personal.

When Bianchi was secured, I turned to Leo and Greta. "I appreciate your help, but neither of you have to stay for this," I told them.

"I'm pretty comfortable here, *cugino,*" Leo said with a grin. "Front row seats and all that shit, you know?"

Greta just cocked one neat eyebrow at me like her answer was obvious.

Well, I supposed it was time to get onto the main event, then.

169

"You took on desperate, incompetent men and sent them after my *family*," I said to Bianchi, approaching the side of the bed where he was bound.

"Please, please, I'm sorry," he sobbed. It was pathetic. In the end, they always sniveled and begged, but Bianchi had gotten there fast.

I shook my head. "Your time for pleading is over; it won't do you any good."

He wailed louder while he tugged on his restraints. He looked pathetic, his face streaked with tears, his puny muscles straining with all their might, his dick shriveled up with fear.

"Your men shot my sister," I said, then nodded to Vito, instructing him to gift Bianchi with a similar wound.

Vito smiled and happily obliged me, firing from close range and putting a bullet right through Bianchi's bicep.

He screamed and shook, his whole face turning red. This man was unaccustomed to pain. He probably hadn't suffered a hardship in his life. Until now.

"The men you sent to my cabin shot one of my people," I said when the screaming had returned to sniveling. "Two bullet wounds that could have killed him."

"No! Please, don't!" he screamed as I turned to Vito and nodded.

Vito took his time, surveying Bianchi's body thoughtfully. I think he might have been looking for the areas that would do the least amount of damage to draw this out for as long as possible.

Finally, he nodded to himself and pulled the trigger, sending a bullet into Bianchi's abdomen, right near his hip. And then he waited until Bianchi's screams had died down once again before pulling the trigger a second time. This one hit the *codardo* high on the left side.

His body convulsed and his screams filled the room, spilling out of the cabin in every direction as blood welled up and trickled down his bare abdomen onto the bed.

When he'd quieted down, I leaned in close.

"I am curious about something. I wonder what you would have done to Heidi if you'd gotten your hands on her. Would you have strangled her like the woman downstairs?" I asked as an image of Heidi flashed through my mind, the stars in her eyes dulled and the pale skin of her neck marred with deep purple bruises.

My hands felt like an extension of the raw and visceral feeling inside me as they moved to Bianchi's neck and squeezed, cutting off his air supply. A little more pressure, and I'd crush his windpipe, but I held back, watching as his eyes bulged and his lips slowly took on a bluish hue.

"This is what that woman felt," I told him, letting up long enough for him to draw in a single breath.

"This is what Heidi would have felt," the raw part of me seethed with my vocal cords as I applied pressure once again.

When I loosened my grip again, Bianchi's lips parted as he tried to speak. He swallowed, then tried again.

"Thompson," he said. "Thompson's idea."

"I don't care whose idea it was." Passing the blame was just another coward's move.

"I couldn't let her lead—lead him to me."

I scoffed. "Thompson's dead, and you know it. You left him in your apartment for me to find so you'd have time to slither away."

His breathing grew shallower, hitching now and again. He was bleeding profusely, and unlike Aurelio, Bianchi didn't have Heidi here to save him.

"I'd make peace with your god, Bianchi. You're about to meet him," I said, then I stood up and walked away.

Now that the "show" was over, Greta and Leo pushed away from the wall where they'd made themselves comfortable.

"Do you want me to take care of this, boss?" Vito asked as I reached the room's doorway.

I turned back and looked at the pathetic asshole on the bed.

He was pale now, nearly as pale as Heidi, but his skin tone was tinged with an ugly purplish hue. There were broken blood vessels in his eyes and bruises from my hands on his neck. His torso was a bloody mess.

"No." I shook my head. "Let him bleed out."

Chapter Nineteen

Heidi

I paced the room like a caged animal while my heart drummed in my chest.

The last conversation we'd had ran through my head in its entirety, over and over again as my emotions bounced all over the bloody spectrum. Betrayal, then guilt, maybe even a bit of understanding, then back to betrayal. *Bloody tosser.*

Amadeo was killing Elio right now. Or maybe the deed was already done. I'd seen Death coming before, felt it reaching out for a patient beneath my hands. But this was different. I wasn't a roadblock now, standing in Death's way. I was merely a bit of rubbish at the side of the road, useless. Powerless.

It made *that* night play over and over again in my mind. The night my parents were murdered. Another night I'd been powerless. I could see them so clearly, and hear my father's voice, my mum's screams. No matter how hard I squeezed my eyes shut now, I watched them drop onto the sitting room's gray carpet. My mother's eyes, they'd looked right at me. Had she seen me? Or was she already gone? I'd asked myself that question more times than I could count.

And I could do no more now than I could then. Would Elio's death haunt me? The knowledge was like a cold block of ice in my chest, and I feared it would never thaw.

I swear I could hear the ticking of a clock. Obviously, it came from inside my head, but there it was, *tick, tick, tick*. Or maybe it was a time bomb, though it was morbidly fanciful to think I could hear Elio's clock counting down.

The bedroom door began to open. I stopped pacing, staring at it, expecting Amadeo to walk in. He'd come to gloat, on doubt. To tell me Elio was dead and there wasn't a thing I'd been able to do to stop him.

But it wasn't Amadeo. It was the big, bald man who stepped into the room.

"Time to go, *tesoro*," he said, motioning toward the door.

Tesoro? I didn't know that word. "And just where are you planning on taking me?" I crossed my arms over my chest and stayed where I was. The last time this man had taken me anywhere, he'd seemed to take delight in letting me know the windows were locked and bulletproof.

"Home," he said.

What? I opened my mouth, but no words came out.

He laughed. "You weren't expecting that, were you?"

No, in fact, I was not. "Aren't you afraid I'll talk to the police?" I asked, raising an eyebrow at him. Why I wasn't making a beeline for the door, I couldn't quite say. Perhaps, I didn't quite believe this carrot he was dangling.

"Not really," he said. He was laughing at me again. For a man who looked like a dark, sinister character, he seemed rather gleeful.

"But there are things I could tell them—"

"You've got no proof of any of it, *tesoro*. All the messes have been cleaned up. After you called into work sick the other day, you probably just took a bit too much cold medicine. It can do all kinds of strange things to the brain, make you think you're seeing things…"

I hadn't "called into work". He'd done that. Or Amadeo had. Or maybe Amadeo had the blonde woman—Greta—call in on my behalf.

"If you're so adept at covering your tracks, why did you have to take me at all?"

The man shrugged. "I think the boss just wanted to make sure you were safe. Now, you are."

The cold block of ice in my chest grew, bitter and sharp. "Elio's dead," I said, though I already knew it was so.

He nodded, watching me, which made it all the worse when tears welled up in my eyes.

"Don't feel too bad for the asshole," the man said. The harshness in his features had softened, and there was no humor in his expression now. "We found a dead woman there with him. What he did to her…" He trailed off, shaking his head. "Don't waste your energy mourning him. He doesn't deserve it."

I licked my lips; they felt dry, like the tears had drawn all the moisture from the rest of me.

"Elio…" I had to stop and swallow to make my throat work. "Elio killed her? The woman?"

He nodded. "He won't be hurting anyone ever again. That includes you," he inclined his head toward me.

I was supposed to be grateful, or at the least, relieved. I could feel the expectation of it in the air between us.

But death did not bring me relief. Perhaps I'd spent too much time battling it to find relief in its victory now.

The man shook his head after a moment and drew himself up straighter. "Come on," he said, motioning to the door once again. "I'll take you home."

Home. It was really over. That at least should have brought some modicum of relief.

I followed him to the door but paused, glancing back at the room—Amadeo's room—then back to the big, bald man who now stood in the hallway.

"Where's Amadeo?" I asked, wondering if this was his way of making it clear to me how insignificant I was to him. After the things he'd said, it did seem likely.

"He's a busy man," the man said, watching me like he'd done before.

Busy? Well, that was fine. The busy tosser could rot in hell for all I cared.

***

It was strange that so much could happen, and yet, everything remained the same.

The worn armchairs in the sitting room looked as cozy as I'd left them. The faux flowers on the tiny kitchen counter hadn't changed a bit. There wasn't even a fresh layer of dust on the flat-screen television that had sat nearly untouched since I'd purchased it six months ago. Unchanged. Undisturbed.

My home was a reflection of me, and yet, it bore no signs of being shaken and stirred and set back down, still reeling.

I felt out of sync here as I stood in my miniscule kitchen, looking over the neat row of clear tea jars on the counter. Chamomile to help with a good night's sleep; peppermint for a morning pick-me-up.

I wondered which tea one might take to combat "recently kidnapped and dumb enough to have sex with her kidnapper". Maybe I could blend it with a tea for "your ex-lover was just murdered" and be feeling right as rain in no time?

I picked up the jar of chamomile tea, the earthy scent stirring up memories from long ago.

"It doesn't smell very good, mum," I say, scrunching up my nose as the steam from the steeping camomile tea wafts across my face.

She laughs. "Well, perhaps not, but it does wonders to settle your father's mind."

My little brow furrows. "Like when my tummy hurts and you give me that drink to settle it?"

She nods as she squeezes a dollop of honey into the teacup.

"Does daddy's mind hurt? Is that why it needs settling?" I ask. He bumped his head on one of the pipes at work today and said a lot of words I'm not going to tell mum about.

She laughs and shakes her head. "Something like that, luv," she says as she picks up the teacup and carries it out of the kitchen to my father.

I gripped the jar tighter. Even with the lid screwed on tight, I could smell the floral, slightly earthy scent of the chamomile tea inside. It made my hands shake and my eyes sting as something livid writhed in my veins.

"You bloody liar," I hollered, and I chucked the jar at the kitchen wall, watching the glass explode into a thousand shards that dropped soundlessly onto the counter.

No sound. Nothing at all.

"It's your fault I can't hear that," I seethed, staring at the shards that lay scattered among tea bags.

"It's your fault," I yelled. My hands clenched into trembling fists at my sides as I thought of every moment I'd spent alone and every night I'd cried myself to sleep. All the times I'd needed them and all the years of missing them so much that it had etched a permanent ache into the center of my chest.

All for money. All for a hidden treasure he never got to spend.

I shook my head and tried to cast the knowledge aside, to shove it down in a box, though I knew it had no hope of staying there.

Stepping around the few shards of glass that had landed on the floor, I moved to my five-by-five dining nook at the back of the kitchen. I pushed aside the blinds that covered the arched window. The stale air in the apartment made it feel stuffy, and after spending too much time locked in rooms, the last thing I wanted to feel was cloistered.

Outside, the sky was still dark. The lamplights cast an orange glow along the sidewalks below and the row of parked cars in front of the building. Most nights, even this late, there were people coming and going from the vehicles, some of them in uniforms, off to early shifts, others still wearing the rumpled clothing of the day prior.

In all the time I'd spent watching the street from this window, though, none of the people down below had ever really noticed me before.

Not like the man in the all-black sports car who was staring up at me now.

Chapter Twenty

Heidi

Three o'clock in the morning. Still there.

Four thirty. Still there.

Five thirty-five?

I slipped my fingers between the gap in the dining room curtains and peeked out.

Gone.

The black sports car that had been parked outside all night was gone.

I dropped the curtains and looked around, holding a kitchen knife tight in my hand. I checked the sitting room, the bathroom. All empty.

I dropped the knife on the olive green vanity and scrubbed my hands over my bleary eyes.

"I don't think tea's going to cut it this morning," I told my reflection, then grabbed the knife and returned to the kitchen for the French press I kept stored in the cupboard above the sink, moving carefully around the glass I had no intention of cleaning up at the moment. But there was also no sense in trying to sleep now, not when I needed to be up for work in half an hour.

Fortunately, the morning passed in a blur—as any shift in an emergency room tended to do. But it was my lunch break, and time had slowed and brought the world into sharper clarity, particularly the woman who stood in front of me at the table in the far corner of the cafeteria with a tray of French fries in her hands.

"Do you mind if I sit down?" Raven asked, then sat down without waiting for a response.

"I don't know what Deo told you about me," she said with no further prelude. "But I hope we've been working together long enough that you know what I am—at least here, at the hospital," she said, pushing the French fries around on her plate.

"Raven Luca is about as steeped in the 'criminal' world as a person can get," Amadeo had said.

My father had been steeped in the "criminal" world, but he'd been a father as well. Could a person be both?

Nothing seemed to fit inside my neat little boxes anymore.

"You're a competent and hardworking nurse," I said because that much was undeniable. "I value having you on my team."

Raven nodded. *"Bene.* But now that we've gotten that out of the way, do you want to tell me what happened?" she asked. "Deo was pretty vague." She was sitting comfortably in the cafeteria chair, and her shoulders were relaxed like we were talking about the weather or the abysmal cafeteria food.

I, on the other hand, felt a knot in the pit of my stomach. I had no idea how to answer her even if I'd wanted to.

"A man I knew," I waded in carefully, "tried to hurt someone close to Amadeo. I believe that man won't be repeating his mistake."

Raven grinned. *"Sì,* Deo has a way of communicating with people, doesn't he?"

"Strip," he'd said.

"Is this what you want, perla?" he'd asked me as he pulled his incredible, pierced cock free and stroked it.

I pushed the memory away as my cheeks suffused with warmth. "Yes, I believe he does," I replied with as much composure as I could muster. "I think I'll go for a walk," I said before Raven saw everything clear as day on my face.

"Enjoy your tail," she said as I stood.

I froze, my hands halfway toward my cafeteria tray. "What 'tail'?" I asked as I dropped my arms.

They felt colder.

The whole room felt colder.

Raven shrugged like she hadn't felt the shift in temperature at all. "I have a feeling Deo's just being over-cautious, but we all kind of get that way. It's hard not to after some of the things we've seen."

"You're saying he has someone following me?" The car outside my apartment? That had been because of him? Perhaps he was more worried about me speaking to the police than the big, bald man had let on.

"It's not a big deal," Raven said as she stood up. She stepped closer. "Whoever he has looking out for you knows enough to hang back; they won't get in your way."

"Oh good. Because that's truly my biggest concern here."

And yet, the thought of his men's eyes on me felt in some way like it was *his* eyes on me, which sent hot and cold shivers chasing up and down my spine, even if it shouldn't have.

I nodded, grabbed my tray, and left the cafeteria. My legs felt a little shaky as I navigated the halls to the hospital's main doors. The moment I stepped outside, I breathed in deep, which was a mistake; the heavy car fumes were hardly a recipe for inner well-being.

I supposed that was one thing that could be said for my forced vacation; the air at the cabin Amadeo had taken me to had been clean and light. It had smelled like crisp pine and warm earth. At least, it had until it smelled like blood and antiseptic.

As I looked around, searching for the "tail" Raven mentioned, a dark gray Mercedes pulled up to the curb right in front of me. I took a step back as a man got out of the driver's side and came around to open the rear passenger door. Though the driver didn't look at all familiar, the passenger did.

"What are you doing out of bed?" I asked as the man I'd performed surgery on in the cabin eased himself up off the back seat.

The driver leaned down to help him up, but the man waved him off and slowly got to his feet.

"You were shot, Mr…" I shook my head. "I don't remember your last name."

He smiled, despite the furrow between his brows and the grimace that made the corners of his lips quiver. "It's Carbone, but call me Aurelio, *per favore.*"

"You were shot, Mr. Carbone. You should be in bed, not—" I slammed my mouth shut as it dawned on me that I wasn't chastising a patient; I was berating a very dangerous man. "What are you doing here?" I asked instead.

"I came to see you, in fact. To say thank you."

That was hardly necessary. "You already thanked me."

"*Sì*, well, you did good work under a great deal of pressure when others would have stood by and let me die. I'm very glad you did not."

He was charming; it struck me a bit like a bucket of cold water. And there was something about him. The cardigan he wore, it reminded me of someone. I couldn't think who.

I motioned to the bench a few feet away. "If you'll not return to bed, will you at least sit down?"

He nodded and didn't wave me off when I hooked an arm beneath his and helped him to sit down, though he very much seemed to be operating under his own power.

All the while, though, I was having a hard time reconciling this man with a killer.

"You seem kind," I said as I sat down next to him, but then an image of this man with his arm wrapped around the lunatic in the ER sprung to mind. There'd been a coldness in his eyes then. Strange, though, that it didn't seem to be there now.

"You're wondering why someone as delightful as me would do the kinds of things I do?" he asked. This time, the corners of his lips twitched with a suppressed smile.

I nodded. I'd come this far, hadn't I?

"My family has been loyal to the Lucianos for a long time, and I assure you, the Lucianos earned that loyalty. It was not freely given."

"What exactly is it you do for them?" I asked. Perhaps it was his job to keep people like Raven safe. That wasn't so bad, was it?

"Unsavory things, Dr. Dawson," he replied with a kind smile that contradicted his words.

Part of me wanted to inquire further; part of me very much did not. Fortunately, my break was just about over.

"I'm afraid I must be getting back," I said, standing up, but then I paused, looking around for the car that had brought him here. It seemed to be nowhere in sight.

"Will you be all right?" I asked.

"I will," he said, nodding without hesitation. "But I do appreciate your concern."

A killer? This man?

I was just about to turn and leave when his lips began to move again.

"You'd be good for him, you know?" he said

I raised my eyebrows at him. "I'm sure I don't know what you mean." Certainly, it had nothing to do with the blond-haired, amber-eyed man who flashed through my mind.

"Amadeo. He needs a strong woman."

I opened my mouth to tell him he was being absurd, that Amadeo was a *criminal.* A bloody murderer. But this man was just like him, and I was finding it difficult to despise him.

"Amadeo made his feelings perfectly clear," I said instead. "Whatever it is he 'needs', it certainly isn't me."

"*I do what I want, when I want, to whomever I want*," Amadeo had said. I was just what he'd wanted to "do" at the time. I wouldn't regret it; I wouldn't shame myself for it—it's what I'd wanted as well. But nor would I let this man try to make it into anything more than it was. Just sex. A physical distraction.

"Goodbye, Mr. Carbone," I said, putting an end to this conversation.

He smiled kindly at me. "Goodbye *for now*, Dr. Dawson."

Chapter Twenty-One

Amadeo

"What the hell are you doing here?" I whisper-shouted as Aurelio hobbled out of the back seat of the Mercedes and made his way over to where I stood by my Ferrari, half a mile from the entrance to GreenVale park.

"I've been in bed long enough, *Signor*," he said, standing up straighter like that helped to prove his point.

"You should be resting," I muttered, knowing no matter how much I persisted, the man wasn't going to budge an inch. At times, I couldn't help but wonder just which one of us was in charge here.

"There'll be plenty of time to rest when I'm dead, *Signor*. And from what I understand, we're here to watch, not to challenge our messenger to a mad dash across the park."

He wasn't wrong, but he'd also lived in this world long enough to know fate had a way of fucking with the best-laid plans.

"All right," I said, shaking my head. "But if this turns into a mad dash, I'm leaving your injured ass behind, Aurelio," I added, grinning, both of us knowing there wasn't an ounce of truth to the threat.

"I wouldn't have it any other way, *Signor*."

That much was true. Aurelio would take a bullet for any one of the Lucianos. He'd taken two just recently; it was difficult to question his loyalty.

I checked my gear one last time, then motioned down the street toward the park. Vito, Bruno, and Carmine were making the same trek from various directions and we had five other Luciano men further back. We'd watch the park from a distance to see just who showed up after the drop at midnight.

"I take it you're hoping we might have an opportunity to question our mystery messenger?" I asked. Aurelio was a help to the Lucianos in numerous ways, but he had a very particular skillset.

He shrugged as he managed to keep pace beside me. "You never know when a little information may come in useful."

When we arrived at the spot outside the park I'd marked out earlier, there were still fifteen minutes to go until midnight. We'd wanted to be in place early, though; no chance of alerting our messenger to our presence here.

I'd intended to let the time tick by in silence. Aurelio had other plans.

"It seems Dr. Dawson has returned to her home..." Aurelio mused, trailing off thoughtfully.

I nodded. I knew he had already been to see her today, though I couldn't fathom why.

"Vito tells me she's quite the woman." He smiled. "I think he's infatuated with her."

What was that now? Though I was certain I'd heard him right, evident by the way my hands were tempted to curl, particularly around Vito's neck.

"She's hot as hell; that's no surprise." I said, brushing it off.

He shrugged. "I think the girl's appeal runs more than skin-deep, don't you?"

Now, it felt like he was leading me, and he wasn't even bothering to try to hide it.

"Do you have something to say, Aurelio?"

"There aren't too many women I know who could have kept their composure the way she did. I found that to be… impressive. You would benefit from a woman like that in your life."

"I have more than enough women in my life, Aurelio, any time I want them." None of the faceless blurs were springing to mind, though; they'd all been obliterated by the image of one prim and proper, pale-skinned brunette with goddamned stars in her eyes.

He sighed. "You're twenty-eight years old; you've had more than enough time to play at being a man, *Signor*. Perhaps, it's time you became one for real."

My spine stiffened. "You know, there isn't another person on earth who could get away with saying shit like that to me?"

"And perhaps that's why it's left up to me to say it. You know I mean no disrespect," he said, meeting my eyes plainly. "But I've seen you with these 'women'. They bore you. They throw themselves at you, you use them, and forget all about them. There isn't a single thing about them that makes them memorable to you. Tell me that I'm wrong, *Signor*?"

"No, you're not wrong," I conceded.

"And Dr. Dawson? Is she not… memorable?"

That was one way to put it. Before I could respond, static crackled in my ear.

"Brando made the drop at the bench," Vito's voice spoke into my earpiece. "He's leaving the park by the east side."

"*Bene*," I replied. "Wait for him to clear the area, then have Bruno bring him back to the house. He stays there with Antonio until I say otherwise."

"You got it, boss."

Now, all we had to do was wait for our mystery messenger.

"You should make an effort with the doctor, *Signor*."

"Do you think we might have more important things to worry about at the moment?" I asked, nodding in the general direction of the park.

Aurelio laughed quietly under his breath. "I think you're more than capable of staring at trees and talking at the same time, *Signor.*"

Probably. But I didn't have room in my head for the prim and proper brunette who hated all criminals, myself included—I'd made sure of that the last time we'd spoken.

"Even if I wanted to take it a little further with Heidi—which I don't—she has no interest in pursuing any kind of relationship with a criminal." Except the physical kind of relationship. She'd been more than willing to pursue that avenue. Willing and pliant and so goddamned wet.

Christ, I actually had to shake my head to banish the image.

"I'm done with this conversation, Aurelio." Because stakeouts and hard-ons were like oil and water—they just didn't fucking mix.

"Of course, *Signor,*" he relented, though I had no doubt the reprieve was only temporary.

Half an hour passed in blissful silence—no more unwelcome advice from Aurelio. But too much time was passing. If no one showed, then it could mean Antonio and his cousin, Brando, were full of shit. It didn't make much sense, though, to tell me all about Bianchi and his whereabouts and then lie about this. And more than that, my gut was telling me we were on the right track.

So, it didn't surprise me when fifteen minutes later, I heard Vito's voice speaking into my earpiece.

"We've got movement, boss," he informed me. "East side of the park, moving toward the benches."

"Hang back," I instructed. "I want to see what this guy does once he's got what he came for."

"Understood, boss."

Since he was coming from the opposite side of the park from where I was standing, I moved in closer. Close enough to get a look at the guy with a pair of night vision binoculars as he reached down and picked up the scrap of paper from beneath the rock where Brando had left it.

The guy looked at the scrap of paper, pulled out his phone, and typed something before shoving it back into his pocket.

And that's when the guy turned in my direction.

"Fuck," I whispered under my breath as Vito's voice cursed through the earpiece. He was seeing what I was seeing.

"It's a kid, boss, maybe fifteen or sixteen years old. What the hell is it with these assholes using goddamned kids to do their dirty work?" he hissed under his breath.

"Because these assholes think it buys them an extra layer of protection," I replied. "They think we won't torture them for intel." And they weren't entirely wrong. I don't think even Aurelio could bring himself to unleash his skills on a child.

Aurelio was chuckling darkly beside me, though, shaking his head. "We won't torture them, but the thing about adolescents is they're all talk. It takes about thirty seconds to scare the piss out of them, and after that, the intel pretty much just flows out too."

True as well. And quite the vivid picture.

But did we follow this kid and hope he led us to the bigger fish? Or pick him up and hope we could scare the fish right out of him?

The kid ripped up the scrap of paper, shoved it into his pocket with the cell phone, then turned to leave, heading in Vito's direction.

"Stay with him, Vito," I told him, my decision made. Because the thing about kids was that the grown-ups didn't often entrust them with a whole lot of intel.

"You got it, boss."

"Come on, old man," I said to Aurelio, motioning back the way we'd come. "I want to catch up with Vito and see where this little shit leads us."

It wasn't long before we were pulling up behind Vito's Porsche outside a shitty apartment building.

"There he goes," Vito said as the kid walked into the building.

I watched, waiting to see a light come on in one of the apartment windows. After a moment, a bulb flickered dimly in one first-floor window.

"All right, let's take a look," I said, moving in while keeping an eye out for trouble from all around us.

Up close, I could see through the kid's half-open blinds that his unit was a bachelor apartment. There wasn't much furniture in it, and certainly nowhere anyone else could be hiding. The kid was already sprawled out on the ratty brown sofa.

"We'll wait five, then I'll go inside," I said. "Stay here, Vito, and let me know if the kid wakes up."

Vito nodded, and precisely five minutes later, I took off toward the building's front door. Though it had no lock, I paused outside it, turning back to face Aurelio who'd remained with me for some reason.

"Where do you think you're going?" I asked. It seemed he kept forgetting he'd been shot recently.

"Someone's got to make the kid piss his pants, *Signor*," Aurelio said, withdrawing a small leather roll from his cardigan pocket.

"And you don't think I can do that?" I asked, because I was fairly certain I had what it took to scare a kid.

"You might exert more… pressure than is necessary," Aurelio said, his lips twitching.

I rolled my eyes. "I'll get the kid secured. Don't do anything that'll rip out those stitches, *capisce*?"

Aurelio nodded, and I turned back to the apartment's front door. It squeaked on its hinges as I opened it, but it closed behind us with a quiet click.

It took less than a minute to navigate the short, stained carpet hallway to the kid's apartment. I grabbed my lock pick and unlocked the door, then withdrew my gun and crept inside. Fortunately, this door was much quieter than the one on the main entrance.

With the curtains open, the light that spilled in from outside was more than enough to illuminate the small space. I could clearly see the kid sprawled out on the ratty sofa; his eyes were closed, and he was snoring quietly. "Like taking candy from a baby" sprang to mind because this was just too fucking easy.

I holstered my gun and moved to the end of the sofa, behind the kid's head, then in one swift move, I covered the kid's mouth and wrapped an arm around his neck.

The kid's eyes shot open and he flailed like a fish out of water.

"Calm down, *ragazzo*," I hissed.

He froze, then muttered something that came out muffled.

"If I remove my hand, you're going to be nice and quiet, *sì*?"

The kid nodded, eyes still wide.

I kept my arm around his neck but removed my hand from his mouth, revealing a face full of freckles. There were just a few across his forehead and chin, but across his cheeks and down his nose, there were so many, they covered most of his skin.

"T-take whatever you want, man," he stammered.

I almost laughed. I looked around the tiny apartment, at the stack of old juice jugs on the kitchenette counter, the dirty laundry on the floor in front of the bathroom door, the stack of empty food containers on the broken coffee table.

"What exactly is it you think I'm here to take?" I asked. It was a fair question, in my opinion. There wasn't a thing worth stealing in this shithole.

"I've got phones. I swear. You can take them, man; just take them and go." His gaze swiveled to the old, beaten chest beneath the window, then back again.

"Do I look like someone who would need to steal a chest of phones?" I asked.

He shook his head emphatically.

I dragged the kid up until his back was flush with the sofa's armrest and looked around for a chair to get him ready for Aurelio.

No chair, though. Apparently, we'd have to improvise.

"My friend here has a few questions for you," I said as I maneuvered the kid around so that his feet rested firmly against the floor.

Aurelio took his cue and moved around in front of the kid, taking up the space between the sofa and the coffee table. He unfastened the tie that secured the leather roll in his hand and let it flop open for the kid's viewing pleasure.

The moment the small, thin knives, pliers, and other pointy things came into view, the kid dug his heels into the floor, trying to push his body back into the sofa.

"God, man. God, no," the kid whimpered. I could feel the sobs starting to choke his chest.

I did not feel like a big, strong man at the moment. The playground bully, maybe, picking on the youngest, puniest kid in the yard.

"You took a little trip this evening," Aurelio said as he withdrew one of his thin knives. "I'd like you to tell me all about it. Do you think you can do that?" he asked as he touched the tip of the knife to his own fingertip, making a drop of blood well up.

The kid nodded. I couldn't see his face, but I had no doubt his eyes were as wide as saucers and glued to the knife.

"Excellent," Aurelio exclaimed. "I'm very glad to hear it."

The kid whimpered.

Christ, this was definitely not my finest moment.

"Tell me," Aurelio began, "who hired you to pick up that note at the park this evening?"

"I-I don't know, man."

Aurelio tsked and shook his head.

"I swear, I don't know his name. I was just minding my own business, and this guy comes up to me. He tells he'll pay me; all I gotta do is pick up a message for him, that's it. No names, I swear, man."

"Describe him, if you don't mind," Aurelio said with an encouraging smile.

The kid swallowed. "It was dark. He was wearing a hoodie, so it was hard to see his face. But he had tats! He handed me a phone, and his hands were covered in tats."

"Tattoos of what?" Aurelio persisted.

"I don't know. I swear I don't. I didn't get a good look at them, but they were black tats; no color at all."

"The phone he gave you, where is it now?"

"In… in my pocket."

"Good. Would you mind handing it to me?"

Christ, Aurelio was one eerie fucker, standing there looking like Mr. Rogers with a blade in his hand.

The kid's hand shook as he reached into the pocket of his baggy, worn jeans. He nearly dropped it when he pulled it out and held it up for Aurelio to take it.

Aurelio handed it to me, and I scrolled through it one-handed. Just one number in the contacts list. Just one text to that number, reiterating the context of the note verbatim. No other activity on the phone. I had a feeling the number led to a burner phone, but that wasn't the kid's fault.

I nodded to Aurelio, letting him know to continue.

"Is there anything else you can think of?" he asked the kid. "Anything else you think might be useful to me?"

The kid's sobs had slowed. He sniffled like he had the biggest cold in the world, then started to shake his head, but stopped.

"A car," he said. "The guy was driving a fucking nice car. Black sports car. I-I don't know anything else about it."

I nodded again to Aurelio. We were done here. And thank fuck.

I unwound my arm from around the kid's neck while Aurelio rolled up his leather bag of goodies.

"That… that's it?" the kid asked. He hadn't moved a muscle.

"Almost," I said.

He swung his head around, looking up at me with wide eyes. To his credit, he hadn't actually pissed his pants.

"You're going to leave, *ragazzo*." I looked around. "Somehow, I don't think it will take you long to pack."

"Leave? Where am I going to go, man?"

"If the man who paid you discovers you've spoken with us, he may not be too happy with you."

"Fuck," the kid cursed under his breath. He was still shaking like the prospect of having to leave was just as terrifying as two grown men here to torture him.

Christ.

"Where's your family, *ragazzo*?" I asked him, lacing my fingers behind my neck.

"My mom's dead," he said, and for the first time, something fierce flashed through the kid's eyes.

"And foster care isn't your thing?"

He shook his head. "Those people are fucked up, man."

Admittedly, I'd heard horror stories.

I dropped my hands and pulled out my money clip. "This is for your cooperation," I said, tossing down five hundred dollars beside him. "Keep in mind that it pays to cooperate with the Lucianos. You'd rather have us as friends than enemies."

The kid nodded, his gaze fixed on the small stack of bills like it was a bucket of gold. It made me wonder how little the asshole had paid him to pick up his message.

I withdrew another stack of bills from the clip, a thousand dollars. "This is to get you where you're going."

"Holy shit," the kid breathed, his eyes as wide as saucers. "You're serious?"

"Do I look like I'm joking?" I asked.

"I don't get it, man."

That made two of us. I couldn't quite say what the hell had come over me, but I felt slimy as fuck for scaring the shit out of a kid. Now, give me a full-grown scumbag, and it was one of my favorite pastimes.

"I'm giving you a chance to choose a different path," I told the kid. Maybe there was some truth to it. "If you keep doing odd jobs for strangers, you're going to wind up dead." A whole lot more truth to that.

He nodded, his gaze going back and forth between me and the bills on the sofa.

I turned to leave but stopped at the doorway. "Don't get caught on the wrong side of my family again, *ragazzo*. There won't be a second warning. *Capisce?*"

He nodded vigorously. He was still nodding as Aurelio and I left the shithole of an apartment and headed outside.

But it wasn't over. At least, it wasn't for me.

"Heidi's the second target Bianchi was referring to," I said as Vito met us on our way to the car.

Vito and Aurelio both looked over at me, expressions curious.

"I had Mario watching her apartment. He said there was a car on the street all night. He couldn't be sure, but he thought the guy in it might have been watching her apartment too."

"A black sports car?" Aurelio asked.

"*Sì.*"

"Well then, I suppose there might be reason to talk about the doctor, after all," Aurelio said.

Damn it, Aurelio. If the man hadn't been shot, I might have been tempted to do it myself, just to wipe the smug smile off his face.

Chapter Twenty-Two

Heidi

I parted the curtains and peeked outside, scanning the lamplit cars parked on the street. All of them were empty. No black sports car. And yet, I could feel eyes on me. They'd followed me home from the hospital, and I could feel them now, watching.

Bloody tosser.

"Over-cautious"? This was just creepy.

Dropping the curtains, I proceeded to pace the six steps across the kitchen, then back, tempted to peek outside for the hundredth time in the past hour.

I'd be dead on my feet if I kept this up all night. Any sane person would either call the police or go to sleep. And since I wasn't about to call the police—for reasons I wasn't willing to scrutinize at the moment—sleep was the only reasonable alternative.

I checked the locks on the front door once more, made sure all the curtains were closed tight, then crossed the sitting room to my bedroom. The bedsheets were rumpled; it wasn't my first attempt at sleep tonight. I slipped off my robe and slid beneath the cool satin sheets where the soft fabric brushed across my bare flesh.

I imagined the millions of touch receptors firing. Each one initiated an electrical signal, and in my mind, I followed one along nerve fibers, through the dorsal root ganglion, and up the dorsal column-medial lemniscus pathway in my spinal cord. Finally, the signal traveled to the somatosensory cortex in my brain where the conscious perception of touch is generated.

There was comfort in the fascinating intricacies of my own body, and I let it pull me under, breathing out the stress and chaos of the day.

When I next opened my eyes, it was clear by my momentary disorientation that I'd fallen asleep for some time. I blinked, then blinked again, and my dark room came into focus, along with the man dressed all in black standing over me.

I opened my mouth to scream when I saw the familiar blond hair and the amber eyes that were quite unforgettable.

"What the bloody hell are you doing here?" I screeched, though it felt raspy in my own throat.

"I figured there wasn't much point in me knocking," he said, smiling wryly.

"That doesn't answer my question," I said, scurrying up further on my bed, but I hadn't made it far when he leaned over me, a hand braced on either side of my head.

"What do you think I'm doing here?" he asked.

"Breaking and entering?"

He smiled, but it was a dark smile, full of sin. "Not the worst of my crimes, I assure you. But you don't know how glad I am to see that you haven't lost all that goddamned prim and proper shit. It makes me hard, *perla*. Everything about you makes my cock hard."

His words, even without volume, wound through my veins like puppet strings, and he was the puppet master, pulling me closer to him.

But it was nothing more than hormones, a chemical reaction in my brain to the man's very potent sex appeal. Adrenaline, estrogen, and serotonin making my pupils dilate and my heart race.

Oxytocin, however, was notably absent from the mix. He'd broken his word, and I hadn't forgotten the last words he'd said to me.

"I take it you're in the mood for a 'dirty little slut'?" I asked, fighting to keep my tone sharp and scathing.

He flinched as I spoke, but he appeared undeterred. "*Sí*, I am. So, get naked right—" He'd begun to pull the bedsheets away, but he stopped talking and his eyes flared with heat when he discovered I was naked beneath the sheets.

"Christ," he said, his hand still in midair, holding the covers away from me as his gaze swept over me from head to toe, heating every inch of me. It felt like millions of touch receptors were firing, though he hadn't laid a finger on me.

I moved my hand to snatch the sheets back, but stopped myself, glaring at him defiantly even as my cheeks suffused with warmth. I wouldn't give him the satisfaction of seeing me rattled.

"As you can plainly see, I am naked," I said with far more bravado than I felt. "Now, take a good last look and get the hell out of my home."

"I'm not leaving," he said as he continued to take his time looking me over, burning me everywhere with his heated gaze.

"That's funny." I forced the words out past dry lips. "It seemed you couldn't wait to leave during our last encounter."

His gaze snapped to meet mine. "I had to do that, Heidi."

I faked a scoff. "A compulsion to kill hardly makes you welcome in my bed."

He shook his head. "The kill was my choice; making sure you didn't feel like the blame landed on your shoulders, that's something I had to do, whether you understand it or not."

"It was an act?" The words slipped out before I could stop them.

"It was me doing what I needed to do."

Simple. Forthright. There was a sincerity in his eyes I wasn't sure could be faked. I think he meant it.

I didn't think it helped.

"But right now, what I need is for you to put your fingers on your clit, *perla*. Get that beautiful cunt wet and ready for me," he said as he pulled off his jacket and dropped it on the floor.

"And if I say no?"

Would he persist? I wondered. An image of him chasing me sprung to mind, and the sick and twisted part of me he'd awakened went haywire, sparking up a terrible fire between my thighs.

He smiled like he could see my thoughts. "You won't."

Cocky sod. "How can you be so sure?"

"Because you're lying there naked without doing a damn thing to try to change that, and beneath that prim and proper exterior, you're loving every second of my eyes on your body."

It occurred to me that I was fighting this for no better reason than I was supposed to fight it. I wasn't supposed to want sex with a dangerous criminal, but sex with this man had been the best sex of my life. Perhaps we were incompatible in every other way, but in this one thing, we were perfect.

So, I slid my hand down my body, taking my time along the valley between my breasts and the concave dip of my abdomen. When my fingers were a hair's breadth from my clit, I paused, watching him.

He was holding his breath, and only when I crossed that small distance and settled two fingers against my swollen clit did he let it out.

I rubbed in languid circles as he undid the buttons of his shirt so fast his hands were a blur.

I pressed harder as he unbuckled his belt. Instead of dropping it to the floor, he held it in one hand while he toed off his shoes, whipped off his pants, then his boxer briefs.

And then his magnificent, pierced cock was right there, right in front of me. My mouth watered; it had never done that before, not at the mere sight of an erection. Right now, though, there were few things I could imagine wanting more than to lean up and wrap my lips around the swollen head, to flick my tongue against his piercing before taking him in deeper.

But before I could act on the urge, he grabbed my hands and drew them both above my head. Now I understood why he'd held onto the belt. He looped it around my wrists, then through the wrought iron headboard of my bed, buckling the belt so that I was trapped.

I should have been afraid; I should have been fighting with everything I had to escape my restraints. But I'd been completely at this man's mercy already; he could have killed me or anything else, but he hadn't. Was it completely insane that from that knowledge, I felt safer with him than I had with any other partner I'd had?

There was no urge to flee shooting down my spine when he climbed on top of me. When his lips covered mine, I hadn't the slightest inclination to pull away. I parted my lips and let him in, reveling in the feel of his tongue exploring my mouth. When he broke the kiss and worked his way downward, I tilted my head back, giving him full access as he kissed, then nipped, then soothed each sting with the sweep of his tongue. Down my neck, across my clavicles.

As he moved, his cock pressed against my thigh, lower and lower, further and further away from the part of me that needed him most. But when I tried to wrap my legs around him to draw him back up, he grabbed hold of my thighs and slammed them down without a word, pinning them to the bed, open wide as he moved lower.

"Push your tits up toward me," he said when his mouth hovered above my nipple, so close I could feel the warm heat of his mouth.

I obeyed, pressing my nipple hard against his mouth right before he parted his lips and suckled me in, so hard, so deep. I cried out as his teeth grazed the sensitive flesh.

This wasn't me; this wasn't the kind of lover I'd ever been, the kind who craved his teeth as much as she craved his lips, the kind who tugged on her restraints, not to escape, but to feel them there, a constant reminder.

He moved lower and lower still. His lips, tongue, and teeth had explored me from neck to mound, but as his breath tickled my clit, he paused and looked up at me.

"Are you going to be a good girl, or do I have to tie your legs down too?" he asked.

Hot shivers traveled everywhere. Up and down my spine, across my skin, between my thighs.

I nodded, not quite sure to which I was agreeing, but he shook his head.

"Tell me you're going to be good, *perla*."

"I'll be good," I breathed.

He smiled like the devil, then released my thighs only to hook them over his shoulders.

For a moment, his breath teased my slick flesh and then he ran his tongue along my slit, a barely-there touch that made my whole body clench with yearning, most notably, the quivering flesh between my thighs.

When his tongue flicked across my clit, it was almost too much. My hips jerked and my fingers wrapped around the wrought iron bars, holding on tight. He flicked once more, then suckled my clit into his mouth. Even there, his tongue continued its work, taking me higher and higher. He slid a finger inside me, stroking the ultrasensitive patch of flesh inside just as expertly as the last time.

The pressure mounted fast, so quickly, I was gasping for breath as I felt the pinnacle right there in front of me. So close.

He stopped.

His finger slid out of me and he leaned away, lowering my legs back onto the bed.

"Bloody hell," I cursed in frustration.

He laughed. "I like it when you curse, *perla*," he said as he climbed off me and off the bed. "I'll have to make sure it happens more often."

He grabbed one of my spare pillows and propped my head up, then leaned back just enough to look at me.

"Perfetta," he said, then leaned over me, his cock once again just inches from my lips as he fiddled with my restraints.

Somehow, he managed to release just one of my wrists.

"Rub your clit," he said as he stepped back, watching until I obeyed.

Then he climbed on top of me, putting that magnificent cock right in my face, so close, I could stick my tongue out and tease the plump head now. So that's what I did, lapping up the drop of precum that had beaded there.

He remained still, letting me run my tongue along the barbell piercing. And then he was pushing past my lips, filling my mouth.

I was no stranger to oral sex, but I'd never had a man so big inside me—any part of me. He was doing all the work, watching me intently as he fucked my mouth, slow and steady. I watched the way his arousal played across his features, gritting his jaw, dilating his pupils, making his sharp cheekbones stand out even more brilliantly.

"Those lips were made for my cock," he said as he ran his fingers around them.

My own fingers worked faster, rubbing harder. The peak was right there again; just a little more. A little longer.

He yanked his cock out of my mouth and clamped his hand down on my arm, stilling my fingers as he climbed off me.

I almost screamed. Every expletive I could imagine hovered on the tip of my tongue until he released my arm and slid his finger inside me. The dual stimulation of my fingers on my clit and his finger in my pussy was too much.

Within seconds, my orgasm overtook me. It exploded in the core of me and blazed outward, engulfing every fiber of my body.

I'd barely begun to come back down when he pulled out and climbed on top of me.

I moved to wrap my arms around him to draw him closer, but I only had one hand free.

"Amadeo, release me," I said.

"No," he said, shaking his head. "In fact…"

He grabbed my free hand and managed to resecure it, leaving me fully trapped once again. He grabbed a condom he'd dropped down on the bed at some point and rolled it on while I watched the glide of his hand over his cock.

Knowing what was coming, my body was already beginning to spark up again.

There was no more teasing, no more delays. He settled between my thighs, lined himself up, and drove in hard. Deep.

I cried out, gripping the wrought iron bars so tight, it was a wonder they didn't bend or break. And just like the last time, there was no pause, no tentative movements as my body adjusted to his girth.

He fucked me hard. Fast. So deep. His piercing hit my G-spot over and over again. With every thrust, it felt like he was driving me deeper into the mattress, and yet, I wanted more.

I wrapped my legs around him and leaned up for his lips, but instead of kissing him, I caught his bottom lip between my teeth and bit down tentatively, wondering just how this would play out.

When I leaned away, searching his gaze, his eyes were lit up.

"You like to play rough, *si?*" The smile on his face made something twist nervously inside me. I wasn't certain what was coming, but God, I wanted to find out.

I nodded, just the barest of movements.

"Me too," he said right before he leaned up onto his knees and hooked my thighs over his shoulders.

He kicked his hips and drove in impossibly deeper so that every thrust hit my cervix in a twist of pain and pleasure that was quickly becoming a drug.

His hands were on my hips, his fingers digging in deep. I'd never felt so confined, everything in me narrowing in, focused on that one spot where we were connected.

I couldn't move. I couldn't writhe. I couldn't claw out some of the energy that was building so fast it had me breathless and made my head spin with the intensity of it.

I was moaning loudly; I could hear it in my ears and feel the vibrations in my throat.

His muscles were tense; even the muscles in his neck stood out as he fucked like an animal, primitive and so bloody good.

"Oh, god, yes," I cried as the coil inside me wound up tighter and tighter.

"Come, *perla*. Now," he commanded.

And my body obeyed.

"Amadeo!" I screamed as the most exquisite explosion started between my thighs and spread out until I felt it tingling in my fingertips.

I didn't think it was possible, but he fucked me even harder as the ripples of my orgasm rocked through my body and made my pussy grip him tight, over and over again.

"Fucking Christ," he groaned loudly as he thrust once more and his cock swelled inside me and he rocked through his own release.

He remained there for a moment, looking down at me. In the aftermath, it should have been uncomfortable, but it wasn't.

Eventually, he slid out of me, leaving my body feeling empty. Without a word, he ditched the condom and unfastened the belt, then he threw on his boxer briefs.

He was leaving, I figured. He'd gotten what he'd come for.

"You made me work up an appetite. I'm going to raid your fridge," he said, surprising me.

I laughed, taking time to find my robe and throw it on as he left the room. When I followed him out a moment later, he already had four pieces of freshly sliced bread on his plate, as well as slices of cheese, lettuce, and the leftover chicken from my fridge. He was currently stacking them up in tall layers.

"Is one of those for me?" I asked, already knowing the answer.

He looked up at me with genuine surprise. "Do you want one?" he asked, reaching for the loaf of French bread.

I shook my head, laughing. "It's a wonder your family hasn't gone broke trying to feed you."

He grabbed the sash of my robe and pulled me toward him, untying my robe in the process.

"Just fueling up, *perla*," he said as his eyes grazed over the flesh he'd revealed with renewed intensity.

"Fueling up for what, exactly? A month-long fast?"

He chuckled, then nodded to the food spread out on my small countertop. "I suggest you fuel up too because the minute I'm done, I'm planning to use that hot cunt again."

"Are you?" I shook my head. "I'm afraid I can't stay up all night having sex. Some of us have work in the morning."

Apparently, it was his turn to shake his head. "There you go being all prim and proper again," he said. "You're just sealing your fate."

I was?

"Call in sick," he said like it was of no concern.

"I'm not going to do that, Amadeo. My work is important to me."

"And making you scream is important to me," he said with every bit as much solemnity. But his gaze met my unwavering one, and he sighed after a moment.

"Fine. Get naked." He nodded to my robe which was no longer covering much.

"I need sleep, Amadeo, I—"

"And I need your cunt. So, hurry up and get naked so I can fuck you, and then I'll let you sleep."

This was hardly a concession he was making here. I crossed my arms over my chest and stared up at him defiantly.

"You can take off the robe, or I can take it off for you, Heidi. Either way, you end up naked with my cock inside you." He shrugged. "Up to you how that happens."

In my mind, I'd already relented. My body was revving up; I could feel the wetness on my inner thighs. But I didn't move. Because the truth was, I wanted him to *take*. I wanted him to tear the robe off me, bend me over the counter, and fuck me ruthlessly.

And sometimes, wishes really do come true, because that was precisely what he did.

Chapter Twenty-Three

Amadeo

"Is everything all right in there, boss?" Vito asked as I slid into the passenger seat of his Mercedes.

"*Sì*, everything's fine."

"It seemed to take an awfully long time to check things out," he said, adjusting his position in his seat so that he could face me. "You run into any problems?"

Problems? Not exactly. One hell of a detour, though. "No problems."

Vito wasn't buying it; he was looking at me with his eyes narrowed, searching for what I wasn't saying.

"She woke up," I said. Why did it feel like I was suddenly getting the third degree?

"You must have been making a hell of a racket to wake up a partially deaf woman. We might need to work on your stealth skills," he said with a straight face. Not many people would have noticed the flicker of humor in his dark eyes.

"I'll see what I can do. Any changes out here?" I asked.

He shook his head. "Same black car," he said, nodding to the black Camaro parked five cars up. "There's no one in it, though. And the license plate checks out; it belongs to a guy in the next building. I doubt he's the one watching the girl."

"You know, the girl has a name, *sí*?" I said, then immediately regretted it. Where the hell had that even come from?

"I did hear something like that," Vito said, not even bothering to hide his grin this time. Vito wasn't the grinning sort; it was unnerving. But he sobered quickly, shaking his head at me. "You look like hell, boss. Go home and get some sleep. I'll keep an eye on *Dr. Dawson*."

He was probably right. I couldn't remember the last time I'd slept. Now that I thought about it, I was pretty impressed that I hadn't face-planted somewhere along the way.

I nodded and moved to get out of the car, but then paused.

"Do we know if the phone we took from the kid was of any use?" I asked.

"Some," Vito replied with a nod. "The phone number he texted was a burner, so there's no record of who bought it, but we got the logs from the number's service provider. We know which cell tower the phone connected to when the kid's message was received, so we know the general area."

"And that area would be?" I prodded. I was too damn tired for a guessing game.

"You're sitting in it," he said, motioning around us.

I pinched the bridge of my nose, trying to stave off an oncoming headache. "Well, doesn't that make me feel all warm and fuzzy inside."

"I'm guessing that's the post-orgasmic bliss," Vito said, lips quirking.

Maybe, but it was sure fading fast now.

"Maybe I should stick around," I said, but then shook my head, negating my own thought. While it was tempting to linger, to keep an eye out myself, I trusted the men who worked for me. "Never mind. I'm not going to be a damn bit of use to anyone if I don't get some fucking sleep."

I opened the car door, then paused. Again. I must really need some sleep.

"Raven mentioned the tail to Heidi," I told Vito. "So, she knows we're watching. If there's any sign of trouble, you let me know and get in there. Fuck stealth."

Vito nodded. "She'll be safe on my watch, boss. And since you look like shit, I won't even comment on how interesting it is that you seem so concerned for the girl." He was actually grinning. What the hell?

"I appreciate that."

Before Vito came up with anything else he wasn't going to comment on, I got out of the car and headed for my own. I could practically hear my bed calling to me from miles away.

But I hadn't made it three blocks toward home when my phone started to ring. It was Bruno; his number flashed across the Ferrari's console, and I pressed the button to answer it, hoping like hell my night wasn't about to get longer.

"*Pronto,*" I said.

"*Buonasera, Signor.* I just wanted to let you know that we've finished a cursory look into Antonio Verdi's history. So far, his story seems to check out."

"*Bene. Grazie,* Bruno." Finally, something was going right. "I still want him and the kid, Brando, kept close. After seeing how easy it was to squeeze an adolescent for information tonight, I'd rather not have to worry about someone getting their hands on the kid."

"Of course, *Signor.*"

As he spoke, I noticed the telltale glint of headlights approaching rapidly from behind. My muscles tensed as the car got close enough to get a good look. A sports car—a black BMW.

"Looks like I've got company," I said as I gripped the steering wheel tighter.

"Can you handle it, *Signor?*" Bruno asked, though it didn't sound much like a question. Of course, I could handle it. But Christ, I was too tired for this shit.

"*Sì*, I've got it," I said, then hung up.

The car drew closer, its engine roaring.

I rolled my eyes. If they thought they could intimidate me with loud noises, they hadn't really done their research, now had they?

With a flick of my wrist, I sent my car swerving around a tight corner, tires screeching against the pavement. The BMW followed, taking the corner at a wider arc.

"Okay, let's see what you've got," I muttered under my breath, a smirk dancing across my lips.

Adrenaline pumped through my veins as I weaved through the labyrinth of dark streets. The BMW stayed close, but it couldn't quite manage to close the distance.

There was a narrow alley up ahead, barely wide enough for my Ferrari.

"Shall we see what you think of tight spaces?" I asked, looking back at the BMW in the rearview mirror. I squinted, trying to get a better view of the driver, but he wasn't much more than a dark blur.

As I reached the alley, I veered sharply into it, my car barely squeezing through the tight space. The BMW followed, but it was forced to slow down; the driver couldn't navigate the narrow passage at full speed.

At the end of the alley, I swerved back onto the main road while the BMW scraped the shit out of its paint job.

"*Asino,*" I said, laughing.

But as much fun as this was, I was too tired to lead this dumbass on a wild goose chase around the city. I needed a destination.

Taking a look around at my surroundings, I took stock of what was nearby. And I knew just the place.

I veered toward the Old Dogs' clubhouse. The sound of the BMW's engine grew louder as I toyed with him, letting him close in on me. But just as he tapped into the back of my car, I hit the nitro button, sending the Ferrari surging forward like a lightning bolt. The sudden burst of speed left the BMW in the dust, his headlights growing faint in the distance. And the way the road flew by beneath me was fucking awesome.

It took several minutes before he managed to catch up, and when he did, the clubhouse was just up ahead, a mile on my right.

Half a mile.

A hundred yards.

The BMW turned left, shooting down the last side street before the clubhouse.

So, it seemed he'd done enough research to know about the Lucianos' alliance with the Old Dogs.

I debated for a moment just passing right on by the club, but I pulled into the gravel parking lot at the last second, parked my car, and headed toward the front door. I could feel the gravel crunching beneath my feet with every step, but I couldn't hear it, not over the old rock music that was pouring out from the clubhouse.

Inside, the scene was everything one might expect from an MC clubhouse: men in leather cuts, beer and liquor flowing freely, and at least half a dozen naked women enthusiastically performing various services for the club's members…. Pun intended.

I got a few curious, even suspicious glances as the door shut behind me, but one of the prospects who recognized me right away stood up, waving as he came over. I thought his name was Cueball, but prospects didn't have their names on their cuts, so I couldn't be sure.

"Is Brute around?" I asked him, half-shouting to be heard over the music.

He shook his head. 'No, sir. He's at home with his… *woman*," he said, emphasizing the last word. "And he left instructions not to be disturbed unless the clubhouse is going up in flames."

I laughed. "Greta gave you hell for calling her an 'old lady', didn't she?"

The guy grinned. "She sure did."

"How about Dynamite?" I asked, reaching for the names of the other members.

The prospect nodded and led me back toward the bar and then off to the right of it where the redheaded Old Dog was sitting in the middle of a black sofa with his arms stretched out across the back of it, getting head from an okay-looking brunette. She was enthusiastic about it; I'd give her that much.

"Hey, Dyn!" the prospect called, getting the guy's attention.

He looked up. "Deo! Good to see you, man."

Uh-huh. "If I see your dick once while we're having a conversation, I'm going to shoot it off," I informed him. I was joking. Mostly.

Dynamite smiled, then turned to the girl. "You heard the man. Put my dick away, honey, and come back in a few minutes."

Not surprisingly, she obeyed and scurried off toward the bar, sidling up next to one of the other members.

"Sorry to interrupt," I said. I was grinning, but I really did feel for the guy. To get shut down half way through a blowjob sucked.

Dynamite waved it off. "No worries; she'll be back."

"Then I won't keep you longer than necessary. The man we ran into the other evening by Cayuga Lake," I said, keeping it vague even here since I didn't know how many of Brute's 'brothers' were aware of what we'd done. "He may have associates. I wanted to give Brute the heads-up, but since he's not here, I figured you could pass along the message for me."

Dynamite nodded. "Sure thing. Any details I should pass along?"

"Not at the moment. I doubt these associates have any interest in the Old Dogs, but since Greta would kill me if anything happened…"

Dynamite's smile stretched from ear to ear. "Yeah, that girl's fierce."

"Well, I'll let you get back to your blowjob," I said. I would have shaken his hand, but no, I wasn't going to do that.

"You're welcome to stick around if you like," he offered. "Plenty of pussy on tap."

I looked around, but I couldn't muster up any interest in the girls who didn't have pearl-like skin and lashes long enough to dust their cheeks when they closed their eyes. No stars in their eyes either. No plump lips that were the best damn thing I'd ever seen wrapped around my cock.

"I'm good, *amico*. But I appreciate the offer."

I turned and walked out of the clubhouse, wondering what the hell had happened to me. Turning down pussy? Christ, I really was tired.

Chapter Twenty-Four

Heidi

"ETA two minutes," I announced as my team stood ready, staring at the ER bay doors. The room was thick with tension; it made my lungs work harder as I counted down the seconds in my head.

"A young male, approximately fifteen years old." I relayed the information I'd received from the paramedics.

A young male. A kid. A fifteen-year-old kid was on his way in. With only me, Raven, and Tom to serve as Death's roadblock.

"Multiple gunshot wounds," I continued. "Entrance wounds on the upper back, just right of the spine, and the lower back, left side."

"Any exit wounds?" Raven asked.

"Two. Right upper chest and the right lower abdomen. Blood pressure is ninety over sixty, heart rate is one-thirty, and respiratory rate is twenty-eight."

Raven and Tom nodded.

I sighed as the team shifted and their gazes swiveled back toward the door. I could vaguely make out the muffled sound of a siren. That meant it was close, right outside.

The moment the doors swung open, we moved. We were like racehorses shooting out of the gate.

"Gunshot wounds, multiple locations," the paramedic closest to me reiterated as he and his partner transferred a freckle-faced boy onto the gurney.

"All right, let's move," I said, taking hold of the head of the gurney.

We sped down the hall to the trauma room waiting for us, and the moment we were inside, we flew to work.

"Start IV fluids and get me a central line kit," I told Tom. "Raven, get me an airway." I cut down the boy's shirt and spread it open.

Bloody hell.

Whatever wounds my patients presented with, I never envisioned their cause. I never allowed myself to look beyond the scope of what was directly in front of me, but this time, it came. Unbidden, the images flooded my mind, the boy terrified, running for his life. I could feel his heart pounding, his whole body shaking with terror. And then the fiery impact as someone shot him in the back, not once, but twice.

"Prepare a chest tube," I ordered Tom, forcing the images away.

A penetration wound through the upper right quadrant of the abdomen risks damage to the liver, the lung.

The moment the blonde handed me the scalpel, I made the incision at the mid-axillary line and carefully inserted the tube between the boy's ribs and into the pleural space.

The blonde connected the tube to the drainage system, and blood began to fill the collection chamber. I was right; the bullet had punctured the boy's lung.

His heart rate stabilized, albeit weakly.

"Get a portable X-ray and notify the OR," I told the blonde, then turned to Raven.

"Administer blood products, type-specific," I instructed her, though she was already moving like she'd anticipated it.

It felt like hours, but it was really only minutes later when we managed to stabilize the boy enough to make it to the OR. Tom and an orderly helped the surgical team to wheel him out of the trauma room and down to the elevator while I sagged against the empty table.

"That one was too close for comfort," Raven said, leaning back against the counter as she tugged off her gloves. "Poor kid," she added, shaking her head.

I swallowed hard. "Do you…" I began, but decided against saying anything more. "Never mind." I dropped my gloves in the rubbish bin and headed for the door.

"That kind of thing makes you think about all the bad stuff out there, right?" she persisted. "It makes you wonder how I can feel bad for that kid when I'm all for some of that 'bad stuff'?" There was no anger marring her expression. It seemed like a genuine question.

"It's none of my business, I'm sorry."

She shook her head. "Don't be sorry. We have to work together, right? If you've got questions, then I'd rather you ask them than have them lingering like a wall between us."

"All right, then yes, I do wonder how you reconcile certain aspects of your life with the work you do here."

She shrugged. "In a perfect world, I'd be the first one to melt down every gun like the one that injured the kid today. I'd turn them into… I don't know. Something useful. But this isn't a perfect world. We work with what we've got, right?"

It was that simple for her, a neat and tidy box. I found myself envying her that clarity.

"Do you think Amadeo feels the same way?"

The question slipped out before I could stop it, but it wasn't entirely my fault. Three days had passed since Amadeo had shown up in my home in the middle of the night. But instead of disappearing like some dark dream, he'd reappeared every night since.

And then there was Aurelio Carbone, who seemed to have made it his routine to "stop by" to sit with me at lunch each day.

And the shifts with Raven throughout which I'd seen her carry herself as nothing but a confident and compassionate nurse.

The only people I had any interactions with were *them*. Lucianos. Lucas. *Criminals*. Instead of shunning them, though, I found myself wanting to understand what made them tick.

Raven started walking toward the trauma room door, but she kept her gaze on me, eyes thoughtful. "I don't know if Deo would ever melt down his weapons, but then, I'm not sure I'd want him to. Some people were made to be healers," she said, motioning between the two of us. "Others were made to be protectors."

Amadeo, a protector? In some lights, I could see it, perhaps. But in others? The coldhearted killer I'd first met? The man who controlled his people with an authority that oozed from his pores? The man who seemed to have taken control of my body with that same power? "Tyrant" felt like a word that fit better.

She stopped at the door and turned to face me.

"Look, I know this kind of crosses the nurse-doctor line here, but I think we've pretty much stepped over that boundary already. So, my friend, Greta, has been setting up a girls' night for tonight. Why don't you come out with us? Spend some time with us and see what you think."

I opened my mouth to respond, but I had no idea what to say. My tongue felt tied, nearly as much as my brain did. In truth, I'd never been invited out to a girls' night before, never mind a girls' night with the cousin of the mafia man I was currently sleeping with.

"Think about it. We'll be at the Onyx nightclub, any time after ten P.M.," she said before I could figure out how to respond. "The place will be crowded, but I guarantee you'll spot us."

She pushed open the door and left the room, leaving me gaping after her—quite like a fool, I imagined.

I sighed and checked my watch. It was my lunch time, and I couldn't help but notice the way my feet gravitated toward the hospital's exit, toward the bench where Aurelio Carbone had been waiting for me each day.

But today, the bench was empty.

I stared at it, not quite sure what to make of the disappointment that welled up inside me. Still, it was for the best that he wasn't here. There was somewhere else I needed to be.

* * *

"All right, so I've been thinking about it, and I think I have to forgive you," I said, standing in front of the small headstones that stood side by side in a remote corner of the cemetery.

The grass had recently been cut. The sweet, green aroma wafted heavily through the air as I laid a single sprig of forget-me-nots on the top of each headstone. They were my mum's favorites; I didn't know if my father had a favorite flower.

I ran my fingers along the face of my dad's smooth, cold headstone. But the face in my mind was not his, but Amadeo's, and Aurelio's, and Raven's. They were the reason I was here, after all. I'd stopped trying to shove these people into boxes in my head; they didn't fit. And perhaps, neither did my father.

"But I'm still angry," I went on. "You're gone, and it's because of that money, isn't it?"

I shook my head and stared at the headstone like it might actually answer me.

Was it worth it? I asked them silently.

I felt a hand on my back.

My breath caught in my throat as I spun around.

I expected it to be someone familiar, but I was quite certain I'd never before seen the man standing there. He was a tall man with dark chestnut

218

hair and warm brown eyes. He was clean-shaven and dressed in an expensive-looking suit—Armani, if I had to guess.

"I'm sorry," he said, holding up his hand. "I was calling to you…"

"I mustn't have heard you." I seldom felt the need to explain my impediment to strangers.

"It's just… it looks like we're neighbors," he said, nodding to the headstone nearest my parents. "My mother… cancer."

"I'm sorry," I replied, looking at the headstone. According to the date of death, his mother had passed away only two months ago.

"My mum and dad," I said, nodding to my parents' headstones.

He eyed the date like I'd eyed his.

"Car accident?" he asked, the lines of his handsome face softening with sympathy.

I shook my head. "They were murdered."

His eyes widened. "I'm so sorry. I didn't mean to pry. I'm just not sure what else to talk about… here, you know?" he said, motioning around us.

He glanced back at his mother's headstone, and his warm eyes grew shiny with unshed tears.

"You could tell me about your mother," I offered.

He looked up at me, and the corners of his lips twitched in a smile. "I think she'd like that."

I watched his lips, waiting for him to continue. They were well-shaped lips, not too thin but not overly full.

"She was kind," he said, but then he stopped and shook his head. "That's what she'd want me to say. What I'd say is that she was mischievous—she could stir up strife or settle disputes with just a few well-chosen words."

I smiled gently. "My father was the mischievous one—secrets and such." The image of my parents had faded in my mind over the years, but I could still see the way my dad's eyes lit up whenever we were conspiring to keep secrets from Mum.

"Does it ever go away?" he asked, his eyes meeting mine. "That urge to turn to them only to realize for the hundredth time they're gone?"

I smiled sadly. "I'm afraid it doesn't. But it does become a little less of a jarring shock, I think. You catch your breath a little easier from it, your heart doesn't feel like it skips quite so many beats."

His lips twitched in an empathetic smile. "Thanks."

I nodded, not sure what else to say.

"Well, maybe I'll let you finish with your visit," he offered, shuffling his feet. "I'll come back later."

"No, please," I said before he could turn away. "I was just leaving, truly."

He nodded and stopped shuffling. "Thanks."

I looked at my parents' headstones once more, fidgeting with the forget-me-nots so that a light brush of breeze wouldn't blow them away.

"...strange and probably highly inappropriate," he was saying as I caught a glimpse of his lips as I turned to leave. "Did you want to get coffee... sometime?"

All right, well, this had taken a quick turn in a direction I hadn't been anticipating.

The man was attractive and well-dressed. He seemed kind and courteous as well. Here in the cemetery, so close to my parents, it was easy to feel their glowing approval.

But he's not Amadeo, a voice whispered from the back of my mind. A trait that should have been this man's most appealing feature. But it wasn't.

"Thank you, but I don't think that's a good idea," I said, all the while wondering what was wrong with me.

I'd felt my parents' cold disapproval on my shoulders the whole time I'd been engaged in a meaningless sexual relationship with Elio, and here I was turning down the chance for a real relationship in favor of sex with a dangerous man, a man who only came to me in the middle of the night.

220

"You're probably right," the man said with a chagrined smile, though it didn't deter him from holding out a business card. He shrugged. "In case you change your mind."

I hesitated for a moment, then took it. When his fingers brushed against mine, I waited to feel the tingling warmth that should have been there, that first moment of contact with a sexually appealing potential partner.

There was no tingling, no warmth.

"Goodbye," I said as I tucked the card into my purse and left, ignoring the slight prickling of unease that was stirring the hairs at the nape of my neck.

***

I stepped off the hospital elevator onto the fourth floor, wondering, not for the first time, what on earth I was doing. My shift was over for the day. I should have been on my way home.

"The multiple-gunshot victim?" I asked at the nurse's station. "He came into the ER this morning—a boy, about fifteen years old?"

A nurse with a long braid down her back and blue butterfly scrubs nodded. "Yup, he's here," she said, scanning through the charts in front of her and holding out the one I was looking for.

"Thank you," I said, taking it and flipping through the chart. There was a name on the chart now. Grayson Thomas. It was just a name, letters on a page, but they morphed the image of the freckle-faced boy in my mind, animating him, making him more than the flesh and bones and billions of cells he should have been.

"How's he doing?" I asked.

"The boy made it through surgery just fine, Dr. Dawson," she replied. "No complications."

"Can you tell me which room he's in?"

A furrow formed between her heavily plucked eyebrows. The dramatic arch to them made it look like she was always a little surprised, but the disbelief she wore on her face now was not due to her grooming habits.

It wasn't that I'd never come to inquire after a patient, but looking in on them, visiting with them was certainly a rare occurrence.

"Um, of course," she replied after a momentary pause. "He's in room four-one-seven; just make a left at the end of the hall."

"Thank you," I said as I turned away, then I followed the tiled hallway to the end and made a left. I pushed open the door to four-one-seven, but my patient was not alone. There was a man with the boy, hovering over him with his back toward me.

As I stepped into the room, the man stood up straight and spun to face me. He looked vaguely familiar, but I couldn't place him. Something about the scene was making me uneasy.

"Excuse me," I said, keeping my voice steady. "I'm Dr. Dawson; I treated Mr. Grayson in the ER earlier today. Can I help you with something?"

He took a step toward me, away from the boy's bed, offering me a faint smile. He appeared to be in his mid-forties, about my height, with a neatly trimmed beard and a calm demeanor. There was nothing inherently threatening about him, but an indefinable unease settled in the pit of my stomach.

"Ah, Dr. Dawson," he replied, his features arranged in a polite expression. "I'm a family friend of Grayson's. My name is Alex. I wanted to check on him while his parents are away."

I nodded, acknowledging his explanation. But I'd seen countless friends and family members visit patients in the hospital. Something about this encounter felt different.

"I appreciate your concern for the boy, but I must ask that you leave," I said firmly, trying to conceal my unease.

Alex's smile faltered, and his demeanor shifted ever so slightly. "Oh, I understand. I just wanted to make sure Grayson was okay," he replied.

"I assure you, he is in good hands. Only immediate family members are allowed in patient rooms at the moment." I glanced at my watch. "And visiting hours are over. If you'd like to visit him, I would recommend coordinating with his parents."

Alex nodded, seemingly unfazed by my request.

"Of course, Dr. Dawson. I understand the need for precautions."

He walked past me then and out of the room without another glance at the boy. *A friend, indeed.* Not that I was an expert. My only "friend" through my teenage years was the neighbor to my last foster family, an old cantankerous Brit who softened a great deal if you managed to work your way beneath the crotchety outer surface.

I looked at the boy who was fast asleep on the hospital bed. He had thick eyelashes, and his lips were parted as he slept. Combined with the mass of freckles on his face, he looked terribly innocent.

There wasn't really much I could do for him. He was asleep and would likely remain that way for some time. I watched his vitals on the monitor for a moment, adjusted his blanket. I was just about to fluff his pillow beneath him when I stopped.

What on earth are you doing?

I rolled my eyes at myself and left the room. Professional distance wasn't a luxury; it was a necessity.

But as I retraced my steps back down the hallway, an image of Alex sprung to mind, and the prickling began again at the back of my neck.

"No visitors in Mr. Thomas's room," I said to the nurse with the butterfly scrubs at the nurse's station. "And keep a close eye on him… *please,*" I persisted, even knowing it was quite ridiculous of me.

I'd never had this type of "radar" before, the sixth sense that others might have called "gut instinct". Surely, it was only my brief foray into a world that wasn't my own that had me making specters out of shadows.

Chapter Twenty-Five

Amadeo

"Who is he?" I snapped the moment Vito walked into the room.

Cielo and I were sitting in the parlor. I'd been sipping on the same whiskey for the past half hour, waiting for answers.

"Whoa. Chomping at the bit, *fratellone*?" Cielo joked.

"Are you telling me you wouldn't be gunning to get your hands on some scumbag just for the hell of it?"

He shrugged, not bothering to deny it. There was a reason why Cielo was good at what he did. Loyal to a fault, for sure, but my brother got a twisted pleasure from the shit he handled so adeptly.

"He comes up clean, boss," Vito went on. "At least, according to a background check. The architectural firm on the business card is legit—" He waved the business card from Heidi's purse. "And his name came up there too—Nathaniel Alexander Sinclair. According to the firm's records, he recently transferred here from the head office in London."

"So, this Sinclair is on the level?" I asked. "I'm not buying it."

It wasn't the chance meeting with Heidi at the cemetery that had my radar up, or even the way the asshole had deliberately touched her when he'd handed her that card—though I would have had no problem ripping off his fingers one by one for doing it.

I shook my head. "The moment I saw him, Vito, my gut told me something about the guy was off."

He nodded. "And your gut might be right," he said, handing me a handful of grainy photographs. "We did what you said and ran the photo we took at the cemetery against the surveillance footage outside the Regalton Arms," he explained.

"Smart," Cielo said, nodding approvingly.

"It took six hours and Aurelio's sharp eye, but there he is," Vito went on, pointing to a photo that was time-stamped six days ago.

Nathaniel Sinclair was there, just standing outside the building. He could have been walking by it or meeting someone nearby. Hell, he worked for an architectural firm; he could have been surveying the site, looking to make a bid on the reconstruction project. All viable explanations.

"Do we know where he's staying?" I asked.

Vito nodded. "You don't think I'm an amateur here, do you, boss?"

He flipped over the photo, and written on the back in Vito's handwriting was an address. An apartment building two blocks from Bianchi's.

"Another coincidence?" Cielo asked, his voice thick with sarcasm.

"That's just too many coincidences in my books," I said. "I want someone keeping an eye on him. If he was outside the Regalton Arms, then I think it's a safe bet to assume he knows about the money. It's only a matter of time before he makes a move to retrieve it."

But what the hell did he want with Heidi?

"You got it, boss. Do you want me to pull Bruno off Dr. Dawson to keep an eye on Sinclair?"

"Hell, no," I snapped before I noticed the way Vito's lips were twitching. "*Stronzo,*" I muttered under my breath, realizing the game he was playing. I'm not sure I liked this new side of Vito. "Since Sinclair seems to have an interest in both Dr. Dawson and the Regalton Arms, I want surveillance on both."

But who the hell was I kidding? Vito was well aware of where I'd been spending my late-night hours. A habit I was very soon going to have to break.

"I have a man in London who owes me a favor," Cielo said. "I could have him look into that firm from his end. It couldn't hurt to see what he turns up."

"I'd appreciate it. *Grazie, fratello.*"

It struck me as odd that Cielo didn't jump on the opportunity to give me a hard time about Heidi. Very odd.

"I'll go make some phone calls," he said, then he left the parlor, pulling his cell phone from his jacket pocket as he went.

I'd only just stepped into the foyer, intending to seek out my father, when a knock sounded on the front door and Giovanni appeared, seemingly out of nowhere, to answer it.

Even without seeing her, it only took about a second and a half to figure out who it was. I think the girl's energy practically radiated into the foyer the moment Giovanni opened the door.

"*Buonasera, Signorina* Agossi," Giovanni said as he stepped back to let Greta in.

A Greta who was dressed in a strapless navy blue dress and stiletto heels, and who had her hair piled on top of her head in some sort of intricate braid or bun or some shit like that.

"Casual night in, *amica?*" I asked, smirking at her.

She scoffed. "*Si*, I got my ass into this dress, all so I could come over here and hang out with you. Hope you're in the mood for an *I Love Lucy* marathon."

"I wish I could. I'm afraid I already made plans to watch grass grow." I shrugged. "Wouldn't want to disappoint the grass."

She smiled, but the devilish gleam in her eyes had me worried. "I have a feeling you'll be changing your plans soon enough, *amico,*" she muttered, almost under her breath.

All right, *that* was concerning.

"Why?" I asked, feeling an uncomfortable sensation in the pit of my stomach. Greta was up to something.

She shrugged. "No reason. I'm just here to collect Freya."

I laughed. "You and what army?" I was shaking my head. "Anything less, and I don't think you're getting her past our father."

"That's what *you* think." She sounded pretty damn confident.

"All right, I'll bite. How do you plan on getting her out of here?"

"Well, let's see." She held up one hand in front of her, fingers wide. "Gabe Costa will be driving us," she said as she lowered her thumb. "I've arranged for a personal escort to Onyx by the Old Dogs." She lowered her index finger. "Our personal escort will remain there outside the building—" Another finger went down. "—while all four Costa brothers will remain inside the club, along with two of their men at each of the exits." There was just one finger left. "And of course, *I'll* be there."

It looked like she had her army.

"Not bad, Greta. You might just be able to pull this off."

She nodded, accepting the praise demurely. "All I have to do is let *Signor* Luciano know that you'll be there, and I'm guaranteed success."

"And how exactly is it you're going to talk me into a night of chaperoning?"

She smiled like the devil, holding my gaze. "That's easy. Heidi's going to be there," she said like it was all the temptation I needed.

And goddamn it, she was right.

"Why is Heidi going to be there?" It was the less caveman-ish way of saying that Heidi was supposed to be at home, safe in her apartment. And waiting there for me.

"Raven invited her out. I think the two of them have been getting closer at work. And by your reaction, Deo, I have to say, I'm very glad Raven invited her." She was grinning like the devil again.

"And why's that?" Like I didn't already know.

"Because I think you've got a thing for this one, and I don't remember you having a thing for anyone. This woman must be something special. I'd just like to get to know her better."

"Greta," I said, all humor forgotten. "Heidi's been pulled into something dangerous here."

"And that's why I have no doubt you'll be tagging along. But remember, this is girls' night. We're letting you boys hang around for your own peace of mind, but if you start raining on our parade, your peace of mind will find its way to the bottom of my list of concerns."

Freya appeared at the top of the stairs, dressed in a blood-red top and dark jeans with her hair pulled back and her makeup done.

"I'll be down in just a minute, Greta," she called, waving to Greta, then winking at me.

Greta waved back, then turned back to me, all signs of humor gone. "You know I'd never do anything to jeopardize you or anyone you care about, Deo. We're fully protected here, and you're welcome to come along to be sure of it."

"I know you'd never be careless like that, *amica,*" I said, and I meant it.

But she could bet her ass I'd be coming along.

Chapter Twenty-Six

Amadeo

The woman in the high-necked, sleeveless black dress writhed and spun on Onyx's dance floor. There was a slit in the dress all the way up to her hip. Every move flashed more thigh, and every time she put her arms above her head, the dress slid up higher.

This was bad. Very bad. Amid all the micro-size club dresses and over-styled hair, she looked sophisticated and tasteful.

And way too damn innocent. Like a lamb thrown into a shark tank at feeding time, she was just begging to be devoured. And if the hungry looks from the men all around her were any indicator, the feeding frenzy was about to begin.

I crossed my arms over my chest and leaned back against the wall next to Onyx's office door. I was armed; I could just shoot the fuckers. Problem solved.

"Having a good time, Deo?" Gabe Costa shouted over the music as he came toward me. He had a drink in his hand and looked like he didn't have a care in the world. *Lucky bastard.*

"I'd be having a better time if your younger brother wasn't eye-fucking women on the dance floor," I said, not missing the way Caio Costa hadn't taken his eyes off Heidi once in the past ten minutes.

Gabe smiled, his green eyes relaxed and way too happy. "Heterosexual men do tend to spend a great deal of time 'eye-fucking' women here, but I have a feeling you might be referring to one woman in particular?" he asked as he spotted Caio at the table next to the dance floor and followed his gaze to where Heidi, Raven, Greta, and the rest of the devil's girl brigade were dancing.

Really, when this particular group of women got together, they were evil. Nothing but trouble.

"Ah," he said as he correctly picked out which woman Caio had been ogling.

His gaze moved on, finding his fiancée, Cait, and lingering there for a moment. She was a pretty woman, with dark hair a little shorter than Heidi's, and she had the most intricate tattoos I'd ever seen. Flames covered the entire left side of her body, reaching all the way to her temple, flames that covered a mass of scarring from a real fire.

"So, one of them finally caught you, did they?" Gabe asked, grinning as he turned his attention back to me.

"Caught? No." I shook my head. But so long as I was fucking her, I wasn't about to share her with a room full of sharks.

Gabe was grinning like an asshole, but there was an understanding in his eyes. If I had to guess, I'd say he wasn't particularly fond of men eye-fucking Cait either.

"I'll be sure to mention to Caio that he'd best do his eye-fucking elsewhere," he said, then turned to look at the girls once more.

"Your woman seems to fit right in," he said, nodding in the general direction of the group. "That's a good sign, *amico*."

I nodded. On the surface, it did look that way, but Heidi wasn't fitting in, not really. I could see it in the tautness of her shoulders and the way her teeth kept toying with her bottom lip even if nothing else about her countenance gave her away.

And it only got worse when the latest song ended and the girl brigade left the dance floor for their seats at a table across the room.

One of the Costas' bouncers followed close behind them, keeping any of the eye-fuckers from trying to trail along after them. A girls' night out with no one to bother them—that's why Greta and the other women didn't mind if we tagged along. And we were damn good at making sure no one bothered them.

Heidi took a seat, and Greta and Raven sat down on either side of her. When Ella—Leo Luca's girlfriend—sat down across from Heidi, it blocked my view until Fallon—Dominic Luca's wife—gave her a shove and sat down. Fallon was shorter than the other women, leaving my view wide open.

The bartender brought them a round of drinks, and I watched as Heidi's head moved as they drank, glancing from one woman to the next and back again. It looked exhausting, and maybe that was why, after a while, her movements started to slow until eventually, they stopped altogether.

But even from across the room, I could see something wasn't right. Her breathing was coming faster, making her chest move at a more rapid pace, and her teeth were burrowing so deep into her lip, it was a wonder she hadn't drawn blood.

She stood up abruptly, said something to Raven, then left the table, headed toward the hallway at the back where the washrooms were tucked away from the main floor.

I stayed put as she disappeared into the hall, and I waited. The Costas had eyes all over the place; she'd be safe here.

But a minute passed, and then three, and then five, and still, she hadn't returned.

I pushed off from the wall and rounded the dance floor, heading toward the hallway. Aldo, another one of the Costas' bouncers, was standing guard at the door that led to the basement, in plain view of the hallway.

"The new girl with the group, did she go in there?" I asked him.

"*Si, Signor,*" he said, nodding. "Third door from the left."

I hovered outside it. I was pretty sure barging into the women's bathroom would be an act Greta counted as 'raining on their parade', but my gut told me something was wrong here, and when I heard a loud thud from inside the room, that was it.

"Key," I said, holding out my hand to Aldo.

The man looked at me, not sure what to do.

"The girl's mine, Aldo. Give me the key, *per favore.* If Nico has a problem with it, you send him to me."

He didn't look thrilled, but he handed it over, and I shoved it into the lock and pushed the door open.

It was definitely Heidi inside the spacious single-stall bathroom. Heidi kicking the shit out of a trash can. Definitely not what I'd been expecting.

Obviously, she didn't hear me come in, so it was only by chance that she looked up and caught sight of me in the bathroom mirror.

She froze for a second, then spun to face me and stood up straighter.

"What on earth are you doing in here?" she asked with that tone I fucking loved coming through even in the midst of whatever meltdown she was having.

She looked incredible. The slit in her dress was parted, her hair was mussed, and her cheeks were flushed.

"I was about to ask you the same question," I said, leaning back against the door.

"Well, don't. Feel free to leave, though. This is the *ladies'* room," she said, motioning around the small room.

"What's going on, *perla?*" I asked, undaunted.

"What's going on is I've made a terrible mistake."

I looked at the trash bin that was looking like it had seen better days. "I'm sure it can be replaced."

She huffed, then shook her head, her shoulders sagging just a little. "I shouldn't have come."

"They're not that bad, are they?" I asked. I mean, as much as I complained about Greta and the others, they weren't actually evil. If they'd said something unkind though...

"No, of course not," she said, shaking her head. "Or at least, I don't think so."

There was more; she was holding it back under the guise of washing her hands in the sink.

Since it appeared the thud had come from her wreaking vengeance on a trash can and she was in no immediate danger, I waited patiently for her to answer.

She looked up at me in the mirror, her eyes a little wider like a cornered animal. Eventually, her lips parted and words fell out.

"With everyone yelling to be heard over the music, their voices get muddled together to me, so I can't make out what they're saying. And when people yell, it makes lip-reading more difficult because it changes the way facial muscles move to produce speech."

Well, Christ, I hadn't even considered that. Not that I knew a great deal about lip-reading.

"It's very frustrating to feel like I'm just a kid again, trying to navigate with no ability to communicate." She sighed. "I think I'd just like to go home."

"I'll take you," I said. It's where I'd wanted her anyway, but I felt very little victory in it at the moment.

She stared at her own reflection in the mirror for a moment, then her gaze shifted to mine. She nodded to me and turned to leave, but then paused long enough to straighten the trash can.

It didn't surprise me at all to find Nico Costa, don of the Costa family, outside the door the moment we stepped out of the bathroom. Aldo would have gotten in contact with him seconds after handing me the key.

Nico was leaning against the opposite wall, his arms crossed over his chest, but his green eyes were devoid of the ice that usually inhabited them.

"Is everything all right here?" he asked as he pushed away from the wall and his gaze moved from Heidi to me. The music was still loud back here, making him raise his voice to be heard.

"Everything's fine. This is Dr. Heidi Dawson," I told him, then turned to Heidi. "Heidi, this is Nico Costa—Raven's fiancé," I said in a normal speaking tone.

"It's a pleasure to meet you, Dr. Dawson," Nico said, following my lead and speaking normally, which did surprise me. He held out his hand, and she took it, shaking briskly before dropping her hand back to her side.

"And you as well," she said, just loud enough to be heard over the music like she was adept at adjusting her own volume accordingly even if she didn't hear the world the same way we did.

"I'm going to take Heidi home. I'd appreciate it if you passed the message along to Raven and Greta."

"Of course," he replied, motioning to the rear exit of the club, saving us from having to navigate back through to the main entrance. Clearly, he'd read the situation correctly.

"*Grazie*, Nico."

Heidi's shoulders were still tense as we left the club and got into my car, but with each mile we drove, her shoulders relaxed a little more and her breathing grew calmer. She was calm and comfortable... with me.

The woman had no radar at all.

Chapter Twenty-Seven

Amadeo

"Why'd you agree to come out tonight?" I asked as I maneuvered into a spot at the curb in front of Heidi's building. She'd been silent the entire drive back, and since it was dark and reading my lips would have been difficult for her, I'd let her be.

I was done letting her be.

"I wanted to see your world from a different perspective, not yours and not mine."

"Why?"

"Objectivity, perhaps." The way she said it sounded dismissive, but she was faking it. Whatever had her taking a closer look at "my" world, she wasn't in the mood to discuss it. Fine by me.

I turned off the car and got out, rounding the hood and opening her door for her—like the perfect gentleman I was.

She stood up, and I put a hand at the small of her back and led her toward the door.

"You really don't have to come up, Amadeo," she said as she rummaged through her purse for her keys.

I almost laughed. "We both know if I leave now, I'm only going to be back here in a few hours." I shrugged. "Up to you, *perla*. Would you rather

235

let me in the front door now or have me showing up in your bedroom later?"

"I get a choice?" she asked without missing a beat.

"I'm all about choices," I lied. I'd already decided how this was going to go.

She looked up at me, eyebrows raised, like she wasn't buying it. Smart woman.

Still, she hesitated. This was different. This wasn't me showing up in her apartment in the middle of the night; this was her having to welcome me into her home. Fortunately, I could fix that.

"Time's up," I said as I took the key from her hand and opened the door. "Get inside."

A grin played at the corners of her lips as she turned away and stepped inside, and I had no doubt the sway of her hips as we headed up the stairs was all for me. This woman who'd been terrified of me not long ago was turning out to be the best thing I'd ever stumbled upon.

She seemed to be moving slowly, though. I think she was trying to draw this out, make me wait. And the dark bastard that I was, I laughed to myself. Because the woman was going to regret this.

The moment we stepped inside the apartment and I'd closed the door behind us, I grabbed her arm and spun her around, backing her up against the door.

"Do you have any idea how you looked tonight?" I asked, clearly remembering the sight of her on the dance floor.

"Frustrated?" she said, looking up at me.

I shook my head. "You looked like the sexiest woman I've ever seen, and I want to see more."

I stepped back. "Strip, *perla*. Slowly."

Her eyes snapped with defiance for just a brief moment, and then it faded, her mind accepting what her body already knew: She *wanted* this.

She reached behind her and worked the buttons at the back of her dress free, then she took hold of the high neckline of the dress and started to pull it downward.

"Slow," I said. It was one thing to strip; it was fast, like ripping off a Band-Aid. It was something else entirely to reveal herself, inch by inch.

She slid the dress down to her clavicles, then the upper swells of her breasts. Her cheeks pinkened as she lowered the dress further, to her nipples, to her ribs, baring her tits while I looked on.

While I was enjoying the show immensely, my cock was already throbbing like a son of a bitch, more than ready to move onto the part where it got to delve into her tight, wet cunt.

But inch by inch, she continued.

Her ribs.

Her toned abdomen.

The flare of her hips.

Another inch, and the dress fell the rest of the way, pooling at her feet.

She wore no bra.

All that covered her now was a tiny piece of black lace.

Her fingers hooked into the sides of the scrap of fabric and tugged. Seconds later, she was completely bare and blushing right down to her tits.

It probably didn't help when I stayed where I was, looking her over, watching her nipples grow taut beneath my gaze.

"I like seeing you like this," I told her, taking a step toward her and closing the distance I'd put between us.

"Naked?" she asked, feigning haughtiness.

I shook my head. "Uncomfortable. But I'm a very big fan of seeing you naked as well. But after tonight..."—and all the men eye-fucking her at Onyx—"...I think there is one thing we should get clear. This," I said, grazing a finger from her throat down the center of her to her pussy. I cupped her there, feeling her wetness against my fingers. "This belongs to me." I slid a finger inside her, crooking it so that it hit her G-spot and made her gasp.

But she shook her head. "It most certainly does not," she argued.

Like hell it didn't. I withdrew from her cunt and grabbed her hand, dragging her fingers between her wet lips. Then I brought them up between us.

"I think your body feels differently," I said right before sucking her fingers into my mouth to taste her.

She was staring at me; the wheels were clearly turning behind her eyes.

The moment I let go of her hand, the look in her eyes changed. I only saw it for a split second, a fraction of a breath before she slipped sideways away from me.

And she ran.

Her long legs carried her into the living room in three long strides, her dark hair swishing across her bare back and her perfect heart-shaped ass shaking with every step. She snaked around the sofa and fled into the hallway, a flash of pale skin in the dim light.

When she glanced back over her shoulder, her eyes were wide and her lips were parted.

But this wasn't fear.

This wasn't like her escape attempts before.

This was all about the chase, the hunt. The game she'd joined me in playing.

And Christ, the woman was fucking killing me here. Just too goddamned perfect.

Every fiber in my body sparked. It lit up as I let her get further into the room before I took off after her.

The moment I caught her, shoving her up against the hallway wall, was the closest I'd gotten to coming without any contact since I was thirteen years old.

I grabbed her arms and trapped them behind her with one hand while I jerked my fly down with the other.

When my cock was free, I let go of her hands and took hold of her hair instead, turning her face toward me.

"Tell me you don't want this," I said as I dragged my cock between her lips and the crack of her ass.

"Tell me if you don't want my cock buried deep in your cunt right now," I persisted, because while I was a sick fuck, if I'd misread the signals here, I sure as hell wanted to know before this went any further.

She licked her lips, but no words came out.

There was no fear in her eyes as I lined my cock up and drove into her tight, slick heat.

Jesus fucking Christ. I'd driven in bareback, hadn't even thought to wrap up, but goddamn it, there was no way I was stopping now.

I let go of her hair and grabbed hold of her hip, pulling her back toward me as I thrust in again, driving deeper. Deeper, but not deep enough.

Without pulling out—because there was no way I was doing that, maybe ever—I pushed her down onto the hallway floor onto her hands and knees, thrusting shallowly until I had her in position.

And then I kicked my hips and drove in deep, bottoming out so that every inch of my cock was sheathed inside her.

She cried out, but at the same time, she pushed her ass back toward me, begging for more. And I was nothing if not the giving sort of man. So, I gave it to her.

Fucking her hard.

Fast.

So fucking deep.

I fucked her like an animal, and she took it, arching her back, letting the force of my thrusts drive her elbows downward until she had her cheek against the floor.

With her ass tilted up at the perfect angle, I took advantage, dragging her wetness from her cunt to her anus and working my finger into her. She didn't flinch or tense up; she just took everything I gave her.

Her moans got louder. Her body pushed back harder until it wouldn't have surprised me to find hip-shape bruises marked on her ass come morning.

"God, Amadeo, yes," she moaned over and over again—the best sounds I'd ever heard. And then she wasn't just moaning; she was screaming, crying out as her back bowed and her cunt gripped me so tight, I'm not sure I could have withdrawn if I'd wanted to.

But I sure as hell didn't want to. I fucked her harder. Faster. What I wouldn't have given to fill her up with my come, but I pulled out at the last second, fisting my cock as I came all over her ass and back.

When she went to move, I put a hand on her hip and held her still and used the other to rub my come into her skin.

"What are you doing?" she asked, looking back at me over her shoulder.

I'd always fucked hard and dirty, but this was something else, some innate urge I'd never really felt before. "I'm making sure every man knows you're mine."

She laughed. "You do realize I shower, right?"

"Then when you do, I'll do it again." Not a problem because the thought of her covered in my scent, making it clear to the world who this body belonged to, had my cock stirring already.

When I released her, instead of standing up, she rolled onto her back and looked up at me. Christ, she was beautiful. Not just sexy as hell, but *more*. Prim and proper, and mouthy, and brave.

"What are we doing, Amadeo?" she asked.

I lowered myself down next to her, propped up on my elbow, and brushed the dampen wisps of hair off her forehead. "I don't know about you, but I'm taking a minute to recharge so I can fuck you again."

She rolled her eyes. "You know what I mean."

"Really?" I cocked an eyebrow at her. "The 'relationship' conversation?" The thought tied like a knot in my stomach.

She shrugged. "I'm not the one trying to mark you like an animal."

"I don't do relationships, Heidi." The words spilled out automatically. I fucked, plain and simple, and seldom the same woman twice. Why I'd come back here again and again wasn't something I was willing to contemplate.

"And I'm not asking you to," she said, but there was a furrow between her eyebrows.

I reached out and smoothed it just because I damn well could.

"But you can't claim this is just sex, no strings attached, and then try to cover me in semen to repel other men."

"You've spent some time in my world, *perla*; you know I can do anything I want."

"Look around, Amadeo," she said, motioning around us. "We're not in your world; we're in mine."

The woman really had no clue if she thought she wanted something more than this.

"You don't want a relationship with me," I said as I took the hand she'd been waving around and pinned it over her head. "The control I want—it isn't an act. It's what I am."

I let go of her hand and grazed my fingers down the soft flesh of the inside of her arm all the way to her shoulder, then toward her throat, laying my fingers around it.

"That's fine in small doses; you get your rocks off on a man who can overpower you, who has no problem doing what he damn well pleases with your body for a couple of hours, carefully slotted into your late-night schedule."

I squeezed lightly, feeling the pulse of her carotid artery beneath my fingers.

Her breath came harder, emphasizing the rise and fall of her naked chest.

"Trust me, *perla,* you don't want more."

When I released her throat and let my fingers graze lower, I could feel the tiny tremors coursing through her body.

She licked her lips. Swallowed.

"I don't think you know me well enough to tell me what I do and don't want, Amadeo."

"That's not entirely true," I said, waggling my brows as my gaze swept over her body, which I'd come to know rather well.

When she opened her mouth to object, I shook my head.

"I know that family is more important to you than money," I said, all at once realizing just how much I did know about her. "I know that you can't stand to see people suffer—that's why you helped Aurelio. I bet it factors into why you became a doctor. I know that when you make an oath, you take that seriously. And I know that despite the shit life has thrown at you, you're not jaded; you'll still look beneath a criminal's surface and see the good in him."

"I'm not sure there *is* any good in you," she said with an uncomfortable little laugh. She'd paled a little as I spoke. I don't think she realized she'd revealed so much either.

"Maybe not, but you saw good in Aurelio." I laughed. "You've got the old man wrapped around your finger. Vito too," I said, not sure how I felt about the effect she had on my men.

Her brow furrowed. "Which one's Vito?" she asked.

I smiled. "Big man. Shiny, bald head."

Recognition dawned in her eyes. "You had him bring me home... that night."

I nodded. I'd intended to have Vito take her home and then never see her again. So much for that plan.

She sighed, and for the first time, looked away, staring up at the speckled ceiling above us.

"After my parents were murdered, every criminal fit in a neat and tidy box in my mind." She shook her head, and the furrows across her brow deepened. "But Raven, she doesn't fit there. Neither do Aurelio, the women tonight… and *you*. In a very short amount of time, you've managed to change the way I see the world. But that doesn't benefit me in any way. It doesn't make me better at my job or fill any holes in my life. So, I can't help but wonder," she went on, turning her head to look at me now, "in what other ways might you influence the way I think, Amadeo? All for this 'carefully slotted couple of hours' that will never be anything more than what it already is?"

"I told you; you don't want more."

"How can you be so sure of it?"

That one was easy. "Because while you're lying here telling me all this deep shit, I'm picturing you on your knees with your hands tied behind your back and a vibrator in your cunt."

Her lips parted and her breathing deepened.

"I'm imagining setting it to low, just enough to keep your body reaching for an end that won't come. I'd shove my cock between your lips," I said, circling them with my index finger. "I'd fuck your mouth and come down your throat." I ran my fingers down the smooth column. "And then I'd sit back and watch you suffer."

She blinked slowly.

"And I'd love it," I continued. "I'd love every second of hearing you moan and beg. I'd love watching you get so frustrated that it makes tears trickle down your cheeks."

Her thighs shifted and squeezed together.

"And if you managed to get off on it and come before I wanted you to, I'd drag you up onto my lap and spank your hot ass until it was decorated in my handprints."

Her whole body trembled beside me as my cock throbbed, hard and ready to fuck again.

"And that's a sedate fantasy in comparison to some of the things I've thought about doing to you, *perla*."

With those thoughts fresh in my mind, I would have liked nothing better than to flip her over and fuck her, but mixed in with the arousal that shone in her eyes, there was something else. Something was really troubling her.

She breathed in and out, slow and deep, deliberate.

"Maybe you're right," she said—which, peculiarly, I didn't care for. "What you're saying doesn't frighten me; it excites me. But what I fear are the changes within myself."

She swallowed. Looked up at the ceiling. Looked back to me.

"A patient was brought into the ER today. He'd been shot in the back. Someone had shot him while he was running away. I couldn't help but see it… imagine it." She shook her head. "It's never happened before. It *shouldn't* have happened."

"I've seen gunshot wounds, *perla;* they're not pretty. And to see someone had shot him in the back like a coward, of course your brain's going to run with that."

"No, Amadeo. I know better than that. I know that what I do requires the kind of detachment that others would call cold and unfeeling. But feeling uses up precious seconds and compromises one's judgment. My judgment was compromised today because there are no neat and tidy boxes left in my head. Instead of a broken body that I could put back together, I saw a poor, freckle-faced teenage boy on that trauma room table."

Her words had my ears perking up, a very different part of my brain tuning in.

"Freckles?" I asked, but it had to be a coincidence.

She looked at me like I was completely missing the point. "Do you have something against freckles?"

The back of my neck prickled. I might have been grasping at straws here, but my gut was telling me I wasn't.

"A teenager, maybe fifteen or sixteen years old?" I asked. "Not many freckles on his forehead or chin, but a shit-ton of them across his cheeks and nose?"

She stiffened. "Yes. Why?"

Reluctantly, I released her and sat up.

"There might be a problem," I said as I stood up and zipped my fly.

"I don't understand," she said as she followed me up.

"If this freckle-faced kid is the same boy I'm thinking it is, I need to get to the hospital right now."

"What? Why?" she asked as she retrieved her dress and put it back on.

"Because otherwise, the kid may be very dead, very soon."

Chapter Twenty-Eight

Heidi

"What exactly is it you intend to do?" I asked as I followed Amadeo to my front door, hopping on one foot as I tried to shove my other foot into my shoe—a pair of flats because there was no way I was sticking my feet back into the high-heeled death traps I'd had on this evening.

"I'm going to go keep the kid from getting any more holes in him," Amadeo said.

"But how—"

"I need to go right now, *perla.*" He leaned in to kiss me, but I took a step back.

"Then I'm coming with you," I said, using the brief pause to shove my other foot into a shoe.

He sighed, but rather than fight me like I'd expected, he pulled out his cell phone from his pocket as he opened my front door. He pressed a button on the phone as he held the door open for me, then put the phone to his ear as we left.

"… hospital… me there… Vito…" I tried to follow his lips, but I kept having to look away to keep from running into walls and tripping down stairs.

By the time we'd arrived outside, he'd pressed a button on the phone—presumably disconnecting the call—and pressed another, holding it up to his ear once again.

"I need… meet… of the hospital." I caught pieces of the conversation as he opened his car's passenger door for me, then circled around to the driver's side.

My breath was coming faster. It was like I was back in the Onyx nightclub again, only this time, I wasn't missing pieces of random conversations that had little to do with me; I was missing out on vital information that somehow pertained to my patient.

"Would you please tell me what the bloody hell is going on?" I demanded as Amadeo slid into the driver's seat. He still had his phone to his ear, but his lips stopped moving.

"*Grazie, cugina,*" he said to whomever he was speaking to, then shoved the cell phone back into his jacket pocket as he started the car and pulled away from the curb.

"What floor and what room is the kid in, Heidi?" he asked without answering me.

"He's on the fourth floor, but—"

"Is there security stationed on that floor?"

"No, none of the hospital's security guards are 'stationed' there. Now, will you—"

"How many staff members are on the ward at night, do you know?"

Well, I'd certainly had enough of this. "Yes, as a matter of fact, I do know. And I'll tell you just as soon as you tell me what it is you're planning to do," I said, fed up with being interrupted.

He was silent for a moment, his gaze going back and forth between me and the late-night traffic. Finally, he shook his head and smiled. "Christ, I love it when you talk like that."

"Like what?" I asked, genuinely baffled.

"Like you've spent the day with the queen of England and really need me to fuck all that fastidiousness out of you."

I pressed my lips together but couldn't stop the corners from quirking in a poorly-suppressed smile. It was short-lived, however.

"That doesn't answer my question," I persisted.

"I plan to take the kid out of there, and I'm asking you all these questions because the less resistance I encounter, the better."

I shook my head. "You can't do that. He was shot, Amadeo. His lung was punctured and there were superficial wounds to his kidney."

"He can't stay there, Heidi. Whoever shot him could come back to finish the job at any time."

My chest went cold; it felt like an Arctic wind blew right through it. *Bloody hell.*

"I think someone already did," I said. I think my voice wasn't much louder than a whisper.

He glanced at me, waiting for me to continue.

"I went to check on the boy at the end of my shift. There was already a man there in the room with him. He said he was a family friend." I shook my head. "It didn't feel right. I told him to leave. What if you're right and he's already come back? What if—" I slammed my mouth shut. Had I really stood in the room with a man whose only purpose there was to murder my patient? A fifteen-year-old boy?

I felt like I was going to be sick.

"It's all right, *perla*. Raven's checking with the hospital. If the kid was already dead, she would have let me know by now."

"If you try to take him off the ward, the nurse will call security. You won't make it out the door," I said as I struggled to shove everything else into a box. This was no different than a medical emergency, I told myself. Identify the problem, then find a solution.

"I will if the nurse doesn't see me take the kid off the ward."

"And how do you intend to do that?" I asked.

There was a tension in the corners of his eyes, creating tiny creases there. "The less you know, the better."

"Why—" I slammed my mouth shut. "Because you don't trust me. If I know what you're going to do, you worry I'll try to foil your plan."

He turned into the hospital's parking lot without confirming or denying my suspicions, but it wasn't necessary. I'd received the message loud and clear, a message that created a far more uncomfortable sensation in my chest than I would have expected.

"There will be three to four nurses on the ward," I said, offering up the information I'd promised as an idea formulated in my mind. "If there is one at the nurses' station, she'll be your primary concern. The others will be busy checking on patients and such."

"So, if we—"

"I can distract the nurse," I cut in. "You'll need someone dressed in scrubs with an ID badge to wheel the boy off the ward into the ward next to it. From there, the staff won't know who he is, and you can use the elevator at the other end to take him down to the parking level. If you're stopped, tell them you're taking him for X-rays—it's the best I can think of."

"Heidi, I—"

"You'll need a cargo truck," I interrupted once again. This boy had been my patient. I'd stood in a room with the man who might have shot him. "He has to be transported on a gurney. Once I'm sure you're off the ward, I'll collect supplies—"

"No." Apparently, it was Amadeo's turn to cut in as he pulled into a parking spot near the side of the building. "I can't let you do this, Heidi. Even if I decide to trust you, if you get caught helping us, it could cost you your license."

He was right. So, was I to abandon one patient to save many? It was a classic philosophical debate, though it seemed there was little to debate for me at the moment.

"It's a risk I'll have to take. That boy was my patient, Amadeo."

"Not anymore." He shook his head again. "We'll take care of him."

"No," I said firmly.

"Excuse me?" He'd turned off the car, and he shifted in his seat to look directly at me. I'd been correct in my assumption that it wasn't often this man heard the word "no".

"If you insist on taking that boy out of the hospital, then it will be under my care. And he will *remain* under my care until I say otherwise." Despite the large, muscular, and very intimidating man sitting next to me, I would not bend on this. I'd stood between my patient and Death once already, and it seemed my job wasn't done yet.

He looked at me like he was seeing me for the first time. "This is about more than being a doctor, *perla;* this is personal to you. Why?"

"I hadn't the skill to save a man once. So long as it's within my power, I won't allow that to happen again, and that includes letting people with no medical training take this boy from the hospital without medical supervision."

Out of the corner of my eye, I saw two cars pull up beside me and three men and Raven exit them. Still, Amadeo looked at me, eyes searching mine.

"All right, we'll do this your way, *perla.* But I advise you not to make me regret this. I'd enjoy punishing you for it far too much."

Hot and cold shivers danced up and down my spine, but I ignored them and nodded demurely like the large, muscular, and very intimidating man sitting next to me hadn't just threatened to 'punish' me. It was easier to do than I'd expected, likely because my entire code of ethics was crumbling before my eyes. I was about to break the law, to become a criminal. And if that was the cost of protecting a fifteen-year-old boy, then the law be damned.

***

"I was reviewing my charts from this morning, and I'm missing information on a patient that was transferred here from surgery this afternoon. Grayson Thomas," I explained to the woman behind the desk at the nurses' station. It wasn't the usual nurse with the butterfly scrubs. I'd never seen this nurse with the short, gray bob and plain purple scrubs, but she gave me the automatic acceptance my badge and scrubs granted me

My heart was already racing, and my hands were cold and clammy. When Amadeo and Raven stepped off the elevator, I swear, half the oxygen in the room evaporated. I forced myself to take slow and even breaths as they made their way toward the hallway, pushing an empty gurney in front of them.

"Of course," the nurse said, leaning across the desk in search of the file.

The position kept her back to my accomplices, but she could turn around at any moment. Raven appeared right at home in her green scrubs, but Amadeo looked out of place in his. The fabric of his 'borrowed' scrubs stretched across his broad back and wrapped tightly around his biceps. Even from this distance, I could see the rough outline of his gun, poorly concealed beneath his shirt.

"Ah, here we go. Is this what you're looking for?" the nurse asked, handing me Grayson Thomas' chart.

"Yes, it is. Thank you," I said, opening it up and scanning from the top of each page to the bottom.

Acute respiratory distress

Posterior incision

Thoracic region

My eyes took in random words, but they could have been gibberish for all my brain could make sense of them at the moment. My hands tried to tremble, forcing me to grip the chart tightly to keep it from shaking.

Out of the corner of my eye, I saw Amadeo and Raven round the corner at the end of the hall, and I had to swallow back the audible sigh of relief that threatened to escape. They'd made it, at least far enough that the likelihood of running into trouble was minimal.

I scribbled a few random notes down on the chart I'd brought with me to stall for an extra moment. If the nurse looked too closely, she'd discover the chart I'd brought was blank.

When enough time had passed for Amadeo and Raven to have transferred the boy onto the gurney and off the ward, I closed my file and handed the chart back.

"Thank you again," I said, then I bid her goodnight and left the ward.

It was a wonder my knees held me up.

The elevator was empty, and I allowed myself to lean back against the wall as it descended to the main floor. From there, I hurried down the hall to the nearest washroom.

Raven had recommended I stop for supplies first, and I was glad I'd heeded her warning. I was in no condition to go sneaking around supply rooms now.

My hands were still trembling as I grabbed the duffel bag of medical supplies from the furthest stall in the ladies' room. Bandages and gauze in hopes all went well. Scalpels and surgical scissors, hemostatic agents, clamps and forceps, sutures and sterile drapes in case it did not.

Finally, vials of morphine. If I was caught with those, my career would be over.

I stared at the zipped bag for a moment and contemplated leaving the narcotic behind. To be caught with bandages and clamps would result in a disciplinary action. They wouldn't take my license for it. But it meant I'd have nothing stronger than acetaminophen to ease the boy's pain.

So, with the fully stocked duffel bag slung over my arm, I left the ladies' room, retraced my steps to the elevator, and took it to the parking level, praying it would not be the last time I set foot in this hospital.

"We're ready to go," Raven said the moment I stepped off the elevator. She was hunched over Grayson Thomas in the back of a cargo truck parked ten feet away with her fingers pressed to his wrist, monitoring his pulse.

Amadeo, Vito, and Nico Costa were standing outside the truck, but right away, the sight of them sent a strange prickling sensation across the back of my neck. It wasn't their tense postures or the adrenaline that seemed to pulse in the air around them. It was their faces. They wore no expression, no tension lines across their foreheads, no creases at the corners of their eyes. No slack-jawed relief. Nothing.

I shivered as I crossed the short distance to the truck. The boy was awake, glancing around warily, though he made no effort to flee.

"Get in, Heidi," Amadeo said as he held out his hand to me.

This man was different from the one who'd come to my bedroom each night, demanding my body submit to him. Even the first time I'd seen him—after stabbing him in the back—there'd been more emotion playing across his features than there was now.

I shifted the strap of the duffel bag so that it sat higher up on my shoulder, then placed my hand in his, half-expecting his fingers to be as cold as stone. But they were warm, and they gripped mine tightly as he helped me up into the back of the truck. The moment I was inside, he let go of my hand and the door swung shut, trapping me inside.

Crouched down beneath the low ceiling, I turned around and faced Raven.

She smiled sympathetically. I had a feeling my discomfiture was written clear as day across my face.

"Don't worry about them," she said, waving in the direction of the closed door. "We had a bit of a surprise, and they're not big on surprises."

Perhaps. Though it felt like absconding with a hospital patient would not have ranked terribly high on their list of offenses. This seemed rather mild in comparison to the no-holds-barred shootout that had taken place at Amadeo's cabin or even the bullet he'd put in the back of Owen Thompson's head.

I didn't ask about the "surprise'" it was nothing I could affect here and now. I turned my attention to the boy, to the reason I was here.

"How are you feeling, Mr. Thomas?" I asked. I focused on an observational pain assessment, searching for tightened facial muscles, clenched jaw, squinting, or rapid blinking, but he seemed to be resting more or less comfortably at the moment.

"I think I've been better, but it could be worse," he said as his gaze shifted to Raven, then back to me.

The truck began to vibrate beneath me, and with a sudden jerk, it began to move. I braced my hand against the side of the truck and duck-walked toward the boy, sitting down next to him.

"Blood pressure is one-hundred and ten over eighty," Raven informed me. "Heart rate is ninety and respiratory rate is eighteen."

All good stats. "Thank you," I said. I was tempted to check on his wounds, but with the truck in motion, it wasn't safe. The slightest bump, and I could end up doing more harm than good.

So, I sat. It only took a moment for the boy's eyes to start fluttering closed. He forced them back open a few times, but quickly gave up the fight and let the narcotic and his body's own need to heal pull him under.

"How are you feeling?" Raven asked when we were the only two conscious people in the back of the truck.

Like I've committed a crime.

Like I've helped to save a boy's life.

Like the man I'd been sleeping with has suddenly turned to stone.

"I don't know," I said when no answer seemed to summarize the mass of emotions roiling inside me.

She nodded. "That sounds about right."

"Does it? Nothing about this feels right."

"When we get to the Lucianos, I can stay to keep an eye on him," she offered. "You don't have to get any more involved than you already are."

I'd helped them abscond with a patient; I'd stolen narcotics from the hospital. "I think my walking away now would be of little consequence."

I looked down at the boy, slack-jawed in sleep, then back to Raven.

"Was he really in danger?" I asked, still baffled that someone could not only shoot the child but then come back to finish the job.

"*Sì,*" Raven replied without hesitation.

I turned to look at Grayson Thomas once more, the fuzz-like hair across his jaw, the heavy spattering of freckles across his nose and cheeks. According to his chart, he was fourteen years old, not sixteen. Just a boy, barely an adolescent.

"I'll stay with him," I said, fighting the strange urge to brush the messy mop of hair off his forehead. Raven nodded and settled back comfortably against the wall.

I couldn't have said how much time had passed when the truck came to a stop and the vibrations beneath me ceased. According to Raven, we'd reached the Lucianos' estate, a place to which I'd never expected to return.

If time had stood still in the truck, then it raced by in a flash now.

The rear door of the truck opened and two men appeared, taking hold of the boy's gurney and whisking him out of the truck and into the massive estate. A hand appeared to help me out, but it wasn't Amadeo's hand; it was Vito's. He helped me down, then offered his assistance to Raven who waved him off and jumped down the few feet to the ground, grinning at him a bit like a precocious child. I had a feeling there was a history between these two.

My gaze flitted toward the house. I'd tried to run from here not long ago, and some part of me felt the same potent urge now, but I stood awkwardly still, my gaze going back and forth between Raven and Vito until Amadeo appeared from around the side of the truck.

255

He wore the same expressionless mask, but when he looked right at me, there was something very troubled in his eyes.

"I have business to tend to, Heidi; go with Raven," he said, motioning toward the house.

With that, he turned away, effectively putting an end to the conversation.

I watched as he shook hands with Nico Costa, then motioned for Vito to follow him back to his own car, parked behind the cargo truck.

A hand touched my shoulder from behind, and I spun around.

"Come on," Raven said, motioning toward the door where the two men had gone inside with my patient. "Let's get the kid settled." She looked over at Amadeo and Vito, her lips set in a grim line. "I have a feeling they're going to be a while."

Chapter Twenty-Nine

Amadeo

"He's still unconscious, boss," Vito said as he reached into the trunk of my car and heaved out the asshole we'd stashed in there.

"*Bene.* Get him inside, *per favore.* Aurelio will be here shortly."

Vito nodded and shifted the guy over his shoulder.

"Tell Giovanni to have Antonio Verdi meet me in the basement. I want to see if he recognizes this *codardo.*"

"You got it, boss," he said, then headed inside with the asshole draped over his shoulder like a sack of potatoes. As he went, I breathed out a sigh and shook my head. Two more minutes, and the kid would have been dead. Raven and I walking in when we did had to have been pure fucking dumb luck.

"I don't suppose you'll be needing any help?" Nico asked. He spoke casually, but I could see the eagerness in his cold, green eyes.

"Too quiet on the home front these days, *amico*?" I asked as I closed the trunk of my car.

He scoffed. "I suppose I should be grateful, *si?*"

"Peace is a wonderful thing until it leaves you with idle hands and no assholes in need of killing," I said—a rather deep sentiment, in my opinion.

"Molto vero," he replied at the same time the front door opened and Raven stepped outside. He smiled up at her, the ice in his gaze melting in an instant.

The man was completely whipped.

"Dr. Dawson… er, Heidi is with the boy upstairs," Raven informed me when she'd reached the bottom of the stone front steps. "She said she has everything under control, so…"

"Grazie, cugina. I appreciate your help tonight. And yours as well, Nico," I said.

Nico nodded, but Raven shrugged. She glanced at the house, then back to me. "It looks like you didn't really need my help, after all," she said, smiling a little too brightly.

It was true, but I hadn't expected Heidi to jump on board this evening. In truth, I was still waiting for the other shoe to drop.

"I like her, Deo, so try not to screw things up, okay?"

"There's nothing to screw up," I replied, fighting the urge to roll my eyes. You spend a few nights with a woman, and suddenly everyone was chiming in with their opinion.

She rolled her eyes, feeling no need to quell the urge, it seemed. "Let me ask you a question: When you told her this kid was in danger, did she question it?"

Come to think of it, no, she hadn't. But I kept my mouth shut.

"And why do you suppose that is?" Raven went on without pausing.

"Because she's madly, deeply in love with me?" I asked, my voice dripping with sarcasm.

She scoffed. "That's pushing it. But it seems to me she trusts you. She put a lot on the line tonight to help that kid, entirely based on what you told her. That's a pretty big deal, in my opinion."

"We'll leave you to it," Nico interrupted, casting me a sympathetic glance as he put his arm around Raven. "Enjoy your evening, *amico,*" he said, his voice just a little wistful.

I was hitting that tired point where I almost would have been willing to exchange places with him. *Almost.*

I watched Raven and Nico walk toward their car as another car turned into the long driveway. It appeared Aurelio had arrived.

It was time to get to work.

Lucky for me, by the time I'd changed out of the ridiculous scrubs I was wearing and Aurelio and I had made our way down to the basement, Giovanni was already waiting there for us with Verdi at his side.

Vito had our latest guest on a chair in the middle of the concrete-walled room. His wrists and ankles were cuffed to the chair, and his hands had been duct-taped so that his fingers lay flat against the chair's wide arms. His chin rested on his chest; he was still unconscious, the consequence of the sedative I'd dosed him with.

I glanced at my watch. It wouldn't be long now.

"Do you recognize him?" I asked Verdi, nodding to our guest.

Verdi took a step into the room without batting an eyelash. He wasn't the least put off by what was about to happen here. He looked at the guy through narrowed eyes, his head cocked on an angle. He shook his head slowly at first, then more decisively.

"No, *Signor,* I don't." He turned to look at me. "Who is he, if I can ask?"

"He's a breadcrumb," I said since that was all we had at the moment. "Time to see where it leads. *Grazie,* Antonio," I said, dismissing him.

He smiled wryly. "Any time. It seems I have plenty of that on my hands these days." He didn't sound angry; he sounded restless.

I smiled. "We'll get you off the bench soon, if that's still what you want. But keep the warning I gave you in mind; I don't make idle threats."

"*Si, Signor,*" he said, then followed Giovanni up the stairs.

I leaned against the concrete wall as Aurelio sat down in an empty chair opposite our guest and busied himself with laying out his 'tools'. Knives and pliers, nails and a tack hammer; Aurelio was old-school.

"I want every bit of information he has, Aurelio," I said, pushing off the wall. "So keep him alive as long as possible."

"Of course, *Signor*," he said. He adjusted a few pieces to lie at just the right angle; I wasn't much for that psychological shit, but Aurelio knew what he was doing. "Dr. Dawson was quite helpful this evening," he observed, his voice deceptively light.

"*Sì*, she was."

"*...it seems to me she trusts you*," Raven had said, but fuck if I knew what to do with that.

"She's a brave woman, *Signor*," Aurelio mused, nodding approvingly. "And I notice you haven't lost interest in her yet; that's a good sign."

Lose interest? Everything about Heidi was interesting, from the way she spoke to the way she fucked. From her dedication to her profession to the way she handled herself under pressure... and the occasional times she let it get the better of her and took it out on a helpless trash can.

I laughed, remembering the sight I'd walked in on in Onyx's washroom.

Aurelio cocked an eyebrow at me while amusement danced in his eyes. "I'm going to take that to mean you agree."

"You can take it to mean I find her interesting, Aurelio, nothing more."

But who was I kidding? No woman had ever held my attention for more than a night or two, and I was still having trouble recalling a single face but hers.

"Of course, *Signor*," he replied, smiling knowingly at the same time the asshole in the chair began to stir.

"Do you suppose we could focus on the task at hand now?" I asked, nodding toward the asshole like Aurelio hadn't noticed the faint stirrings going on behind him.

But of course, he had. He was already reaching for the bottle of water he'd let the asshole sip from before he got down to business.

"That's it," Aurelio said encouragingly as he put the bottle to the man's lips. "Take a drink and get your bearings," he went on like he was everybody's fucking next door neighbor.

The man drank back every drop he was offered, losing some in his eagerness as it spilled down his carefully groomed beard. As he gulped the water back, his smallish, close-set brown eyes darted around the room, eventually settling on Aurelio, then on me. Recognition dawned in his gaze, and the tension that snapped in the air all around him shot off the charts. He choked on his final gulp of water, spluttering as he jerked in his chair, yanking violently against the unyielding restraints.

"There now. That's enough." Aurelio screwed the lid back on the bottle and set it down on his table of otherwise nasty shit. "We'll start with something simple, shall we? Tell me your name, *per favore.*"

The asshole glared, still yanking against his cuffs like he had a hope in hell of escaping. Bound so tightly, he couldn't even loosen the duct tape.

Aurelio sighed, shaking his head as he grabbed the pliers and got a good hold on the man's left index fingernail.

"Fighting me will only prove painful, *Signor.* And in the end, it won't help you," he said, then tugged slow and steady, yanking off the nail while the man screamed and his whole face turned red.

The sound reverberated around the room, starting a steady throbbing in my temples.

"We'll try this again," Aurelio said once the guy had calmed down. "Tell me your name, *per favore.*"

The asshole glared while his chest heaved. "It's Edward. Edward Sterling," he spat, his British accent thick.

Aurelio nodded. "My name is Aurelio Carbone. It's a pleasure to make your acquaintance," he said like the two of them were meeting across a backyard fence.

I had to fight back a laugh. Aurelio Carbone was so damned cordial, even when torturing scumbags.

Edward Sterling, it seemed, wasn't seeing the humor in it. He kept on glaring, shooting daggers from his small, brown eyes.

Aurelio dropped the fingernail in a bucket he kept near him for just such a purpose, then turned his attention back to Sterling.

"I'd like you to tell me why you felt the need to try to murder a child, *Signor* Sterling," he went on. "I presume you're also the one who shot the poor boy." He shook his head disapprovingly.

Sterling turned his head to look at me. "That kid's nothing to you," he spat. "Why would you give a fuck if I offed him?"

Aurelio got hold of another fingernail with his pliers. "I'm afraid that doesn't answer my question, *Signor* Sterling," he said, then yanked.

More screaming. The chair shook as a red-faced Sterling did his damnedest to get free. By the time he settled back down, the tears in his eyes had spilled over.

"Let's not get off-topic again," Aurelio advised him, cool and pleasant-sounding as ever as he dropped another fingernail into the bucket. "Tell me why you felt the need to try to murder the boy."

"He was a loose end, you wanker," he seethed. His accent was much more pronounced than Heidi's, but I had to say, it wasn't doing much for me coming from this asshole's mouth.

Aurelio nodded encouragingly, ignoring the insult.

"A loose end?" he asked. "You paid the child to do a job for you, and then you tried to kill him for his efforts." Aurelio *tsk*ed reproachfully. "That's just poor business practice, in my opinion."

Sterling glared, but since Aurelio hadn't asked an actual question, he was wise enough to keep his mouth shut.

"You paid him to retrieve a message from Elio Bianchi and to deliver it to you," Aurelio continued. "You were working with Bianchi, then?"

"That arsehole's dead," Sterling spat. Okay, maybe not so wise.

"That is not the question I asked," Aurelio said as he picked up his tack hammer and slammed it down on one of Sterling's knuckles, breaking it.

My temples pulsed as Sterling screamed. I'd have to remember to store some earplugs down here from now on.

"You were working with Bianchi, *sì*?" Aurelio asked again once the worst of the hollering had passed.

"Yes," Sterling hissed, then he leaned his head forward and to the side and spat blood onto the floor. He'd bitten a hole through his tongue; I'd seen it happen before.

Aurelio nodded, unperturbed by the blood. "I presume you're not the mastermind here. Who do you work for?"

Sterling turned to me once again. "If you let me go, we can make it worth your while," he cajoled like I gave a flying fuck about his pathetic bribes. But all right, I'd play along and see where this led.

I waited for Aurelio to administer Sterling's punishment, smashing the second knuckle of his left middle finger.

When he was finished and Sterling had stopped screaming, I held up a hand, interrupting Aurelio's interrogation.

"If you mean the 'treasure' we stumbled upon at the Regalton Arms," I said, addressing the man for the first time, "you're a little late."

He shook his head. "That toolbox you wheeled out of there wasn't big enough to hold a quarter of what we're looking for."

It made some sense. Heidi's father had been careful—no identification, no paper trails. It stood to reason that he wouldn't have put all his eggs in one basket—or toolbox, in this case. It still begged the question: Where the hell had Heidi's father gotten all that money?

"You expect me to believe that someone stashed boxes of cash and gems around the city like Easter eggs?" I asked, curious just how much Sterling knew.

The man smiled, revealing a mouth full of blood-covered teeth. "You don't know who Heidi Dawson is, do you? You help me get the information out of her head," he went on without pausing, "and you'll be rewarded with plenty of money and a powerful ally."

"Signor, I have more money than I could ever spend, and I've been collecting allies faster than I know what to do with," I said lightly. "But humor me. How exactly do you propose we get this information you're talking about out of the woman?"

"I don't think my boss is picky, mate. You get her in a nice, cozy chair like this one," he said, nodding down at his own comfortable accommodations, "and I'm sure your friend here–"he nodded to Aurelio"– could convince her to think real hard about where that money is."

Unbidden, images of Heidi in Sterling's place sprung to mind. That's what this asshole would have done to her if he'd gotten his hands on her. He would have fucking tortured her for information she might not even have.

White-hot rage shot through me, so fast and so potent, it was the first time I could recall having to struggle to keep a straight face, to hide the urge to rip this fucker apart like a wild dog. I leashed it. *Later.*

Sterling flinched like the sheer force of my fury had struck him.

"But you didn't only promise me money, *amico;* you promised me an ally," I said in a voice that gave nothing away. "Tell me who."

He stared at me, then Aurelio, then back to me again. The wheels were turning behind his small, dark eyes. Weighing his options, perhaps? I don't think the fucker realized he had none.

When his mouth set in a firm line, I could already tell what was coming.

He shook his head. "I can't tell you that, not until you get what we need from the girl."

Perfetta. I'd needed an excuse to hurt this motherfucker, and now I had one.

Aurelio was already holding out the tack hammer to me; he knew me well.

"You've got five seconds before this hand won't ever be the same again," I said, nodding to Sterling's uninjured right hand as I took the hammer.

"Five." I slammed it down in the middle of his little finger without pause.

"You fucking tosser," he hollered. "You're going to pay—"

"Four." The knuckles of his right index finger gave with a stomach-turning crunch, barely audible above his roar of pain.

"Three."

I kept going.

"Two."

His screams echoed off the walls, swirling around and around until it felt like they might reverberate forever.

"One."

I stepped back, waiting as tears rolled down his red face and blood dribbled from his open mouth. His hand was a mangled mess, and the other one, with two broken knuckles and missing fingernails, had certainly seen better days.

"Do you have a name for me, or should I start again?" I asked, nodding to his less-injured hand.

"Nathaniel… Sinclair." He forced out the name between body-wracking sobs.

The man from the cemetery. The legitimate CEO of Windsor Crest Architecture.

"I told you what you wanted to know. Now, let me go, for mercy's sake."

Mercy? Was that what I should have been feeling? I wondered. Remorse for disfiguring the man and inflicting an enormous amount of pain?

As I stared at the man, I felt neither. No different than he would have felt had he been the one standing here with Heidi as his captive.

I shook my head. "You're not going—"

The heavy metal door squeaked open, but by the time I'd swung around, I was too late.

Heidi's eyes were as wide as saucers.

Shit.

She gasped as she threw her hands over her mouth, her gaze swinging back and forth between Sterling, Aurelio, and me.

"Bloody hell," she whispered as her gaze settled on Sterling's disfigured hand.

Her face behind her hands went impossibly paler, and she was shaking her head like she could will the scene before her out of existence.

"What are you doing down here, *perla?*" I asked in the calmest tone I could find. But it didn't matter; she couldn't hear my tone, and she wasn't looking at my lips to know what I was saying.

She took a step back from the gory scene, her eyes still wide, her hands still over her mouth, and her breath coming so fast, she was going to hyperventilate

"Heidi!" I said loud enough for her to hear me, but no part of her seemed to register the sound.

When she took another step away, her back hit the hallway wall behind her, and then she did what any reasonable person who'd stumbled upon the scene she'd just walked in on would do.

She ran.

But this was one-hundred percent *not* the kind of chase that excited me.

Chapter Thirty

Heidi

A gunshot sounded as I ran down the concrete-lined hallway.

The same muffled sound I'd heard from Amadeo's cabin.

The same muffled sound I'd heard in Elio's dining room.

The sound I'd heard loud and clear the night my parents were murdered.

After seventeen years, so much of that night had faded. I couldn't recall what my mother's face had looked like when she'd been torn from my bed. I couldn't remember if my father had been looking at me when the gunshot sounded. But that sound, so loud it felt like it had gone off inside my brain, had been etched permanently into every neuron. And then the ringing. Dear God, the incessant, shrill ringing.

I could hear the ghost of it now as I flew up the stairs and across the marble floor to the front door. There was no one around to stop me, but the moment I stepped outside, an enormous man with a thick, dark beard stepped into my path. The same man who'd stepped into my path the last time I'd been here.

"Is there a problem, *Signorina?*" he asked. He hadn't reached for his gun, but I could see the muscles tighten along his forearms. Adrenal glands release epinephrine to trigger the fight-or-flight response—

I drew myself up and forced slow, even breaths from my lungs. "I'm not leaving," I said with all the calm and precision I could muster, "and I'm *not* a prisoner here." God help me, I'd come here of my own volition.

He nodded like he had no particular objection to what I'd said, but he didn't move from my path.

"I'm simply in need of some fresh air. Some space," I added, gazing pointedly at the small distance between us.

He eyed me warily for a moment, then nodded and took a step to the side, letting me pass. I noticed, though, as I descended the front steps and veered right through the ornate gardens that sprawled across the front of the house and around the side, that the big man followed at a distance.

Each time I looked back, he was there, perhaps fifteen feet back, keeping an eye on me.

"If I'd intended to escape, I would not have taken the scenic route through the gardens," I told him when I'd reached the back edge of the house, and still he followed.

I turned away before he could reply. There was an open expanse of grass, like a no man's land between the well-kept gardens and the dense wooded area surrounding the house.

I stepped out onto the grass, and it was strange that at that moment, what I wanted, perhaps more than anything, was to feel the cool, soft living carpet beneath my feet and between my toes.

Living.

Alive.

Cells multiplying and dividing.

Growing.

Thriving.

Out here, there was life.

In that basement, there was death. Or perhaps worse, the process of dying. A man, bound and broken. Blood had spilled from his mouth and his mangled hands. But how much blood? I tried to envision it, to remember how much blood had pooled on the floor beneath him, but I couldn't be certain.

I kicked off my shoes, pulled off my socks, and dug my toes into the cool grass. The blades tickled the edges of my feet. To my follower, I must have looked mad. I smiled, perhaps a little manically. To this man, the sight I'd stumbled upon in the basement was probably the norm; I was the bizarre sight here.

But when I turned around, my follower was gone. Amadeo had taken his place, but he'd come much closer, just a few feet from me. The lights that surrounded the house cast little more than a faint glow around him here, but the moon was full and the sky was clear, casting lights and shadows across his features.

"Nice night for a walk, *perla?*" he asked. His facial muscles moved with relaxed ease, but his shoulders were taut and his stance was uncertain, like he wasn't sure whether to make a grab for me or give me my space.

"How could he do that?" The question spilled out before I'd even fully realized what had truly bothered me in that gruesome scene. Not Amadeo; I'd known from the first moment I saw him that he was a violent man. I think I'd even come to accept Raven's explanation that it was part of what made him a "protector", as she called it. But Aurelio?

Amadeo's brow furrowed as he took a tentative step closer.

"You're not afraid?" he asked, though it didn't feel much like a question even without being able to hear the inflection in his tone.

I curled my toes in the grass, then stretched them out. He was right; I wasn't afraid. I was overwhelmed and horrified by what I'd seen, but not afraid that I would meet the same end as the broken, bleeding man in the basement.

"Who was he?" I asked, though even in his battered state, I'd recognized him. The man from the hospital, the man who'd started an itch in my brain because something about him had seemed terribly familiar.

"He was the asshole who tried to kill that kid," Amadeo said, nodding back toward the house. "You were right to send him out of the kid's hospital room, but he just waited for shift change at the hospital to come back to finish the job."

"How do you know that's why he was there? Would a man really admit to such a horrific thing?"

Amadeo crossed his arms over his chest in a semi-relaxed stance, but I could see the way his hands were curled into fists.

"Raven and I walked into the room and he had a pillow over the kid's face. I'd say his intentions were pretty clear."

"Bloody hell."

I felt sick. A moment or two longer, and the boy would have been dead. A boy whose blood had seeped out around my gloved fingers this morning. A boy whose tachycardic pulse had thudded beneath them.

Death was sneaky, it seemed. Even when I'd bested it, it had come back, slinking through the shadows and creeping into a boy's hospital room late at night.

But Amadeo had done the same thing I'd done; he'd stepped in, thwarted Death. He'd saved Grayson Thomas's life, even if he'd gone about it in a different way.

I licked my dry lips and took a shaky breath.

"I understand why you killed that man," I said, and I truly did, even if I wasn't sure I would ever have been able to stand in his shoes and pull the trigger. "But you didn't just kill him, Amadeo. You *tortured* him. Aurelio tortured him. Why?" I pinned him with a gaze that wasn't quite accusatory, but it was far from accepting.

He laced his fingers behind his neck, shaking his head slowly. "You might not like what we had to do—and if you hadn't been wandering where you shouldn't, you never would have seen it, Heidi—but it needed to be done."

"I can't imagine—"

"Do you want to know what that asshole proposed I do to you?" he cut in.

"Me? What have I to do with this?"

"He thought I should tie you up and torture *you* until you led me to a fortune."

I scoffed. "Have I not already done that?"

"He thinks your father stashed more—a lot more."

"This was all about money? Grayson Thomas's life? Brutal torture?" I looked up at Amadeo warily. Was money what *this* was about as well? I wondered.

"Christ, you know me better than that, *perla*," he answered like I'd spoken aloud.

"Do I?" I asked, but even before the words were out, I realized I did. When that had happened, I wasn't quite sure.

He took a step closer, closing the distance between us in one long stride.

"I do want to tie you up," he admitted. His lips moved with less enunciation than usual, and I imagined his voice was little more than a whisper. "But when I make you scream, it will be in pleasure, I guarantee it."

Hot and cold shivers raced up and down my spine.

"And just to make sure we're clear; I don't give a flying fuck about your money."

"It's not my money," I said, trying to sound composed even as my breath was coming harder and a fire ignited between my thighs. It felt wrong, so wrong that it made my stomach roil a little to think of becoming aroused so soon after the horrid thing I'd seen.

"It was your father's money—however he came by it—which means it's now yours. If you don't want to look for it, don't. I really don't care, *perla*."

He put a hand on my hip. It wasn't a light touch; it was firm and possessive, his fingers curling around and digging in just a little.

I'd been so caught up in my own chaotic emotions, I hadn't noticed the wild energy that had been radiating from him until now. His eyes were hooded, and his broad chest heaved with every deep breath. When he leaned in and his nose grazed along my jaw, scenting me, it dawned on me what that energy was even as my pussy clenched and my breasts grew heavy.

"You're turned on," I said, clearly stating the obvious. But it wasn't just arousal, it was something even more innate than our basic, carnal urges. It was feral and fierce, and it made every fiber of my being come alive.

He nodded and leaned away just enough that I could see his lips. "Right or wrong, what I do creates a lot of adrenaline. And you look like a goddamned forest nymph, *perla,*" he said as his gaze grazed over me from head to bare toes. He shook his head slowly. "So perfect, and so ready to be fucked."

"Maybe I am," I said, meeting his heated amber gaze boldly. "But you'll have to catch me first."

I spun on my toes, yanking myself out of his grip and taking off at lightning speed toward the woods. I don't know what it was he'd awakened inside me, but whatever it was throbbed in my veins with every step. It had every sensory receptor on my body waiting, tingling with anticipation.

I kept running; I couldn't hear his footsteps behind me, but I could feel him there, closer and closer with each passing second.

My heart pounded, and my lungs chased the air. The feeling that raced through me was so much akin to fear, and yet, not quite. I didn't know when or how his touch would come; would he grab my arm and yank me back to him? Would he tackle me to the ground? How long would it be before he was tearing off my clothes and shoving his cock inside me?

The tree line was right in front of me. So long as I made it beyond that line, whenever he caught me, we'd be alone, hidden from view, nothing but the trees and their nocturnal inhabitants to witness what happened next.

But just as I put on a burst of speed, his hands were there. They grabbed hold of me as his weight hit me, tackling me to the ground. Instead of the hard impact, though, he twisted his body as we fell, taking the brunt himself before rolling me beneath him in the cool grass.

I'd barely had time to register that I was no longer upright and moving when he grabbed hold of my hands and pinned them above my head. His face loomed right above me, his eyes filled with a primal heat and his teeth bared, as he shifted his weight and shoved up my scrub top and bra, exposing my bare breasts. His breath was hot against my neck as he reached down further, dragging down my scrub pants and thong.

No more than a second or two had passed, but I was bare to this man who sent more hot and cold shivers through my body than I'd ever thought possible. With his free hand still between us, I could feel his free hand still between us, deftly moving, unzipping his trousers, and then it wasn't his hand between us; it was his cock, hard and thick as he lined himself up. I could feel the tantalizing barbell near the tip teasing me.

Even as I anticipated it, I had to fight my body's innate urge to tense, knowing the brutal thrust that was coming, the hard drive that would bury him hilt deep all at once. But he didn't thrust; he paused, and his eyes met mine.

"Tell me you don't want my cock buried in your cunt, *perla,*" he ground out between clenched teeth.

It was the same thing he'd said the last time. This man who'd tortured another human being moments ago wouldn't take from me without permission, without knowing for certain this was what I wanted.

An unexpected tenderness welled up inside me. Up to this point, nothing I'd felt toward Amadeo could have been described as tender, and yet, there it was, warm and soft.

I want this, I told him silently since my tongue was having trouble with words at the moment, and just in case he hadn't heard it, I shoved my scrubs off my ankles with my feet and wrapped my legs around him.

It was all the confirmation he needed.

With my hands still pinned above my head, he kicked his hips and thrust in. Hard. Fast. Right to the hilt. He filled me so full, my inner walls burned with the stretch, but it was a burn I'd come to savor, proof that he filled every molecule of space inside me.

He watched me as he withdrew and rammed back in, his thrust so hard, my body inched upward along the blanket of grass.

Then again.

And again.

"Don't look away, *perla*," he instructed as he leaned down lower and suckled my nipple into his mouth.

He sucked hard, drawing me in, and the sensation traveled straight down a line inside me to my throbbing clit. He kept his gaze locked on mine even as he unsheathed his teeth and sunk them into my sensitive flesh. A little more, then a little more.

It was strange and erotic to watch him as he hurt me, and yet, he wasn't hurting me. It was like something had gotten crossed as the sensation traveled along my nerve pathways, reinterpreting it as it went so that by the time it exploded in my brain, it was pure unadulterated pleasure.

I moaned and mewled as he finished with one nipple and moved on to the other, giving it the same treatment as he fucked me hard and steady.

I tugged on my wrists, but he shook his head as he released my nipple.

"I like you like this, *perla*. Out in the open. One hundred percent at my mercy."

My breath caught in my throat. I'd completely forgotten that we were not, in fact, shrouded by hundred-year-old trees. And yet, I swear I could feel dopamine activating every neuroreceptor in my brain, flooding it with pleasure. Dear lord, I was drowning in it.

He smiled like the devil. "You like that, I see," he mused, though the way his jaw remained clenched told me he was no less affected.

"Yes," I moaned as the coil inside me spun faster, winding up so tight, there was no way I could hold off much longer. Every thrust ground his barbell against my G-spot. Every time he bottomed out, his pelvis rubbed my clit.

It was like he was made for this, and for a moment, I allowed myself to fancy that he had been. Just for this. Just for me.

"*Bene,*" he said, but rather than returning to his task of a moment prior, he pinned me with his gaze just as surely as he had my wrists pinned. I couldn't look away, couldn't have if my life depended on it.

He thrust faster. So hard, and impossibly deep. It should have had me crying out in pain, but I couldn't stop the moans of pleasure that tumbled from my lips, one on top of the other. It was wild and primal. And so much more intimate than I'd ever imagined a physical act could be as he held my gaze while hot shards of bliss exploded in the core of me and shot out through every part of me.

"Christ, you're fucking perfect," he groaned out, loud enough I could just make out the sound of his voice.

He shifted, ready to withdraw since we'd used no protection, but I clasped him tight with my ankles around his hips.

"I've got an implant," I said because I wanted this; I wanted to feel him coming deep inside me. And maybe just a little, I wanted to be marked by the scent of him.

"*Perfetta,*" he said, the word nearly distorted by the harsh line of his jaw.

Then I could feel the vibrations of his groans against my chest when he leaned in, suckling my neck as he thrust hard and deep.

His erection swelled inside me and for the first time in my life, a man's semen filled me, spurt upon spurt until my pussy had milked every drop he had to give.

Chapter Thirty-One

Amadeo

"It doesn't make any sense," I seethed as I paced back and forth across the office floor. My father sat behind his desk as usual, Cielo, Vito, and Aurelio in the chairs opposite him. "Nathaniel Sinclair's the CEO of a British architectural firm. Why is he after that money? How would he even know about it?"

"I'm still waiting to hear back from my contact," Cielo said as he scrubbed his hands over his five-o-clock shadow. "But from a cursory look into Nathaniel Sinclair, he isn't just the CEO of Windsor Crest Architecture. He's recently inherited four other corporations owned by the Sinclair family, previously by Edward Sinclair."

If I was a dog, my ears would have been standing straight up. "That name sounds familiar," I said. It rang a bell, but a distant one—not a name with which we had regular contact.

"It should." Cielo picked up a folder he had tucked in the chair beside him and laid it on the desk.

My father flipped open the file, and I stopped pacing long enough to peruse the pages inside, scanning a brief summary of the family's holdings. And there were a lot of big numbers in that summary.

That's when the name clicked.

Edward Sinclair, the British business magnate, but that wasn't all he was.

Edward Sinclair was a crime boss.

He had no fingers in any pies in our territory, so he'd never really ended up on our radar, but he and his family were on it now.

"Edward Sinclair passed away about a year ago," Cielo continued, "leaving everything to the youngest of his two sons."

"Youngest?" I interjected because that seemed to go against most typical family structures. "Do we know why the eldest son was passed over?"

"Not a clue," Cielo said, shaking his head. "But it's strange, right?"

"*Sì*, it is," my father said as he stared at the open file with a furrow between his brows.

Aurelio and Vito had both been uncharacteristically quiet, but they were nodding their heads now.

"I imagine there must have been a significant falling-out between father and son," Aurelio posited lightly.

My father leaned back and steepled his fingers over his stomach, the furrow still firmly etched across his forehead. "Sinclair is worth billions. If he's looking for this money, this is personal."

It hit me like a goddamned brick to the head. It should have hit me sooner.

"*This* is where Heidi's father got the money; he stole it from the Sinclairs."

Heads nodded in agreement on both sides of the desk.

"He hasn't come to *steal* William Dawson's money," I continued while an uncomfortable sensation writhed in my gut. "He's come to take it back."

It was an awful lot of hassle for a man who clearly didn't need the money, but I understood it. If anyone stole from the Lucianos like that, it would be the last thing they ever did.

277

"We could find the money and get in contact with Nathaniel Sinclair," Vito proposed. "Give it back to him and hope the man goes on his merry way."

Cielo shook his head. "I wouldn't be surprised to find Sinclair wants more than his money back; he wants revenge on whoever took it. If William Dawson isn't available, his offspring might be the next best thing."

The uncomfortable sensation turned into lava, coursing fast and hot through my veins. If Sinclair thought he could use Heidi to get his revenge, he was very fucking mistaken.

I breathed out, making room, keeping the lava contained inside.

"Even if we decide that finding this money is a feasible option," I said, my voice calm as a placid lake, "there's nothing saying Heidi has any clue where her father stashed the rest of it."

Aurelio's eyes met mine, and I could see what he was thinking.

Hand over the money from our own coffers, his gaze said like it was the simplest solution in the world. That he was on board with handing over millions of dollars to keep Heidi safe sure said a lot about how much she'd gotten to him.

I shook my head. "Sinclair will want what was stolen from him returned. He won't accept Luciano money as a substitute."

Cielo's eyes widened. "*Fratellone,* you weren't seriously considering—"

"No."

There was no sense in considering whether I would have done it had Sinclair been willing to accept it. Because he wouldn't.

"*Bene,*" Cielo said with an exaggerated sigh. "Because otherwise, if you've found pussy that's worth that, I'm taking it for a test drive."

Like hell he was. "*Vaffanculo,*" I cursed at him, mostly in jest.

"We need a way to have eyes and ears on Sinclair, *Signor,*" Vito said, refocusing the conversation.

"If he's been watching the young doctor," my father said, tapping the tips of his fingers together over his stomach, "then he's likely aware that our family has been… involved with her."

It was a fair point. If we had our men getting close enough to keep an eye on Sinclair, it was possible he'd recognize them. But perhaps, there was another option.

"We have several shell corporations," I said, working through the possibility in my head.

"Arrange for one to be in need of Sinclair's services?" Aurelio asked.

I nodded, but Cielo was quick to shake his head.

"It poses the same problem as surveillance. If we arrange a meeting with the man, he'd have even more opportunity to recognize our men and—"

"He wouldn't recognize all of them," I said, warming up to this plan.

Eyebrows raised while my father stopped tapping his fingers.

"Antonio Verdi," I explained. "We've been keeping him and his cousin 'comfortably situated' here. Perhaps, it's time we give Verdi the opportunity to prove himself."

My father's eyebrows joined in and reached for his hairline. "You want to utilize a man who's been playing around with the Free Birds?" His tone clearly said he didn't approve.

I shook my head. "Verdi wasn't there to be one of those fucking birds; he was there to keep an eye on his kid cousin."

"And you believe him?" my father persisted.

I turned to Vito, giving him the floor.

He nodded. "His story checks out, *Signor*. We've been able to verify where he was raised and the missing persons reports filed for his mother and sister. He's got a military record—signed up at eighteen and selected for special forces by twenty-one. What he did in his four years of service afterward is classified. It'll take time to dig deeper, but in the meantime, I think it's safe to assume he ran covert ops."

So, he was either one hell of an asset or a big fucking problem.

All eyes swiveled back to me.

"My gut says he's good for this," I told them, and I'd learned to trust my gut. It knew what it was doing. "He wanted an opportunity to prove his loyalty, and here it is."

While my father mulled it over, I noticed Aurelio's attention remained on me. There was a sly light in his eyes that concerned me.

He cleared his throat and sat up straighter. "It seems to me, though, that whatever Sinclair is after—whether that be money or revenge—it now has little to do with the Lucianos." He kept his eyes on me as he spoke. "Our issue was with Bianchi; Bianchi is dead."

"That hasn't escaped my attention," my father said. Once again, all eyes in the room turned to me, waiting expectantly.

I glared at Aurelio, knowing full well what he was doing. The old man was trying to make me step up and declare that Heidi was more than a casual fuck.

Well played, vecchio.

"I dragged her into this," I said since he wasn't the only one who could play. "It wasn't intentional, but the result was the same, nonetheless. Letting Sinclair get his hands on her? Torture her, and fuck only knows what else?" I shook my head. "I'm just not good with that. If you want to read into that, *amico,*" I continued, looking pointedly at Aurelio, "be my guest."

My father's fingers were back to tapping while the wheels turned behind his eyes. "Greta's effect seems to be spreading," he mused aloud. The corners of his lips actually twitched.

I chuckled. "Maybe."

Cielo was nodding. "For a woman who works for the mafia, she is one hell of a do-gooder… even if she does go about it in a bit of a murder-y way."

My father heaved a heavy sigh and dropped his hands. "Fine. We can arrange for Verdi to get a meeting with Sinclair. That shouldn't be a problem. What do you propose we do once he's in there?"

"If we can get Verdi into Sinclair's office, we'll use him to bug the room and get a tracker on Sinclair," I explained.

"Do you think Verdi can pull it off?" Cielo asked. "He'd have limited time, and Sinclair will be watching him closely."

"*Sì*, I do. The guy had balls, driving right up to the Luciano estate the way he did." That, or a serious lack of mental acuity, but I preferred to go with balls of steel.

"If he could do that," I continued, "then he can certainly handle a twenty-minute corporate meeting. With a little practice, he'll be able to plant what we need him to plant."

Cielo nodded. Of all of us in the room, he likely had the most experience with spy-type shit.

I glanced once more at the open file on the desk. Edward Sinclair. I shook my head. Of all the men in the world to steal from. What the hell had Heidi's father been thinking? "In the meantime, I'll have a conversation with Heidi and see if we can figure out where the rest of Sinclair's money is hiding."

Everyone nodded but Cielo.

"Do you really think Sinclair will be amenable to taking his stolen money and flying home?" he asked, his tone thick with doubt.

I shut the folder and headed toward the door.

"He can be amenable to it, or he can be dead, *fratello*. Either way, he's not getting his hands on Heidi."

I could hear Aurelio chuckling as I closed the office door behind me. *Well played, vecchio.*

Chapter Thirty-Two

Amadeo

It didn't take long to find Heidi. After I'd fucked her out in the yard, she'd pretty much glued herself to her patient.

I cracked open the door to Grayson Thomas's suite and found her bent over the young man with a syringe in her hand, injecting something into his IV.

She stepped back after a moment and jotted something down on a chart she was keeping. The way she moved, she was in her element here, just like she'd been when she saved Aurelio's life.

If anyone had been made for a particular calling, it was her.

Watching her from the doorway, she leaned over the boy again, pulling back bandages in a way that didn't even make the kid flinch. Though that might have had something to do with the steady stream of morphine that was being pumped into his system.

She was talking to him; I couldn't hear her words at first, so I opened the door further, just enough to slip into the room without drawing her attention.

"After his heart attack," she was saying, "I knew I could never do that again; to stand there and be useless while someone I cared about slipped away right in front of me…" She paused.

I could hear the shaky inhale and exhale of her breath. Then she shook her head like she was clearing it.

"I started volunteering at the hospital not long after," she said as she did something to his wounds I couldn't see from my position. "Academic grades are important, of course, but modern selection committees are looking for more well-rounded applicants," she explained to the kid.

"Someone like me doesn't go to medical school, Doc," the boy replied, his voice slightly sluggish.

She scoffed as she stood up straight again. "Because you're poor?" she asked. "So was I," she went on without pausing. "Because there will be hurdles for you to overcome?" She pointed to her ears. "I understand those quite well. Don't sell yourself short, Mr. Thomas, and don't be the obstacle that gets in your own way."

Well, damn, who would have guessed the woman could be a motivational speaker? And who wouldn't buy whatever motivational shit she was selling when she was a kickass, competent doctor who looked like a dark-haired angel and spoke like British royalty?

For reasons I wasn't willing to analyze, it was tempting to just stand here and watch her, listen to her, but unfortunately, some things couldn't wait.

I started to cross the room, but she caught the movement out of the corner of her eye and spun around.

She still had her mouth open, like she'd been about to launch back into her motivational speech, but she closed her lips when she spotted me and her cheeks flushed just a little. Not quite embarrassment, but… something.

"Can I speak with you, *per favore*?" I asked before I got hung up on figuring out exactly what that "something" was.

She looked at me for a moment, then to the boy, then back to me. "Of course."

She said something quietly to the boy, then followed me out of the room and down the few steps to mine.

I'd intended to dive right in the moment I closed the door behind us, but clearly, there was something on her mind. Her hands fidgeted in front of her, and her teeth were digging into her bottom lip.

"Spit it out, *perla*," I said, now fighting the urge to take her place and sink my own teeth into that ridiculously plush lip.

Still, she was silent for a moment while she continued to fidget. Whatever was on her mind, it was taking her a lot to get it out.

She dropped her hands and clasped them together behind her back. "I'd like to ask a favor of you," she said, prim and proper as fuck.

I could think of about a hundred different 'favors' I wouldn't have minded performing for her at that moment.

"And what favor might that be?" I asked, because maybe it was my lucky day and she had the same kind of favors in mind.

The way she swallowed and her eyes flickered up to me, then away, though, suggested otherwise.

"You have… resources, the means to look into a person—their life, their background, that sort of thing."

It didn't sound much like a question, but she looked up at me, waiting for me to respond.

I nodded slowly, not sure where this was going. "I might have that type of resource."

She swallowed again, licked her lips, then nodded like she was pep-talking herself into continuing.

"According to Mr. Thomas, the living accommodations you found him in were… subpar."

I scoffed. "That's one way to put it," I said, remembering the shithole of an apartment where we'd found him.

Her brow furrowed. "His mother died six months ago. She was struggling to make ends meet at the time, leaving nothing to Mr. Thomas and his seven-year-old sister."

"A sister? That apartment isn't big enough for one, never mind two people. And one of them a seven-year-old child?"

"I didn't tell Mr. Thomas this, but I remember the woman, Amadeo. It was a car accident."

She swallowed and something flickered in her eyes like she was having difficulty maintaining the cool detachment that had earned her the title of Ice Queen.

"You treated her." It didn't take a rocket scientist to piece that together.

She nodded curtly. "The patient presented with significant multisystem trauma. Multiple fractures, including bilateral long bone fractures in the lower extremities, rib fractures, a collapsed lung, organ damage. Traumatic brain injury." She paused, took a shaky breath, then continued. "The immediate cause of death was recorded as hemorrhagic shock resulting from polytrauma."

She called the woman 'the patient' like she was cool and detached, but it didn't escape my notice that she recalled every detail of the woman's injuries.

"I don't often lose patients; it's difficult to forget those I do." She still had her hands clasped together behind her back, and her speech was just as prim and proper as ever, but it was clearly a cover, not so different from the straight face I could put on no matter the situation.

"Heidi, this isn't your fault," I said, seeing the aloofness for what it was. I reached out my hand toward her, but she leaned away.

"According to Mr. Thomas, he was a straight-A student prior to the accident, even if he did struggle with attendance at times. After his mother's death, he was forced to take whatever work he could find to support himself and his sister. Even then, it wasn't enough."

The kid still has the apartment, and he hasn't died from starvation. "Enough for what?"

She sighed and dropped her hands like the aloof act was tiring her. "The Administration for Children's Services were called three weeks ago; they took his sister."

Ah fuck. And there was a decent chance that was why the kid hadn't run like I'd told him. Well, didn't I feel like an asshole. But it still begged the question, "What is it you want me to use my resources to look into?"

She looked at me like the answer was obvious. "Mr. Thomas' story, of course."

"Why?" If the story was true, I felt for the kid, but what did that have to do with Heidi?

She looked at me, meeting my gaze head-on, but when her chin tilted up even higher, I had a feeling I wasn't going to like whatever came out of her mouth next.

"If Mr. Thomas' story is legitimate, I intend to do whatever is necessary to become a foster parent to Mr. Thomas and his sister."

"You're not serious," I said, shaking my head. I was damned impressed with myself that I'd stopped my jaw from dropping.

I'd never describe Heidi as cold; that prim bitch persona she gave off at times was just a cover and I damn well knew it. But taking on a troubled kid and a seven-year-old little girl who might be just as fucked up?

"Why not?" she asked like what she was suggesting was perfectly reasonable.

I could think of a few reasons right off the top of my head, starting with an adolescent male living under the same roof as Heidi with no protection around. Nope, I didn't like that one bit.

I cocked an eyebrow at her, waiting for a better explanation.

She stared back at me, weighing me somehow. Her chest deflated after a moment and she nodded.

"Because the foster system is abhorrent, Amadeo. I'm sure there are a plethora of good foster parents, but there are also many who—" She slammed her lips shut.

She wasn't speaking hypothetically.

"What did they do to you?" I asked, because suddenly, the kid and his problems were about the furthest thing from my mind. My blood was heating up, heading toward a full boil. I had no problem with going on a foster-parent killing spree and taking out any asshole who'd ever laid a hand on her.

She shook her head. "Nothing."

"What do you mean 'nothing'?" I think the blood in my veins got confused. Were we all go for murder here or not?

She still had her lips pressed together like she had no intention of letting any more words out.

That wasn't going to fly here. "If you want my help, *perla,* you're going to give me more than that."

She huffed, and the look she flashed me wasn't one of those 'you're so going to get laid for being such a concerned guy' kind of looks.

"Nothing—that is exactly what they did, Amadeo. Nothing. It was like I didn't exist. They didn't beat me; they didn't starve me. They... *nothing*-ed me."

Something in my chest felt like it was cracking—must have been some strange-ass heartburn. It couldn't have had anything to do with what she was telling me, if for no other reason than because I just couldn't fathom Heidi being 'nothing' to anyone. No fucking way.

And yet, nothing about her screamed "I'm lying here". She'd been unloved. Left alone. Invisible.

"All right," I said. I think she could have asked me for the whole fucking world in that moment, and I would have found a way to serve it up on a goddamned silver platter. "I'll look into Grayson Thomas," I conceded, not that I was getting on board with the kid moving in with her.

"Thank you," she said. There was something raw in her voice, exposed. I'd dragged something out of her she hadn't wanted to offer up, and I can't say it left me with tingly good feelings here.

"But the kid isn't leaving this house until the shit we've been dealing with is squared away. And on that topic, we need to have a conversation."

"A conversation about what?"

I sighed, hoping like hell Raven had been right about the whole trust thing.

"I need to know where the rest of the money is, Heidi."

Chapter Thirty-Three

Amadeo

A row of seats had been set up, side-by-side. Nearly every seat had been filled. The buttery scent of popcorn filled the air.

You'd think I'd just walked into a movie theater, not the surveillance room in the estate.

"Popcorn," I asked Greta as I closed the door. "Really?"

She shrugged without turning around. "Like you don't want some?"

Vito and Aurelio chuckled. Even my father smiled.

Well… I could eat.

I shoved my fingers into the bowl and snagged a handful, watching on the central monitor as Sinclair's middle-aged secretary typed away behind her desk. Her phone rang. She answered it, muttered something, then stood up.

"Mr. Sinclair will see you now," she said, looking straight at us. Well, looking right into the tiny camera on the lapel of Antonio Verdi's Armani jacket.

The picture shifted as Verdi stood up and turned toward a set of double doors.

It had taken us four days to lay the background we needed and secure this appointment. I took a deep breath and hoped like hell Antonio Verdi did not fuck this up.

"All right, boys," Greta said, adjusting her position like she was settling in. "It's showtime."

My father looked over at her from the opposite end of the row of seats, shaking his head while the corners of his lips twitched.

All eyes returned to the screen as the camera—and Verdi—approached the double doors. The sound was coming in clear; we could hear every footstep as he crossed the marble floor and opened the office door.

Beyond it was an enormous glass-walled office, sparsely but tastefully furnished. A man sat behind a wide glass desk on the far side of the room, right in front of the windows that overlooked the city from the fifty-fifth floor.

The man, Nathaniel Sinclair, stood up as Verdi approached, not rounding the desk, but stretching his hand out across it. The man was about the same height as Verdi with dark hair and eyes, and the way he wore his high-end suit, he was born in it, born to it. Plenty of money. Plenty of power.

They shook hands, exchanged pleasantries. Then it was down to business.

"Tell me how I can help you, Mr. Verdi," Sinclair said, watching Verdi with shrewd eyes.

"I've recently acquired a vacant property," Verdi explained. Then, just like we'd coached him, he offered up the location of the property and the basics surrounding the future build there.

Sinclair nodded at all the right times, but it was clear he was waiting for something, the particular reason Verdi had sought out his firm and had managed to wrangle a meeting with the CEO.

"This is what I need from you, Mr. Sinclair," Verdi said, withdrawing blueprints from his briefcase and handing them across the desk.

Sinclair perked up, glancing over the blueprints, searching for what Verdi was after. What he was looking at was a very incomplete blueprint, but I don't think it took Sinclair long to figure out why.

"Interesting," he said, placing the blueprint down on the desk in front of him.

"I need nine rooms," Verdi explained. "Three in the basement and two on each of the first three floors. These rooms will not be recorded with the New York City Department of Buildings, nor will they be detectable to anyone who doesn't already know of their existence."

Sinclair sat back in his chair, his gaze fixed on Verdi. He was sizing Verdi up, the same way I was sizing up Sinclair, watching him, looking for tells.

If Sinclair didn't buy his act, this wasn't some lily-white businessman who would shoo Verdi out the front door. If Verdi fucked up, it was possible he would never see daylight again.

"I'm intrigued," Sinclair said after a long moment of silence. "Tell me, what might a person do with these… phantom chambers?"

Verdi shifted; the camera angle changed like he'd crossed his leg, turning his body just a little. As he did, his hand moved to his knee, just beneath the desk. With the flick of a finger, he stuck a listening device with an adhesive backing to the underside of the desk.

"I can't quite say what they might be used for, Mr. Sinclair. My clients depend on me for the utmost discretion, and to that end, I seldom find it beneficial to ask too many questions."

Sinclair nodded.

This would have come as no surprise to him. Cielo had worked his magic to set Verdi up as the head of a successful real estate firm that dealt with a very particular clientele. And I had no doubt Sinclair had done his research before he'd agreed to this meeting.

"All right, Mr. Verdi. I'll consider your proposal and get back to you."

So, he was intrigued, but still suspicious. That was fine. By the time Sinclair had managed to dig deep enough to give credence to his suspicions, he'd either be dead or on a plane headed back to London.

"Fair enough, Mr. Sinclair," Verdi said, then rose to his feet.

"Come on," Greta urged, her gaze glued to Sinclair. If he stayed behind the desk, there was no way Verdi would be able to plant a tracker on the man. We'd have ears in his office, but no way to follow his movements.

Sinclair stood up, and when he circled the glass desk, the surveillance room-turned-movie theater let out a collective sigh.

Parting pleasantries were exchanged. Then the handshake. The view from the lapel of Verdi's jacket didn't extend down far enough to see what was going on, whether he'd managed to plant the tracker undetected.

So, I watched Sinclair's eyes for any sign he'd recognized what Verdi was up to.

And then it was over. Verdi turned and we watched him retreat from the glass-walled office, out through the marble-floored reception area, and onto the elevator that would take him down to a car we had waiting for him outside.

"All right," I said, turning to Vito. "Turn them on." *And hope like hell he'd managed to plant the tracker.*

"*Si, Signor,*" Vito replied as he stood up, turned on the tracker and the microphone, and transferred the feeds onto the monitors in front of us.

The monitor that would project the microphone remained black while a GPS map popped up on the other with a little red dot to mark Sinclair's movements—assuming Verdi had managed to plant the tracker. And since the tracker wasn't moving out of the building and down the street with Verdi, I was going to call it a success.

The sound of Sinclair typing projected from the monitor's speakers. And more typing. A knock at the door.

"Here's your coffee, Mr. Sinclair," the receptionist's voice spoke as high heels clicked and clacked across the office floor.

"Thank you, Janet," he replied.

Greta shifted in her seat again like she was getting antsy. "I've got to say, this show isn't nearly as interesting as the trailer made it out to be." She smiled as she set the popcorn bowl on the ground. It was empty. The woman had practically inhaled it.

Now I was hungry. I was just about to go rummage through the kitchen for something to eat when a phone rang, the sound coming through loud and clear from the monitor's speaker.

I almost laughed when every pair of eyes in the room swiveled to stare at the blank monitor screen.

"Hello?" Sinclair's voice answered the call.

"Turn it up to full," I said, hoping to catch more than muffled snippets of the caller's voice.

Vito nodded and adjusted the volume.

"You were right, Mr. Sinclair," an unfamiliar British voice said, coming through the speaker clearly.

"Bloody hell," Sinclair sighed. That was Heidi's curse; it was just fucked up to hear it coming from this man even if it wasn't exactly uncommon.

"The Luciano family seemed to have scooped her up, sir."

My spine stiffened, and my adrenaline amped up another three notches. It seemed Sinclair had been keeping a close eye on Heidi.

"But it's strange," the unfamiliar voice continued.

"How so, James?" Sinclair asked.

"You saw her at the cemetery, sir; she didn't look injured or scared. She hasn't left their estate for the past four days, but I have a feeling that has something to do with the boy. Nothing about this feels like they're holding her against her will."

If you'd been here two weeks ago, you might be singing a different tune.

Sinclair sighed. "So, they're trying to use the same approach Bianchi used."

"I think so, sir. The eldest Luciano son was with her every night before the move to their estate."

All eyes stayed fixed on the blank screen, but I could feel the fucking smiles on their faces.

Stronzi.

"So," Sinclair continued, "they know what they found at the Regalton Arms wasn't all William had in his possession, and they're trying to get the rest out of her." Sinclair sighed again. From the frequent sound, I got the feeling there was a lot of weight on this man's shoulders.

The unfamiliar voice said something, but it was too quiet for the mic to pick up.

"We're going to have to put an end to this, James. The less digging they do, the better."

"How would you like me to proceed, sir?"

I sat up straighter, silently begging Sinclair to say the words, to send this asshole after a Luciano. The second he did, this fucker was all mine.

"Perhaps it's time to stop playing games, James."

"Do you want me to find a way to retrieve the girl, sir?"

Silence.

Say yes. My hands bunched into fists. If he went after Heidi, he was just as dead as if he'd threatened my family. *Say it, goddamn it.*

"No, not yet," Sinclair replied.

Damn it.

"Let's find out all we can about the Lucianos first, shall we? They've been useful so far."

"Of course, sir."

Sinclair hung up a few seconds later.

"I want to know everywhere they're poking around for information," my father told Vito the second the call disconnected. "Limit the flow as much as you can."

Vito got up and headed for the door. "I'm on it, boss."

"I could talk to Hack," Greta offered. Hack was the Old Dogs' resident tech guy. He knew just about everything there was to know about computers and networks and all that shit. "He could probably lock a lot of shit down and let you know if anyone's trying to get in," she continued.

My father's jaw was tight, his lips pressed together, but he nodded after a moment. This alliance shit was going to take him a while to get used to.

"*Grazie*, Greta," he said with another curt nod.

She got up, grabbed her phone out of her pocket, and punched in a number as she left the room.

I turned to Aurelio, then my father.

"Useful?" I asked, honing in on what Sinclair had said. "How the hell have we been 'useful' to Sinclair?"

My father's expression said he could make no more sense of it than I could. "We located the fortune William Dawson had hidden at the Regalton Arms, but that put it out of his reach. I don't see how that was useful."

It took me a minute—maybe I was off my game—but when it hit me, it hit hard.

"Unless it kept someone else from getting their hands on it."

"You think there may be another player, *Signor*?" Aurelio asked.

"If that asshole, Sterling, was correct and there's four times what we found hidden somewhere, there could be a lot of players looking for it." I said, tamping down the urge to wring a dead man's neck. Heidi's father had to have known that people would come looking for that money. He hadn't just been careless with his own life; he'd been careless with his daughter's life.

My father and Aurelio both nodded.

"Are you any closer to locating the rest of this fortune?" my father asked.

"Hell, no," I said, frustrated. "She was nine years old when her parents died. She doesn't remember much from before that." And after four days of Heidi trying to remember anything that could be useful, I kind of just felt like an asshole for making her dredge it all up.

Aurelio nodded. "The Regalton Arms helped to jog her memory, but without knowing what else might do that…"

The obvious hung in the air between the three of us: It was quite possible Heidi would never remember, and that was assuming there was anything to remember, that her father had left her clues in the first place.

"All right," I said, getting to my feet. "I'll keep at it." I didn't relish the thought of grilling Heidi any more on the topic.

Returning to Heidi, though, I was just fine with that. I'd left her in my bed two hours ago—lightly tied, so she could get free if she really wanted to.

Now, she was either waiting for me, tied up, naked, and ready for more. Or she'd gotten herself free, and it was time to drag her back and tie her up all over again. Seemed like a win-win situation to me.

My cock was already stirring when I reached the office door. It was not impressed, though, when the door swung open and Cielo strode in, blocking my path and just about colliding with me.

"I've heard back from my contact in London," he said without preamble, his jaw tight as his gaze moved back and forth between our father and I. "You're going to want to hear this."

I sighed as visions of my naked, willing captive went up in smoke.

My cock was not impressed at all.

Chapter Thirty-Four

Heidi

The hospital looked different today.

It wasn't the five days I'd been away from it. It wasn't that the building itself had changed. Or that the hustling and bustling people moving in out of the front entrance appeared in any way different.

It was me. It was the nervous knot in the pit of my stomach and the cold dampness of the palms of my hands.

Keeping my head straight as I approached the building, I glanced surreptitiously to the right, then to the left.

Did they know?

Could they see what I'd done, written plain as day across my face?

Fired.

Arrested.

Imprisoned.

All these words whirled around in my head as I crossed the threshold and stepped inside. The hospital would know about the missing narcotics by now. And the magical disappearance of the boy who'd been my patient.

Amadeo broke the law on a regular basis. How did this gnawing paranoia not consume him?

The tall, blond nurse I worked with frequently fell into step close by me. Not with me, but headed in the same direction toward the ER. I was still fairly certain his name was Tom.

"Good morning, Dr. Dawson," he said when he realized I'd noticed him.

"Good morning…" *Say it? Don't say it?* "…Tom."

His step faltered. A furrow formed between his pale eyebrows.

Bloody hell. I'd gotten it wrong. I could feel my cheeks warming.

"I didn't realize you knew anyone's name," he said as the furrow vanished.

"Only the names worth knowing," I replied.

Was that a joke? Did I just joke with this man?

He laughed.

Dear Lord, I did just tell a joke.

He stood up straighter, shoulders back. Not offended, but chuffed.

"Have a good day, Dr. Dawson," he said, then veered toward the men's washroom.

Have a good day? My throat grew tighter.

"*Have a good day, Heidi-girl,*" my father had called to me from our car as I hopped out of the passenger seat and scurried toward school. That was the last time anyone had wished me a good day.

I shook off the memory and hurried toward the ER, but the moment I stepped onto the ward, I could feel every eye on me, though no one was looking at me.

No one was looking, but they knew. They had to know.

My breathing came faster as some of the oxygen in the room seemed to evaporate. My palms were cool and clammy again.

Raven spotted me from the nurse's station. She smiled, raised her hand to wave, then dropped it and made a beeline in my direction.

Without a word, she grabbed hold of my hand and towed me along toward one of the empty treatment areas. She pulled the curtain behind us and turned around to face me.

Fired.

Arrested.

Imprisoned.

The words were back, swirling in a chaotic, formless mess in my head.

"You've got to calm down," she said, her lips moving slowly but not exaggeratedly. "You're pretty pale on a good day; today you look like you've been moonlighting as a marble statue."

She was right; this wasn't me. I took a deep breath. Let it out. I was cool under pressure. The Ice Queen.

I nodded my head. "Thank you. You're right."

"You're all covered here," she said, leaning in closer like she was whispering. "There's nothing to worry about." There was a certainty in her blue eyes, a certainty I felt I could trust.

"Thank you," I reiterated. "Both for this and for the other night."

She smiled brightly. "No worries, *amica.*"

Friend.

I hadn't even realized how starved I'd been for that, for that kind of connection to another person. I'd had colleagues, mentors, sexual partners. Not friends. And not whatever it was that had developed between Amadeo and me that was dragging me deeper into a criminal world filled with... friends.

"Deo needed help; that's kind of what we do," she continued.

I shook my head. "No, not for that. I mean, yes, of course that. But also..." I huffed a frustrated breath.

Maybe you should stop talking while you're ahead, Heidi-girl, my father teased me from the back of my head.

"You were exceptionally understanding *that* night," I persisted despite his nonexistent teasing. "I appreciated it."

Raven's smile brightened even more. "Any time," she said as she winked at me and threw open the curtains.

And it turned out, when Raven said there was nothing to worry about, she'd meant it. I saw no mention of missing narcotics all morning, no lips flapping about a boy who vanished from the hospital in the middle of the night. Somehow, she—or Amadeo—had covered it up.

There were no more terrifying words whirling about in my head by the time I grabbed a sandwich from the cafeteria at lunch and headed toward the hospital's entrance. It wasn't by conscious effort. My feet gravitated toward it of their own volition. Out the door, across the concrete walk to the bench. To *our* bench—mine and Aurelio's.

I hadn't spoken to him since seeing him in that terrible room, had pretty much boarded myself up for four days, only moving back and forth between Grayson's room and Amadeo's. But there he was, leaning back comfortably with his legs crossed at his ankles and his hands resting in his cardigan pockets.

My brain hesitated, but my feet had a mind of their own, it seemed, and they kept moving until I was standing in front of the bench.

Aurelio smiled at me as I perched myself next to him and set the plastic-wrapped sandwich down between us.

He didn't look like a killer, like a man who could torture a human being without breaking a sweat. Amadeo did. It wasn't his stature or the weapons he carried, but rather the way he could stand cold, like stone, no matter what was going on beneath the surface. But Aurelio? Cardigans and kind smiles?

When I could think of nothing to say, I stared at the plastic wrap, following the wrinkles and folds like capillaries.

"Go ahead," he said; I caught the movement of his lips out the corner of my eye.

I frowned. I wasn't quite certain with what I was to "go ahead".

"You have questions, *cara mia*; I can see them in your eyes."

I did. I had many questions, but one stood out most prominently.

"How can you do what you did?" I asked.

He nodded like I'd asked the question he'd been expecting. "I imagine very much the same way you do," he replied.

"What?" Surely, I'd read his lips wrong.

"When you cut a man open, you don't see a man, do you?" he asked. "You see a problem," he went on without pausing. "And you do whatever must be done to fix it."

That was the simplified version, yes. "But you're not fixing—"

"Am I not?" he asked. The way he looked at me, it was like he was urging me to think harder, to look deeper.

And so, I did. Or at least, I tried.

"That man was going to kill Grayson Thomas," I said, thinking out loud. "You stopped him." That was the reason the man was dead, I supposed, though, it didn't explain the disturbing scene I'd stumbled upon.

Aurelio nodded but said nothing, still urging, still waiting.

"But that man trying to kill Grayson wasn't the 'problem'," I went on. "Or, it wasn't the source of the problem. You needed to find the source to stop it from happening again, like finding the source of a bleeder. So, you were doing it… to *keep* Grayson safe."

He nodded. "In part."

"In part?" I could think of no other "part" to his motivation.

He smiled. "Your safety was my concern as well, *cara mia*."

A warmth unfurled in my chest, but even as it did, my stomach roiled. Warmth was not the right response. There should be no warmth to hear that this man had tortured a human being for me. I should have been appalled. Disgusted.

"I think I do not belong in your world, Aurelio," I said, less for his benefit and more because I needed it to be true.

He shook his head, smiling gently. "We live in the same world, *cara*. You are simply living without blinders on now."

It felt like whatever world I'd been living in stuttered on its axis. But of course, he was right. There were no more separate worlds than there were literal boxes in my head.

I sighed and clenched my hands together in my lap. "I am having difficulty seeing the benefit in losing those blinders."

Aurelio shook his head, quick and sharp, like he didn't believe it for a moment. "With blinders on, Dr. Dawson, would you have gone searching for this?" he asked as he picked up a folder that had been lying on the bench beside him.

"What is it?" I asked as he handed it to me.

"The information you requested about young Mr. Thomas."

I stared at the file, a boy's life all summed up on a few pieces of paper.

"Do you know what's in here? What it says?" I asked, still staring. The boy's story was either confirmed or refuted by what laid inside this folder.

He nodded. "*Sì,* I do."

"And?"

He smiled gently. "Trust your intuition, *cara mia.* What is your gut telling you?"

Trust my intuition? With a patient, certainly, but to weigh a man's words? To judge the subtle nuances of his body language?

Aurelio was waiting patiently, still smiling, still urging me to think harder, to look deeper.

"I think the boy has been telling the truth," I confessed.

His expression remained unchanged as he nodded again to the folder, encouraging me to open it.

School transcripts. A clean criminal record. A half dozen hospital reports for his mother. And one for Grayson—a broken arm and a split lip, five years ago. That's when his mother had fled with her two children and filed a restraining order against an abusive husband.

A lump formed in the back of my throat. I'd worked in this woman's body, had her blood on my hands. In some ways, I'd known this woman more intimately than anyone else, and yet, I'd known nothing. I'd inquired about nothing. She'd died, and I'd moved on. To the next patient, to the next broken body.

The Ice Queen.

I nodded, swallowing back the lump. "Thank you, Aurelio," I said, back stiff, hands clasped on top of the closed folder in my lap.

He shook his head and laid a hand on mine. "In that room," he nodded toward the hospital, "you do what you have to do. You keep yourself distant, detached, because deep down, you know that's the way it has to be. There is nothing wrong with that."

"I suppose you speak from experience."

He squeezed my hand. "I do."

He was right again, of course. I remained detached because I did care. To regret that would be to regret the lives I had saved.

He returned his hand to his lap, and we sat in a comfortable silence, though it didn't last long.

He shifted in his seat after a moment, turning to face me directly. His movements were a little stiff, thanks to the recent gunshots. "You do know he's never going to let you take him home with you?" he said when he had my full attention.

"I believe Grayson would be amenable to the idea."

He shook his head. "Not him. Amadeo."

"I don't think he would care one way or the other."

"Don't you?"

"I—" I closed my mouth.

In all honesty, I had no idea. Sexually, we were more compatible than I'd imagined two people could be. But the last time I'd tried to make sense of what it was between us, Amadeo had shut me down. Whatever 'it' was, I had a feeling there was still an expiration date. But it didn't matter; the Ice Queen wouldn't care.

But you do, Heidi-girl.

I sighed. I missed my boxes and blinders terribly.

"Thank you for this, Aurelio," I said, holding up the folder.

"It was my pleasure, *cara mia.*"

I stood up, not missing the knowing light in Aurelio's eyes.

"My lunch break is nearly over," I explained. I picked up the sandwich I'd left on the bench, though I had no desire for food at the moment.

"Of course, Dr. Dawson," he said, still smiling. But then the smile disappeared, and he sat up straighter, his expression stern. "Someone will be here to pick you up when your shift is finished."

I was about to tell him that wasn't necessary, but although I hadn't spent a great deal of time with these people, I knew better than to argue.

I started to leave but stopped after a step and turned around.

"Until tomorrow, then?" I asked, praying the bubble of hope in my chest hadn't worked its way into my voice.

"I'll look forward to it."

And I would as well, far more than I should.

Chapter Thirty-Five

Heidi

My back pressed hard against the passenger side door of Amadeo's car. His hands gripped my hips, pulling me close, crushing my breasts against the hard planes of his chest. His lips devoured mine like I was the only sustenance that could satisfy him.

"If we don't leave now," he said as he tore his lips away, "I'm going to spin you around, shove down your scrubs and panties, and fuck you until you don't give a damn who's watching."

His words sent hot shivers down my spine and straight to the throbbing, empty ache between my thighs.

But we were standing in the hospital parking lot. This couldn't happen no matter how much my body screamed otherwise.

"We need to leave," I said, though I had my fingers digging into his shoulders, and I made no move to release him. He was so close, so warm, so hard; I could feel his erection digging into my abdomen.

But Amadeo didn't make idle threats. We either left now, or I had no doubt, he'd have me half-naked with his cock buried deep inside me in front of every staff member, patient, and visitor around.

With conscious effort, I released one finger after another. He let go of my hips and stepped back.

"I thought you liked it when I fucked you out in the open," he said, grinning like the devil himself.

A fiery jolt of arousal shot through me as memories from the night at the edge of the woods flashed behind my eyes.

"I do," I admitted.

It was strange how easy it was to be honest with him about my sexual interests, even those I hadn't pursued prior to him. But he made me feel like there was nothing I could ever propose, ever want, that would change the way he looked at me.

The devilish grin remained in place as he leaned in and kissed the top of my head.

"Then let's get you home, *perla*. And we'll see just how far you get when you run from me tonight."

The fiery jolts continued, like mini fireworks inside my body, but at the same time, one word stood out from all the rest, pulling on something inside my chest.

Home.

"*...let's get you home, perla,*" he'd said.

He opened the passenger door, and I slid inside.

Perhaps I was reading too much into it.

I stayed silent as Amadeo got behind the steering wheel and revved the engine. But it was dark out; if I wanted any hope of a conversation, it would have to be now before we left the bright overhead lights of the parking lot.

"What are we doing, Amadeo?" I asked, just like I had before. And in truth, I was expecting the same answer now as I'd gotten then.

He let out a sigh that deflated his chest, shaking his head to himself with a wry grin.

"Fuck if I know, *perla,*" he said, still wearing a wry grin. But then the grin vanished and he met my gaze. "Whatever it is, I've never done it before. We're in uncharted territory for me."

"Me too," I replied. My chest filled with warmth even as a knot twisted in my stomach. We were more than sex, but to have more meant there was more to lose.

He shrugged, and the grin returned. "We've got time to figure it out, and I've got plenty of ideas on how to spend that time."

The grin turned devilish, but there was something in his eyes that wasn't right, a tension in the corners that concerned me.

Before I could decide whether to inquire about it, he turned away and started us on the drive back to the Luciano estate. To his estate. To... home?

He was silent on the drive out of the city, but that didn't surprise me. I tried to watch his lips, but he had to know it would be difficult for me to keep up any kind of conversation in the intermittent light of streetlamps.

I found myself relaxing as he turned onto the highway, and I must have dozed off because when I opened my eyes, we were no longer on the highway, but on one of the long stretches of road that led to the estate. The lighting was even more intermittent here, just enough that I could make out where the edge of the road turned to grass, whipping by beside me.

I turned my head, but the moment I saw Amadeo, my breath caught in my throat.

"Find. Him," it looked like he said, the movements of his lips exaggerated like he was speaking very slowly and clearly.

He hung up and shoved the phone back into his pocket, his movements brisk. The muscles in his clenched jaw twitched and his gaze moved back and forth between the road in front of him and the rearview mirror.

"Find who?" I managed to force out past the panic that was taking root in my chest.

I don't think he answered.

"Find who, Amadeo? Are you talking about Grayson? Where is he?" Questions tumbled out one on top of the other, as images of the boy's bullet-riddled body flooded my brain.

He shook his head. "Grayson's fine," he said, turning his head just enough that I could see his lips better as he spoke. But he said nothing more.

We were speeding up, flying down the road at twice the speed limit.

"Amadeo, what's—"

The impact came out of nowhere.

Hard.

Fast.

It was as if time itself had shattered, and the world was a jumble of jagged edges and broken shards.

My body strained against the seat belt, held in a painful limbo between movement and restraint.

A symphony of pain erupted as my muscles tensed, the force of the collision coursing through every fiber of my being. I was weightless and weighty all at once, suspended in a space where a split second felt like an eternity.

And then the airbag erupted like a brutal awakening. A relentless explosion of white-hot force, it slammed into me with an unforgiving violence. The impact drove me back against the seat, and my head collided with a merciless hardness.

Stars burst in my vision, a kaleidoscope of agony and confusion.

And then my world went black.

Chapter Thirty-Six

Heidi

My ears were ringing.

The sound brought me up from the darkness, louder and louder. It was a sound I had not heard in a very long time. A sound that should have been accompanied by a horrid pain in my ears, but here, there was no pain, no body. Just sound.

I floated in it, like the sound itself was carrying me. Higher and higher.

The pain came next, not in my ears but at the back of my head. A throbbing that traveled down my body to my stomach where the sensation twisted and turned into nausea.

The ringing.

The throbbing.

The roiling.

I gasped and tried to reach for my head to somehow quell the sensations, but my hands wouldn't budge.

Paralyzed.

The word chilled me to the bone and sent my lungs racing for air.

I tried again, and this time I felt the hardness that encircled my wrists, trapping them, keeping my hands from doing what I demanded of them.

I nearly sighed in relief until it dawned on me what was trapping them.

Shackles.

I was lying on my side on something hard and rough with my hands shackled to something behind my back. The arm beneath me was nearly numb, sending prickles all the way from my fingers to my shoulder.

It took far more effort to force my eyelids open than it should have. They felt weighted, and every second it took made the throbbing and ringing worse.

When I'd managed to drag them open, the world around me appeared out of focus, so I blinked, then blinked again.

Concrete. There was a concrete wall inches in front of my face, the rough texture and the cracks that ran through it clear as day now.

My heart beat harder. It took no time to make sense of the wall, the shackles, the throbbing. And though I had no name, no face to put to the culprit, I hadn't a doubt in my mind why I was here. They had a "problem"—the hidden money—and they intended to fix it.

But what had they done with Amadeo?

I lifted my head up, searching, but there was only a concrete wall in front of me. I tugged on my shackles. They were tight around my wrists, but whatever they were secured to, there was some give to it.

Like a turtle on its back, I rocked my body, but it slammed into something behind me, a post or a pole. So I clenched my abdominal muscles tighter and forced my upper body upright.

I could sit, it turned out, and I could maneuver around on my backside to the other side of the pole so that I faced the opposite side of the room. A very small room.

There were no more than eight or nine feet between myself and the opposite wall. Between myself and the man who was shackled to the pole in front of it, out cold on his side.

Amadeo.

His eyes were closed, but even in sleep, there was a furrow between his brows. There was also a nasty looking bump above his ear, just behind his temple. It would have been nearly hidden in his hair if it weren't encrusted with blood and slicked to his head.

My pounding heart beat even harder, so hard, I could feel it banging against my ribs. He could have skull fractures, a temporal hematoma, intracranial hemorrhage, even a cerebral contusion.

There was nothing I could do about it. I couldn't reach him. I had nothing with which to treat him.

"Amadeo!" I tried to whisper-shout. If our abductors were nearby, I had no desire to alert them to my state of consciousness.

He didn't move.

I stared at his chest, watching for proof that he was still breathing. Doubts tried to crowd in, but they were not difficult to beat back. Because he couldn't be dead. Whether this was my world, his world, or any world at all, there was no world in which Amadeo Luciano did not exist.

His chest moved up and down, strong and steady.

He's alive. I'm alive. It was like a heartbeat. And so long as there was a heartbeat, it wasn't over. And it was up to me at the moment to figure a way out of this.

"Assess," I said aloud, or perhaps, I mouthed the word. It was the first step of any triage situation, and focusing on the logical was all that was keeping me from coming out my skin.

So, I surveyed the room, and despite seventeen years in a very quiet world, I held my breath and strained my ears. Of course, I heard nothing. Nothing but the ringing that continued. *Tinnitus*, the perception of sound even in the absence of external auditory stimuli. It was a common side effect of a concussion.

There was not much more to glean from a visual inspection. A narrow, concrete-walled room, perhaps nine feet across and twenty feet long. The two posts were all that occupied the floorspace aside from a steep set of wood stairs that led up, but from my position, I could not see what was at the top of them. A door, presumably. There were no windows in the room, so that door—which might or might not exist—was the only means of escape.

I tugged on the shackles. At first, it was meant as a cursory tug, just to confirm that I was indeed trapped. But after the first tug, I tugged again. And again. And again. Once I'd started, I couldn't stop.

I maneuvered up onto my knees and leaned forward, pulling with all my might.

My wrists and shoulder joints screamed, but I kept pulling. Tugging. This was the only way out; there was no escape from this room unless I escaped these shackles.

My wrists grew slick. Blood. I'd drawn blood, but I couldn't stop.

My lungs were gasping for breath and my pulse thudded in my ears. My shoulders screamed; I was on the verge of dislocating them.

"Heidi!" Amadeo shouted.

I froze.

He was awake. Awake and sitting up with his arms trapped behind his back. He was leaning against the post with his legs drawn up loosely in front of him.

"Thought I'd lost you there for a minute, *perla*," he said, and the corners of his lips turned up in a gentle smile.

It was utterly absurd that he was smiling, and yet, the gesture slipped inside me and helped to slow my racing pulse.

"What are they going to do, Amadeo?" I asked, not certain I was prepared for the answer. But if anyone knew what was to come, it was him, was it not?

"I don't know, *perla*," he said, but there was something guarded in his eyes.

"They want the money, right?" The money was the problem, and I was the solution. All they had to do was crack me wide open, and the money would come pouring out. Or it would, if I had the slightest clue where it was hidden.

"*Sì,*" he said and then his gaze met mine.

He held it, silent, but a crack appeared in his stone-like mask. Just for one moment, one crack, one narrow fissure, and then it was gone. But I swear what I'd seen was jet black and ice cold. It was fury unlike anything I'd ever imagined.

It told me everything they were going to do to me, everything neither one of us would be able to prevent.

Bound.

Trapped.

Shackled.

I'd just taken the place of the man from Amadeo's basement, and that knowledge made me tremble so hard, my teeth clacked together.

"I don't know where it is, Amadeo. I don't. I—"

"Listen to me, Heidi," he cut in. "You're going to be okay. Do you understand me?"

I nodded, but the choppy movement flung loose tears that had gathered in my eyes.

"I do a lot of bad things, *perla,* but tell me, have I ever lied to you?"

"No." I breathed in a ragged breath and let it out. "You haven't."

"I'm not lying to you now," he said, meeting my eyes once again. There were no cracks this time, nothing to reveal what was going on beneath the surface.

I wanted to believe him, but how on earth could he be so certain?

"Tell me something I don't know about you," he said as he shifted like he was searching for a more comfortable position.

I just stared at him, for surely, I hadn't read that right.

"You saw what I said. I want you to tell me something you haven't told me." Though I couldn't hear it, I could feel the command in his tone.

I tried to think past the terror, past the trembling and the racing heartbeat.

"My only friend when I was a teenager was a man in his sixties," I blurted out the first thing that came to mind.

He cocked an eyebrow at me, expecting me to continue.

"He was a cantankerous, old Brit who lived next door to the last foster family I had." I shook my head wistfully, remembering the old man with a full head of white hair, more wrinkles than a well-read map, and a different cardigan for every day of the week.

Of course. "That's who Aurelio reminds me of," I said, shaking my head. It was no wonder he'd moved so easily past my defenses.

"I'd gotten locked out of the house after school one day," I went on. "I don't remember the reason. It was raining, and the house had no overhang. Trumble was on his front porch—Mr. Algernon Mortimer Bertram Trumble. He once told me his parents must have hated him from the day he was born to give him such a horrific name."

"It is a mouthful," Amadeo said with a wry smile.

I nodded. It really was. "Trumble waved me over, but I remember I just blinked because I didn't think he'd ever acknowledged anyone. And then he yelled, *'Quit dawdling, you numskull, and haul your sorry self out of the blasted rain'.*"

"Pleasant fellow." Amadeo shook his head, but he looked amused.

I shrugged. "I 'hauled my sorry self out of the blasted rain' and sat with him on his porch until Tracy—my foster mum—got home. And after that, he waved me over every day after school until I just started coming on my own. He told me stories of his childhood and helped me with my homework. I tidied the house and made dinner for him on days his 'blasted joints' ached too much to do it himself."

I smiled, but it was fleeting, as was our friendship.

"He died," I said as my heart clenched painfully. "It was at the beginning of my final year of high school—I was set to graduate two years early—and Trumble and I had been talking about my college admissions. I hadn't quite settled my mind on which career I intended to pursue."

I shrugged again, but this time, my shoulders felt heavier.

"He had a heart attack. I didn't know CPR; I barely had the presence of mind to call for an ambulance. And then I sat there next to him. I just... sat there, willing him to breathe. But he didn't, not ever again."

"And that's why you decided to go into medicine," Amadeo said. There was no question in his expression, but still, I nodded. I'd vowed never to just sit there again.

"So, now you know two things about me," I said, letting out a shaky breath. "I believe it's your turn."

He looked at me like he was weighing something in his mind, then nodded. "I'm morbidly afraid of heights," he confessed, but surely, he was joking.

"I can't imagine you afraid of anything."

He shrugged. "I won't let fear or anything else stop me from doing what needs to be done, but I sure as hell prefer doing it with my feet on the fucking ground."

I laughed. Bloody hell, he'd made me laugh. Shackled and awaiting torture in a concrete prison, and he made me laugh.

"Thank you," I whispered, for I had no doubt why he was doing this.

I made the mistake of looking around, and I swear I could feel the walls moving closer, the ceiling sinking lower. There was no water here; we could die of dehydration in a matter of days. But I had a feeling we would not be so fortunate, nor would our wait be that lengthy.

"How can you be so sure we'll be okay, Amadeo?" I asked, fully aware of the tremble in my voice.

"Because I won't let anything happen to you, *perla.*" The lines of his jaw were fierce, but the conviction didn't quite reach his eyes.

"Do you know who they are?" I asked, feeling no need to explain to whom I was referring.

He was silent for a long moment, then nodded. "The name's Sinclair. The family owns several corporations in London, but there's more to them."

I licked my lips that had gone dry. There was no missing the meaning of what he'd meant by 'more'.

"I don't know where it is, Amadeo," I said, though it couldn't have come out as more than a whisper. My voice felt strangled, like something had wrapped tightly around my throat.

"I know, *perla,*" he replied. The fainter movements of his lips meant he was whispering too.

His gaze shot to my left, toward the stairs that led to a door that might or might not have been there, and he shot to his feet, his hands still cuffed behind his back and secured to the post by a length of chain.

My body shook. My teeth clacked together.

I had a feeling there was a door.

And that door had just been opened.

Chapter Thirty-Seven

Heidi

There were feet on the stairs. Feet dressed in shiny, black oxford shoes. Then legs, covered with perfectly tailored black trousers.

A matching suit jacket. Jet black cufflinks. A black tie that nearly blended with the shirt beneath.

And then a face.

The moment I saw it, my breath escaped my lungs like I'd been punched.

The face smiled at me as he stepped down onto the concrete floor.

And the spider legs on his cheek wriggled.

I couldn't breathe. He'd sucked all the oxygen out of the room, and no matter how hard I tried, my lungs couldn't get enough. They chased the air over and over again but came up empty.

The spider-man came toward me. I don't think he even spared a glance at Amadeo. It was like he wore blinders, and I was the only thing in his sights. I could envision the gun he'd held that night, the way he'd smiled at me then.

And just like that night, terror flowed through my veins as he took another step, and then another.

My knees wobbled. I'd climbed to my feet. When that had happened, I couldn't be sure, but the urge to slink back down to the ground was potent.

To cower, to escape, to put as much distance between the spider-man and myself as possible.

Across from me, Amadeo was eerily still. Nothing but his lips were moving.

"Don't you touch her," he seethed in a tone that I imagined was eerily calm. So calm, so cold, it sent shivers down my spine.

The spider-man laughed, unperturbed, and kept coming.

"I've done many unsavory things, mate," he said, half-turning to look at Amadeo, "but touching my own niece?"

My insides turned cold. Not shivers. Ice cold.

But it couldn't be true. This man had killed my parents. His own flesh and blood?

The spider-man shrugged. "I suppose we all have our limits."

Limits? What limits? He'd murdered my parents right in front of me.

"But Jasper here," he continued as he motioned toward the staircase, to the feet, the legs, the torso of another man descending them. "He has no such blood affiliation, nor do I think he'd be bothered if he did."

The man stepped off the stairs. A man with a shaved head, his scalp covered in black tattoos. His eyes were nearly as black as his tattoos, and when he smiled at me, I could see his black soul.

I gripped the post behind me as the spider-man stopped moving and the man with the black soul kept coming. Closer and closer until he stood right in front of me, so close, I could read some of the words of the tattoos.

"And fear not them which kill the body, but are not able to kill the soul: but rather fear him which is able to destroy both soul and body in hell. Matthew 10:28," read the tattoo across his right temple.

"And I looked, and behold a pale horse: and his name that sat on him was Death. Revelations 6:8," was written just beneath the first.

Bloody scriptures. What kind of psychopath tattooed biblical scriptures about death and murder on his head? There were more of them, on his neck and even on the backs of his hands, all of them verses about murder and death.

He took one more step, and I could feel his hot breath against my cheeks. He reached up and ran one finger down my tear-streaked face, and though his finger was warm, his touch felt cold. When I jerked away, he grabbed my chin with his other hand, and his fingers bit into my skin, holding tight.

He turned my head toward the spider-man.

"Where's the money, Heidi dear?" he asked, enunciating like I was a toddler, making the spider legs wriggle with every movement.

"How the bloody hell would I know?" I asked, tilting my chin up as much as the grip on it would allow and feigning a courage I most certainly did not possess.

"I suggest you think very hard... unless you want Jasper to help jog your memory."

Jasper-the-psycho smiled as he released my chin and withdrew a small knife from his jacket pocket. He flicked it open with a skill that did nothing to bolster my courage.

I tried to circle the post to escape, but his free hand shot out and grabbed me by the neck. His fingers dug in on either side of my throat, holding me still without compressing my trachea.

The hand with the knife moved. I could see the glint of the steel, and every muscle in my body tensed, waiting for the fiery stab of the blade.

Instead, he slipped the knife beneath the top button of my shirt, dug in, and flicked, nicking my skin as the button popped off.

The nick burned, like I'd doused a cut in alcohol. I bit down on my lip, fighting the urge to cry out.

He moved lower, slipping the blade beneath the next button. When he sliced the thread, he nicked my flesh deeper, and a warm trickle ran down into the fabric of my bra beneath my breasts.

He smiled when I cried out, and in that smile, I could see everything he intended to do to me. My death wasn't to be quick. It would be slow and painful, rife with every agony and defilement a man could inflict.

My heart pounded like a drum. I could feel the blood whooshing past my ears. Every ounce of courage I'd try to muster threatened to flee.

"Heidi!" Amadeo shouted so loud it reached my ears clear.

I looked at him, and I couldn't say whether it was a comfort or not to see the cold stone expression he wore.

"Just look at me," he said when he had my attention. "It's going to be all right, *perla.*"

Jasper dug the knife into my flesh and popped off another button. This time, he paused to drag the tip of the knife down the opening he'd made.

I screamed as my blood welled up and ran down, and though the doctor in me recognized it was by no means a fatal wound, the fiery sting was a terrible foreshadowing of what was to come.

My breath was coming so hard and so fast, every movement dug the tip of the knife in deeper.

Amadeo's lips kept moving, but my vision was blurred by tears. I couldn't make out what he was saying.

Focus on what you need to do, Heidi-girl, my father's voice whispered inside my head.

What I needed was to stop the tears so I could see. And with a task in mind, I latched onto it, breathing slow, forcing what was happening into a box and closing the lid.

Another breath, and then another.

"Tell him where it is, *perla,*" Amadeo was saying.

But I didn't *know* where; he knew this. So why would he have—

Oh.

I looked at Amadeo for another moment, and now I could see it; I could see his eyes willing me to understand what he was saying. But what he was saying was an extraordinary gamble. At best, it would stall for time, nothing more. I could only trust that he knew what he was doing.

"I'll tell you what you want to know," I told the spider-man even as Jasper slipped the knife beneath the next button.

He held up his hand, staying Jasper's movements, and then he smiled at me, the spider legs of his scar writhing and making me feel like they were crawling up my spine.

"Go on, dear," he said. There was a light in his eyes like he was salivating, a predator about to sink his teeth into the most delicious prey.

"In the house where you… where you killed my parents, there was a room in the basement," I lied.

He shook his head. "I searched every room in that house, Heidi. Don't lie to me."

He nodded to Jasper, who flicked away the button on my shirt.

"I'm not lying," I cried.

He raised his eyebrows at me, but he held up his hand, staying Jasper's movements once again.

"I hope for your sake, you're not," he said. There was no smile this time.

I took a deep breath. "In the laundry room in the basement," I went on, "there's a false wall behind where the washer was—just like at the Regalton Arms. It looks like the rest of the concrete block wall, but this section is hollow. It's light. My father showed it to me a few…" The rest of the words got stuck in my throat, and I had to force them out. "…a few weeks before you killed him. He said that if he ever told me to hide, it was the perfect place."

I blinked, and tears cascaded down my cheeks. "I thought he meant when we played hide-and-seek."

The spider-man laughed. "He never quite got the chance to tell you to hide that night, did he?"

It was like there was a switch inside me, and with a few words, he'd hit it, slammed his hand right down on it. In the blink of an eye, terror gave way to rage as he stood there laughing over the death of my parents like it was a joke.

If I could have gotten free in that moment, I wouldn't have run—not away, at least. I would have run straight for him. I'd never been a violent person. The images that flooded my mind, the things I would have done to him had I been able, would have appalled the woman I'd been just a few short weeks ago.

I glanced at Amadeo, wondering if this is what he'd felt. Was this the white-hot feeling that had coursed through his veins when Elio had hurt his sister?

He shook his head. It was a warning. *Don't let it out,* the gesture screamed.

But this feeling was too raw and too exposed to leave it alone.

"Why the bloody hell did you kill them?" I shouted, glaring at the spider-man.

He looked at me, eyes appraising like he was deciding whether he wanted to tell me or kill me.

"Your father was an obstacle," he said after a long moment.

"An obstacle?"

He shrugged. "He was the eldest of the Sinclair brothers. There were four of us; now there are two."

Sinclair? It's the name Amadeo had used, but thinking about it now, I'd seen that name with my own eyes. It had been on the business card from the man in the cemetery. Nathaniel Sinclair.

"And if you're hoping your men will come running to your rescue," he said, turning his attention to Amadeo, "I'm afraid it's rather unlikely. Your phone is on its way to Nathaniel as we speak. My brother will be very surprised when your men follow it there. Surprised… and very dead." He chuckled. "And then there will only be me."

"That was the move all along, wasn't it?" Amadeo asked him. "You tried to use the Lucianos to take down your last remaining obstacle."

The spider-man grinned from ear to ear, but the smile faltered when Amadeo smiled right back, a smile that I could only describe as malevolence incarnate.

I swear I saw the faintest hint of a shiver as the spider-man's Adam's apple bobbed.

"Why are you smiling?" he asked Amadeo.

"I'm just thinking how much I'm going to enjoy cutting you up into pieces. One big jigsaw puzzle," he said, the words leaving his lips slowly and surely. He wasn't yelling at the man; he wasn't taunting him with false threats. He meant every word.

The spider-man scoffed. "I hardly see that happening when you're there,"—he said, nodding to Amadeo's position, cuffed to the post—"and I'm here."

Amadeo's malevolent smile didn't waver. "I guess it will come as a surprise then."

The spider-man stared at him for a moment with no expression on his face, then turned to me.

"Jasper's going to make a short trip to your old family home, back to the place where it all started."

He nodded to Jasper who then flicked the knife closed right in front of my face and dropped it back into his pocket.

He stared at me with his black, soulless eyes for what felt like an endless moment before he turned away and headed for the stairs.

"Heidi," the spider-man said when the man was halfway up. "You'd better not be lying, dear. Jasper doesn't care much for liars."

Bloody hell, I was so screwed.

Chapter Thirty-Eight

Heidi

Jasper was gone, at least for now. I fought the urge to sink down onto the cold, concrete floor while I heaved in great gasps of breath.

I was breathing too fast—I was going to hyperventilate—but I couldn't seem to stop. There wasn't enough air getting in, no matter how deep, how fast I tried to draw it in.

"Heidi!" Amadeo yelled.

My head shot up.

"Breathe with me, *perla,*" he instructed. "In and out," he said as my gaze was divided between his lips and the rise and fall of his chest. "In and out."

I nodded and tried to follow suit, watching the movements of his chest and forcing my lungs to mimic them. It could have been seconds or minutes, but eventually, I could breathe again.

All the while, I could feel the spider-man's gaze on me. When I looked up at him, he was watching me with amusement in his dark eyes. My discomfiture amused him, like I was a caged animal in a zoo.

He came toward me and didn't stop until he was directly in front of me.

"It's such a shame you're family," he said, grazing a finger down my cheek.

"Since when did you give a damn about family?" I hissed.

Foolish perhaps, but despite the fierce and unrelenting fear that was twisting my insides, the rage, raw and visceral, was still there. It was not just emotional; it was deeply biological, the hypothalamus orchestrating a symphony of stress hormones, flooding my bloodstream with cortisol while my prefrontal cortex struggled to maintain its grip.

His finger paused against the edge of my jaw, and his other fingers joined it there, gripping tight, forcing my head up higher.

"Perhaps, you're right," he said while his eyes grazed over me, making my skin writhe like there were insects beneath it.

I caught sight of Amadeo out of the corner of my eye. He was nodding at me, as if encouragingly.

"Scream," he said. I think he was mouthing the word by the slightly odd movement of his facial muscles.

That I could do.

I opened my mouth and let out a short burst of the terror that was lodged in my chest. It actually felt good to make noise I could hear, something other than the chilling silence.

The spider-man's eyes widened, and his grip on my jaw tightened painfully.

"You want me to gag you, do you?" he said as he dropped his hand. He was about to turn away, to go in search of a gag, no doubt, but I couldn't let that happen. Not now.

Because Amadeo was moving.

He no longer stood trapped against the post across the room. He was coming toward us, moving slow and carefully. If the spider-man turned around now, he'd see him.

Amadeo would lose the element of surprise.

So, I did the first thing that came to mind and brought my knee up hard and fast, slamming it into his groin.

He cried out as he doubled over, stumbling back, but he only made it one step before Amadeo was there.

He moved like lightning, so fast his hands were a blur as he wrapped them around the spider-man's neck from behind.

The man struggled, shoving his elbows back into Amadeo's ribs, but whether by accident or intent, Amadeo was compressing the man's carotid arteries, and it wasn't ten seconds before his eyes rolled back in his head and he slumped, unconscious, in Amadeo's grasp.

Rather than releasing him, Amadeo dragged the man across the room, dropped him to the floor, and shackled him to the same post where Amadeo had been trapped just a moment ago.

"You did good, *perla*," he said as he stood up.

All signs of the malevolent smile from earlier were gone, but the look in his eyes was wrong, like something had taken all the light out of them.

Without another word, he crossed the narrow room. He had something in his hand. It looked thin, a bent piece of metal. A bobby pin, perhaps, though it looked twisted out of shape now.

I looked at it, then back at him. "Where on earth did you find that?"

"Never leave home without it," he said when he was right in front of me. "It took time to shape the pin," he said, his jaw clenched tight. "I couldn't carry it twisted into the right shape—it would have been too noticeable."

Without touching me, he circled around me and then he was working on the cuffs. The tiny metal pin scraped against the cuff, sending vibrations through my wrist.

It only took a moment, and then the shackles were gone; my wrists were free.

Free.

I let out a cry of relief, but when I went to throw my arms around Amadeo, that same worrisome look in his eyes brought me up short. It felt like he was holding himself distant. There was a wall between us now, one it felt like he didn't want me to cross, so I wrapped my arms awkwardly around me instead.

His gaze perused me, lingering on my chafed and bloody wrists, then the narrow slice down my chest from the tip of Jasper's knife. His Adam's apple bobbed as he swallowed. He reached out like he intended to take my hands in his, but then he dropped his hands to his sides.

"I'm—" he started, but then closed his mouth and shook his head.

"Time to go," he said instead. He glanced up at the door, but the movement was unhurried. Without looking, I knew there was no one there. For now.

"But there could be—"

"I *will* get you out of here, *perla*," he cut in like I'd called the possibility into question.

"I know," I said, nodding.

How he intended to do it, I hadn't any idea, but if anyone could, it was Amadeo.

His lips quirked in a smile that didn't reach his eyes.

"What?"

He shook his head. "We'll talk about it later," he said. He glanced up toward the door, then back again.

"My men should be here by now, but you're going to stay here until—"

"No," I said, shaking my head for emphasis.

The exasperated look on his face reminded me he wasn't used to being told no.

But while my heart was pounding, and I was terrified of what—or who—we would run into on the other side of that door, I wasn't leaving him.

"I know the help I can offer is limited, but even the most inexperienced nurse or technician can mean the difference between life and death so long as she keeps her wits about her. I *will* keep my head clear, Amadeo."

He eyed me, and I could feel every one of my inadequacies. I wasn't a skilled fighter. I had no training with weapons. My hearing impediment meant my use as a lookout would be limited. But this was what he had to work with. So, he could take it, because leaving it wasn't an option.

"I need you to stay right behind me," he said, acquiescing with far less difficulty than I'd expected.

Perhaps he'd recognized my merits as a human shield, I thought morbidly.

"If I move, you move," he continued. "You keep your eyes on me, *perla;* I need you watching in case I have to tell you to do something."

I nodded.

"And if I give you an order, you do it, *si?*"

I nodded again. I'm not sure what it was he expected.

If he was worried I was going to transform into G.I. Jane and start flouting his directions in favor of my own extensive knowledge of daring escapes, then perhaps, he'd confused me with someone else.

"I mean it, Heidi. Tell me you understand that no matter what I tell you to do, you'll do it."

If it meant getting out of this horrid basement and far away from the spider-man who claimed to be family, I think I would have been willing to two-step, duck-walk, and flap my arms like a bird if that was what he asked me to do.

"I understand," I said, though the moment the words were out, an uncomfortable sensation prickled along the back of my neck.

He took hold of my hand, gripping tight but carefully, his fingers away from my wrist, then led us up the stairs to what looked like a heavy, metal door. He stood there on the top step, his body turned slightly sideways, enough I could see the look of concentration on his face. He was listening while tension rolled off his body in waves.

After a moment, I took hold of his free hand and leaned forward to place his palm against the metal door.

He looked at me, eyes questioning.

"If they're quiet, you might feel the vibrations of movement before you hear it," I whispered, nodding to the door.

He nodded, and even when he motioned for me to drop my hand, he kept his against the door.

Seconds passed.

I could hear them ticking, like the sound of my father's wristwatch. *Ticktock. Ticktock. Ticktock.*

"I need you to scream again, *perla,*" Amadeo said. "Loud and long."

With pleasure.

I let out a scream, sharp and piercing even to my own ears. As the noise escaped, it felt like it was taking some of the pent-up tension inside me with it.

"*Bene,*" he mouthed, then he angled my body more thoroughly behind him and released my hand.

A second passed and then another.

He dropped the hand that had been against the door as it started to open. And then it was a blur.

A man appeared.

Deo moved.

A gun fell to the step right below me.

Amadeo's hands were around the man's neck. He dragged him toward us, onto the top step. With what seemed like a flick of his wrists, the man's neck twisted unnaturally. An instant death. Gone in a fraction of a second. I could envision the dislocation of the cervical vertebrae beneath my fingers.

I'd seen Amadeo kill men; it was the first thing I'd ever seen him do. But this, death brought about by his bare hands, it was different. Intimate and terrifying at the same time.

He lowered the man to the ground and grabbed the gun that had fallen onto the stairs.

"…on me," Amadeo was saying.

I snapped my gaze to him.

"Eyes on me, Heidi," he said, exaggerating the movements of his mouth a little, but I felt it was appropriate to let it slide on this occasion.

I nodded.

"Let's go."

The door had partially closed. Amadeo moved to push it open, but it swung open the rest of the way, seemingly on its own, and the blonde woman—Greta—stood there with a gun in one hand and a smile on her face. Behind her stood a very, very big man, blonde and wearing a leather vest. He had a gun in one hand as well and the other was wrapped around Greta's hip.

"Fancy meeting you here, *amici,*" Greta said, winking at me. But her eyes were perusing Amadeo, then me, and when they settled on the blood down the center of my torso, her eyes narrowed, then flickered up to Amadeo.

He nodded, his jaw clenched tight.

She nodded back in some silent conversation.

"One of them already took off," Amadeo said. "He's headed to the house where Heidi grew up."

"Already taken care of, my friend," the big man in the leather vest said. "Cielo and Dynamite picked him up two minutes ago. They're just getting him gift wrapped for you as we speak." He smiled in a grin that stretched from ear to ear as Greta leaned back against him, and the hand he had on her hip wrapped around her waist.

"My kind of present, *amico. Grazie,*" Amadeo said.

Greta and the big man in leather both smiled.

"We've got the perimeter secured," Greta explained. "Vito took a bullet to the arm, but he says he's fine." Her lips moved lightly and easily, but the worried expression on her face said she wasn't convinced. "Maybe the doc could take a look at it?"

"We'll see," Amadeo said. "I want to get her away from—"

"Of course," I said at the same time.

I met Amadeo's gaze. His amber eyes were filled with a look that was telling me to back down, but he'd forgotten something.

In fighting and killing, this man might have been king. But when it came to bullet wounds, we'd just entered my domain, and here, the Ice Queen reigned supreme.

Chapter Thirty-Nine

Amadeo

"Don't you dare argue with me," Heidi snapped from the back seat of the Lexus LS. She took hold of Vito's arm and went to work inspecting it whether he liked it or not.

She'd already wrangled him into the car—a feat I would have paid good money to see on any other day—and the doctor was taking no shit from her patient.

She prodded at the wound—or whatever the hell it was doctors did—while Aurelio drove.

"I saw that," she said when she caught Vito grumbling under his breath.

Aurelio laughed.

I was still seeing red. Blood. Heidi's blood.

"The bullet nicked the subclavian artery," Heidi said, and the tone of her voice made it clear this was no small matter.

Vito sat there stoically, having been thoroughly chastised by the woman sitting beside him, but there was no denying he was looking a little pale. Blood had saturated through his jacket and shirt sleeve before Heidi had yanked them off, and it was still pouring out at a pretty good pace.

"He needs a hospital," she said, her eyes flitting toward me in the front passenger seat, then back again. She was wrapping the discarded shirt around his arm now, above the wound.

"No hospital, Doc," Vito said, shaking his head adamantly.

She rolled her eyes. "No worries, we'll just leave this tourniquet tied around your arm until you develop your own brand of fashion-forward gangrene," she said. "Or, if you're feeling particularly medieval, we can skip the hospital and fetch a saw. I hear amputation was all the rage back then, but I'm not sure it'd be the highlight of your day."

My heart swelled with pride for this woman. No matter what she went through, there was no quelling her spirit.

Vito was right, though; the hospital wasn't an option.

"You still have the supplies from the hospital, *sì?*" I asked her.

She dug her teeth into her bottom lip and looked at me, but I looked away. I couldn't look at her. I just fucking couldn't.

"Yes," she admitted begrudgingly.

"Do you have what you need to repair the artery?"

She shook her head. "I only have morphine. I have no means of sedating him. He'll be awake."

I looked at Vito, who nodded without hesitation.

"He'll be fine," I said, then pulled out my phone without waiting for her to reply.

"One of the guest suites needs to be transformed into a makeshift surgical suite in the next ten minutes," I told Giovanni when he answered the phone. "Make sure all of Dr. Dawson's supplies are brought there and ready for her."

"Of course, *Signor*," he replied like it was an ordinary request.

"*Grazie*," I said, then hung up the phone and called Raven. I was fairly sure Heidi could use an extra set of qualified hands for whatever it was she was going to do.

I glanced over at the side mirror. Greta and Brute were on bikes right behind us, and Bruno and Carmine were in the car behind them, with the asshole from the basement—Dorian Sinclair—trussed up like a turkey in the trunk.

I clenched my hands into fists, then stretched out my fingers, staring at them consideringly. I'd brought about countless deaths with these hands, but I couldn't say I'd ever particularly enjoyed it. Torture and murder, they'd always been necessary evils. A means to an end. But what I was about to do to Dorian Sinclair and the asshole who'd cut Heidi had nothing to do with necessary evils.

And I was sure as hell going to enjoy every fucking second of it.

By the time Aurelio turned into the driveway of the estate, there was so much adrenaline coursing through my veins, it was a wonder it wasn't boiling out of my pores. I watched as Bruno and Carmine drove past Greta and Brute, circling around the house to take Sinclair in through the side entrance and straight to the basement.

It took every ounce of restraint I could muster to help Heidi get a slightly woozy Vito into the house. Once inside, Giovanni took over, hooking Vito's good arm over his shoulder and leading him up the stairs while Heidi followed behind them.

At the top of the stairs, she turned back, looking right at me with troubled eyes. Like a fucking coward, I looked away. It was too soon. Maybe it would always be too soon.

I headed for the parlor where Greta had already poured out three fingers of whiskey for me. Brute stood next to her, eyeing me just as warily as Greta was.

"Are you all right, Deo?" she asked while I tipped the drink back.

When it was empty, I stared at the glass, contemplating a refill.

"No," I said, both to Greta and to the refill. I wanted my head clear for what was coming.

"She's fine," Greta said, seeing right through to what was eating at me.

"We both know it could have just as easily gone the other way," I said, and she knew it was the damn truth.

If Sinclair had found the pin I kept hidden against the seam of my pocket.

If Heidi hadn't been able to bullshit him.

If he'd given that asshole Jasper free rein with her.

I shook my head and squeezed my eyes shut, trying to banish the images that had been rolling in ever since I woke up in that basement.

"You got her out of there before shit went bad, my friend," Brute said, smiling sympathetically.

I had to admit, he knew firsthand what it was like to know bad shit could happen to the woman he cared about, but he'd never had to stand there, tied to a fucking post, forced to watch it happen.

I slammed the glass down on the coffee table. There wasn't fuck all I could do about that now. But what I could do was make sure Dorian Sinclair and the asshole with the knife paid for their sins.

And when it came to meting out punishment, the devil had nothing on me.

***

The basement was cold.

We kept it that way deliberately. It was a natural way to slow blood loss, to draw out a man's torture a little longer.

Goosebumps raised across my arms as I entered the room where Aurelio and I had done some of our best work.

He was standing in the room now with Cielo nearby. In front of them, Dorian Sinclair and the man named Jasper had been secured to chairs, their wrists and ankles cuffed, their hands and feet duct taped to the chairs.

"Dynamite thought you'd appreciate the wrapping," Cielo said, nodding to Jasper who had an actual bow wrapped around his shaved head, covering most of the inked scriptures. I'd have to remember to thank him.

"Leave, *per favore*," I said to Aurelio and Cielo without looking at them. This was between me and the assholes in the chairs. Their blood, their pain, belonged to me and no one else.

I could feel my brother and one of the men I trusted most both eyeing me, but I wasn't in the mood to explain myself and Greta had already tried to talk me down. It wasn't happening.

"Leave," I said when neither of them had moved.

I saw Aurelio nod out the corner of my eye, and Cielo clapped me on the shoulder.

"Just holler if you need us, *fratellone*."

I nodded, then stood there as they left the room and closed the door behind them. I walked over to the door and locked it, not taking any chance of Heidi walking in this time.

And then it was just me and the men who'd put their hands on her, the men who'd shackled her to a post in a fucking basement. Who'd touched her, cut her. And there hadn't been a goddamned thing I could do to stop them.

I had no doubt about what that fucker, Jasper, would have done to her. I'd felt the combination of bloodlust and pure, blatant lust in the air, just like I'd felt not so long ago in *El víbora's* compound when I'd been there to help take that asshole down.

And while I hadn't been able to stop Sinclair and Jasper in that basement, there was plenty I could do to them now.

I looked at the gift-wrapped man. He was glaring at me, but the gag in his mouth kept him from hurtling the insults I could see written plain as day across his face.

I yanked out the gag and ignored him while I looked down at his hands. He'd touched Heidi with them, used them to hurt her. I don't think I'd ever forget what it felt like to watch the asshole drag that knife down her flesh. It was worse than any agony I'd ever felt, like the man had been cutting me, not her, and not just my flesh but straight into my goddamned soul.

"You made a very big mistake tonight," I said to both of them, my voice cold, devoid of emotion. "If you'd come after me, perhaps I would have granted you a quick death." I shook my head, letting them know the end for them would not be swift.

Aurelio had laid out a dozen tools on his table.

I picked up the sharpest knife, one that didn't look so different from the knife Jasper had used on Heidi.

With that horrid image fresh in my mind, I sliced. One finger after another; they all needed to go.

Jasper screamed as his blood sprayed, warm and slick against my skin, but he'd only made it through the third finger when his eyes rolled back in his head and he passed out.

No worries. I finished the job and cauterized each stump to keep the man from bleeding out. The room filled with the scent of charred skin and burnt flesh.

While I waited for Jasper to regain consciousness, I pulled the gag from Dorian Sinclair's mouth.

"You thought if you killed Heidi's father—your brother—you'd be next in line to inherit the Sinclair fortune, didn't you?" I asked him. "You'd be number one, *sì*?"

When Cielo had come to me with information he thought I needed to see, it was little more than the Sinclair's family tree, but it had spoken volumes.

"You care about the girl, don't you?" Dorian asked, ignoring my question. "Without me, you never would have known her, you know? And she wouldn't have known about the blood that courses through her veins. Sinclair blood."

I scoffed. "You think she cares about your family's money?"

He laughed. "Sinclair blood isn't just rich, it's powerful. It's been powerful since good ol' Queen Vic. Blood that is more powerful than yours will ever be. And blood that our enemies will be after now that the secret's out. You won't be able to protect her, mate. At least I would have made it quick."

"If you're trying to goad me into killing you quickly, don't bother," I said at the same time Jasper started to moan and come around.

As soon as his eyes were open, I leaned in, knife still in hand. The guy was wearing a Henley; there were no buttons to slice through. So, I dug the knife into the neckline of the shirt, right at the same spot he'd dug his knife into Heidi.

I dragged the knife down, cutting through layers of flesh until I reached his navel and his flesh gaped open.

His whole body convulsed as he begged and screamed.

If he was hoping to find mercy here, there was none.

I closed my eyes, and though the screams echoing off the walls were giving me a headache, I drank them in, trying to assuage the feeling inside that had started the moment I'd woken up and seen Heidi cuffed to that fucking post.

But no matter how loud or how long I made them scream, the feeling never left.

It stayed with me through every slice and stab. No matter what I cut or severed, it refused to leave. Even when Jasper was long dead, and Dorian Sinclair's screams had turned to lifeless whimpers, it stayed with me.

I dropped the hammer I'd used to break Sinclair's jaw and stepped back. I was covered in so much blood, it dripped from my clothes and I could feel it becoming tacky as it started to dry in my hair.

The feeling remained as I unlocked the door and left the room. Adrenaline still surged through my veins as I climbed the stairs.

"Holy shit," Greta gasped when she saw me as I reached the top. It took a lot to startle Greta Agossi. I imagined I looked like something straight out of a horror movie at the moment—not that I gave a damn.

She was standing in the front parlor. Brute was still there next to her. Cielo and Aurelio had joined them.

"Remind me not to get on your bad side," Brute joked, but he was nodding. I think it was in approval.

"Dr. Dawson is still upstairs, *Signor*," Aurelio informed me. "She and Raven finished with Vito, and last I saw, she went to check on her young patient."

"*Grazie,* Aurelio," I said, though I stayed put, making no move to go seek her out.

Greta sighed and took a step toward me. "Look, I get it, Deo. Feeling helpless fucking sucks, and when it's the person you love that you can't help, that sucks a thousand times more. But you got her out of there with no lasting damage done. We've both seen the kind of damage men like those assholes can do. You got her out of there, Deo. Take the goddamned win, shower that shit off," she said, waving her hand up and down me, "Then kiss and make up with that woman, or I'm going to go kiss and make up for you."

She shrugged when I cocked an eyebrow at her.

"The doc's hot as hell," she said. "And I'm pretty sure Brute wouldn't have any problem with it." She glanced over at Brute as if for confirmation.

It was his turn to shrug. "If you feel the need to engage in a little girl-on-girl action, darling, be my guest."

She looked back to me. "So, what's it going to be, *amico*? It sounds like one of us is going to show her a good time tonight. Up to you which of us it's going to be."

Chapter Forty

Heidi

Just breathe, I told myself for the umpteenth time.

I'd treated dire injuries, saved lives, even stood toe to toe with killers. What came next was nothing in comparison.

I'd nearly had myself convinced too, until Amadeo's bedroom door opened and he walked in. He was covered in blood, so much that his shirt stuck to his torso, molding to his chest. His blond hair was slick and red, and blood was smeared on his face. And his hands... there was no flesh. Only blood.

He looked at me—but not into my eyes—and he didn't speak a word. He looked and then he looked away, and then he crossed the room and disappeared into the en suite without a word, shutting the door hard enough behind him that I heard the slam.

Well, that was enough of that.

I stood up from where I sat perched on the edge of his bed and followed the path he'd taken, following the bloody footprints he'd left across the rug.

The en suite door wasn't locked; the handle turned easily beneath my hand. And thank heaven for that. I hadn't the skill to pick the lock, nor was I entirely certain of the strength it would require to break down the door.

Inside, he had his back to me as he adjusted the shower faucet, and though I hadn't any doubt he'd heard me come in, he did nothing to acknowledge my presence.

"Turn around," I said, quite pleased with the Ice Queen I could feel alive and cold in my veins.

He turned slowly, still dripping with blood. In the confines of the en suite, the metallic scent was overwhelming. He stood up straighter, then stood still like he was allowing me to look my fill, to take in the man who was more blood than man at the moment.

"I don't know what it is you're trying to do," I said, "but it won't work."

He cocked one eyebrow like he highly doubted it.

Well, this was it. I was either right, and my world wouldn't crumble tonight. Or I was wrong, and it would.

"I couldn't understand what you were feeling tonight, why it seemed you'd built up this wall between us. But then I thought about what it feels like to lose a patient, that helplessness, that bitter guilt that eats at my insides no matter how hard I worked to save them."

I paused, hoping the cold stone expression he wore would miraculously fall away and prove me right.

But it remained firmly in place.

"You saved my life tonight, Amadeo. You didn't lose me; you saved me. I'm sorry you were forced to feel that helplessness, but whatever this is between us, I believe it is stronger than that feeling, is it not?"

He didn't speak. His chest rose and fell a little harder than usual, but nothing about his countenance gave him away. And then a crack formed, just a single crack like before, and I caught a glimpse of the hurt and anger that lay beneath.

"It's love, *perla*. That's what I feel; that's what this is between us. And it scares the hell out of me because what I felt tonight was the worst fucking thing I'd ever experienced in my life. I don't know if I could survive it if it happened again."

I shook my head. "You don't let fear or anything else stop you, remember?"

His lips twitched in a ghost of a smile.

"I never intended for this to happen," he said. He wasn't talking about what had taken tonight but about us, about what had developed between us in such a short amount of time. "I never wanted it. I still don't."

I shrugged and then took a step toward him. "Neither do I," I admitted. "The only people I've ever loved, I lost; they all died right in front of me, Amadeo. And the life you live…" I shook my head as emotion tried to well up in the back of my throat. "…I don't know if I could survive it if it happened again," I reiterated his words back to him.

But here was the kicker, here was what perhaps made me the most foolish woman in the world: "But I'm willing to risk it, Amadeo."

I closed the remaining distance between us and placed my palms against his cheeks, grazing downward, through the blood, through the scuff of his five-o-clock shadow. Down his neck to the buttons of his blood-soaked shirt. As I unfastened them, blood coated my fingers. I had no doubt it was the spider-man's blood. The blood of the man who'd claimed to be my uncle. The blood Amadeo had spilled in retribution.

When I'd finished with the buttons, he didn't stop me from slipping the shirt off his shoulders, but he took hold of my hands then, pulling them up between us where he glanced at the bandages I'd put on after taking care of Vito's wound.

He took hold of the edge of one bandage and carefully unraveled it, then the other. The shackles had cut deep, slicing through layers of skin when I'd tried to yank them off. I'd treated them with a lidocaine and antibiotic ointment, so when he brought them to his lips and kissed the ugly, raw wounds, I felt nothing more than a light tingling from the contact.

He raised my hands above my head when he was done, then took hold of the hem of my shirt. I cringed a little as he lifted it over my head—not in pain, but because the wound wasn't a pretty sight. I'd closed it with surgical glue, and covered it with a waterproof, transparent dressing, but it ran from just below the hollow of my throat to the bottom of my sternum, just beneath my breasts.

He dropped my shirt on the floor, then raised a hand like he was going to trace the wound between my breasts but then stopped, following it with his gaze instead. He swallowed hard, and I could see the pain in his eyes.

"You should see the other guy," I tried to joke, though I also tried very hard not to envision what that "other guy" might look like now.

"He's dead, *perla*," he said, finally settling his hand on my bare breast, directly over my heart.

"I know."

There'd been no doubt in my mind what Amadeo would do to him, and I'd grappled with my own feelings about it, or more accurately, I'd grappled with the realization I had no feelings about it. No guilt, no sorrow for the loss of a human life.

"Sinclair wasn't lying," he went on. "He was your father's brother, and I killed him too, Heidi. I killed a man whose blood runs in your veins."

"I know," I replied again. I'd already made peace with it. To say that murder was wrong was too black and white for a world I'd come to discover was filled with more shades of gray than I'd ever imagined possible. "I don't know if I could have done what you did," I admitted, "but that man has haunted my dreams since I was nine years old. I'm not sad that he's gone, Amadeo. I'm… grateful."

He sighed and lowered his forehead to mine. "I'd rip a thousand men apart with my bare hands for you, *perla*," he said, leaning away just enough I could see his lips move.

He meant it. It should have revolted me; a few weeks ago, it probably would have. But now, my heart swelled and filled with so much warmth, I could feel it in every fiber of my being.

Love was a chemical reaction—that's what I'd always told myself. The complex interactions of various neurochemicals and hormones in the brain and body, and nothing more.

But this was *more*. So much more.

"But that's not all I would do for you," he said, and this time, he leaned fully away and put his hands on my shoulders. "I'd let you walk away, *perla*," he said, conviction etched across his features even as his hands gripped my shoulders tighter like his body was railing against that conviction.

"I thought about it," I confessed, "while I was clamping Vito's artery. He was shot because of his involvement with me. And so was Aurelio. And you... you were trapped in that basement with me... because of me. But I suppose I'm a selfish woman, because no matter how I tried to convince myself it was the right thing to do, the truth is I don't want to walk away, Amadeo."

"Nothing that's happened was your fault," he said, shaking his head. But then he gripped my shoulders a little tighter, his gaze boring into mine. "But Heidi, you'd better be sure, because I don't think it's an offer I can make again. If you choose to stay... you're *mine*."

Not surprisingly, his words sent hot and cold shivers down my spine, a feeling to which I had not only become accustomed but addicted.

I shrugged. "I'm not going anywhere," I said, tilting my chin up.

His lips quirked in a smile even as his eyes flashed with a possessive heat that ignited my insides.

"Last chance, *perla.*"

I stared back at him.

When I made no move to leave, the heat in his eyes grew brighter. Hotter. And when his lips descended on mine, it felt like more than a kiss. The crushing pressure of his mouth was a brand. The sweep of his tongue along the seam of my lips, a claim to his territory. And when I parted my lips and let him in, I hadn't a doubt that I'd just sealed my fate.

"Can you shower?" he asked when he eventually let me up for air, nodding in the direction of the wound on my chest.

I nodded, but I'd barely managed the movement of my head when he grabbed hold of my hand and dragged me beneath the hot spray with him.

"Hands against the wall," he said right before he spun me around.

The hot water cascaded down us, washing away the blood that covered him as he hooked his fingers in the waist of my scrubs and panties and dragged them down.

He'd no sooner gotten them off my feet when I felt his lips against the backs of my thighs from my knees all the way up my backside, kissing and nipping as he went.

When he'd left every inch of me tingling and stinging sweetly, he grabbed hold of my hips and pulled them back so that I was nearly bent right over at the waist, my hands still hard against the wall. And then it was his tongue I felt, gliding along my slit, lightly at first like he was sampling me, and then harder, parting my lips and tasting me at the source.

I felt the vibrations of his groan right before his finger took over, sliding into me on that perfect angle that hit my G-spot from the very first stroke. The man worked my body like a master, fingering me so that every stroke drove me higher, but so slowly, it kept me reaching for it, yearning for it, but I could quite touch the precipice. It was right there, right in front of me.

"Faster," I pleaded.

But he withdrew instead, grazing his finger up to my anus and penetrating me there, slowly. It wasn't the first time he'd touched me there, but this time felt different, particularly when he'd worked one finger in and started on another, scissoring his fingers and stretching me. Thrills and chills shot down my spine. I wanted what it seemed he was gearing up for, but this was also uncharted territory for me.

It surprised me, nonetheless, when his fingers disappeared after a moment. From my bent position, I looked over my shoulder to watch as he began to shed the rest of his clothes, yanking off his soaking wet trousers along wit his boxer briefs until finally, he was gloriously naked, the pierced head of his cock glinting at me, making my mouth water.

He moved behind me, and the plump, pierced tip of his cock pressed against my slit for the span of a heartbeat before he grabbed my hip and thrust in hard. Deep.

The stretch, the burn, the way his piercing grazed over my G-spot, all of it twisted inside me and shot me toward the precipice so fast, it made my head spin with the intensity of the sensations.

His free hand moved to my breast, squeezing and pinching my nipple. But even in this mad race to orgasm, his hand was more careful than usual, keeping far away from the wound down the center of my chest. And perhaps it was only the stimulation his fingers were providing, but I think it was more that reached into the core of me in that moment and drew an orgasm up from the depths that rocketed through my body with the force of hurricane that made me scream and left me gasping for breath.

He slowed his strokes as my inner walls spasmed around him, and then he withdrew entirely. A whimper rose up in my throat at the loss, but it got strangled there when the tip of his erection slid up and pressed against my anus.

He grabbed my wet hair with one hand and yanked my head back to look at him.

"Relax for me, *perla*. I want to be in every part of you."

It was easier to nod than I'd expected. A part of me still feared that he wouldn't fit, but there was no denying my heart was pounding, not in fear, but because I wanted this too.

"Do it," I said, loud and clear.

He looked at me for a brief moment like he was surprised by my easy acquiescence, then turned his attention to his task, grabbing hold of my hip as he pressed forward, driving the head of his cock into my virgin ass, little by little.

The stretch, the burn; it hurt, but I dug my fingers into the shower wall and held on, knowing he'd make it good for me.

He stilled when he was all the way inside me, his hips against my backside.

"Christ, you feel incredible," he said, loud enough I could hear his voice.

Rather than withdraw, he slipped a hand beneath me, and his fingers settled on my clit, rubbing, pinching.

By the time he withdrew and then thrust back in, I was climbing again, and the new sensations sent me higher. Faster. So fast, the pleasure receptors in my brain felt overloaded. And when he picked up his pace, fucking me faster and rubbing my clit harder, everything went haywire. It was too much and not enough and so much more than I could handle.

He still had his grip in my hair and he used it to turn my head back to him again.

"Come for me, *perla*," he commanded, his jaw clenched tight.

He kept his grip on my hair, watching me as the first shockwave of my orgasm hit me, and then another and another.

He kept his fingers on my clit as he yanked his cock out of me, and I felt the hot spurts of his come across my back and down my backside.

I leaned hard against the wall, feeling spent, like every muscle in my body had been worked thoroughly, so I didn't mind at all when he stood me up and turned me around, gathering me into his arms.

Instead of stepping out of the shower, though, he stood still, his eyes meeting mine. There had been a great many times in my life when I'd missed my hearing. This was not one of them. I could see everything he was feeling in his eyes. And knowing he could hide it so well when he chose to do so, there wasn't a doubt that this was deliberate. It was his intention to let me in like this, just as much as I'd let him inside me.

"I love you, Amadeo," I said, words I'd never thought I would say.

"*Ti amo, perla*," he said. "Always."

Epilogue

Heidi

The air in the room snapped with tension.

I could feel it coming from Vito and Bruno behind me and from the two bulky men in black suits who stood just inside the parlor doorway. And I could certainly feel it in the pit of my stomach, gnawing at me with each passing second.

And yet, Amadeo sat next to me, looking perfectly at ease in the front parlor of a house that belonged to a stranger. If I weren't sitting right next to him, I would never have known that his muscles were taut, alert and ready. I found that both comforting and disturbing at the same time. The man was an expert at projecting only those things he wanted others to see. A master of disguise, really.

I'd watched him dress for this meeting, and while I'd been taken with the hard planes of his magnificent body at the time, now I was painfully aware of the holsters that wrapped around his shoulders and concealed the weapons he wielded like an expert. And there were more, a gun in the holster around his ankle and a knife in a sheath inside his jacket.

"You don't have to do this if you don't want to, *perla,*" he said, rubbing my knee soothingly.

I tried to smile to reassure him, but the movement was stiff. "I want to do this," I said, repeating aloud the same thing I'd been telling myself for the last several hours.

I hadn't the chance to say more when the tall, dark-haired man from the cemetery walked into the front parlor of the house where he was apparently staying while in the country.

The men in black suits closed ranks behind him, following him into the room toward us. Without looking, I could feel Vito and Bruno stand up straighter behind us as Amadeo and I stood up.

"*Buongiorno,*" Amadeo said as he shook hands with Nathaniel Sinclair, but when the man took my hand, he clasped it in both of his, looking at me with an expression that was caught somewhere between a smile and disbelief.

"You lied to me," I blurted out. It wasn't how I'd intended to greet the man who was supposedly my uncle, but my mouth had its own agenda, it seemed.

He smiled apologetically as he released my hand. "You're quite right, I did. And I do apologize for it."

He looked at me, silent. If he was hoping that was enough, he was sorely mistaken.

"What I told you was not entirely a lie, my dear; my mother did pass away two months ago, just a few short months after my father's passing."

There was the same sad look in his eyes I'd witnessed at the cemetery. He was either a terribly good actor or the sentiment was genuine.

I nodded, accepting his apology and mourning just a little, the grandparents I would never have the opportunity to meet.

"I'm glad we have a chance to meet now, Heidi," he said as he motioned for Amadeo and I to retake our seats.

As I sat down, I glanced to Amadeo, who nodded encouragingly. I'd never been part of any type of clandestine business transaction before, and that was very much what this felt like.

I licked my lips and turned to address Nathaniel.

"I did come to meet you," I said, "but I've also come to tell you that I have your money—or at least, a portion of it. I found it hidden in the basement of the Regalton Arms—as I'm sure you already know. I've been informed that there is more, but I don't know where it is. Should I come upon it, I *will* return it to you."

His brow furrowed as he looked at me, then his gaze flickered to Amadeo and back again.

Out of the corner of my eye, I could see that Amadeo's expression hadn't changed, but some of the tautness left his muscles.

Nathaniel shook his head. "That money does not belong to me, Heidi."

"I was given to believe it does."

The furrow between his brows deepened. "I don't know what you've been told, but to the best of my understanding, when William… when your father left, he took with him only those things which belonged to him, his personal fortune included."

"The money was his?" It took a great deal of effort to keep my jaw from dropping.

Nathaniel nodded.

But if that were true, then my father hadn't been a thief. Though, as part of the Sinclair family, perhaps he'd been worse. The thing was, I didn't care anymore. I'd embraced the shades of gray, and I didn't think it was possible to turn back now.

"But I'm confused then," I admitted, because it had been my understanding that he'd come here in pursuit of that money. "If you hadn't come to retrieve the money, then why are you here? Why did you lie to me in the cemetery? Or approach me at all, for that matter?"

He smiled. "You speak your mind," he said, nodding approvingly.

I could see Amadeo's scoff in the movement of his sculpted chest. "Indeed, she does."

He smiled at Amadeo, looking back and forth between us for a moment before his gaze settled on me once again. "Your mother was very much like that."

She was? I wished I could recall. But I supposed there were snippets that suggested she'd certainly never had trouble telling my father precisely what she was thinking, particularly when he'd gotten himself in trouble.

Nathaniel sat back in his wingback chair and scrubbed a hand over his jaw. The way his shoulders lifted and dropped, it seemed like he was sighing rather heavily.

"For the longest time, we didn't know about Dorian or what he'd done," he explained, his lips moving slowly like this was not a comfortable topic. "When he returned from the U.S. seventeen years ago, he told my father that William and your mother... and *you* had been murdered. My father was devastated."

He shook his head slowly, his eyes caught up in memory.

"As the eldest son of the Sinclair family," he continued, "your father had known he was a target, had escaped two attempts on his life in a very short period of time. And so, he left everything—everything he'd ever known—to try to keep you and your mother safe, and it had been for nothing.

"Over the years, Dorian did things to... alienate himself from the family. After our father died, leaving him nothing, I had my men keep a close eye on him, following him to New York, and eventually to a young woman who looked terribly familiar."

He withdrew a photograph from his jacket pocket and placed it down on the coffee table between us. A photo of a woman in her mid- to late-thirties with dark hair and pale skin. And blue eyes that had the same pale flecks in them that mine did.

I couldn't stop my breath from coming out all at once, like someone had hit me in the solar plexus, knocking the air right out of me. All this time, I'd been trying so desperately to remember what she'd looked like, and here I'd been staring at her every time I looked in the mirror.

"...I knew he'd lied all those years ago," I caught most of what Nathaniel was saying, thanks to Amadeo's hand squeezing my knee to draw my attention. "So, I followed him myself and saw him pair up with that tosser, Owen Thompson, then Elio Bianchi. But I didn't know why, not for certain, until the Lucianos had gotten involved."

"And the rest is history," I finished.

He nodded.

"I appreciate you sharing this with me," I said. But inside, my stomach was twisted in knots. There was still one more issue to address, and despite Amadeo's assurances that all would be well, I had my doubts.

I glanced up at the bulky men in black suits. They stood behind Nathaniel, their hands at their sides, but there was no mistaking the bulge of the weapons beneath their jackets.

"Dorian Sinclair is dead," Amadeo said out of the blue. He stood up as he spoke, drawing me up with him, but there was no expression on his face, no sign that he was preparing to defend himself or strike first.

Nathaniel stood up, his gaze fixed on Amadeo's, but I could read it no better.

"Yes," he said after far too many seconds had passed. "I imagined that was the case."

"He hurt her," Amadeo said, nodding to me, "and he would have done much worse. I wasn't going to let that happen."

Nathaniel sighed, nodding. "My brother was..." He nodded some more. "It had to end. I'm in your debt, Mr. Luciano, for taking that burden on yourself."

Amadeo shook his head. "There is no debt. you owe me nothing. All I want is your word that this is finished; there's no ill will harbored here."

"You have my word," Nathaniel said, extending his hand, "and whether you consider it a debt or not, you have my gratitude for keeping my niece safe."

Amadeo nodded and shook the man's hand.

I wasn't particularly fond of being talked about while I was in the same room, but I understood it.

These weren't just two men engaged in idle conversation, they were two powerful leaders in the criminal world where misunderstandings could easily cost lives.

And it seemed our meeting had come to an end as Amadeo motioned toward the front door, but I couldn't resist turning back to Nathaniel as a man dressed in a butler uniform opened the door.

"Nathaniel?"

"Yes, dear?" he asked.

"You wouldn't happen to have a picture of my father, would you?"

He smiled, then returned to the parlor and came back a moment later with a photograph of the man I hadn't seen since I was a little girl. He was, perhaps, a few years younger in this photo, but he was smiling, and the mischievous light I remembered so clearly lit up his eyes.

"Thank you," I said, forcing out the words past a lump in my throat.

"There are many, many more in London... if you ever feel the inclination to visit," he offered with an expression that looked rather hopeful to me.

"I'd like that," I said as a tiny fizzle of excitement bubbled in my stomach.

To see the place where my father grew up, where he met my mother and married her.

To see the place that was home to our small family before we'd moved to New York.

"I'd like that very much," I added quietly.

***

"What are you thinking, *perla?*" Amadeo asked me from the driver's seat of his Ferrari. He'd started the engine, but seemed to be in no hurry to leave Nathaniel Sinclair's driveway.

I laughed a little and the movement felt light and buoyant, like there was nothing holding me down.

"I'm thinking that a few weeks ago, I would have been terribly relieved to discover my father wasn't a thief, and equally appalled to learn what he really was."

"And now?"

I smiled and leaned over to graze my fingers down the side of his face. The scrape against his five-o-clock shadow left them tingling pleasantly.

"And now I don't care one whit about what he was, only what he was *to me.*"

"From the sounds of it, he loved you very much. And now, thanks to him, it seems you're a very rich woman," he mused with a wry smile.

I shrugged, figuring now was as good a time as any to delve into the topic. "Not really," I said.

He cocked an eyebrow, waiting for me to continue.

"If that money truly belonged to my father, then I'd like to set it aside for Grayson and his sister, Alice."

He smiled. "That's quite a college fund."

I shrugged again. "Between my work and your… ill-gotten gains…" I smiled. "I hardly think we'll be lacking. And I don't believe I'll find a better use for it than two children who've had a rather difficult start in life."

"I take it that means you're still intent on fostering the kids?" he asked, though there wasn't quite the same amount of disapproval in his voice this time.

"I am."

"You do realize that means you're moving in with me, *sì?*"

My breath caught in my throat.

We hadn't known each other long enough for this to be happening, and yet, it was. But it wasn't that simple.

"Do you realize that would mean that a sixteen-year-old boy and seven-year-old girl would be moving in as well? Are you sure you want that, Amadeo?"

He scoffed. "I'm definitely getting the better end of the deal, *perla*. You seem to be forgetting that by moving in with me, you'll be stuck with my cranky father, psychopath brother, and Freya—who, just keep in mind, has been giving you space, trying not to scare you away. That won't last forever. Then there's Greta, who drops by—generally unannounced—at pretty much any time, day or night. And you haven't even met my youngest brother, Matteo, yet."

"And Aurelio?" I asked.

He cocked an eyebrow. "Do I need to be worried about leaving you two alone?"

I shrugged. "You could always mark me with your scent, and then you'll have nothing to worry about." I waggled my eyebrows. "I promise I'll only shower it off when you let me."

His jaw dropped. Perhaps, not a full hit-the-floor kind of drop, but I'd most certainly caught him unsuspecting.

I couldn't help but smile, but the smile fell away and I dug my teeth into my lower lip when his gaze heated in an instant and turned predatory.

Without a word, he maneuvered the car out of the driveway and kept his eyes on the road in front of us all the way back to his estate while the confines of the car snapped with a whole different kind of tension, like electric sparks in the air all around us.

By the time we pulled into the long driveway of the Luciano estate, the sun had set and it was a wonder the sparks in the air hadn't set anything on fire.

He turned the car off at the top of the drive, but he made no move to get out. He looked around the property, then looked at me. And even before he spoke, I could see it in his eyes, the man turning into the predator, the hunter preparing for the hunt.

My breath caught in my throat as arousal hit me so hard, it felt like I'd been struck by a tidal wave.

My teeth were biting into my lower lip, my muscles taut, anticipating it.

He smiled, the look filled with every dark and sinful promise imaginable. And then he said the word that had my heart racing and my thighs clenching against the onslaught.

"Run."

THANK YOU FOR READING: MAFIA KINGS:
CORRUPTED BOOK 7: CORRUPTED SEDUCTION

DON'T MISS THE FREE SIZZLING BONUS CHAPTER

EXCLUSIVE FREE BONUS CHAPTER

Something gripped my chest as I looked at her. Because this was more than just kink.
She'd handed herself over to me, offered up every one of her senses to me. Absolute trust.
It was a far more potent aphrodisiac than I ever could have imagined.
Her body jolted at the unexpected contact, but then a quiet moan slipped out as I kept
up the slow glide. I'd barely touched her. She was slick, ready for it; ready for me.
I stood up and stepped back. Christ, she was beautiful.
And one-hundred percent mine.
"Be careful what you wish for, perla," I warned her because I had no problem giving it
to her.

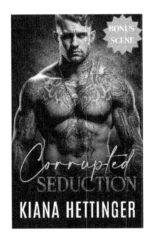

Can't get enough of Heidi and Amadeo? Download the free bonus
scene for one more steamy chapter.

Download the FREE bonus chapter here -
https://geni.us/corruptedsdbonus

What's Next?

Wow, I hope you enjoyed *Corrupted Seduction!* Your support means the world to me.

The next book in the Mafia Kings: Corrupted Series is Corrupted Deception.

If you enjoyed Amadeo and Heidi's story, you're going to want to read Cielo's story, Corrupted Deception!

By Kiana Hettinger

Corrupted Seduction is the seventh book in the Mafia Kings: Corrupted Series.

Mafia Kings: Corrupted Series

#0 Cruel Inception

#1 Corrupted Heir

#2 Corrupted Temptation

#3 Corrupted Protector

#4 Corrupted Obsession

#5 Corrupted Vows

#6 Corrupted Sinner

#7 Corrupted Seduction

#8 Corrupted Deception

Standalones

Stolen Bond

Brutal Oath

Forbidden Romeo

Calling all Kittens! Come join the fun:

If you're thirsty for more discussions with other readers of the series, join my exclusive readers' group, Kiana's Kittens.

Join my private readers' group here -
facebook.com/groups/KianasKittens

CAN YOU DO ME A HUGE FAVOR?

Would you be willing to leave me a review?

I'd be over the moon because just one positive review on Amazon is like buying the book a hundred times! Reader support is the lifeblood for Indie authors. It provides us the feedback we need to give readers what they want in future stories!

Your positive review would mean the world to me. You can post your review on Amazon or Goodreads. I'd be forever grateful, thank you from the bottom of my heart!

Printed in Great Britain
by Amazon

33971792R00205